LIGHT RISES

RACHEL WESSON

Copyright © Rachel Wesson, 2022, 2023

Previously published in 2022 by Londongate Publishing.

The moral right of the author has been asserted.

To request permissions, contact the publisher at rights@stormpublishing.co

Ebook ISBN: 978-1-80508-131-9
Paperback ISBN: 978-1-80508-132-6

Cover design: Debbie Clement
Cover images: Arcangel, Shutterstock

Published by Storm Publishing.
For further information, visit:
www.stormpublishing.co

ALSO BY RACHEL WESSON

The Resistance Sisters

Darkness Falls

Light Rises

Hearts at War (WWII)

When's Mummy Coming?

A Mother's Promise

WWII Irish Standalone

Stolen from Her Mother

Orphans of Hope House

Home for Unloved Orphans (Orphans of Hope House 1)

Baby on the Doorstep (Orphans of Hope House 2)

Women and War

Gracie Under Fire

Penny's Secret Mission

Molly's Flight

Hearts on the Rails

Orphan Train Escape

Orphan Train Trials

Orphan Train Christmas

Orphan Train Tragedy

For Ruth and Annie.

Now one knows better how to love you, protect you and bother you like a sister does!

* * *

Note to readers: As before in fitting with the characters being French, we adopted the French style of non capitalisation for nouns including maman, papa, mémé and where applicable the word resistance.

ONE

AUGUST 1942

Sophie ran a hand under her hair to stop it from sticking to the back of her neck. Her blouse had come back from the laundry only slightly less grey than when it went in. The lack of soap was affecting everyone and, combined with the heat and their once-weekly bath, she was aware of her body odour. If only she'd had time to pack suitcases of her old clothes or those of Adèle's before she had to flee Paris. For a split second, she wanted to run away down the hill back to Perpignan and from there go anywhere.

The camp was located about a fifteen-minute drive outside Perpignan, but it might as well have been in a different world. There were rows and rows of barracks as far as the eye could see. Although they were well made from concrete and once had glass windows, they had fallen into a bad state of disrepair. Overcrowding was a huge problem with insufficient shelter available for the number of Jews being housed here.

Nothing grew in the sandy pebble covered ground, no grass, trees or anything else.

Sophie walked towards the barbed wire, the wind buffeting

her, making it difficult to stay upright, all the while trying to keep her eyes open despite the sand grains flying into them.

Inside the barbed wire fence, it was almost impossible to believe she was still in France. There were armed guards at either end of each barracks, which were filled with straw and nothing else. The people were sitting or lying down, with nowhere to go and nothing to do.

Many adults and children were showing signs of severe malnutrition, food being scarce everywhere. But the adults who appeared to have given up all hope were the ones who worried Sophie the most. They had to fight back – otherwise, they were doomed.

The heat was affecting Mary too, who wasn't her usual cheerful self when she met her. "The parents, they won't hand over the children to be evacuated to safety. I can't make them understand it's the only chance the little ones have to survive." Mary scratched the side of her head. "They believe Pétain will protect them, and understandably they don't want to be sepa-rated from their children. I can't blame them. How could anyone believe someone would cause any harm to a child?"

Sophie didn't have the words to comfort her friend. "Someone said the Germans are afraid of the children more than the adults. If the children grow up, they will take revenge on the German people."

Mary rolled her eyes. "They shouldn't be doing anything to warrant revenge. Why do people judge others and find them so wanting just because they follow another religion or way of life?"

Sophie knew the question was rhetorical. Mary had told her about her own home in Ireland being burned down during the Troubles. Sophie didn't know what the Irish problems were, but she knew it was something to do with Catholics and Protestants. Here it was Gentiles and Jews. She shook her head. Now wasn't the time to think about the world's issues. They had to fix the problem right in front of them.

"We have to convince the parents. In an ideal world, we'd save all of them. The clock is ticking. We must get them out. Haven't they heard what happened in July? The *rafle* in Paris. I was there – it was horrific, and it wasn't just foreign Jews. French ones were caught and deported too."

Mary nodded as she listened to Sophie, who continued. "The same will happen here. If Laval has his way, the children will go with their parents. In fact, he says it is more humane."

Mary snorted, but Sophie barely noticed.

"How is it humane to pack anyone into those cattle trains? They should send him for a trip and see how he likes it."

Mary gave her a hug before standing back and pushing the hair way from Sophie's face. "Are you sure you aren't Irish? Sometimes I get the feeling you have our temper."

Sophie came to a decision. "I'm going to ask if I can live in the camp. That way, the parents will get to know me better; they may trust me more."

"That's dangerous. You could get caught up in the deportations."

That wasn't likely. Nobody knew mémé had been born Jewish but converted to Catholicism when she got married. They'd only found out after her grandmother left Paris to live in Lyon. Sophie wasn't on any list, not having two Jewish grandparents or practising as a Jew. And she was single.

"It's the obvious choice. You have more contacts in the countryside. You need to be free to find places to hide the children."

Mary kissed her on the cheek. "I can't argue with your logic. Go and see the commander. He might not agree."

"He will." Sophie wished she felt as confident as she sounded. Still, she had to try.

* * *

She approached the camp commander's office. Knocking at his door, she walked in, determined to remain calm.

He didn't look up, his attention focused on a pile of papers on his desk. She stood waiting for an acknowledgement, but none was forthcoming. His greying hair was brushed to the side. Was it to conceal the balding patch in the centre? His uniform looked a little large for him, buckling around the stomach area as if he had lost weight recently. Not that it was unusual given the rations they were on, but usually, men of his position remained unaffected by those rules. She urged him silently to notice her, but he continued to examine the pile of papers, occasionally pushing the glasses up on his nose.

She focused on the picture of Pétain above his head, counting back from ten in her head. She had to remain polite and not display any *hysterical, feminine* behaviour. She stifled a grin – her nerves playing up and making her want to laugh. What would Adèle do if she were here? She wouldn't be standing like an idiot waiting; she'd already have purred and charmed her way into getting his agreement on everything. Where was her twin? Was she being entertained by high-society men in England?

Finally, the commandant spoke without looking up. "Dr Bélanger."

"Thank you for seeing me, commandant. I wish to request permission to move into the camp."

His eyes shot up from the papers, meeting hers. "You? Move in here. Are you insane?"

"No, sir."

"But why? The fences are there to keep people out."

His attempt at humour fell flat. She didn't appreciate the joke, and he knew it. He flushed slightly.

"Explain why you wish to live here. It is not necessary for your work."

"I believe it is." For her real work, at any rate. "As you know, I treat patients suffering from a range of maladies. Their temperatures often spike at night, and this is the time when I should be here. I can't travel back and forth, so, therefore..." She shrugged, hoping he'd agree without asking more questions.

"But where would you live? You can't move in with the inmates; you would fall sick yourself. I don't have the facility to give you a room."

She wanted to give a pointed look at the space he enjoyed, with his massive desk only taking up a quarter of the office, but she needed his help.

"I will sleep at the medical hut. We've cleared one of the buildings and turned it into a clinic." It was barely more than a shack. "I really would like to be close to my patients. You should understand."

"I should?"

She closed her eyes, wishing Adèle was here. Her twin could twist any man around her little finger. But Adèle was miles away, safe in England if she played true to form, and Sophie was on her own. The children and their parents needed her. She smiled in what she hoped was a flattering manner but not too flirty. The last thing she needed was for the man to get the wrong idea.

"Yes, commandant. You have a duty to your men and to our government. To France. You fulfil your duty to the best of your ability." She saw the small smile even though he did his best to hide it. "I wish to do the same."

He shuffled some papers, letting the silence linger, but she knew better than to fill it. She stayed quiet, focusing once more on the picture above his head. Then he removed his glasses and looked at her. She saw his pupils focus. Did he need the lenses, or were they a barrier to hide behind?

"Dr Bélanger, I will agree on two conditions. You will go to Miss Elmes's home every Sunday and stay the night. This will prevent you from falling ill from exhaustion, and you should be able to eat better too."

"But..."

"I haven't finished. You will not choose quarters in Block K."

Block K was where the Jewish inmates were held, surrounded by a barbed wire fence since early July. She hesitated. She needed access to the Jewish inmates if she were to convince them to give up their children.

"I need to be able to see patients in Block K."

"Yes, of course. But you will not sleep there. Do you understand?"

She stared back at him. Was he trying to tell her something, or was that her imagination? She hesitated.

"Dr Bélanger, these are my conditions. I'm a very busy man. I think it would be best for us both if you accepted without further argument."

For a brief second, he reminded her of her father – or at least what he had been like as a parent when she'd been younger. Adèle had often been in trouble at school, but Sophie had taken the blame. Her father had known but played along. Why did the commandant's behaviour bring up that memory? "Yes, sir, of course. Thank you."

He nodded in dismissal, and she walked to the door stopping when he spoke again.

"I will send a cleaning detail to clear out a hut for you to use. Miss Elmes will not be happy should you fall ill."

He was trying to help. She turned, but his head was down, his eyes focused once more on the papers in front of him. Was that why he reminded her of her father? He knew what was happening but wasn't about to admit it.

"Merci." She choked out the thanks and left.

* * *

Sophie moved among the children as they queued up for the bowls of rice provided by the Quakers, the milk from the Red Cross and the odd red apple the staff smuggled in.

"This is the worst camp we have been in, Dr Sophie." Madame Goldman spoke as she spooned rice into the mouth of the listless child on her lap. The five-year-old was too tired to feed himself. "In the other places, the children could go outside but here, the sand filled winds make it impossible. See his cheeks. That red glow – once, I would have wished for my children to have rosy faces, but here it means the sand has cut into them. It's painful, and we have no salves. Why would anyone want our children to suffer so?"

Sophie reached out to hold the child while Madame Goldman ate her own ration. "I don't know." Sophie dropped her voice to a whisper. "You must think about giving David and Rosa to Miss Mary. She will find good places for them to stay; they will get better food and be away from the wind. But most of all, they won't be put on the trains."

Madame Goldman snatched David back, causing him to squeal in protest, but even the effort of crying was too much for him. He sank back against his mother's chest, his too-big eyes staring listlessly out of his little face.

"I can't. My children are my everything. You don't have a baby. How could you ask me?"

"I want to save your children. I know you love them."

"Yes, I do. But I can't give them to strangers. I heard about Miss Mary's friends. They want our children to become Catholics. Those very people who tell us we murdered their Jesus."

The woman's strident tones were attracting the wrong attention. Sophie hushed her. "Please, just think about it. Nobody is going to force Rosa and David to be anything but alive." Sophie stood up and, with a small smile at David, walked out of the barracks, heading for the medical hut, as the inmates nicknamed one barracks. It was in slightly better condition than the other barracks: the windows still had glass in them, and the walls had been whitewashed recently. They changed the straw daily, a concession from the camp authorities when she pointed out typhus and other contagious diseases didn't care if the victims were French police or foreign Jews. As she walked, she heard someone call her. Turning, she found herself facing a woman with three children, including a baby.

"Doctor, you need to take my children. Give them a chance. I heard what you said to Madame Goldman. I love my babies, but this is not the place for them. Here they will only die. Out there..." The woman looked into the distance beyond the barbed wire. "...they have a chance."

"Come inside out of the heat, madame..."

"Silberman. This is Johann, Adolf, and the baby is Sarah after my mother."

Adolf? What Jewish mother gives her son that name?

Madame Silberman must have anticipated her reaction. "He's almost twelve. We didn't know Hitler when he was born. My husband..." The woman blinked rapidly, her eyes glistening. "His father was called Adolf, and a nicer man you wouldn't ever meet. But now they need to change his name. His whole identity. How will I ever find my children? You know, after the war? When this madness is over. If you take them away, will I ever hold them again, feel their soft kisses against my cheek? Feel their little arms around my neck? I won't, will I?" The woman was fast becoming hysterical.

Sophie ushered her into the medical barracks, pushing her towards the office the staff used at the very back: a small room with one window and a door. She closed the door behind them before pulling open the drawer of the desk and producing two small, wizened apples. She handed them to Adolf and Johann and indicated they sit on the floor near the door, but the mother had a different idea.

"Adolf, take Johann back to our room and stay there until I come."

"Mama, please don't give us away. We want to stay with you."

"You will do as you are told. You remember what your father said. You are to do what I say. Always."

The boy blinked hard before nodding. He took Johann's spare hand, the other one holding the apple in a tight grip. "Come on, Johann, but eat your apple on the way. If we get back to the barracks, someone will steal it."

Johann pushed the entire apple into his mouth before Sophie advised, "Eat it on your way back, one bite at a time."

They waited until the children left before she addressed the woman.

"I swear to you we will keep your children's real identities safe. Do you have any family?"

"Alive?" the woman spat back before she immediately apologised. "I'm sorry. Do you mean outside France?"

Sophie nodded.

"Yes, in America, but they wouldn't help us."

No, but they might be able to take the children after the war if there is nobody else. If you go on the trains. Sophie didn't put that thought into words.

"Perhaps you could give us their name and address just to be safe. That way, after the war, you can write to them for news if you have any problems finding me or Miss Mary."

The woman closed her eyes, her mouth moving. Was she praying? Sophie waited to give her a little time.

"My husband, they told him if he went to a labour camp, they would leave us alone in Belgium. I knew it was a trap; I begged him not to go, but he didn't believe me. He said he had to go. He never came back. They put them on a train ... like the ones that they want to put us on." The woman shuddered. "There was nothing but people on those trains. No toilets, no seats, nothing. People died, but there was nowhere to put the bodies. Old people, young people, men, women, and children. All with only one thing in common. We were all Jews."

"I'm sorry." Sophie had heard stories of how the Nazis had tricked younger men into going away to work in labour camps in a bid to save the rest of their families. They had been shipped east, and nobody had heard from them again. She didn't want to think about what that meant.

The woman seemed to remember what she'd come about. "My name is Perla Silberman. If you give me a piece of paper, I will write their names and dates of birth. What Madame Goldman said about the Catholics... Is that true? Will they be forced to become Christians?"

Sophie shook her head rather than speak a lie. She had no idea whether they would or not. Some children were hidden in Christian orphanages and would have to, at the very least, pretend to be Christian. Others would be hidden with families higher up in the mountains where it was hoped the Nazis wouldn't look for them. Still others, the more Jewish-looking ones, would be smuggled out to Switzerland, but none of this information would help Madame Silberman. Telling her could place them all in danger.

"I can't make any promises to you, Madame Silberman, but..."

"It is better they live as Christians than die as Jews."

Sophie swallowed the lump in her throat as the woman bravely fought back her own tears.

"Nobody can change what is in their hearts, Madame Silberman. If you want to write a short note for your children, we will keep it with their details."

"Will they think I didn't love them?" She stared straight into Sophie's face.

"No, Perla, on the contrary: they will know you loved them more than any mother could."

One tear trailed down Perla's cheek as she handed the baby to Sophie to hold. With a sigh, she took the pencil Sophie had on the desk and the scrap of paper and started writing.

"I'm sorry about the paper, but it's the best we can do. Everything is in such short supply."

"Yes, doctor, everything but hate."

* * *

When Mary came back to the camp that afternoon, Sophie took her to see Madame Silberman. Adolf's eyes were red-rimmed from crying, but when he saw Miss Mary, he stood up and kissed his mother on the cheek. Johann clung to his mother's neck until Adolf spoke sharply to him, and then he, too, kissed Perla. With a last lingering kiss on the baby's forehead, Perla passed her over to Sophie. "Look after my children, Miss Mary. Dr Sophie said you would keep them safe. Adolf is a brave boy; he will help you."

Perla's voice shook with emotion, but her eyes remained dry, her white knuckles standing out as she gripped her hands in front of her chest.

"Thank you for trusting us, Madame Silberman. You are a very brave, loving mother."

With a sob, Perla turned away. Sophie carried baby Sarah to the car. Once there, she placed her in Adolf's arms. "You are a credit to your parents, young man."

Adolf couldn't answer. He just stared into the distance.

TWO

The clock was ticking faster than anyone realised as two days later, the camp commander came to find Sophie and Mary. When he looked at them, the expression in his eyes frightened Sophie. His hands shook as he held out a piece of paper. "This is a copy of the list they gave me. The first train leaves tomorrow, 11 August, and must have four hundred people on it. There are fifty children on the list. They are going to take the little ones." He couldn't look at them but stared at the ground.

Sophie couldn't stop herself. "You knew they weren't going to let them live here forever."

Mary put her hand on Sophie's arm. "Thank you, commandant, for giving us notice."

"Make the children disappear. Just do it."

He walked away, leaving them staring at him for a couple of seconds. Mary recovered first. She scanned the list.

"Sophie, quickly – gather as many of the children as you can. This transport will go to Drancy to join the cattle trains going somewhere in Poland. We know they won't have food or proper shelter. We have to take them now."

Sophie scanned the list and headed for the families whose

names she recognised. The first stop was Madame Goldman. She found them in the barracks. Madame Goldman was rocking back and forth on the ground, her children lying by her side.

"Madame Goldman, you've heard?"

The woman raised her tear-stained face. "Yes. Our names. They are on the list. The children too." The woman went back to rocking.

"Madame Goldman, please give us the children. Let us try to save them."

"And me? You can take me too? I don't eat much, and I'm a good worker. In Belgium, I was known for my needlework and my stitches – they were the best." The hope flared in the woman's eyes as she stopped rocking, her hands reaching for Sophie. "I can do anything. I can cook, clean... Please don't take my children. Take us all."

Sophie just listened, her heart breaking. She couldn't take the woman, and they both knew it. Getting adults out of the camp was next to impossible, and any attempts to do so put the whole organisation at risk.

"You won't even try..." Madame Goldman whispered, dropping Sophie's hands.

Sophie leaned in and took the woman's hands back in hers, caressing them. "I wish I could. I would try, but it is too dangerous for everyone, most of all the children. But I can take David and Rosa. They have a chance."

The woman's shoulders shook as she sobbed. "I can't give you my babies. We should be together."

"But..."

"We die together."

"Madame Goldman, think about what you are saying. If you give us the children, you have a chance at life too. You are young and a talented seamstress. You can work for the Nazis. And when this war is over, you can come back here and find David and Rosa. This is the best way. The only way."

Madame Goldman glanced around her, but nobody was interested in them. They were all overwhelmed by their own tragedy. "I love them so much. I don't want them to die. You know that."

"Yes, of course I do."

"But to give them to strangers? They will be devastated."

"They will, but they will be alive. Children are resilient. Show them how much you love them. Give them to me. Now, please. There is very little time."

"Mutti, I don't want to die. Please let us go with Miss Mary. My friends went last week. I want to see them. I don't want to go on another train." David's words shocked his mother. Her face paled. Rosa didn't speak, but she moved closer to her brother, holding his hand so tight, Sophie saw the boy wince, but he put his arm around his sister, not rebuking her.

"You want to leave your mother?" Madame Goldman asked.

"No, Mutti, I want you to come too, but I don't want to go on the train again. I couldn't breathe the last time, remember? Daddy had to hold me up high, and he's not here."

Sophie had to turn away to wipe the tears from her face. *Dear Lord above, how could you let this happen?* For the first time, she was glad she hadn't got pregnant with Jules's baby. She couldn't have borne to be in this situation.

Madame Goldman's face hardened as she stood up. "Take them. They want to go. Take them now."

She walked away without looking back. The children burst into noisy tears as Sophie gathered them into her arms and lifted them both up. As they walked to the car, she reassured them again and again that their mother loved them.

"No, she's angry."

"No, David, she's very sad. She doesn't want to be away from you. Remember how much she loves you."

David didn't answer. When Sophie put the children in the car, she saw him put his arm around Rosa and pull her close.

Sophie turned to Mary. "Mary, if you can, please try to find a family to take both Goldman children. Their mother... She didn't handle it too well."

Mary glanced at the children. "I'll do what I can. Where are you going now?"

"To find Madame Goldman. I'm worried this was too much for her."

Mary patted her arm, but what could she say?

When Sophie did find the children's mother, she was too late.

* * *

Over the next few hours, Mary drove back and forth to the camp, and Sophie repeated the agonising process of persuading mothers to part with their children countless times. The guards turned a blind eye, obviously working under orders from the commandant. As darkness fell, Mary drove away with the last group of children in her car, saying she would return as soon as she could to collect Sophie.

"I'll stay here. I want to be here tomorrow."

Mary frowned. "I don't think that's a good idea."

Sophie leaned in and kissed Mary's cheek. "I'm not asking for permission. I have to do this. It's the least I can do for them." Sophie gestured to the crowds of women standing around, some in silence, others chattering like magpies.

Mary reluctantly nodded and drove away.

Sophie watched until the car was out of sight before she went to the medical area and gathered more paper. Then she visited as many parents as she could, taking note of any family details they could remember, including addresses for relatives. Sophie worked as quickly as possible, promising parents she would make sure their children were safe.

She calculated that they had saved over thirty children.

Despite their best efforts, some parents refused to hand over their offspring. And she couldn't blame them. They couldn't help the adults, and maybe it was easier for them to believe the Nazis' claim that they were going to live in a family camp somewhere. *Maybe they are.* What if the rumours of what happened in the east were just that, rumours, and they had split up families for no reason?

"You doubt you did the right thing?" Madame Silberman's voice broke into her thoughts as Sophie stared at the barbed wire fence.

She turned to look at the brave mother, who continued talking.

"You shouldn't. If you had seen the things I saw in Belgium, you would believe everything you hear and worse. You were in Paris during the *rafle*, yes?"

Sophie nodded.

"Then you know. I read *Mein Kampf.* Have you?"

"Hitler's book? No, but I've heard of it."

"Everyone should have read it. He said in there what he planned to do. But nobody wanted to believe him. They still don't."

"Madame Silberman..."

"My name is Perla."

"I wish I could help you to escape. I..." Sophie pushed down the nauseous feeling in her stomach. "I can't imagine how difficult..."

"Please don't. You have helped us more than you know. Moving in here, working with us, treating us as real people. Saving our children. Bless you, doctor."

Perla turned to walk away.

"Perla."

The woman turned back, cocking her head on her shoulder.

"Tell them you are a talented worker."

"Me? I don't know how to do anything. You wouldn't think

it now, but I had a very cultured upbringing. My parents were doctors in Vienna. They saw the threat early and moved us to Belgium. My husband, a doctor, was of the same mind; he wanted us to emigrate, but I wanted to stay near my parents. I was their spoiled youngest child. If I had made different choices, I wouldn't be here."

"Don't do that. None of this is your fault," Sophie whispered as she moved to hug the woman.

"Nor yours." The women embraced in silence for a few seconds.

"Lie, Perla. You speak French and German, you are well-educated – tell them you were a secretary or something. Do whatever you have to, but stay alive. Come back. Your children need you."

Perla bit her lip, her eyes swimming in tears as she swallowed hard. "Will you stay with us tonight? A group of us have become friends, and we are going to spend the evening telling stories. Please join us?"

Sophie nodded. "I'd love that."

* * *

Sophie and the other inmates sat on the straw-lined floor in the sole barracks designated for those going on the train the next day. She listened to their stories and their songs while passing out paper and pencils.

"Write something for your child, and I will give it to them."

A mother stared at the paper in Sophie's hand as if it was poisonous. "What should I write?"

"Whatever you wish. You could tell them..."

"Tell them to live a good life. You'll never see them again." The man glared at Sophie. "Why are you filling these people with false hope? There's no coming back from where we're going. You know that, I know it, we all know it."

Sophie shook her head. "Nobody knows what is going to happen. There's always hope. You may come back at the end of the war, your children will have been kept safe, and then your family will be reunited."

"That's easy for you to say. You don't have children, do you? You're not going on the train. I know you pretend to be one of us, living here and everything, but you can walk out of the camp any time you wish. You're free."

Sophie drew back from the vitriol in his attack.

Perla Silberman remonstrated with the man. "How can you behave like this? Sophie, Miss Mary, and the rest of their people have always treated us as human beings. Don't you know Dr Sophie would stop these transports if she could? She is doing her best. If you can't see that, the Germans have won. You've become the animals they think we are."

The crowd murmured in agreement, but nobody was as brave as Perla to stand up and face the man.

He spat at the ground near Sophie's feet. "I hope this makes you feel good." He stalked off to the other end of the barracks.

Perla used her fingers to gently wipe away Sophie's tears. "I'm sorry. Some people are finding it more difficult than others."

Sophie tried to smile but failed dismally. "I can't blame him. Or anyone. What is happening here? None of us understand, but I must have hope. Without it, what is there?"

Perla shook her head, but she didn't say anything.

* * *

The next morning, Sophie stood and watched as the chosen inmates were loaded onto the trains. She could barely see through her tears, but still, she waited until everyone was on board. At the last minute, the man who'd spat at her last night broke free and moved closer to her, throwing a scrap of paper in her direction before the guard roughly pulled him back into line. The man turned his head, despite the guard beating him on his back, forcing him forward, and called out, "I'm sorry for what I said last night. I hope to see you again, Dr Sophie. Thank you."

Sophie bent down to grab the piece of paper. She'd read it later, her eyes locked with those of the man who'd climbed into the train and now stood facing her direction. She lifted one hand in a wave; he nodded in acknowledgement before he turned and disappeared into the mass of people being pushed into the carriage fit for animals, not humans.

Sophie held the messages the mothers and fathers had written tight to her chest. She would bury them in the garden of the home she was sometimes staying in, together with details of the children's new identities. Sophie couldn't bear the thought of the families being separated forever – when the war was over, the children and parents could be reunited.

THREE

AUGUST 1942

Sophie wearily climbed the hill to the orphanage they used as a halfway house to shelter the children rescued from the camp. The location away from the centre of town helped with safety, but it was a very tiring trip. She moved the basket she carried from one arm to the other, trying to lighten the load. *You should be happy people were so generous.* The voice in her head sounded just like her grandmother's. She missed mémé. How were her mother and grandmother coping in Lyon – and where was Adèle? Had she decided to stay in Britain?

She was delighted the locals had given so freely. The basket held fruit and vegetables, which would help the orphans battle not only hunger but also scurvy.

Esmée, another volunteer, took the basket from her as Sophie walked through the door.

"Thank goodness you're back. Mary came earlier; she brought seven boys with her. The poor things don't even speak French. They seem terrified."

Sophie could only imagine how they were feeling, being separated from their parents. The first convoys to leave Gurs and Rivesaltes were en route to somewhere called Auschwitz, and Mary was determined to stop as many children as possible from going there.

Esmée followed Sophie into the kitchen area, where she began unpacking the basket. Only slightly younger than Sophie, she was a wonderful cook, a miracle worker who could turn almost anything into an edible meal. She often joked how the children had hollow legs given how much they wanted to eat, but Sophie knew Esmée herself often went hungry, putting her own portion back in the pot to feed the youngsters.

"They have nasty-looking flea bites. We tried to wash them, but they refused to undress." Esmée looked uncomfortable. "Two are sitting in the bath in their underpants."

The bath was kept outside in the yard due to the level of lice and other bugs the children were infested with. Sophie hurried outside and came to a standstill when she saw the group gathered there.

The children tried to hide – even the boys in the bath. They crouched down and curled in on themselves to look smaller. Sophie smiled, but it did nothing to remove the look of distrust on their faces. They wouldn't meet her gaze but stared at the water, as if by not acknowledging her, they could pretend she wasn't there. The other boys moved closer together, their eyes flitting around the yard, looking for an escape route. Not one of them looked over nine years old. The smallest was probably three or four.

"My name is Sophie. I'm a doctor and here to help you. You're safe."

Their eyes widened as she spoke German. They understood what she was saying; at least, the older ones did. They remained silent, their entire bodies still as statues.

"I work with Miss Mary, the lady your parents trusted to keep you safe. Please do not be scared."

She took a step closer to the bath, but the children screamed and jumped out, hiding behind the tallest boy. Sophie addressed him.

"Are you the eldest? What is your name, and how old are you?"

"Dirk, and I'm ten."

He blushed at the lie. That wasn't his real name. She didn't call him out. "Dirk, we need you and your friends to get washed so we can bring you inside for a meal. I'm sure you're hungry, and Esmée is a wonderful cook. She's making fried potatoes."

Dirk swallowed but remained standing. The boys around him looked towards the source of the tantalising aroma now coming from the kitchen. She hoped their hunger would overcome their fear.

"The sooner you have a bath, the quicker you eat. I will turn my back while you get in, but then I need to wash your hair." She took a step forward and then hunched down so her face was on his level. "Please don't worry – nobody will hurt you here. We know you are Jewish. That's why we brought you here. So we can wash you, give you nicer clothes and some food before we find safe homes for you."

She turned at the sound of scratching coming from the abandoned dog's kennel. She stood up and moved over to the kennel, carefully, in case it held a wild animal. Peering inside, she saw a small boy.

"Hello, what's your name?"

The boy shrank back inside.

"Come out and stay with the other boys. You're safe."

"I'm not a boy. I'm a dog. Dogs don't get sent on the trains."

Sophie's voice failed her. A lump in her throat, she clenched her fists as she fought the tears, not just of sadness but frustration. What type of world were they living in?

Turning back to Dirk, she held her arms out in a gesture of surrender. "Please tell the boys they are safe."

He stared at her for a second or two before he gave a small

nod and stepped into the bath – but without making any move to remove his underwear.

How could anyone do anything bad to these children? She examined each one, deciding not to further traumatise them by insisting they remove their underwear. Their parents had obviously told them to hide, at all costs, the fact that they were circumcised.

Esmée brought out some clothes. She clipped a blanket to the clothesline before addressing the boys. "You can dress in private."

Sophie smiled her thanks before handing each boy a set of clothes, starting with Dirk. One after another, they slipped behind the curtain and changed. They picked up their discarded clothes, throwing them in the bath as they passed it on their way to the kitchen.

Even once they were seated at the table inside, facing plates full of steaming fried potatoes flavoured with wild garlic and onions, they didn't speak. There was none of the boisterous behaviour Sophie would expect from boys of their age.

She watched as Esmée filled each boy's glass with milk and encouraged them to eat up. Dirk helped the younger boys before feeding himself. They had two helpings each and would have eaten more if it were possible.

"There will be more food in the morning. I don't want anyone falling ill from overeating," Sophie said. Their little stomachs had shrunk from starvation, so she didn't want to tempt fate. "You will sleep upstairs. Esmée and I will stay here, so if you need anyone, come and find us."

The boys hung back, looking to Dirk to see what he did. Esmée stood up. "Who'd like a story?"

They followed her up the stairs.

Sophie stood in the kitchen and cried as the sound of Esmée's voice echoed down the stairs.

* * *

Only once the boys were in bed did she sit down to eat.

Esmée filled Sophie's cup with milk. "You're looking thin, Sophie; you need to eat more."

"The occupation is good for the figure, n'est-ce pas?" Sophie joked back. How could she eat more when so many were starving?

"You will have to move the children tomorrow," Esmée said. "Mary plans on bringing more out; she's worried Vichy will ramp up the number of trains. They seem to fall over themselves trying to please their German masters."

Sophie sighed, wondering where she could take the children.

Esmée looked at her with concern in her eyes. "You seem tired. You should take time off. Mary has a place she goes to near the Swiss border; maybe you could go too?"

"Thank you, but not yet. I have too much to do. Maybe in a few weeks' time." Sophie did not want to admit how tired she really was. But she couldn't in all conscience leave. Not now, when children were at risk. She could rest when the war was over.

FOUR

"Sophie, have you heard?" Mary walked into the hospital hut where Sophie was bandaging the arm of a young boy. They both looked up at the angry note in Mary's voice.

"Laval's gone back on his promise of a thousand visas for the children. He promised to let them go to America, but now he's changed his mind. He didn't like the articles written about him in the press, blaming him for the deportations."

"Then he shouldn't have agreed to them." Sophie had no time for their prime minister, who was, in her mind, worse than Pétain.

Mary gave her a rueful smile before asking the boy she was treating, "What happened to your arm?"

"One of the guards didn't like my attitude."

Sophie wanted to hit the guard hard. "He hit Paul with his pistol. Paul was lucky; the bone isn't broken, just bruised, but he will have to rest it over the next few days. We'll hide him in sick bay and tell the guards he has typhus. They will leave him alone and give us time to get him out. We can't let him back into the general camp; that guard has a nasty streak."

They were interrupted by the sounds of cheering outside.

Exchanging a look, they moved as one to the door. Sophie put a hand on Paul's good arm. "You stay here; we will come back and tell you what's going on."

Sophie followed Mary out the door into the camp area. People were jumping up and down, throwing their arms around each other or shaking hands. Some of the guards even wore a smile on their faces.

"What's going on?" Mary asked.

"The Allies landed in North Africa. Many believe the war will be over in weeks."

Mary paled and Sophie caught her friend before she fell. The guard helped her carry the Irish woman back into the hospital area.

"Mary, what is it? What's wrong? That's good news, surely?"

"I'd love to think so, but the Germans won't sit back and do nothing. Somehow, whenever we hear good news, it is the people in these camps who suffer most."

* * *

Mary's ominous words proved true as the Germans marched into the free zone on 11 November, closing all the borders.

Sophie was at Mary's home enjoying a few hours' break when the news came. They were sitting on the little balcony overlooking the gardens when a trusted friend dropped by to tell them.

The two hundred and fifty children they had succeeded in getting to Lisbon from where they were to sail to America would be returned to Marseille.

When the friend left, the two women sat discussing the news. "Sophie, you will have to go to Marseille and help find new places for those poor dears. To think they were so close to safety." Mary dissolved into tears – the first time Sophie had seen her friend so upset.

She rushed to her side. "Mary, you need to rest. This is a huge setback, but we will prevail. You've seen it for yourself. The sentiment among the people is changing. They may have accepted the deportation of foreign Jews but not the children. Laval, Pétain, and the Nazis have made the biggest mistake insisting on deporting the little ones; it will have turned the people to our side."

Mary clasped Sophie's hands in hers. "I hope you are right. All the Americans have been ordered to leave Vichy. If they don't, they will be detained."

"And you? Will you have to go too?" Sophie didn't want to lose her friend despite knowing she'd be safer in Ireland.

Mary shook her head. "No, I will stay. Ireland is neutral, so they won't detain me. I'll continue working but will be based in Toulouse, I think. They want you in Marseille."

* * *

Two weeks later, the Rivesaltes camp was closed with only forty-eight hours' notice. Sophie didn't bother trying to hide her tears as she helped those being deported to the transport. The wind howled and it was very cold. The locals said it was the worst that season. Sophie couldn't help feeling nature was protesting at the total injustice of putting innocent people on those awful trains.

FIVE

14 NOVEMBER 1942

Over the noise of the engine, Adèle ignored her uncomfortable surroundings and rehearsed her cover story again. She was going into France as Elise Delattre, a young married woman whose husband was missing, presumed dead. She was from Paris originally but was travelling to family in the countryside to recover from influenza. They had entered a history of TB in her medical records, just in case she got into difficulty.

Her identity card and ration book would be in the name of Elise, and this was the name she would use in France. Only network members used her cover name, Claire. Confusing as it seemed, this was one way to protect the agents from being discovered by the Gestapo.

"Nearly time, miss."

She wondered if she looked as green as she felt. She swallowed, hoping she wouldn't vomit. Then she heard "Go", and she was off, plunging out of the aeroplane. She couldn't remember what to do next. *Don't panic.* Her parachute opened, and her training kicked in. She looked down, trying to make sure there were no trees in her way. Even if there were, she couldn't steer the parachute. Where was the landing field? She couldn't see any lights from the reception committee. Was anyone waiting for her? What if it were the Germans? She couldn't fail the minute she landed.

As she drifted down, she landed softly in the snow on the edge of a field, avoiding the hedge. She shivered slightly, wishing she'd taken her camel-hair coat despite Miss Atkin's protestations that she had to look the part. The same for her silk stockings and stylish shoes, though she was thankful for the heavily bandaged ankles – the guys back in England had said they would protect her bones and tendons, and they had.

She stripped off the wool coat she wore over the regulation army overalls. Glancing around to make sure she was alone, she tore off the overalls to be buried with her parachute. She patted down the wool skirt she had on underneath, hoping it didn't look like she'd slept in it, before putting her coat back on. She tapped the pocket containing her revolver, her knife sitting comfortably and hidden from view in a modified pocket in her waistband.

In her bag, she had several changes of clothing, all suitable for her new identity as a lowly secretary recovering from TB – although how that girl was supposed to explain away the one million French francs she was carrying in her purse was anyone's guess.

* * *

She had to bury her parachute but, on looking around for a suitable spot, froze on seeing a man walking toward her.

"The priest sends his thanks for the vegetables for the children."

Adèle stared at him for a second before realising she had to reply. "They do not take away all the hunger pains, but they will help."

"Bonsoir, Claire. My name is Luc. Come, we must move quickly. You are slightly off-course. The drops usually are."

Adèle turned to complete the burial of the parachute.

Luc stopped her. "My men will see to that. Come now."

His tone brooked no argument.

Adèle shrugged; he knew the area, so she should listen. His men, approaching from the edge of the field, moved towards them, carefully picking their way, looking left and right as they moved.

She saw the gleam in the men's eyes as they stepped towards the parachute. They would barter rather than bury it. She only hoped they weren't too obvious about it.

As they set off, she gave Luc more information about her new identity.

"Not sure how anyone could concentrate on their job with you as their secretary."

She glanced at him, taking in his cheeky smile. He took her bag. His impeccable manners and cultured accent suggested a wealthy background.

"We are going by train. Stop looking so worried. Everything will be fine. We have a lift. Jump on."

He pointed at a pushbike. Adèle hoped he was joking. Seeing he wasn't, she climbed up and settled herself on the crossbar. He put her bag on his back before taking his seat. The bike wobbled the snow making it difficult to ride. Adèle's white knuckles gleamed in the moonlight. They rode in silence to the outskirts of a town.

When they arrived, she jumped down, whispering, "It's a relief to be off that bike."

He raised a finger to his lips, put the bike against a gate and then took her hand and led her to a small shed. He walked inside, made sure the blackout curtain covered the window before turning on the electric light.

She blinked at the bright light before assessing the man in

front of her. Tall with lean, muscled arms, wide, deep-set brown eyes, which somehow seemed full of hidden sorrows despite the playful smile on his face. He pointed at the blanket and a picnic basket before glancing at her, his eyes teasing. "A lovers' feast."

"I hope you brought your own. I'm starving."

Luc burst out laughing. He was older than she'd first thought. About twenty-eight. What had led him to join the resistance?

"Eat then rest. I will be back to collect you when curfew ends. Don't be afraid. You are safe. Sebastian will see to that."

At the sound of his name, a dog came running. It appeared to be half wolf, half hound. Adèle drew back, her hands tightening on the knife at her waist.

"Seb will look after you. I will be back soon. Stay."

Adèle didn't ask him if he was speaking to her or the dog, her eyes fixed on the beast in front of her. Sebastian came towards her, saliva dribbling from his mouth. Adèle shuddered. Did he think she was his lunch? If she survived, she would skin Luc alive. What was he thinking? Sebastian sniffed then licked her hand before holding out his paw. He stared at her, as if daring her to take it.

"Nice to meet you. Are you hungry?"

Sebastian's tail thumped the ground. She opened the basket and took out a piece of ham and a chunk of a loaf.

Splitting it in two, she gave half to the dog. He wolfed it down in seconds.

"Sorry, Seb, but it's been a long time since dinner." She devoured her share of the sandwich almost as fast as the animal had his. Her eyes fluttered shut but she fought the urge to rest. She had to stay alert. She stood up to stretch her legs but when she walked, Seb growled. She sat back down again.

"Steady, boy."

He licked her hand and inched closer to her. "You're a big pussycat really." She whispered as the dog turned over so she could rub his belly. She found his presence oddly comforting. At least she knew there were no strangers around as the dog lay under her hand.

* * *

When Luc returned, he had to wake her. She couldn't believe she had fallen into such a deep sleep. Some agent she was. Embarrassed, she muttered an excuse.

"There's no need. You were exhausted, and Seb here is the best guard dog for miles. If the Germans or anyone else had come near you, you would have known. He doesn't like Fritz."

Adèle patted the dog's head. If only all her countrymen could be so faithful. "What do you mean, the Germans?"

"Didn't they tell you the Boches have invaded the free zone the day before yesterday complete with their Gestapo, SS and all?

"No, I was waiting for the plane. We weren't allowed listen to the news."

"And there are many French only too happy to help them." His bitter tone suggested he knew from personal experience. "Didn't London warn you about traitors?"

She stayed silent; it was one thing being warned about the enemy when sitting in the safety of an old country house in the English countryside, another when sitting on the floor of a shed with only a man and his dog for company.

"Sebastian. Go home."

The dog whimpered, but Luc repeated his command. With one last look at his master, the dog turned and set off.

Luc handed her a canteen of water before he went to pick up her bag. She put her hand out to stop him.

"I'll carry my own stuff."

"Not here, you won't. I don't know what you were taught,

but men carry the bags, women their purses. We need to appear as normal as possible."

Chastened, Adèle took a long drink before handing the canteen back.

"The station is ten minutes' walk from here. There are no signs of extra soldiers. We think your arrival went unnoticed."

Given the noise of the plane, Adèle found that hard to believe, but she wasn't about to argue. This man was her only link with the network.

The walk to the station passed without incident. She spotted skinny schoolboys, walking down the street escorted by priests. The townsfolk paid them little attention as they went about their business. The delicious scent of garlic made her taste buds water, but there wasn't time to stop. They couldn't afford to be late for the train.

At the station, the ticket clerk yawned as he sold them the tickets.

Adèle's heart hammered. Would her papers stand up to inspection? The train arrived and departed on time. That was something she would change. London had been specific. They wanted the network disrupted, her mission included blowing up tracks and generally acting as a thorn in the Germans' side.

She leaned back on the wooden seat, wishing they could travel by first class, but that was only for collaborators. They would stick out like sore thumbs, especially the way they were both dressed.

"The ersatz-Gestapo are coming." Luc gave her hand a subtle squeeze.

She forced herself to feel calm and stared out the window as if she hadn't a care in the world. What did he mean by *pretend* Gestapo?

"Papers, please." The voice got nearer. Adèle couldn't help herself; she glanced up to find her gaze locked with that of a man, his close-cropped hair emphasising his pale blue eyes and chiselled face. He was gorgeous in a cold-marble type of way. Her heart stuttered, for a moment she thought he was a member of the fearsome Sûreté Nationale, the organisation responsible for the decimation of the first SOE group in Marseille. She could picture Miss Atkins, tears in her eyes, as she told the story of how a rogue agent had invited all the local agents to the Villa des Bois where the Sûreté Nationale force waited and gleefully picked them off, including Bégué, the only wireless radio operator. In one night, they had destroyed the SOE operation in the free zone. As she appraised the man in front of her, she wondered, was he one of those who liked to use a blowtorch on the bare feet of his victims to solicit information?

She pinched herself to focus, he was SS. The Germans had disbanded the Sûreté Nationale, replacing them with their own outfits.

Heat flushed through her body as she tried to keep her anger in check. How could a young man like this believe in the teachings of the Nazis? She forced those thoughts out of her mind. Despite being tempted to act like the old Parisian Adèle and flirt with him, she remembered to behave like the ill secretary she was supposed to be.

She held her papers out, her arm steady, her face a closed mask. He didn't take his gaze off her.

"Name?"

"Elise Delattre."

"Where were you born?"

"Paris."

"Where are you going?"

"To Lyon for a few days." Lyon was on the route for the train but they would be disembarking at a different station, not that this man needed to know that.

"Why?"

"I wish to see a chest specialist to seek a second opinion. I have recovered from a nasty flu, and the doctor mentioned TB."

His composure slipped. She hid a smile. He addressed Luc. "Are you travelling together?"

"Yes."

"You are a couple?"

"You don't think I would let her go alone?" Luc put his hand on her skirt, just above her knee.

Adèle cringed at her companion's bold gesture, but it seemed to work. The officer returned their papers and moved on.

She went to lean back but Luc muttered, "Don't move and don't speak." He kissed her on the cheek, running his hand up and down her leg, before wrapping his arm around her shoulder.

Adèle held her breath, the reason for his caution becoming clear as another officer walked right past. That had been close. Too close.

She didn't speak until her companion did. "They often travel in twos or threes. They watch to see how you go with the first inspection, then pounce on the second or third. You did well; the TB was a nice touch."

"You didn't have to paw me." She fidgeted, pulling down her skirt, and adjusting her coat, feeling uncomfortable that she hadn't known how the SS operated. What else had her training missed?

"I couldn't kiss you, seeing as you have suspected TB, but I am supposed to be your red-blooded companion! Why not take advantage of the situation we are in? It has a few perks."

Luc flashed her such a charming smile, she had to laugh.

"You sleep now. I will stay awake and warn you if we have any more unexpected visitors." His eyes danced. "I'm as reliable as Seb."

She didn't argue, just closed her eyes. But sleep took a long time to come. It was impossible to relax when her heart was beating a thousand miles a minute.

SIX

The rest of the train journey proved uneventful. On leaving the train at a small station, they passed through the barrier, ignoring the contingents of both uniformed and plain clothed policemen.

Luc took her arm as they walked down the street. "You must be hungry?"

"Starving." Despite the fright on the train, her appetite had returned with a vengeance. Her mouth watered at the thought of a decent French meal after the bland English food.

They walked arm in arm to a small restaurant. On entering, she let Luc order in case she made a mistake, using the time to observe her fellow countrymen. If anything, they looked in worse shape than those she'd left in Paris.

"I didn't expect the food supply to be so bad. Not here in the country."

"There's plenty of food for everyone who has money, although they struggle to obtain sugar. But for the rest of us, it's boiled acorn coffee, overcooked vegetables, and, if we are lucky, the tiniest sliver of red meat."

* * *

After their meal, Luc and Adèle made their way to the rendezvous point unmolested. Once they reached the village, a teenage girl, sullen to the point of rudeness, met them with a glare at Luc. She didn't acknowledge Adèle, who raised her eyes in question at Luc, but he ignored her.

"Are the others already there?" Adèle asked their guide, but the girl was either stone deaf or pretended not to hear her.

Luc whistled as if this was a usual occurrence.

It didn't take long – just a ten-minute walk outside the village – for their guide to deliver them to the meeting point. As they walked along the road, the tall grass swayed in the fields to the left and right of her. Adèle's unease grew, her stomach churning as they continued down a snowy path towards a house. Was this it? Where were the lookouts? The lack of security bothered her – they didn't even have a dog.

The girl didn't knock at the door. Did she live there? She walked inside, leaving it open for Adèle and Luc to follow her.

Inside, four men sat around smoking, glasses of wine on the table along with empty plates. They didn't stand in greeting; one muttered to the girl that she was late and the dishes needed to be done. Their guide's mood didn't improve as she gathered the plates noisily before walking through an open door into what was presumably the kitchen. Adèle heard the back door open and then the sounds of water gushing from the pump.

Luc introduced her using her code name. "This is Claire; she's highly trained and here to help lead us in victory."

The men looked up, and she soon wished they hadn't as, to a man, their faces showed disdain. Maybe she had underestimated the difficulty of getting her countrymen to accept a woman in their ranks, never mind taking orders from her. Feeling uncomfortable under their close examination, she glanced around the room before her attention focused on bits of rubberised fabric lying on the floor.

She walked over, bent down and picked up a piece, waving it in the direction of the men at the table.

"You can't leave this lying around. The Germans and their French supporters know we use it to cover the charges and detonators to keep them from getting damp. Why would you be so careless?"

The men ignored her and continued smoking.

"I asked you a question. Do you want to get caught?"

Luc caught her eye and gestured for her to follow him. They headed out the back door, past the grumpy girl washing the dishes.

Luc lit up a cigarette as he walked over to lean on a small wall.

"Careful, Claire. These men have been fighting the enemy for months. They won't take kindly to a stranger telling them off, particularly not a woman."

She rolled her eyes. What did it matter that she was a woman? If she'd been a Nazi supporter, they would all have been arrested. "But you have to see, it is risky."

"Yes, and *I* will speak to them. But you would do well to judge less and listen more. Forget the theory you've been taught in London. Down here in the trenches, life is very different. We live with the threat every day, unsure as to who is friend or foe." Luc's grimaced as he looked into the distance. "Some of us have already lost everything we took for granted. The men inside may be old-fashioned and not trained to your standards, but they are brave and willing to lay down their lives for France. Don't undermine their efforts."

She opened her mouth to say she'd suffered too but shut it again as it was clear he wasn't finished.

"You have your mission, and you won't achieve it by alienating those on our side. It is difficult enough to get those in the resistance to work together; some are die-hard communists, and others are Gaullists. Some believe it is disloyal to be working with the British. Most agree on one thing: women belong at home."

Chastised, Adèle fell silent. He was right. The last thing she needed was to get on the wrong side of the people she needed to train.

"I'm sorry; I should have handled it better."

Luc grinned at her. "I think apologising is something you struggle with." With that, he flicked some ash at her, and she found herself laughing rather than being insulted.

"They're good men. I'd trust them with my life."

He squeezed her arm to reassure her before they headed back into the house.

The men didn't even look up when she apologised, but Luc intervened again.

"Claire is well trained and our connection to London. She will train us in the art of sabotage. If we want supplies, we must work with her despite her being a woman and rather bossy."

Adèle rounded on Luc but caught his cheeky wink directed only at her. One of the older men, a cigarette hanging from his lip, handed her a glass of red wine. "Drink and listen."

She took a sip and spluttered as the rough red wine caught the back of her throat.

"See, she can't even drink."

Adèle took another gulp, earning her a clap on the back from the man sitting to her right. "I'm François, a schoolteacher by day. Welcome to France."

"Merci."

Letting it seem he was in charge, and she was his backup, Luc explained the structure of each unit. She got the impression he was talking to the men just as much as her. So he was worried about security.

"Claire has messages from London. They are very pleased with our work." Adèle kept her eyes on the floor for fear anyone would see he had made that bit up. "But our current role is to make life difficult for the Germans and their supporters. In time, when the British are ready to invade" – a couple of men mumbled at that remark, but the others stayed silent; they were listening – "we can blow up everything and kill as many Germans as we wish. But for now, the reprisals are too high, as we've seen from Paris."

Adèle swallowed hard. She didn't want to think about Jean-Pierre, her brother, even if he hadn't died in a reprisal. She forced herself to concentrate on what Luc was saying.

"Our mission now is to gather as many men as we can to join our fight. We can harass the enemy. If lorries carrying food supplies en route to Germany were to suffer a tyre blow-out or seize up due to sugar in their tanks, there is nobody to blame. They will not shoot their own drivers." Luc's gaze moved from face to face, ensuring he had their attention. "We train like the soldiers we are, but for now, it is our eyes and ears the British need."

The men all spoke at once, most angrily demanding they do more, not sit around like a group of old women. Adèle bit her lip, wanting to tell them sometimes they had to fight with their brains first. The British needed intelligence; they needed to know how many troops the Germans had in France, where and what type.

Silence fell at the knock on the front door. Adèle breathed through her nose to calm her heart palpitations, putting her hand on the knife secured at her waist. *The enemy wouldn't knock.*

The men around her stood as a well-built, swarthy man entered the room. Adèle recognised him instantly and saw the flicker of acknowledgement in his tawny-brown eyes, the grey flecks becoming more noticeable as he stared, and she held his gaze. Adèle couldn't believe her eyes – and he looked as shocked as she was.

She opened her mouth, but before she could say a word, he

embraced her in a large hug, his lips on hers. The men cheered at the kiss, their lewd comments making her blush.

He brought his lips to her ear. "Come with me."

She didn't have much of a choice, as he picked her up in his arms and headed for the door. Given her training, she could have fought back, but the men were all staring with open curiosity.

"Excuse us; we have some catching up to do." His comment only increased the men's remarks.

She let her arms hang loosely around his neck, playing the part, resisting the urge to choke him for embarrassing her. Her eyes met Luc's over the man's shoulder. He wasn't even bothering to hide his amusement but raised his glass of wine in toast.

Her feminine side was very aware of the muscled chest cradling her. His strength was attractive in a very earthy way. She forced that thought from her mind. Only when they were out of sight, near to the trees surrounding the property, did he put her back on her feet. She expected admiration from him, at finding her there of all places, but instead, he glowered at her.

"Adèle, what on earth are you doing here? This isn't some game. Why aren't you in Paris getting your hair done or going out to tea, or whatever it was you did with your life?"

Just her luck – she had to bump into Georges Monier, her brother Jean-Pierre's obnoxious communist friend. Jean-Pierre had introduced them back in 1938 as a lark, knowing they would hate each other, with his communist views clashing with Adèle's society ways. Jean-Pierre had teased Adèle, saying she only hated his handsome friend because Georges was the first man who hadn't fallen head over heels for her charm.

"Stop calling me that; you'll blow my cover."

"Your cover – will you listen to yourself!"

"Get your hands off me." She glared at Georges, trying to loosen his grip. "I swear, I'll—"

"What will you do?" His taunting expression was too much.

She grabbed him by the wrist and, in one move, had him on the ground, sitting on top of him almost before the smirk left his face.

"This is interesting." He ran his hands down her arms, obviously enjoying the feel of her body on his. Her breath quickened as a shiver of pleasure passed through her at the look of desire in his eyes.

Frustrated with his reaction, she growled, "I'm here to do a job. Can't you pretend you don't know me?"

His fingers caressed the skin on her arm, making it difficult to concentrate. Even his voice was sexy. "I would if I could, but I have a horrible feeling you are the agent I was expecting. The message was from the song 'À la claire fontaine'. Since a man is singing the song, I expected a man, not a wisp of a girl named Claire. There was also the fact I requested a sabotage expert."

Ignoring his unspoken question about her abilities, she broke the physical contact, brushing his hand away and standing. "They told me I was meeting Caesar. Is that you?"

He got to his feet and bowed. "At your service. But I can't believe you are here. What does Jean-Pierre think about you volunteering?"

His words had the same effect as a cold shower. Adèle looked at the ground. She wasn't prepared to speak about her brother; it was still too raw and painful.

He reached out, putting a finger under her chin, gently forcing her to look at him. "Adèle? I mean, Claire."

"Jean-Pierre is dead. Murdered by the Boches. Now, what's my job? You requested a sabotage expert, London told me to recruit and train more members."

His face paled, his eyes widening in shock. "Jean-Pierre – dead? I didn't know. How? When?"

"He was involved with the Musée de l'Homme. They shot him earlier this year along with Boris Vildé and the rest of the group."

Georges sighed. "I'm sorry. He was a good friend."

She shrugged her shoulders, trying to pretend she was fine.

He whispered, "Sophie, your parents, your grandmother? How are they?"

"Sophie is in Paris. I haven't spoken to her for months. My mother and grandmother were fine last time I saw them. I have been away a while." Could she tell him about her father turning his back on them? Where was he now? Did he regret what he'd done?

"How did you get to London?"

"I met a friend in Lyon. He took me over the Pyrenees, and the rest is history." She moved away from him, his maleness too disconcerting. Lack of sleep must be affecting her judgement. This was Georges Monier.

His pinched mouth suggested he misinterpreted her response. "I have little use for a woman in my group. The men won't take orders from you."

She gaped at him. Could he hear himself? It was 1942, not the Dark Ages.

"They will if you tell them to. Why can't women fight for the freedom of France? It's our country too. Jean-Pierre worked with women, and they took the same risks he did."

"Were they shot too?"

His pointed question got her back up. "Alas, the Germans shot two of them and sent the other three women to Germany." The I-told-you-so look on his face irritated her. "Can't you see? It makes more sense for us to use women to fight back. Women have greater freedom of movement and less risk of execution."

She waited a few seconds for him to say something. He stayed silent. "I have a job to do, Caesar. If you don't want me, I will find a unit that does."

A smile played around his lips.

"What?"

"You haven't changed, have you?" he said. "You are still a regular little brat."

"And you are an opinionated, self-important chauvinist."

"And your boss! Did London teach you about loyalty and obeying the rules?" he said.

"Did your mother teach you any manners?"

"Touché." He smiled, causing butterflies to explode in her stomach, irritating the daylights out of her. She was his equal, not a conquest. She forced herself to pay attention.

"What did London send with you? Guns, ammunition? Our supplies are low."

"None of that." She saw his eyes narrow and continued. "I have to give London details of a drop. They will send in supplies then. But Georges, London don't want you blowing things up. They want to build a network of support, an army if you will."

He cursed under his breath. "What do they think we've been doing?"

"They are worried about reprisals. Hostages being shot when Germans are killed or wounded. For now, we train everyone in how to use explosives, how to spot targets, gather information, and irritate the regime. In short, they want us to become a pain in the—" Her face flushed as his eyes held hers; she left the rest of that sentence unsaid. She turned away, pretending to look around as if assessing their location. "I have to contact them with the location of a drop zone for money and other supplies."

"You're a radio operator?"

Was that worry in his voice? She turned to look at him. She wasn't about to admit she failed to secure a high enough speed to pass.

"No. They said you already have one."

He inhaled sharply. "We did. My cousin Michel. The Vichy police caught him and killed him last week."

"I'm sorry." She couldn't remember if she had met his cousin, but any death was a tragedy.

"At least they killed him outright, before he could betray anyone."

Despite his cold words, she sensed his loss and a hint of guilt. Had it been his fault a member of his group was caught?

"It means we will have to send your message via another cell. Have you picked out the location yet?"

She shook her head. "I have only just arrived. Luc brought me here. The safe house was a surprise."

"Why?" His eyes bored into hers.

She wished she had said nothing, sensing he wouldn't appreciate criticism, but it was too late to back down now.

"One glance from a passing German sympathiser would be enough to expose it as a safe house. We arrived unannounced, there were no signs of security. There were bits of rubber lying around. I told the men who appear to live there it wasn't acceptable."

To her surprise, he burst out laughing. "I bet you did."

Annoyed at him for laughing at her, she walked away.

He strode after her. "Where are you going?"

I need to get away from you. "To get Luc. We need to find a location for the drop zone. I don't have time to reminisce about the good old days."

Despite her disdainful tone, he continued to laugh. He was still laughing when they entered the old farmhouse via the front door. Now more than irritated, she ignored the curious stares of the men, picked up her bag and snapped, "Luc, we have a job to do."

She turned on her heel and walked back outside, not waiting to see if Luc was following. She could hear Georges still laughing. She wished for a bucket of water – or preferably a large lake. She would push him right into it.

When Luc finally came out, he wiggled his eyebrows, his amusement obvious. She had to regain control.

"We need to find a good place for an aircraft to land if I am to get the supplies we need."

"You trying to get on the right side of the boss?" Luc challenged as he strode along beside her, hands in his pockets as if they were off on a country stroll through the snow. You wouldn't think there was a war on or that they were risking their lives. Hurt by Georges's laughter, she turned on Luc. "I can't understand why you all take this so casually."

Luc looked at her, his eyes blazing, knuckles white as he clenched his fists by his side. "We've lived with the threats. Everyone has their own way of coping. I prefer to joke around; if I stop to think about my friends and family I've already lost ... Michel, our radio operator, he was my best friend."

"I'm sorry, I guess I'm all het up. I want to show everyone I can do the job."

"Everyone, or just Caesar?"

Adèle stomped on, not wanting to answer that. Why did Georges's opinion of her matter? He was a communist, for goodness' sake, a rebel without a cause. Her mind flew back to the meal in Paris when her father had warned Jean-Pierre not to have anything to do with him. What would papa think of what she was doing?

Luc ran ahead and broke off a twig loaded with red berries. She didn't know the name of it but laughed as he bowed and presented it to her. "Truce?"

She took it and nodded.

He pointed north. "This way, the field is just over that road behind an abandoned farmhouse. The old man died; his son disappeared, fighting for France. Nobody comes here, and if they do, we can see them for miles."

She followed him, pleased to see he was right. In the distance, she could see the red-bricked façade of a chateau, but it was far enough away not to pose a threat. The field, while not huge, was free of trees and outbuildings, so would be perfect for a landing. The remoteness of the area worked in their favour, fewer people were likely to hear the plane land. But how would they transport the supplies?

"The men you met earlier have carts and a couple of oxen. They can move whatever we get to a safer location."

* * *

Glad they had found a suitable spot, they returned to the safe house in a much better mood. As they walked, Luc told her about the men – the ones he trusted, the ones he was wary of.

"Romain – he wasn't in the house, but you will meet him later – you can trust with your life, but not his sense of direction. He can't tell his left from his right." Luc grinned as if remembering something. "He's as loyal as Seb and can be just as fierce. He's a natural leader. The men look up to him despite his youth. He's been in more tight spots than Houdini but always comes out on top. François, the teacher, is more a lover than a fighter, but he has brains. Gustave, the red-haired man with the moustache, he is not a fan of the British. His wife ran off with an artist before the war started."

"Bet he won't care that the explosives he gets will come from Britain."

"Of course not; he hates the Germans more." Luc shrugged but she got the impression he wasn't a fan of Gustave. "What about Caesar? Did you know each other before the war?"

She ignored the flare of interest in his eyes. Honestly, he was worse than any woman. But his intense stare didn't help the blush on her cheeks.

"I knew him before the war, that's all."

"I thought so. Were you lovers?" Luc asked as they walked along. She stopped but he was a couple of paces ahead of her before he realised. He turned, seeing her expression, and threw up his arms. "What? It's a natural question, it's obvious you two have a..."

He thought Georges liked her too. She caught herself. She was here for a reason, and romance had no part of it.

"A business relationship and nothing more."

He raised his eyebrows but didn't comment further. "Yes, our paths crossed some years back. We weren't friends, but he is our leader, and I respect that."

"Good. His word is law around here."

It was. She was here now. She'd build her own resistance group and show London.

SEVEN

When they got back, she spotted a lookout on the road. She hid a smile, sensing Luc wouldn't appreciate her commenting on the change. She looked but didn't see any sign of Georges.

A man came forward to greet Luc with a hug.

"Claire, meet Romain."

Romain's head tilted to the side as he crossed his arms across his chest, his tone curious. "The boss said you had a message for London."

She glanced at Luc, who nodded. "Romain has a contact in another circuit."

"Give me five minutes to encode it."

"I will wait with the men."

Romain turned to leave, but Adèle stopped him by asking, "Where is Caesar?"

"He will be back in a few days." Romain's eyes held hers, his tone slightly contemptuous. "He said to tell you to stay out of trouble until then."

Adèle stared at the man for a few seconds. What had Georges said about her? It was difficult not to tell him to tell his boss to go and play with the Germans. She would sort Georges out when he returned.

* * *

She coded the message, inserting a phrase for the BBC personnel to read out. If they heard the phrase 'She wears a yellow dress', it meant the drop had been approved.

Three nights later, she sat with the group around the T.S.F, listening. Adèle smile on hearing the opening notes of Beethoven's Fifth Symphony. She knew enough morse code to understand the choice of music, the rhythm – dot dot dot dash – corresponded to the letter V. For victory.

Around her, the men all smoked. Gustave drank heavily, demanding the surly girl, Beatrice, produce more food. Romain shushed him as he leaned over and turned up the wireless. It was seven thirty in the evening. The first messages would start.

"Et voici maintenant quelques messages personnels...The cat has had a good walk, the goldfish was caught by a sparrow, she wears a yellow dress..."

François, the teacher, was the first to react. "That's it. The drop is on."

Adèle swallowed her relief, not wanting to show weakness. "They will repeat it at nine thirty this evening if it is, but for now, we must get ready. Luc, have you and Romain already picked your team?"

"Yes. All ready to go."

"Can I come too, please?" François begged. Adèle was tempted; he had been the only one who'd made an attempt to be pleasant to her. But a glance at Luc's face told her not to interfere. She put a hand on François's arm. "Next time, my friend."

* * *

At nine thirty, the announcement came on again. The drop was on. Adèle's heart fluttered with excitement. This was it. Her chance to prove to all of them that she was a proper agent with value in the field. She wished Caesar was here to witness it, but he seemed to have disappeared.

* * *

The small group cycled to the drop zone with Adèle keeping pace with the men. On their arrival, they spotted another ten men with a wagon and some oxen. Romain jumped off his bike and greeted the man on the wagon warmly, throwing his arms around him.

"His cousin," Luc whispered, but Adèle was too busy trying to recover from the ride. Thanks to her training, she was fitter than she'd ever been, but the pace set by the male cyclists through the snow had been taxing. She wasn't the only one out of breath.

"I told you we should have brought a lorry," Gustave complained as he leaned over the handlebars.

"It would be too conspicuous and easy to identify," Adèle replied. "It's hard enough to keep these drops a secret given the noise of the aircraft, not to mention some items drifting off target." *Or the pilot being totally off course.* But she kept those thoughts to herself. "Remember to count the number of parachutes. We don't want any packages falling into the wrong hands."

Luc handed a torch to Romain. "You and your men take the south; Gaston and his, the east; Marius, go west, and we'll take the north. And wait for Claire's signal."

The men dispersed. Adèle turned to Gustave, who was still breathing heavily from the bike ride. "You should post some lookouts just in case the aeroplane catches the attention of any patrols."

"Out here? Our gendarme friends are tucked up in their warm stations, not parading the countryside like us fools."

Luc gave Adèle a look, warning her to keep quiet. They made their way onto the field, leaving Gustave with the bicycles.

The time passed by so slowly Adèle gave up counting the seconds. She paced back and forth. The plane needed to arrive, it just had to.

Gustave whistled before shouting at them to abort the mission. "I told you she was a waste of time." His voice carried on the silence of the night.

"Shut him up, Luc, or I will." Her eyes scanned the sky, willing the plane to appear. Luc muttered something she didn't catch but moved off to speak to Gustave.

Then she heard it. Yes, it was a plane. The other men heard it too; she heard their excited whispers. She turned on her torch and flashed out the code.

The plane flew right over them. *No, no, no. This can't be happening.* They had to have seen them. The snow had stopped. The sky was clear, with the moon shining bright. The men grumbled.

Then Luc whispered, "They are coming back."

Sure enough, there was the sound of the motors. She switched on her torch and flashed the code again. One of the men lit the torch at the edge of the drop field. She counted six parachutes falling from the belly of the plane.

The men ran forward to claim the containers, eagerly cutting the parachutes loose.

Luc grunted as he pulled one container loose. "I didn't expect them to be so large or so heavy. Maybe we should have brought a truck instead of the wagon."

"Quit complaining and hurry up." Adèle pulled at one cylindrical metal container, hoping it contained some real coffee in addition to the guns and ammunition she'd requested.

"Leave that to me; you collect the smaller parcel over there. Where is the radio set?"

"Likely to be in a smaller package rather than a cylinder. Probably that one Romain is carrying."

Despite his earlier comments and attitude, Gustave was an asset as his bulky shoulders carried the weight of the six-foot-long cylinder like it was a small stick. They gathered all six packages and loaded them onto the wagon which Gustave would drive to a safehouse with a barn.

Adèle whispered to Luc, "We should get out of here." He nodded and, a couple of seconds later, whistled and gave the order to disperse. Everyone took a different route but all knew they would meet back at the safe house.

As they cycled, Adèle complained to Luc, "London said to bury the parachutes; they are too conspicuous."

"A French man bury silk that could be used to get him into his wife's – or any other woman's – good books? Are they mad?"

"Do you ever think of anything else?"

"Food, sometimes."

She burst out laughing.

At the safehouse, Adèle opened the cylinders in the barn, the men's eyes widening at the contents. Keeping quiet, they showed their approval by placing their arms around the other's shoulders or clapping each other on the back as she unloaded guns, ammunition, explosives, grenades, cigarettes, coffee and a few personal items marked "Claire".

She distributed the contents among the men. When the cylinders were empty, they were thrown down an unused well, the noise as they hit the walls on the way down sounding louder than the planes to her ears.

Walking from the barn to the house, her heart stilled as she saw Georges arriving, a cigarette hanging from his mouth.

"You've charmed the men, I see."

"Hardly. The guns and ammunition worked wonders, though. The coffee helped too."

He laughed, a lovely sound. This was ridiculous. She didn't have time for a man. She pushed past him, going outside to secure her bike to the fence with a chain.

"Are you worried about thieves?"

She whirled around at his mocking tone, but when she saw the look of admiration in his eyes, her retort caught in her throat.

"You did really well, Adèle."

"Don't sound so surprised." She tried to pretend his praise meant nothing, but she wasn't that good of an actress. Their eyes locked as the air between them sizzled.

Romain's voice interrupted, "Claire, you'd better come quick and show us how to use the plastique before Gustave blows himself and the rest of us to kingdom come."

EIGHT

Determined to prove her worth, Adèle mentally reviewed a list of targets Baker Street had provided. The objective was to harass the enemy and what better way than to derail a train. She packed a small satchel with some plastique, a blasting cap, some wire and a magneto blasting detonator courtesy of the previous drop. She put a dress and some underwear on top hoping that if they were stopped, the soldiers would assume the bag was full of clothing.

She approached the group of men gathered at the safe house.

"I need two volunteers to come on a mission with me."

Luc immediately stepped forward, but she shook her head. "Caesar would have my head." She glanced at the men, some looking at her, others staring at their cigarettes. "Anyone else?"

She waited, sweat pooling around her collar. The seconds ticked past before Romain stood up, ground out his cigarette and stepped to her side. He pointed at another man and with a jerk of his head ordered him to join him.

"We'll do it. Where and when?"

"Come with me, we'll talk on the way." She wasn't about to

disclose details of the operation to the crowd. The less everyone knew the better.

Romain and his friend stayed quiet as she moved to the bicycles parked out back. "We're going to derail a train and in the process you will learn how to do it the next time." The men's faces lit up. "I've found a suitable place in the track. A small explosion will be enough to derail the train while lowering the risk of anyone being killed."

Romain turned on her. "Why do you care if we kill Fritz?"

"I don't. But orders are orders." Adèle would love if the train derailment cost hundreds of German soldiers lives but she had to obey command. To do otherwise risked being recalled and sent to the cooler, a remote Scottish location, for the rest of the war.

They travelled in silence, the snow-covered ground helping to muffle the sound of their bicycle wheels. She indicated when to stop. Dismounting, they hid their bikes under some bushes. Putting her finger to her lips for silence, she gestured to them to follow her. The poor weather meant there were few people around. A few dogwood sparse bushes stuck out of the snow here and there.

On reaching the track, she pointed to where two sections of the track met. She removed four of the lag screws and using a small tool, separated the track sections, holding them apart with a screw. The men watched her as she scooped out some gravel. Taking the plastique from the bag, she affixed a blasting cap and ran the wire to the detonator. She indicated the men move back to the shadows, just in case something went wrong. They hesitated, she glared at them and they retreated. All crouched down to wait for the train.

Adèle bent down to place her ear next to the track, when it vibrated slightly, she signalled to the waiting men the train was coming. Ignoring her racing heart, took a deep breath, put her satchel back on her back and waited.

As the train came closer, she willed her hands not to shake. She couldn't detonate too soon but she had to be careful not to cause causalities, conscious of the risk of reprisals. As the train barrelled down the tracks, she detonated the charge, triggering a blast. The train jumped the track, shuddering to a stop but didn't overturn.

She gestured at the men to run. It took several seconds for the dust to clear and the German soldiers to recover their composure but then machine-gun fire traced over their heads as her team raced to where they had hidden their bikes. Luck was on their side as the bullets whizzed past them. All three pedalled away.

The Germans had the line repaired in a couple of hours but Adèle was elated. The operation was a success, the men looked at her differently. She hadn't killed anyone and there were no reprisals against the local community.

Romain approached her. "Can you teach me how to do what you did the other night? I mean properly. When we are allowed to kill, I want to send as many Germans to the next world as possible."

She knew she should try to reason with him but how could she when his words echoed her own feelings.

NINE

It was almost Christmas but apart from the snow and the freezing temperatures, you wouldn't have guessed. The people of Lyon wore miserable expressions and who could blame them with the ever-increasing restrictions put in place by the Germans.

"I wish I could order a real cup of coffee." Adèle brushed the hair from her face as they entered the café. They'd made little progress in recruiting members to their circuit and the men living in the forest wanted to go home. Not just because they were missing their families, but it was difficult to stay warm given the harsh weather and food was scarce. "I can't imagine what they are using to make the drinks they serve."

"Possibly best we don't know," Luc replied. "I like your hair that way; it suits you, ma chérie."

She raised her eyebrows, but he was staring over her shoulder. She leaned forward and kissed him on the cheek. He sensed something.

"Good afternoon, Monsieur Cheval. You seem to have adapted well to retirement here in Lyon.

Adèle stiffened at Luc's tone. She glanced towards the man

who sat at the next table, drinking proper coffee. The smell was tantalising.

"Good morning, Luc, mademoiselle. Please join me?"

Adèle looked to Luc, part of her hoping he would accept.

"Merci, but we have to meet a friend." Luc bowed slightly in the man's direction before flirting outrageously with Adèle as he led her to their own table, choosing one in the centre rather than one in the corner. She went along with it, all the while conscious of the man's scrutiny. A gendarme entered the café, took a seat at the man's table as Luc stiffened in response.

"That was close."

She couldn't contain her curiosity. "Who was he?"

"Monsieur Cheval. He is so cosy with Fritz, it is rumoured he has a swastika tattooed on his chest. He would sell his own mother into slavery. He has denounced countless people. He had to get out of Paris; seems he was over-enthusiastic even by the Germans' standards. I'm suspicious as to why he landed in Lyon."

"You think he might be a spy?"

Luc nodded.

"So why is he still alive?"

"He is clever. If he is killed, Fritz will seek reprisals. They protect their own." Luc's eyes raged with hatred. "He will be dealt with later. After the war."

Adèle exhaled sharply. "Should we not leave too?"

"No, they are probably keeping watch on the café. It is best to act normal."

Adèle didn't have time to question Luc as they were once more interrupted.

"Good morning. Your wife is a pleasure to look at." A small, darker-skinned man of a similar age to Luc joined them. His hand shook as he ran it through his hair, as if he was suffering from nerves. It was unlikely to be a hangover given the lack of alcohol available due to the shortages.

"She's not my wife; I leave her indoors. Elise is much better company." He leaned in and kissed her on the cheek. "Jozef is a friend."

Adèle picked up on the hint, this man was part of Luc's broader network. Luc glanced in the direction of Cheval as he and the Gendarme finished their drinks and left.

Jozef sat down as Luc insisted on buying him a drink. The man leaned in closer, whispering, "There have been more arrests. We must be more careful. Tell our friend they know his name."

Adèle's ears pricked up – they were talking about Georges. Was he in danger?

Before she could ask anything, a dainty, well-dressed and striking-looking young woman came into the café. She glanced around; her blue, almost purple, eyes lit up when she spotted Luc and his friend. Adèle glanced at Luc, curious to see his reaction to the girl. She sensed some hesitation on his part.

"Monique, what are you doing here? Is your mother well?" Luc stood up with his back to Adèle.

Monique's tongue darted out, wetting her lips as she put her hand on Luc's arm. "She's fine."

Adèle pretended to find her drink fascinating, but she couldn't resist watching the woman's actions. Something was off. She seemed ... not overcome with infatuation with Luc, although she was making all the right moves of someone who adored him. Was she playing with his affections? Or using him to make someone jealous? Whatever she was up to, Luc seemed immune to her considerable charms.

"Luc, I need you to introduce me to the resistance. I want to fight for our country. I'm sick of living like this."

"Don't shout it from the rooftops. Sit down before they arrest you." Luc pulled out a chair on the opposite side of the table to where Adèle was sitting.

"They wouldn't. I haven't done anything. Your men won't

let me." Despite the woman's sulkiness, she was very good-looking and younger than she first appeared. She was wearing quite a bit of make-up, making Adèle feel underdressed.

"Elise, this is Monique. She is a friend from my town. Her brother and I were in school together."

Monique gave her a sideways glance. Adèle suppressed a grin; it was the same look she'd used on other women in the past. Hopefully, she'd been a little more discreet. Monique moved the seat closer to Luc as if laying claim on him.

"He thinks he is protecting me. I want to help the resistance, but nobody will let me join." Monique gave a deep sigh before pursing her lips tightly together.

Nervous about who might overhear them in the café, Adèle laughed.

"A young girl like you should have better things to do. I know I have. Now tell me, where can I get my hair done like yours? The cut is beautiful. Classic, but suits you." She heaped on the compliments, hoping the girl would think her a socialite and nothing else.

But it didn't work. Monique dismissed her with a wave of her hand before focusing her large eyes on Luc, batting her eyelashes.

"Did you see there were more men rounded up last week? Why hasn't the resistance rescued our heroes?"

Luc shrugged, his face registering total disinterest. "Monique, what can I do? I have a full-time job and have no interest in fighting anyone. The Germans are in charge. We might as well accept it."

Monique threw back her chair so hard it landed on the floor. "I despise you, Luc. Thank God your father is dead and buried and can't see what a spineless coward you have become."

Luc stared after Monique as Adèle exchanged a look with Jozef.

"I think it's time to let her in." Jozef ground out his cigarette. "She is fiery and immature, but she loves France."

Luc shook his head, but his hands curled on his knee, his body tense. "She is the youngest daughter of one of my mother's friends. She has a rather protective big brother. I can't involve her. He would kill me."

Adèle glanced at Luc. Was he really scared of someone's brother? Surely the maquis needed all the help they could get. But mindful of what Georges and Luc had said about her interfering and coming across as if she knew everything, she kept quiet.

"But I can. He doesn't know me." Jozef sounded like a forty-a-day smoker, his voice raspy. He was painfully thin, too, much more so than Luc. His suit was well cut and once had been of decent quality, but now showed signs of wear; the knees of the trousers looked shiny, as did the elbows of his jacket. War shortages were affecting everyone, but he seemed to be even worse off than most.

"Leave it, Jozef." Luc's tone brooked no argument. "She is not joining our group."

Jozef didn't respond to Luc. He took a gulp of his drink, not hiding his distaste. "Pardon me – I think I might sell my mother for a cup of real coffee." He laughed at his own joke, then his face grew serious. "Is Caesar going to do anything to help the Jews?"

Luc shrugged. "He does what he can, but it is not his prime focus."

Jozef helped himself to one of Luc's cigarettes, his hands shaking slightly. "It should be if those rumours are true."

Curiosity got the better of her. "What rumours?"

"The children are being left in the camps," Jozef replied, "while their parents are deported. Then they are sent in groups on their own to Poland."

"But I thought Laval said he wanted families to stay together?" Luc picked up his cup but finding it empty put it back on the table.

Jozef spat on the floor. "That serpent has a forked tongue. We need to help them."

Adèle listened as Jozef told them story after story of what had been happening in France. She couldn't help but feel sorry for the children. An image of Zeldah, her family's former maid and the mother of her brother's child, escorting orphans onto the ship to America, flashed into her mind. The children were innocent – children like Jean-Pierre's own baby. Was there something she could do to help?

TEN

Sophie fidgeted, wondering what the delay was as the tram stopped on the boulevard Gambetta.

"Mon Dieu." The man sitting beside her crossed himself, his lips moving as if in prayer as the German soldiers were marching in Marseille. Just as they had done in Paris, the troops behaved like conquering heroes, marching in unison in their pristine uniforms and shiny boots. A few people on the tram started to cry, the tears falling silently down their cheeks. Sophie clenched her hands as she tried to calm her stomach. Where were they going to send the Jewish children now? Nowhere seemed safe.

She returned to the apartment she'd been staying in since leaving Perpignan. Situated in the Vieux Port, she felt safe, despite it being a district everyone else usually avoided. She opened the door, pleased to find her friends Liliane and Renée waiting for her. The twenty-year-olds sat at the table with several packages of pasta and bags of sugar, some tobacco, salt – and was that chocolate in front of them?

Renée smiled at Sophie's shock. "Business was good last night."

"I can see that. But why bring it all here?" Sophie took off her coat and hung it over the back of the chair.

"Carlos told me to take it, or he'd sell it. He was drinking again and in a foul mood." Renée picked up a bag of sugar, her mouth trembling as if she was about to burst into tears. "We thought you'd be pleased."

Chastened by their disappointment, Sophie sought to reassure them. She sometimes forgot they were so young, their lives on the streets made them appear older.

"I am. I worry about you both. Carlos is playing a dangerous game. You must be more careful. Especially now."

The girls exchanged a look and shrugged. They'd grown up on the streets of Warsaw and could look after themselves, or so they thought.

* * *

But over the next few days, Liliane and Renée's moods changed. Their smiles disappeared, worry lines appearing at their eyes.

Sophie jumped as the apartment door slammed.

"The rumours are true. Darnand is recruiting from the prisons." Renée unwrapped her scarf before removing her coat and gloves. "Isn't it bad enough we have to fight the Germans without having to deal with a French militia too?"

Sophie had heard Darnand boasted about recruiting thirty thousand Frenchmen to join his Milice. She'd been heartened to hear that the recruitment drive had failed to drum up enough volunteers, but then Darnand had convinced his Vichy cronies to offer those convicted of serious felonies a choice between jail time or joining up. Now those men were working with the German Gestapo, rounding up anyone who opposed the Nazi regime and, of course, the Jews.

Between the Gestapo, the black-market police and the usual gendarmes, she had her work cut out for her as she moved across the city looking for safe places to house children, secure extra food, papers, and, of course, money. She didn't want to think about how difficult it would be if Darnard got his Milice up and running.

"I think it's time you left Marseille. Take refuge in one of the mountain villages," Sophie said as she dished up a plate of pasta with some boiled cabbage. "Sorry, it was all I could find today."

Renée didn't respond, which was unusual. She picked up her fork and began to eat. "Where's Liliane? Isn't she back yet?"

Liliane had gone to Toulouse to see Mary Elmes. She'd been due back the day before. Sophie pretended not to share the younger girl's concerns. "Maybe something came up. Don't worry – as you so often tell me, you girls can look after yourselves. Now go to bed. We've to get the Levin girls out tomorrow. You'll take them to the farm."

Renée nodded. "I'll try to bring back some eggs or maybe a rabbit."

Sophie smiled. "Just come back safe. Now the Germans are here, you can't spit without hitting one of them."

"Now, there's a thought." Renée grinned before she headed towards the bedroom.

Sophie hoped she'd sounded more confident than she felt. Liliane was the more reliable of the two girls; it wasn't like her to worry them.

* * *

Before Renée set out the next morning, Liliane arrived back just after ten. "Sorry, there was a *rafle* at the station. They checked everyone's identity cards and kept us all in the train until they were satisfied they had got everyone they wanted. At least we know Mael's forgeries work."

Renée didn't give her a chance to say anything else before enveloping her in a hug.

"I brought you both back something." Liliane dug out two green hats complete with feathers.

"What's this?" Renée put on one hat and modelled it in front of the mirror.

"All the French women are wearing them. The green feather symbolises a green bean – *les haricots verts* – the nickname given to the Germans."

"I don't think you girls should wear them." Sophie couldn't stop herself being protective of her two Jewish friends.

"Why not? I think they suit me." Renée smiled at her reflection. "It may be a simple form of resistance, but it will help me feel better."

"Sophie, let her keep it. You should wear one too, or else people might think you are German." Liliane put the hat on Sophie's head. "See, it suits you too."

The smell of burning, corresponding with the sounds of whistles and marching feet, interrupted their joking.

Ashen-faced, Renée turned to Liliane. "Did you see anything?"

"No."

Sophie moved to the door. "Stay here; pack the emergency bags."

She was gone before they could protest. She made her way down the street, several of her neighbours doing the same, heading towards where many gendarmes had gathered.

"What's going on? Was it a bomb?" someone asked.

One gendarme spat on the pavement. "No. It's a long-overdue clear-out."

Looking over his shoulder, Sophie could see people being pushed out of their houses, men, women, children, old people – it didn't matter what condition they were in. "Where are they taking them?"

The gendarme held Sophie's gaze. "Sending them back where they came from. There's no room for their sort in France."

She turned on her heel, returning to their apartment. The girls had to get out before the police decided to do the same to their building. Liliane and Renée each held a small carpetbag full of clothes and a few black-market items.

"Leave the black-market stuff here. Don't argue with me. You can't give them any excuse to arrest you." Sophie stood over them as they repacked the bags.

Renée griped, "Can't we take the sugar, at least?"

"No, leave it. Now go. Don't look back or stop for any reason. I will come to Hugo's farm as soon as it is safe."

She embraced both the girls and wished them bonne chance.

Once they'd left, she repacked as much of the black-market produce as she could into bags. Then she called the concierge, Madame Lambard, to come up and distribute the bags as she saw fit.

"This is the worst day of my life," the concierge said. "I never thought I would see Frenchmen behaving like animals. They are burning down all the houses, the stores, everything. And sending all those people to the trains." She shook her head. "What did those families do to anyone? Maybe I should try to get this onto the train too?"

"No, Madame Lambard, take it and give it to those in need. It's from the black market, so warn people to hide it well."

"Bless you, Sophie. Go before they get here. I will tell them Carlos gave it to me. Nobody will dare to denounce me then."

Sophie smiled although she wanted to cry. Before the war, Carlos was one of the most feared pimps in Marseille. Now he was their hero.

ELEVEN

FEBRUARY 1943, LYON

Adèle nursed the cup of real coffee in her hands, courtesy of a recent drop, taking advantage of the lull in operations to stretch out on the couch. The apartment was situated above a lingerie shop, the owner storing weapons under piles of lacy underwear in the back stores. The Germans couldn't get enough of her products, gifting them to their French mistresses or sending them home to their wives. Many in Lyon believed Madame Marchand to be a collaborator, which suited Adèle's purposes. The Germans wouldn't think of searching the apartment above the shop looking for resistants, let alone escaped airmen. In addition to the entrance through the store, the apartment had a back entrance allowing them to come and go without being seen.

Yet she couldn't fully relax as her eighteen-year-old companion paced back and forth across the floor.

"Harry, can you sit down? The customers in the store downstairs are likely to complain about the noise with you stomping all over the floor."

Harry paled and sat immediately, his reaction making her smile.

"Relax, they are on our side. I was half-joking. Want some coffee?"

He got up, shaking his head, rubbing his hands together as he resumed pacing. Had he taken something? She knew pilots took pills; many agents took them too to keep themselves awake. At her pointed look, he resumed his seat, but his knee kept shaking.

"Spit it out. What's the matter?"

"I can't believe the French people have been so kind to us."

She arched an eyebrow.

"I mean, we drop bombs on them, blow their cities to bits, and they risk their lives hiding us. They told us back home the locals might help but we had to be careful. Everyone I met from Paris to here, they've all been so nice."

"And?"

"The Germans will treat us as airmen and so send us to prison."

"If you're caught."

"Yeah, right. But if they catch those sheltering us, like you, I mean, they will torture you before they murder you. I heard they did that to whole families, like the children and all."

What did he want her to say?

"I just, well, I'd like those who helped me to know I'm grateful. I wish there was a way I could pay them back."

"You can. Get back to Britain and bomb Germany to bits. End the war."

He pulled at the shirt he was wearing; it was too small, but it was the best they had. British men tended to be taller than French, but Harry was over six foot three. Finding shoes, not easy given the shortage of leather, had also been an issue, but a local undertaker had come up trumps.

"Please sit down, Harry, you're giving me a headache. Why don't you try to sleep? You've a long trip tomorrow."

"Am I leaving then?"

She shrugged. "That's the plan, but we'll see."

A knock on the door caused him to slide into the chair, his face the colour of milk. She pulled her weapon and moved to the window, but the street outside was deserted. The knock came again.

She indicated Harry go into the bedroom before she opened the door, her handgun at the ready in her pocket.

"Did you miss me?" Georges winked as he walked past her into the apartment.

"You nearly gave us both a heart attack. What are you doing here, and why didn't you use the coded knock?"

"Did you think I was the Gestapo? I doubt they would be as polite."

Even as he joked, she saw the drawn lines around his eyes and mouth, the sadness lurking in his eyes. She moved closer, dropping her voice so Harry couldn't hear her. "What's wrong? Where's Dr Macy?"

"Burned. Romain got word to me just now. The lookout was distracted, and nobody noticed the black Citroën until they screeched to a halt outside the clinic. The whole place was surrounded. They didn't have a chance."

Adèle bit her lip, drawing blood in the process. Dr Macy, a lovely man in his early sixties, had been a key part of the resistance community. Not only did he patch up bullet holes and other wounds, but he also carried several packages in his car.

Georges grasped her hands in his. "I'm here to get Harry out. You need to go too, Adèle. The doc knows about this apartment."

"His wife? Michelle and Suzette, his daughters?"

He put his hand out to push the hair back from her face. "You can't think about them now. Go to Marie – the doc doesn't know about her; she'll give you shelter until tomorrow. Thank God we have time before curfew. When it's safe, get to Luc."

"But what of you? Harry isn't going to pass easily as a

Frenchman." She spoke too loud; her voice must have carried as Harry opened the bedroom door.

"What's wrong? If the Germans are here, I'll give myself up. I'll tell them I forced you to hide me."

Georges went over to shake his hand. "We need to get you home. The RAF need their pilots back – even the ones that crash their planes."

Adèle flashed Georges a small smile. During a crisis, he was trying to make the boy feel better. She moved around the apartment, throwing things into the bag she always kept by the door. Georges raised his eyebrows.

"They're not getting my coffee. If anyone stops me, I'll tell them I slept with an officer, and he paid me in kind."

Georges walked over and kissed Adèle full on the lips, whispering, "Don't even joke like that," before gesturing to Harry. "Come on, let's go."

Adèle kissed Harry on both cheeks, with another for luck. "Bon voyage."

She watched them leave before running to the window to check the streets remained clear of cars. There was nobody about. With a final check to make sure there was nothing incriminating left behind, she was about to leave when she heard someone outside her door.

Merde. Could they have found her so fast? Had Georges been trailed? She took off her coat, throwing it over the back of the kitchen chair. She'd have to bluff her way through, pretend, but she couldn't do that with a handgun in her pocket. She took it out and hid it behind some books in the bookcase. If she went with them, they might not search the apartment.

The knock was a surprise.

She took a deep breath, ran her hand through her hair and opened the door.

"Yes?"

TWELVE

FEBRUARY 1943

Sophie looked up from the bed where the twin Archer boys were sleeping. Both had high temperatures and would be better if separated into two beds rather than sharing, but they refused to be parted. She'd given them tepid baths, a little aspirin and taken them outside in the cool air, but nothing would bring their fever down. She pushed the hair back from their foreheads as they called out in their sleep for their mother.

The door to the room opened as one of the nuns from the convent entered and said, "Sophie, come. Gaëlle will take over. I need to speak to you."

Sophie passed the cold cloth to the young volunteer who often helped with the little children. "Try to get them to drink if you can." Gaëlle nodded, her eyes wide in her face as her hand felt the heat coming from the little ones.

"I will be back as soon as I can," Sophie murmured as she followed the nun out of the room. It had to be something bad to take her away from their sickest patients.

"Sophie, brace yourself. I have bad news." The nun's grave expression turned Sophie's stomach. *Adèle? No, it can't be.*

Nobody knew she had a sister. Her mother, grandmother? Her father? Her mind whirled.

"Tell me, please."

"Mary Elmes was arrested by the SS."

Sophie fell back against the wall, thankful for its support. Mary in the hands of those monsters. What would they do to her?

"But they can't. She's Irish."

"They don't care. Helga and Ima from the Toulouse office tried to visit her, but they weren't allowed in. But at least the guard took a package of necessities. Poor Mary didn't have anything with her when they drove her away."

"What have they charged her with?" Sophie asked. She wondered if she should go back to Mary's home and dig up the names in the garden. *What if the SS discover them? We will never match up the children with their parents when the war is over... What can I do to help Mary?* "Someone must tell the Irish Embassy."

"That's been done. The Nazis say she has been spreading propaganda showing them in a poor light."

Sophie laughed. Of all the things they could have charged her friend with. "She did no such thing. Mary just told the truth. They shouldn't act badly if they don't want people to comment on it."

"Getting angry isn't going to help anyone. We need to get you out of here. We're going to send you to a hospital near Cannes."

"Me? Why?" Sophie didn't want to leave. The children needed stability. They had been sent from camp to camp, torn from their parents and from safe houses to land here in this children's home. Here they felt safe.

"Sophie, if Mary is tortured, she may reveal what she knows. None of us are safe. We will have to move the children. There was talk of doing it anyway. Many believe keeping a group of Jewish children together will only serve the Nazis. They would grab the whole lot together if they came here." The nun crossed herself.

"Surely they wouldn't?" But even as she put the thought into words, she knew it to be stupid. There was no depth to which the Nazis couldn't sink; hadn't they proved that already?

"Have they hired a lawyer? Someone to intercede on her behalf?"

"Efforts are ongoing, but in the meantime, we must concentrate on the children. We will have to find families to place them with. Mother Superior believes you would be a good person to find these homes as you have a way of convincing people to do what you ask."

Sophie barely heard the nun, her mind swirling as she remembered her last days with Mary. Her friend had been so concerned with everyone else's safety; what risks had she taken that she'd come to the attention of the SS? What would happen to her?

"Sophie."

"Sorry, I was thinking about Mary. Of course, I will do anything you ask. But first, I must get back to the twins and check on them. If their fever doesn't break tonight, we may lose them. And I won't let that happen. We have lost enough already."

The nun patted Sophie's hand. "We will pray for Mary and the twins. Now go back to Gaëlle and the boys. Mother Superior will send for you later. She is making a list of people who she thinks may be able to help."

Sophie returned to the sickroom where Gaëlle was sponging down the boys.

"Let me stay to help you, please. My brother ... he was their age when the Nazis took him and my mother. Being here with them makes me feel closer to him."

Sophie nodded, too choked up to speak. She tried to get the

boys to drink more water, all the while wondering what Mary was doing and how she was coping.

THIRTEEN

Adèle's heart raced as she stared at the man in front of her. He wasn't Gestapo.

The visitor was dressed in French clothes, his bandaged arm in a sling. His green eyes shimmered – were those tears? His shoulders slumped, his face lined with exhaustion.

"I'm sorry, I didn't mean to scare anyone, but they're after me. Please help me. Sorry, it's so late, but I had to make sure I wasn't being followed."

Adèle kept the door partially closed, preventing the new arrival from seeing the inside of the apartment.

"Who are you? What do you want?"

The man glanced over his shoulder before whispering, "They said I was to come here, that you'd help me. Although they didn't tell me you were so young and pretty."

She ignored the flattery, her heart thumping as she scanned the hallway behind him. Was this a trap? How had he found this address?

"Flying Officer Edward Hillary Church at your service. My plane was hit by flak, and I bailed out, but it was too low so I hit the ground with a bang. I crawled through some fields before I passed out." He indicated his arm. "A farmer found me before the patrol. He took me to his home, got a local vet to set my arm, did a pretty good job too."

The man's French was passable, the accent English. He seemed to be who he said he was.

She opened the door wider. "Come in, please. I can give you a drink of water, but I don't know what else you expect from me."

Letting him in, she waited for a second, listening out for footsteps or a car door slamming, but there was nothing.

He stood against the wall, just inside the door, as if he would fall over if he took another step.

What was she going to do? She couldn't afford to stay in the apartment. If the doc talked, he knew this location. But she couldn't take a stranger to Marie's. He might be genuine, but if he wasn't, she was putting her friend at risk.

"Who told you to come to this apartment?" She watched as he gulped down the glass of water, her senses on high alert listening to the street outside. No cars.

"The Royers."

She stilled her face, not wanting to show him she recognised the name.

"They have a farm just north of here. Lovely old couple with a son in Germany; he's a prisoner of the Germans. They gave me some of his clothes." He fingered the shirt he was wearing.

He was trying too hard to appear relaxed, but was that nerves due to being on the run in a country full of his enemy, or something else?

He went to stand up, but his leg gave way under him, and he sat down with a bump. "I should leave. You obviously don't want me here. I'll try to find someone else."

"You hurt your leg as well?" Her stomach twinged with guilt.

"It's not as bad as my arm, but yes. A little."

If the poor man had escaped from a plane fighting for her country, he deserved better. "It's not that I don't want you here, but we've reason to believe the Germans will arrive shortly. We need to leave."

That made him stand up, a look of panic crossing his face. He had to be who he said he was; nobody was that good an actor. She knew the Gestapo had infiltrated many of the lines; maybe the bad news about her friend being picked up had made her paranoid.

Picking up her coat, she put it on before she retrieved her handgun from the bookshelf. She couldn't leave him here.

"I will help you as much as I can, but we have to leave." Her softer tone earned her a smile.

"If you are in danger, you should go; I'll only slow you down."

Her opinion of him rose higher. "Nonsense. We go together."

"Where?"

It wasn't her training kicking in; she had no idea where to go. She wasn't bringing him to Marie's. But where? "You'll see."

She went ahead, checking there was nobody waiting outside before beckoning him to follow her. She led the way through the walled streets, up the stairs, keeping her eyes open for anyone looking in their direction. It was close to curfew, and the few people on the streets were hurrying along, no doubt wanting to get home in time.

She set the pace and, to his credit, he kept up without complaining. They left the town behind, now walking across green pasture, which seemed to be more difficult for him. He didn't talk; his breathing became a little heavier. After an hour of walking, it was obvious he was tiring; she spotted sweat on his upper lip despite it being late evening. She handed him her wine bottle. "It's only water, but it will refresh you. We will stop soon. The house is just a little farther on."

He nodded but didn't say a word. She led the way to a farmhouse they used occasionally. As they walked up the lane to the house, a dog's barking made the airman jump. Adèle whistled, and the dog came running towards them, jumping up on her with joy. "Hello, Seb. Long time no see. This is a friend of mine." Seb licked Adèle's hand, but he growled at the airman, who backed away. "Don't worry. He's friendly. Unless you're German or a traitor, of course."

Edward's face didn't move a muscle, his eyes locked on the dog.

"Come on, Seb, take me to your master."

The farmhouse door opened, the small light from the fire illuminating their way. "Who's there?"

"It's me, Monsieur Abreo – Elise."

"Come in, girl, out of the cold. Who's that you've got with you?" Madame Abreo came to the door, rubbing her hands on her apron before she hugged Elise to her ample bosom.

"This is Edward. He's RAF, trying to get to Spain. He came to the apartment we use in town, but it's likely the Germans know about it. I'm sorry to call so late, but it's curfew soon, and we can't afford to be on the street. Not tonight."

"You don't need any excuse to come. We love seeing you, don't we, Adrien. Sit down, Edward. Any friend of Elise is a friend of ours. You must be hungry; you young people always are."

In no time, Madame Abreo dished up a tasty vegetable soup with some chicken on the side. "She stopped laying, so I couldn't waste her. If only I had some butter and a little garlic."

"This is perfect, thank you so much." Edward's atrocious French made them all laugh.

The evening passed pleasantly, with Edward answering the couple's questions. No, he hadn't met Winston Churchill or de

Gaulle in person but had seen them from a distance when he visited London.

Adèle watched the interaction, wishing she could shift the feeling causing the hairs on the back of her neck to stand up. She kept topping up Edward's glass with more wine, despite his protests.

"It will help you relax and sleep; you need to rest. Going over the mountains at any time is rough going, but winter must be the hardest."

He raised his glass to hers, and she took another sip. When he excused himself to use the outside toilet, she topped up her glass with water.

Monsieur Abreo, a determined look on his face, patted her hand. "I'll get us more wine."

While he went to the barn to fetch another bottle from the hidden cellar, Madame Abreo pulled her chair closer. "Elise, something is bothering you. Tell me."

With her eye on the back door, she whispered, "I hope I'm wrong, but there is something bothering me about Edward. I need to get to Caesar. I'll leave a handgun in your bedroom, under your pillow. If you have any doubts, shoot him."

The look of horror in the other woman's eyes was quickly replaced by determination. She stood up, walked over to the kitchen cabinets and, reaching on her tiptoes, retrieved a small box from the top shelf. Coming back to the table, she quickly opened it, removed a small pill and, breaking it open, poured the contents into Edward's wine glass. She mixed it up with a spoon.

She glanced at Adèle and said, "It won't kill him, but he will sleep. Adrien can deal with him when he wakes up. You do what you must, but be careful."

Adèle wiped her eyes with her arm, embarrassed at the sudden tears. "You are so brave. I'm sorry I brought him here, but I didn't have any other choice."

"I'm glad you trusted us. Luc will know what to do if you can't find Georges." Josette put a hand over her mouth at her slip. "I mean, Caesar."

Adèle smiled despite the implication she needed to check with the men. She had another reason for trying to find Georges.

Edward arrived back at the same time as Monsieur Abreo. Adèle caught the look that passed between the old couple. He'd gone out deliberately to watch Edward. She smiled as she picked up her watered-down wine. "Cheers to victory."

Edward raised his glass and took a large gulp of wine, and then added his own toast to the RAF. Josette toasted her son, explaining to Edward, "He's a prisoner of war in Germany." Adèle had to look away. Félix Abreo was with the resistance in Paris.

She watched as Edward's eyelids drooped, his speech becoming slurred. Adrien suggested he help him to bed.

"I'm sorry, it's been a long time since I had such a nice meal and lovely wine. It must be a good year." Edward tipped his hand to his forehead to Madame Abreo before taking Adrien's arm and, leaning heavily on the old man, allowed himself to be taken to the bedroom. Adèle helped Josette clear the table as they waited for Adrien to return. It didn't take long.

"He is fast asleep. Like an innocent child." The gruffness of his voice told her he shared some of her concerns.

"I hope he does turn out to be a real pilot. He has nice manners." Josette hugged Adèle. "Keep your gun. We have one; Félix gave us one the last time he was home. Be careful. Adrien fixed the puncture on the spare bicycle. Take it."

Adèle hugged the older woman, kissed both her cheeks and headed out the door. She had a lot of time to make up; she had to get to the camp before Georges moved Harry on to the next contact.

FOURTEEN

CANNES

Sophie walked along the street, enjoying the sound of children laughing and playing just like they had done prior to the war. Everywhere she looked, she spotted different nationalities, but here, they mingled without looking over their shoulders. The Italians refused to give up Jews to the Germans. Not only that, but they put guards on the synagogues so people could practise their religion if they wished. She'd also heard rumours about the Italians dating Jewish girls. It was all so different from the hatred shown by the Nazis.

She stood at the side of the market as the Italians came marching along the street, the Bersaglieri or light infantry dressed in black with feathers adorning their helmets.

"They don't look like they are starving. Look at the state of those uniforms." A woman standing beside Sophie commented. "I heard they are the reason we can't find anything to eat in the shops. My children would eat their own bare hands. They're that hungry."

Everyone complained about the scarcity of food much more than the presence of the Italians. Following the Allied landings in North Africa, ships filled with olive oil, wheat, and other foodstuffs no longer arrived. The locals were prevented from taking their boats out to fish.

Vichy responded to the shortage in food by reducing rations. It didn't really matter what the allowance was; the lack of salted fish, vegetable oil, wheat, tomatoes, eggs, and virtually every other essential in the shops meant people found it difficult to find any food. Most of the younger patients Sophie saw were showing signs of severe malnutrition. On top of that, the sheer number of people crowding into the Italian zones, all living on top of one another, enabled the spread of scabies, lice, and contagious illnesses.

Sophie studied the woman more closely, seeing her sunken cheeks and glassy eyes. "I'm a doctor at the hospital attached to the convent. Come up to see me tomorrow, and I will find them some food." She crossed her fingers as she promised. They had little enough, even with the donations given to the nuns. The convent grew its own vegetable and some fruit. They'd find something.

"Thank you so much. I wasn't begging." The woman blushed. "I just ... well, it's difficult."

"Don't worry, we are here to help."

Sophie carried on with her shopping, taking her turn to queue. Some women were comparing the two occupiers, and to her horror, the Germans seemed to be winning.

"At least the Germans have nice manners." Two housewives in their mid-forties, ahead of her in the queue outside the boulangerie, didn't even lower their voices.

"Those Macaronis are arrogant, hogging the footpaths, pushing French citizens to walk on the road." Her companion agreed, folding her arms across her flat chest. "They can't keep their hands to themselves. My bottom is sore from being pinched so often."

A young girl beside Sophie whispered that they must be desperate to be flirting with women of their age. Sophie stifled a laugh. The girl reminded her of Adèle. Where was her sister?

FIFTEEN

Adèle cycled to the safe house where Luc was based, thinking that 'house' seemed the wrong word for the shepherd's hut with barely more than a cement floor and an old sofa.

"We've a problem, another escaped airman."

Luc barely glanced up. Like all the resistance networks, they'd had their fair share of escaping airmen. The Royal Air Force had their own networks, but occasionally these routes were overcome by sheer numbers or were blown due to the Gestapo catching up with them.

"I think he might be a German agent."

That got Luc's attention, and he leaped up from his seat. "What have you done with him?"

"I took him to the Abreos' farm."

Luc ground out his cigarette on the floor, turning his blazing fury on her. "You did what? You put them in danger!"

"What choice did I have? The apartment was blown; I couldn't bring him here. Anyway, Josette and Adrien can look after themselves. Josette drugged him, and Adrien was suspicious before I said anything."

"Why?"

"Seb barked and growled at him."

"Good old Seb, but I meant, why were *you* suspicious? What was it?" He stared at her, waiting for her answer.

She hesitated, reluctant to put it into words. But he needed an explanation.

"There was something about Edward – that's the name he gave me. He seemed too friendly or something. Look, I don't know what it was; just get Romain to check out his details with London, please. As soon as he can." She scribbled down the rank and other information Edward had given her.

Luc took the note, saying, "Stay here; the wireless operator is at the main camp. I'll be back in a couple of hours. You need to rest."

"I must find Caesar. I'll be back at dawn."

"Listen to me. If London say they don't know him, you don't need Caesar. Rest. This is the best way; no point in both of us being outside after curfew."

She knew he was right.

Luc took the slip of paper and, borrowing her bicycle, set off for the main camp. She gulped down some water before lying down on the couch and throwing her coat over herself. But it was no use; she couldn't sleep. She paced back and forth until she heard the bike's wheels on the stones outside.

"Well?"

"It's all fine. London confirmed they're missing Flying Officer Edward Church. You can relax."

But she couldn't. Despite the evidence, she couldn't get rid of her suspicions.

Luc watched her closely. "You don't believe he's on our side?"

Adèle picked at her skirt. She was the only woman in their ranks and was often teased for that, but she was a fully trained agent. She had to listen to her instincts.

"No, I don't. I can't say why but there is something off. I

thought if I could get Harry – the pilot we know is the real deal – to talk to him, he could tell us for sure."

Luc's reaction surprised her. "Trust your gut."

"You believe that?"

"Not really, but you said Seb didn't like him, and I trust Seb." His face turned serious again. "I believe in you. Go and do what you have to."

She tucked her skirt up again and headed off into the darkness.

* * *

She found Georges and Harry at an abandoned farmhouse they sometimes used to store arms and their supplies after a drop. It was only known to them and a couple of trusted men. Even Romain didn't know about the location, not because she didn't trust him – she did. But she'd insisted on better security since she'd started working with the group. It was too dangerous if everyone knew everything.

As she arrived, she put down the bike and whistled a tune Jean-Pierre had taught her. Then she walked carefully towards the house, not wanting Georges to shoot her. He came out of the house, only putting his Sten gun down when he saw her face.

"Adèle, what are you going here? I told you to get to Marie and to safety."

"Change of plan. We have a problem."

Georges waited, his eyes not moving from hers.

"I think a German agent infiltrated the escape route; he arrived just after you and Harry left. I brought him to Adrien Abreo. He's keeping an eye on him." She was speaking too fast, but she had to prove to him that this was a serious doubt, not her overreacting. "Romain checked his details with London, and a pilot with his name was shot down. But ... but I need Harry to come back with me."

Georges lit a cigarette, taking a deep drag before blowing out the smoke. He indicated they both return to the house before saying, "The contact is due to take Harry the day after tomorrow. If he misses this chance, he probably can't get over the mountains and will be stuck here for another month."

Adèle stayed silent.

"He's just a boy, Adèle. He can't speak French, and one look at him tells the world he's English. How he stayed free this long is beyond me, but his luck won't hold. Let him get back to his parents, his fiancée."

"He's older than Jean-Pierre was when he first got involved. We don't have the luxury of sentimentality."

His eyes widened, but whatever he was about to say was lost as Harry appeared, obviously having heard the conversation.

"What's wrong? You spoke too fast for me, but I know something's wrong."

Without looking at Georges in case she gave in, she told him about Edward.

"We've checked with England, and they have a record of him being shot down..."

"But you're suspicious."

She nodded. "I can't tell you why. Just woman's intuition, I guess. Seb doesn't like him either."

Harry's eyes widened. "Is he another pilot?"

"No, he's a dog."

Harry let out a nervous laugh. "If the dog says he's a traitor, I guess I have to check him out."

Georges interrupted, "No, you don't, Harry. You are going back to London. We'll get rid of Edward."

Harry's mouth fell open, his upper lip curling back. "You can't just murder him. What if he is one of my lot?"

Adèle scratched the back of her neck. "Ordinarily, Georges would be right. In cases like this, the death of one to save many is justified. But it isn't as simple as just getting rid of Edward. He's come a long way from Paris. How many of our people has he met? Has he already given up their details if he is an enemy agent? We need to warn the line that it's blown if he does turn out to be an imposter. That's why we must be sure. Otherwise, we risk not only the good people who helped along the way but also any chance of getting more pilots like you out of France." Although the explanation was for Harry, she stared at Georges, willing him to understand. She'd send Harry back in an instant if it weren't for the innocent families at risk.

"I'm not going now. If he is one of ours, I won't let him die just because I wanted to get home. Where do I go?"

Georges ground the cigarette out with an oath. "You stay here, both of you. I'll fetch the man and bring him here."

"Be careful." Adèle stepped towards him, reaching for his arm, but he moved too fast for her.

SIXTEEN

The hours passed slowly until she heard a truck in the distance. She took out her Sten and got a spare from the cupboard for Harry.

"If you have to shoot, aim for their stomachs."

He took the gun, gripping it so tightly his knuckles whitened.

"You ever shoot before?"

"In training. I wasn't very good at it."

She didn't have time to worry about that. Moving back to the window, she waited as the truck made its way up the lane outside. It wasn't the Germans, as they wouldn't drive a *gazogène*. The truck stopped, and Georges jumped out of the driving seat, quickly followed by Luc on the other side.

Between them, they dragged Edward out of the back of the truck, with another man she didn't recognise covering them with a pistol.

Edward looked totally dishevelled, but she suspected that was due more to the wine and sleeping draught. He had no obvious signs of injury.

"I know you have to be careful but do you really need to

wave that gun in my face?" He complained as they led him towards the house. "Can I have some water? My throat is rough. And any aspirin? My head is pounding."

"He's brave." Harry muttered as they watched the men walk up the path. "He sounds just like a BBC newsreader too. I think you're wrong about him."

Harry rushed over to the table, filled a glass with water from the jug and dashed outside. Adèle watched from the window as Harry approached Edward, saying, "Here you go. Been a long time since you had a good drink. Come inside. They're a friendly bunch really."

Edward's eyebrows shot up, but he took the glass and gulped down the contents. "Thanks, mate."

Adèle saw the smile fall from Harry's face. He stood staring at Edward's back as the men pushed him in to where Adèle was waiting.

"Sit there." Georges pulled out the chair for Edward.

Adèle walked past them and out to where Harry was still standing. "You doubt him too?" She whispered, so that Edward wouldn't hear.

Harry looked up, an agonised expression on his face. "I don't know. He speaks with a BBC accent, but officers like him don't say 'mate' like that. Do they?"

Adèle shrugged her shoulders. She didn't know.

Harry pursed his lips, shaking his head slightly. "I can't condemn him just because of that."

Adèle's patience was running thin; she was starting to feel stupid. "Nobody is asking you to. Come inside and talk to him. You know more than we do about your operations. Ask him about the bases he operated out of, the pubs he went to, that sort of thing. I will be here too. The decision is mine, not yours."

His forehead wrinkled, a downcast expression on his face as he walked into the house like he was the condemned man. Adèle followed.

Edward was quite convincing. He answered lots of the questions Harry asked, and they even shared a couple of jokes at the expense of French cuisine. Georges glanced over at Adèle with a told-you-so look on his face, and then he and Luc headed outside to talk.

Harry stood up. "Come on, mate, let's go for a walk too. I can't sit still for long."

Edward's relief was palpable. He stood up and walked around to the table to Harry's side. Adèle was about to apologise for doubting Edward when Harry punched him in the face, knocking the man off his feet. Harry kicked out viciously, punctuating each word with a kick as the man on the floor curled into a ball.

"You swine. You evil-minded b—"

Adèle pulled her gun as Edward swore he was innocent and yelled at Harry to stop kicking. Georges and Luc burst through the door, guns drawn.

Harry backed away, chest heaving, holding the hand he had used to land the punch under his other arm. "He's a lying weasel. He's spent time in England, but he's not one of us. He's a spy."

Georges looked up from the curled-up figure. "Are you sure?"

"Absolutely. I asked him how many stones he'd lost after his escape, food being scarce and," Harry flushed, "not what we English are used to."

George looked from Harry to Adèle and back. "Stones? What has that to do with food?"

"Exactly. You're French so you don't understand. We use stones and pounds to measure weight. Europeans use kilograms." Harry glared at the man calling himself Edward. "Men like him, he hunts all those decent, honourable French people who help downed pilots and aircrew at risk and..." Harry burst past them and out the door. Luc followed him, leaving Georges and Adèle staring at Edward, who'd pulled himself to a seated position.

He looked just like any other young man who'd been in a fight, not a devil with horns. Yet he was the enemy, and she couldn't let him live. She slammed her fist on the table, "Hälst due mich für blöd?"

"Natürlich nicht."

He saw the triumph in her eyes, flushing as he realised his mistake. He couldn't deny the truth now.

"What did you say to him?" Georges kept his Sten aimed at Edward.

"I asked him if he thought I was stupid, his reply was he didn't. Now Harry doesn't need to feel guilty when I kill him."

Edward paled slightly before his bravado reappeared. "There is no difference between you and me. I fight for my country just like you fight for yours. Neither of us wears a uniform."

She gritted her teeth. She wasn't a bit like him.

Georges pulled him to his feet. "We don't kill innocent people. Or let sadists torture men, women, and children. There is no comparison between you and us."

Edward didn't look at Georges but kept his eyes on Adèle. Maybe he believed he'd got under her skin.

Curiosity got the better of her. He seemed well educated; he'd spent time in England. "How can you justify what your so-called Führer does?"

"I never said I agreed with Hitler. But I am German. You, a woman who could be at home raising children, are fighting for France. How are we so different?"

"Have you betrayed those who gave you shelter on your way here?"

His eyes fell to the ground along with her heart. The Royers. Were they even now being picked up?

"You will die. It's your choice whether that's by my hand or

I give you over to my men. They've lost family at the hands of the Gestapo. They are itching for revenge and will ensure you endure a long, painful death."

He blanched but quickly recovered. "You'll shoot me?"

She didn't take her eyes off him, not reacting as he smirked.

"I find that difficult to believe. You have a soft heart."

"Your people murdered my baby brother. I have no heart. Now, what's it to be? Tell me the truth about your contacts and how you found out about the escape route, and I will let you die like a man or..."

SEVENTEEN

Adèle set up her own safe house in a village called Brive-la-Gaillarde. From there, she set about finding and training new recruits. She enforced strict security, trying to adopt the measures recommended by Buckmaster. Each group should be self-sufficient and have as little to do with the other groups as possible although given the number of families and friends in the surrounding areas, this wasn't always feasible.

Georges was away a lot meeting with Max and other top people in the resistance. Luc was her main contact with his network, but she occasionally met Romain. He'd been an excellent student and was now teaching other members of the cell, turning young men into soldiers.

* * *

On one of her recruiting drives, she bumped into Monique at a café. The young woman didn't look as glamorous as before. Her make-up was smudged as if she'd been crying, and her gaze kept roaming around the café as if she expected someone to come in.

She didn't intend to greet her, but Monique recognised her and invited her to join her for a coffee.

"Please – Elise, isn't it? I hate sitting alone."

Adèle sat and allowed the woman to order an ersatz coffee for her. Monique was all questions about what Elise was doing and whether she was working with Luc.

Adèle played her role. She had to convince this woman she was unwell. "Luc? His firm doesn't use women. And I am not sure my doctor would allow me to work full-time. I am still recovering from a bad chest infection."

She didn't know if it was just the fact Monique was an attractive woman or it was something else, but she felt uneasy in her presence. Luc had never explained his reasons for not wanting to involve Monique, but she didn't buy the story of the older brother.

"Have you seen Jozef?"

The question surprised her, but, thanks to her training, she covered it. "Who?" Adèle pretended not to remember.

"The tall, skinny man with you and Luc, that time we met. Do you not remember? I want to speak to him about becoming involved. I must join the resistance."

Adèle shifted in her seat, sensing desperation from the young woman. The hairs on the back of her neck rose as she glanced to her left and right, assessing the other café patrons. Was this some sort of trap? She checked the exits: out the front door to the street or through the bar and out via the kitchens.

"But why? From what I hear, the resistance circuits don't like women much. Anyway, imagine what it would do to your hair and your nails." Adèle forced a shudder. "I can't imagine being on the run all the time, sleeping in fields and whatnot."

Monique stared at her, making Adèle wonder if she had gone too far. Then the woman brushed away the tears as they flowed down her cheeks. Adèle hated anyone crying, but, especially in a public place. What would Sophie do if she were here? She'd offer comfort, and try to be a listening ear. She opened her bag, searching for a hanky. Handing it to Monique, she moved closer. "What's wrong? What did I say?"

Monique grabbed the hanky and blew her nose in a very unladylike way. "My brother was with the resistance, and they caught him. The Gestapo killed him."

Gestapo. Adèle risked looking around; this time, several people were paying attention to them. Was it just because of the scene the woman was making, or was it something more?

"I'm so sorry. How horrible for you." She moved to get up. "Come on, let's get you home. You should be with your family at a time like this."

Tears suddenly forgotten, for a brief second, Monique resembled a cat Adèle once had, all claws. "I don't have one. He was my family." She almost spat out, her lips thinning. "I *must* avenge his death." She grabbed Adèle's arm, hurting her as she held her in a vice-like grip. "Promise me you will tell Jozef or Luc. I must see them."

Adèle's patience evaporated. She removed the woman's hand, saying firmly, "I think you would be better talking to your brother's friends if you really are serious about joining up, but you shouldn't be making a spectacle of yourself. The Gestapo or the Milice or both could be watching you. Take your crazy theories somewhere else. I haven't seen Luc since that day." She stood up and turned to go, closing her eyes as her own brother's image popped into her head. She turned back. "I'm so sorry for your loss, Monique."

Her calmness had more of an effect than her warning.

Monique wiped away her tears, stood up and faced Adèle. "Thank you."

She took her handbag and walked out of the café. Adèle decided it was best to wait rather than walk outside. It was safer not to be seen with that woman.

"You handled that well." Someone spoke quietly behind

her, but when Adèle turned around, everyone seemed caught up in their own business. Opening her bag, she left some francs on the table and walked out.

She took the long way home, stopping at several shop windows as if she was examining the merchandise. Instead, she scanned her reflection to check nobody was following her. Her throat hurt, guilt making her chest tight. She knew what Monique was feeling; hadn't she experienced the same loss? And her reaction had been similar. She'd wanted to fight back. Monique wanted revenge, and who was she to stop her?

She walked on. It was pointless asking Luc to reconsider. He was as set in his ways as an eighty-year-old grandfather. But the decision lay with Georges. He was the leader. She'd visit him and ask. Her step sped up a little, butterflies forming in her stomach. If anyone had predicted she'd lie awake at night wondering what Georges was doing, where he was, and who he was with, she'd have denied it with every bone in her body. But she couldn't deny he'd made an impression on her, and not just physically.

She stopped off at a café, nursing a warm drink while her mind went over everyone she knew. Who could possibly have the contacts she needed to build extra resistance groups? Maybe Monique could help her if Georges said she was trustworthy.

She looked up when someone coughed beside her. Her heart almost stopped as a strange man sat down at her table.

"Good morning, mademoiselle. May I join you?"

She wanted to tell him to get lost but after the scene with Monique in the last café she was reluctant to draw attention to herself. She decided to ignore him, hoping he'd take the hint.

"You looked so sad. I had to come over to see if I could cheer you up."

Adèle didn't answer.

He signalled the waiter to bring more drinks. "What do

they say? A problem shared and all that. What is a pretty woman like you so worried about?"

"I don't know. Perhaps the war." Her reply was loaded with sarcasm.

His eyes narrowed, but then he smiled. "I think the war has caused a lot of short tempers, but it will soon be over. The Germans are winning. Soon Europe will be defeated, and we can all get back to living."

The waiter set their drinks on the table. Real coffee arrived this time, the smell making Adèle's mouth water.

"You are a Frenchman. Don't you want France to win?"

"I am a practical man. Now tell me, what is your name?"

Adèle wanted to stand up and walk off, but she couldn't. She was trapped.

"Elise Delattre."

"Raphaël Allard."

"Excuse me, monsieur Allard, but I must get back." She drank her coffee quickly, the temptation to enjoy the brew too much to waste it by refusing to taste it. She inched her chair backwards, but to no avail.

"Please don't leave." The request was a command, and they both knew it. She sat waiting as he finished his drink. She refused to show fear, though she had to cross her legs to stop them shaking.

"You are a very busy woman, mademoiselle Delattre."

She studied him without replying.

"You travel a lot. All over the place, if reports are to be believed."

So, she was being watched – but was he warning her or baiting her? She wasn't sure.

"I do a lot of charity work, monsieur Allard. So many loyal Frenchmen are away working for Germany, leaving their families needing help."

"So, you help *French* families."

She didn't like the emphasis he placed on 'French' but pretended she hadn't noticed. She wasn't in the mood to play games. Her back and stomach ached, making her mood even worse than usual.

"I am sorry, monsieur Allard, but what did you want?"

He held her gaze, "I wanted to know if I could be of help."

Every one of her senses was on high alert. Who was he? Was he a Gestapo agent?

"But of course. We always need food. I can go with you now if you wish to buy vegetables, so I can make the poor families some soup." She moved to stand up.

He reached for her hand, his grasp so tight she winced.

"I think you should stop playing games with me and tell me what you are doing."

"Take your hands off me, you cretin! How dare you manhandle a woman! What type of man are you?"

She stood up quickly, her outburst leaving him at a loss for words. Other people in the café quickly voiced their disapproval of his actions. She was tempted to smack his face, but that was going too far.

"Do not follow me. I do not wish to date you; your wife is a friend of mine."

With that, Adèle quickly walked away. The uproar in the café behind her told her the other diners were giving the man a piece of their collective mind. She allowed herself a brief smile, but she knew her time in the town was over. Elise Delattre needed to be buried, and another woman arise in her wake.

EIGHTEEN

APRIL 1943

Only when she was sure she wasn't being followed did Adèle make her way to the rendezvous point. Her heart beat faster seeing Georges up ahead; he looked good despite his lifestyle. The few grey hairs suited him, as did his more pronounced muscles. Maybe he was slightly too thin, but what Frenchman wasn't? Her eyes met his; he looked annoyed, but she thought she could see concern in his eyes too.

"You had a lucky escape earlier."

"You heard about that already?" Was he monitoring her? When would he realise that they were equals in their fight against the enemy?

"We were tailing Allard, your new friend. He's been a suspect for a while. We had no real proof, but after this morning, we didn't need any. He has been eliminated. That was some move you played. Risky, but effective."

"Thank you, I think." Despite her sarcasm, Adèle was relieved. Dead men couldn't talk.

"Leave now. Far too many people are talking about it."

"Where do you need me to go?"

"Not sure yet. You will stay at a safe house for now as you

need new papers. You should dye your hair as part of a new disguise."

She nearly screamed at him. Was he mad? "Over my dead body! Have you any idea how many women would kill for a hair colour like mine?"

Georges's snort told her he was trying hard not to laugh.

"What?"

"Underneath, you are still the same Adèle Bélanger – vain through and through."

"I am not the least bit like my old self. I think it would be silly to dye my hair a colour the Germans hate. When they see me, they think I am Aryan. It gives me certain advantages."

Adèle tensed, waiting to see how Georges would respond to her revelation. She hadn't told Georges about her grandmother. Would the fact she had Jewish blood change his opinion of her? As soon as the thought hit her, she dismissed it – she didn't care what Georges thought of her. He was a comrade, that was all. When he didn't react to her comment, the silence grew uncomfortable.

"I was talking to a lady called Monique in the café earlier. She is very interested in joining us."

That got his attention. He held her gaze. "What did she say?"

She gave him a summary of the conversation, including the bit about her brother being murdered. She also told him about how Luc had reacted.

"You trust her?"

She took a moment to answer. "I don't have much experience trusting women."

He smiled at that.

"But I related to her. I couldn't help it. She lost her brother just like I lost Jean-Pierre. But there was something about her. I don't know what. Maybe you should check her out. Her brother died for France."

Georges shrugged his shoulders as if to say Monique's brother wasn't the only one. Adèle knew that. So many men and women had laid down their lives for freedom, yet they weren't any closer to achieving it. She sighed loudly.

"What's with the sigh? This morning playing on your mind?"

Did she imagine a hint of disquiet in his voice? This morning must have rattled her if she thought Jean-Pierre's friend Georges would pay her any attention. As far as he was concerned, she was little better than the Germans – a spoiled brat without a care for anyone but herself.

"No, not really. That man, Allard, said the Germans are winning."

"He would."

"But aren't they? I mean, every news bulletin talks about their victories." She didn't want to sound defeatist, but was there any point in kidding themselves?

"You can't believe what you hear on the radio – even those reports from the BBC. They are designed to help keep morale up, so the Allies will say they are winning, and the Germans the same."

"Don't you ever question why we are doing this? With so many just doing their best to survive?" Adèle spoke without thinking. Her stomach cramps were making her wish for a warm bed and the touch of her mother's comforting hand.

She stopped talking when she saw the sullen expression on Georges's face.

"You know why we are doing this. For Jean-Pierre, for Michel, for all those whose names we don't even know. Victory will come, and then we will deal with those who didn't stand on the right side."

Georges finished cleaning his weapon as he spoke. She knew he meant every word, but for her, it was different. Jean-Pierre, her hero, had been murdered by the Germans. She didn't know where Sophie was, or if her mother and grand-mother were safe. She didn't want to think about her papa, a cold-hearted collaborator but his face occupied her nightmares. Even he'd be alive if the war hadn't started.

"Come on, Adèle, you must pull yourself together. We need your persuasive charms. We still have to get those ration books for the children."

How could she have forgotten she'd promised to help feed the hidden children?

"Claude Diderot will help us," she said.

He gave her an incredulous stare. "Did you hit your head this morning? He's the head of the general supply office in Lyon."

"I know what he is, but he is on our side." She knew she sounded tetchy, but she hated how he questioned her. She'd been working as an agent for months; didn't he know by now that she knew what she was doing?

His cheeks flushed at her tone. "How could you possibly know that?"

"As you said, my feminine charms are useful. He was very happy to help me. I can go and see him again." She let the insin-uation she had given him good reason to be of assistance hang in the air. Would Georges be jealous?

His lips pursed. "No, you can't. We don't know who Allard was working for or how much they already suspect you. I will send someone else. Are you one hundred per cent sure, Adèle?"

"Yes." She flung her hands up in the air, not hiding her frus-tration. "I wouldn't say it otherwise. He will help us; I know he will."

Georges stared at her for a few seconds. "All right. We will send someone to see him, but first, we need to get you to a safe house outside Lyon."

Could she go to the same safe house as maman and mémé? She'd avoided going near her grandmother's house since coming back to France but the desire to see her family was over-whelming.

He was looking at her intently. "It wouldn't be wise to check on your family now, Adèle. They've left your grandmother's house and moved elsewhere. They are safe."

She glared at him. How had he read her thoughts so well? How did he know about her mother and grandmother?

He put a hand on her arm. "You have spent the last six months tearing around the countryside, here, there and everywhere."

She glared at the implied criticism.

"Stop looking at me like that. You've done very well, building up numerous contacts and resistance cells. You've earned the respect of my men."

Had his view of her changed? She knew he found her attractive but was it more than just physical?

"You've worn yourself out, and that will make you careless. You need to live a normal life for a few weeks to regain your perspective; if you can't do it for yourself, do it for those dependent on you." She opened her mouth to protest, but he continued. "I could arrange for you to go back to London."

"Please. Please don't do that."

"Stay at my mother's farm and help. My mother will find plenty for you to do. You won't have time to wallow in your thoughts."

His mother? She almost groaned. She had met Madame Monier years ago; the woman was intimidating, and that was putting it mildly. She was a hard taskmaster and had little time for spoiled rich brats, as she had told Adèle the last time they met.

"Farming? What do I know about that?"

"Nothing, but you will learn fast. Mother would have made a good German."

* * *

She followed Georges down an overgrown path, a wisp of smoke the only sign of life until they came to the clearing where the farmhouse lay. Half a dozen chickens pecked around the yard, and a lone goat was tethered to the fence. She could smell pigs, but thankfully there were none in sight. A small, well-tended vegetable patch lay to the side of the farmhouse.

Georges's mother stood in the doorway, her frown suggesting she didn't relish the prospect of Adèle being there.

"Maman, you remember Jean-Pierre Bélanger? And his sister Adèle? She is going to stay with us for a while."

"I remember her. She doesn't look like a farmer."

"Bonjour, Madame Monier. No, I am not."

The woman ignored her. She began to remonstrate with Georges, telling him Adèle had no place here and would be better suited to a city location. Adèle stood by in silence while Georges repeated their cover story: she was recovering from TB and was there to convalesce. She couldn't agree with his mother's view more, but it wasn't as if she had much of a choice.

Georges ignored his mother's tirade and told Adèle to follow him inside. Two skinned rabbits were turning on the spit over the open fire. Adèle looked around the rest of the room. It was small and sparsely furnished, with only two crude wooden chairs, a table, and a bench. Towards the back, a ladder led up to what she assumed was a sleeping platform in the back.

Madame Monier slammed cutlery on the worn wooden table before dishing up stew. She poured red wine into their cups before motioning at them to sit down.

Adèle sat. She was exhausted and starving. His mother was an excellent cook, and the meal was simple but extremely tasty. The wine was rough but warmed her stomach.

"Adèle's been busy the last few months. Don't work her too hard, maman."

"She will help with the farm. I don't have time to be looking after anyone."

"I will help." She was eager to show this woman she was a useful member of the human race.

"You need a bath." The woman sniffed the air and Adèle fumed. "Georges, bring in the bath and fill it. Then leave us."

Her annoyance faded as she watched Georges's mother order him around, and she hid a smile of amusement.

He didn't complain. Having brought in the bath and filled it to his mother's liking, he gave her a smile and left her to enjoy her bath.

Adèle got undressed and climbed in.

"Here."

She looked up to find the woman handing her some rough soap. For a second, her mind flashed back to her mother's favourite lavender-scented soap, but then the memory was gone.

"Tonight, you rest. Tomorrow, you work."

Adèle nodded, too busy enjoying the feel of the hot water against her skin to care what tomorrow might bring.

* * *

Georges hadn't been joking. Madame Monier set her to work harder than she had ever worked before. She milked the cows, collected eggs – earning herself some quite painful pecks on the hand – and fed the scraps to the pigs. That was the job she hated most.

A few days passed, and then it had been a week, and then another one came and went. She grew restless at the lack of news, but his mother kept her busy.

"Have you heard from Georges?" She asked the question every morning, but the answer was always the same. A shake of her host's head and a note to pay attention to whatever farm chore needed attending.

She developed muscles she never knew she had, and her fingers were covered in calluses. Madame Monier handed her a basket one sunny afternoon with instructions to go down to the cold cellar and collect some squash and a few carrots. "Tomorrow, we will have company, but for tonight we'll do with a simple supper."

Adèle's ears pricked up at the word 'company', her heart beating faster. "Georges?"

"Non. A friend. A local priest."

"Oh!" She caught the grin on her host's face but pretended she didn't. Every night she dreamed of Georges, but she wasn't prepared for anyone else to examine her feelings.

She didn't mind Georges's mother; in fact, she had grown to respect the woman for her hard work. It was difficult living on a small farm, trying to coax food from the ground. Living alone wasn't for everyone. Georges's mother delighted in telling her tales of her son when he was younger. Tales she doubted the man himself would appreciate at times. But it was nice to think someone different would be around tomorrow. Maybe they would have news of the outside world. Could they be coming to bring her back to work?

Over time, she got used to the work and found a certain pleasure in eating the food she had helped to grow. Georges's mother showed her how to do a lot of things, including how to cook a rabbit stew, from trapping the animal through to the finished dish.

"You've changed. I expected a Parisian like you to turn and run at the sight of blood."

Madame Monier indicated the bloodied carcass Adèle was cleaning. Adèle remained silent. If only Georges's mother knew. The Parisian woman, the one who'd gone through her whole training without killing anything due to her squeamish stomach, was now a killer. The White Witch, the men said the Germans had nicknamed her. She'd lost count of the numbers she had killed by blowing up trains or patrols, and then there were the men she'd killed close-up. Her thoughts flickered to Edward Hillary Church or whatever his real name was. She'd shot him through the heart.

The older woman also taught her about herbs and flavourings to add to the simple meals she made. How to find food in the forest and make a meal out of almost nothing. Adèle even learned how to bake bread.

As she stood at the kitchen counter preparing a rabbit pie for the priest's visit, she realised it was the first time Madame Monier had allowed her to cook alone.

"You are smiling?"

"Oui. I was thinking of our maid Zeldah and how she would laugh if she saw me now, my face covered in flour and my hands like this." Adèle wiped the worst of the mess on her apron.

"I think most people who knew the old you would be surprised to see you now. At least you no longer burn water."

Adèle looked up, but Georges's mother had walked out the door to the rear garden. She had sounded almost as if she liked Adèle. Smiling, Adèle went back to preparing the pie. Once it was baking, she set the table using a red-and-white-checked cloth and the best dishes. As she moved around the small space, her mind went back to the lavish dishes her family had once enjoyed. Separate courses spread over several hours, especially if they had company. Her father and Jean-Pierre discussing – well, arguing – about politics. She gripped the knife so hard, it sliced into her finger.

Madame Monier chose that moment to return from the garden. "What have you done? Silly girl." The woman grabbed her hand and put it into the bowl of cold water. Only when she was satisfied it wasn't deep did she wrap it in a piece of cloth.

"Sit down; I'll finish. Where was your head? Thinking of my handsome son, no doubt?"

Adèle blushed, her cheeks hotter than the cut smarting under the bandage.

"I wasn't born yesterday. I see the way you look to the door each day, hoping he will come. He's the same, keeping you here in safety when they need your help."

Adèle stood up too fast and had to sit back as her legs went a little weak. "I'm not hiding here. I want to get back to work."

"I know that, chérie. Whatever else you were, you never lacked bravery. The priest will bring us news. Now drink up and change your dress. Soak it in cold water, or those stains will never come out." She patted Adèle on the arm before she moved towards the oven to remove the pie. That was Georges's mother's way. She wasn't given to gestures of affection.

Adèle ran to change, not wanting the older woman to see the effect of her words.

NINETEEN

JULY 1943, CANNES

"Sophie, I have wonderful news." Sister Edith came rushing into the kitchen where Sophie was peeling some potatoes. She liked the young nun, who, at thirty, was only a few years older than herself. They had found they had a lot in common, having younger brothers and a love of reading. "Mary Elmes was released from Fresnes last Friday. She's going to say with Roger Danjou in Normandy for a month or so before she returns to Perpignan."

Sophie flung her arms around the nun before realising her error. She jumped back with an apology, which the nun brushed off.

"Don't apologise – it's good news at last. We were all so worried when she disappeared, and nobody knew where she was. But the Irish luck held, she's alive and no doubt the lovely Mr Danjou will look after her. I've heard he is head over heels in love with her."

Sophie hid her smile. Despite Sister Edith's vow of chastity, she was a true romantic and had confessed to loving the Brontës' books before entering the convent.

"Now, tell me, are you going to return to Perpignan?"

Sophie shook her head. "I'd love to see Mary, but I'm sure there will be loads of people fussing around her, which she will hate." Sophie hesitated before confiding, "I love being a doctor, but I'd prefer to be helping with the escape routes. Getting the children away from here before the Germans arrive. We know that's going to happen; there're already rumours about the Italians' loyalty. What happens when they leave? It will be Marseille all over again. There must be more I can do." She glanced at the mountain of potatoes. "There is so much need."

Sister Edith's eyes danced with laughter at the reference to boiling vegetables, which took hours. "I was hoping you would say that. Mother Superior and I have been talking, and we believe you should go to Nice."

Sophie listened, curious as to what had been planned for her.

"There are thousands and thousands of Jews who went to Nice and the surrounding areas because of the Italians. We know the Germans are just waiting to move in if the Italians do leave, as everyone suspects they will."

Sophie didn't want to think about that.

"How do you feel about becoming a nun?" Sister Edith grinned.

"A nun? Me?"

"Yes. When you get to Nice, you will join a convent as Sister Agnès. Given what happened to Mary and also the latest string of arrests by the Italian secret service, we've been told you would be safer disguised this way. Then nobody will suspect your motives for visiting people or working with sick children."

That made sense, but Sophie wasn't at all sure she had the acting skills necessary to make a good nun. Her friend obviously shared some of her concerns as she said, "I wish I could see you in your new role. You must be obedient – especially to the priests."

Sophie sighed. She knew her regular arguments with Father

Michel over the best way to care for the children had spread fast around the convent. The nuns treated the priests like they were on a pedestal. She refused to do that. A priest he might be, but Father Michel was no doctor.

"Sure you don't want to come with me?" Sophie asked, half-joking. It would be nice to have a friend with her in the new convent.

"Maybe next time." Sister Edith smiled. "Come, I will give you one of my habits." The nun helped Sophie pack a bag before escorting her to the door of the convent. "I will miss you. Take care."

* * *

Once again, Sophie found herself on the way to a new life with another identity. She walked to the train station trying not to pull at the neck of the habit; the fabric itched her skin. The head covering was worse with the coif, secured by a wimple and a veil, making her feel hot and sweaty. How did real nuns cope? Was this a way to teach patience and humility? How she missed her simple cotton dress she wore in Rivesaltes. She closed her eyes and, for a second, could see Jean-Pierre and Zeldah laughing at the way she was dressed. They wouldn't be as bad as Adèle. She shook her head; it was too painful to think about her twin. She stopped fidgeting when she saw another train passenger looking at her curiously, holding her hands in prayer, praying for the war to be over.

TWENTY

The smell from the rabbit pie had Adèle's mouth watering by the time the priest finally arrived. He knocked once on the door before entering, carrying a bottle of wine, which he presented to his hostess.

"Father Jacques, take a seat, please."

"My nose led me all the way here, as usual, my friend."

Adèle saw Georges's mother's blush as she ushered him to the table. "I can't claim any credit. Elise prepared everything. I don't think you have met; she's the granddaughter of a very old friend of mine. She has recovered from TB, and her grand-mother agreed the country air would benefit her lungs."

"It is lovely to meet you, Elise. Although, it is not the best time to visit. Everyone is frightened now the Milice have become so active in the area."

Madame Monier opened the wine, placing it on the table. She also poured the priest a glass of water. "But why? It is the Germans who are our real enemies, surely."

"They are the more obvious enemy. The Milice is made up of our own countrymen. They are better positioned to identify those who have reason to hide. People such as Jews and resistants."

Adèle didn't get involved in the conversation. She didn't know if the priest was just recounting his thoughts or was trying to warn them. The militia was the more dangerous of their enemies. The men attracted to these groups were a lethal combination of cowards and bullies. Many used their position to settle scores against their neighbours.

"I hate to say this about my own congregation, but there are some who will use their position of power for their own base needs. You'd do well to stay away from the village, young lady. Your beauty will draw attention, and then questions will be asked about your presence here."

His rheumy old eyes caught hers and their gazes locked. He was warning them. She waited until Georges's mother was distracted before giving the man a discreet nod. He looked towards their hostess and blessed himself.

A shiver of fear went down Adèle's spine. Had she brought trouble to Madame Monier?

The priest ate as if he didn't know where his next meal was coming from. "Did you know the blacksmith has begun putting shoes on cows? The farmers need them to pull the ploughs since the Germans took all the horses. Never thought I'd see the day."

Georges's mother tutted, but Adèle wanted to know more. "Are the Germans visiting farms or sticking to the towns?"

"They usually leave the farms alone unless they head out in a group. Travelling around here in twos and threes can prove rather dangerous. There are a lot of strange beasts in the wild, you know. And the boars and other animals leave no evidence of their catch. They hunt for food, and nothing is wasted."

The wild? It was hardly the middle of Africa. But then she caught the gleam in his eye. "You would be out there with the maquis if you were younger, wouldn't you, Father?"

"Me? What a thing to ask of a holy man. I pray for peace. That's all I can do."

Madame Monier pushed a large piece of cheese onto his plate. "Of course, Father."

Adèle didn't believe him, but she kept her own counsel.

TWENTY-ONE

Adèle was desperate to get back into the fight, and – after the priest's visit – was concerned about her stay attracting attention, but she had to wait on Georges.

She stopped counting hours as the days passed. Georges sent word he hadn't been able to get her new papers yet. She had to stay at the farm, hearing titbits of news from the rare visitors who came to see Madame Monier.

* * *

One morning, lost in thought as she returned to the house after an early start tending the livestock, she glanced up to find Madame Monier staring at her.

"You will make a farmer's wife yet," Georges's mother said.

She was so tired, she couldn't reply. She sank into the chair by the fire.

"Drink this; it will help you."

She didn't ask what the vile-smelling liquid was. She had learned the hard way: Georges wasn't lying when he compared his mother to the Germans.

"Georges will be here later. You are leaving this afternoon. I will miss you."

Adèle couldn't hide her surprise – not just at the news she was leaving, but at Madame Monier admitting she would miss her.

"You have come a long way from the girl I knew who visited her grandmother. The old lady would be very proud of you."

Tears sprang to Adèle's eyes. She wiped them away furiously, not wanting to show any weakness.

Georges's mother pretended not to see. "It is a difficult time for everyone. We must all do our bit to get rid of those animals. Victory will come. Never lose sight of that."

"Have you news of my grandmother?"

The woman shook her head, but Adèle got the impression she was lying. She wanted to beg for information but knew it was futile. It was safer for everyone if people kept information like that to themselves.

"If you know of anyone who can take her a message, please let her know I am alive and I love her. I can't remember the last time I told her that."

The woman moved closer and laid a hand on Adèle's arm. "She knows you do. She is very proud of you, Adèle." Her soft and gentle tone was Adèle's undoing, and Adèle bent her head, giving in to her tears.

"Let them out. Tears are not a sign of weakness, but a sign of strength. They prove you still have a heart and feelings. If the tears disappear for good, then the Boches might as well win."

She pulled the older woman into an embrace, and they hugged for several minutes.

* * *

She watched out the window, not wanting his mother to catch her reaction when she saw him again. Her eyes studied him as he walked down the lane towards the house, his shoulders hunched as if he carried the weight of the world on them. She longed to run to hug him, to tell him she'd share his burden, but she remained where she was. She waited for him to come into the house and greet his mother in private. Only when Madame Monier called for her did she appear. Their eyes met, and he was the first to look away. He pulled out an envelope from his pocket.

"Here, new papers. Your name is Éléanor Breton. You are seventeen years old, the pampered daughter of doting parents who has just left school."

She stared at the papers. So that was why his mother had insisted she wear her hair down when she had the photographs taken.

"You think I can pull that off?"

"You have to," he replied gruffly. "Otherwise, you will end up working for them. The STO applies to women over twenty-one, you know. Edouard will take you to the next rendezvous, where you will meet your contact, Charlie." Georges didn't look at her even once as he spoke. Was he angry with her?

"Did you get the ration cards?"

He finally looked at her and smiled, his admiration obvious. "You were right; Claude did help us. I shall miss your instincts, Adèle."

She held his gaze. "I will miss you too, Georges."

"After the war, we must have a drink and laugh about these times. Perhaps by then, you won't smell like the pigs."

Adèle opened her mouth for a retort but stopped when she saw he was teasing her. She caught the look of approval on his mother's face, and felt warm inside.

"Thank you, Madame Monier, for all you have done for me."

"My pleasure, Adèle. I didn't think I would ever say this to you, but you are welcome in my home any time, day or night –

and not just because you are on our side." Georges's mother hugged her.

"Come on; we must go. Edouard won't wait long. He is the impatient type." Georges's brusque tone didn't match his suspiciously watery eyes.

Adèle said her goodbyes and followed Georges out of the door without a backwards glance. Saying goodbye never got easier.

Once they were well away from the farm, he gave her a pistol.

"You must never come back here, Adèle, no matter what. I believe we have a traitor in our midst."

She stopped moving.

"You can trust Edouard; he was a friend of my father's. Do exactly what he says."

"Georges, your mother—"

"Will be moved. I am sending her away tomorrow. But whatever you hear, do not return. You have important work to do."

She didn't care what he thought. She flung herself at him and kissed him, twining her arms around his neck.

Then she leaned back and looked at him. "Be safe, Georges, please."

She kissed him again, and, stunned as he appeared to be, he returned the kiss. The passion between them lit up, but, with a sigh, he pushed her gently from him.

He stood facing her, brushing her hair back from her eyes. "Now is not the time. After the war. Come." He held out his hand, and together they walked through the woods until they came to a hollowed-out tree. Georges whistled, and soon the answer came. An older man walked towards them.

"This is Éléanor Breton. Éléanor, meet Edouard. He will take you to Charlie."

The old man didn't look at Adèle, keeping his gaze focused

on Georges. "Be careful. That rumour about the traitor has merit."

Adèle presumed Edouard was talking about the risk to Georges's network. She wanted to beg Georges to come with her, but she couldn't. It would only upset him. The best thing she could do for him was not to add to his worries.

"Thank you. Bonne chance, mon ami." She shook his hand, despite wanting to embrace him. The look in his eyes told her he wished to do the same. Then he was gone.

"We must go quietly. These woods are usually safe, but now..." Edouard shrugged his shoulders.

She kept her hand on the pistol in her pocket as they walked carefully through the woods. She did her best not to make any noise, and Edouard walked in silence beside her. Soon the gaps between the trees widened, exposing their cover.

"We will wait to continue our journey until night falls. It is too risky to be caught on the roads now."

"What happened?"

He gave her a dirty look.

"He and I are old friends. I can't bear to think about him or his mother being in danger."

The man snorted. "This is no picnic for any of us."

"I know that. I am not stupid. But you mentioned a traitor."

"The woman, Monique – her story has proven false."

"You mean her brother wasn't killed by the Gestapo?" Who would lie about something like that?

"No – he was arrested, all right, but they let him go."

"The Gestapo doesn't let men go; they send them to Germany."

"Exactly. The only reason they are allowed to go is if they have been turned. The brother gave Monique up when some of our men spoke with him."

She knew immediately what he meant by 'spoke with'. The young man had been tortured. "What if he had been innocent?"

"He denounced a nun for hiding resistance members. She was shot; the other members of her convent were shipped to Germany. Don't waste your pity on him."

"And Monique? You cannot condemn her because of her brother."

"Of course not. She is guilty of her own crime. Her lover is a member of the Wehrmacht. Their pillow talk must be very interesting."

Feeling sick, Adèle thought back over the last few weeks before going to the farm. Had she entrusted any information to Monique?

"You tell her anything?"

"No. I had a drink with her, and she told me she wanted to join up as her brother had been murdered. I felt sorry for her. To be honest, I am not a woman's woman."

Edouard chuckled. "That much I have heard. You don't like the competition."

The old Adèle would have argued, but she knew better now. She had enjoyed being the centre of attention; other girls, especially pretty ones, were rivals.

"What will happen to her?"

"She will be dead by noon, if all goes well."

Adèle crossed herself. Monique and her brother might be traitors, but they were two more people who would die before this war was over.

"Edouard, can you get word to me if something happens to Georges?"

The older man looked at her for a moment and then shook his head. "You must forget him and concentrate on your own work. Now is not the time for love."

"When is? You and I both know the chance of us being alive when this war is over is remote."

"You will guarantee your death, and that of others, if you try to return to see Georges. Forget him for now. He has work to do, as do you. Now get some sleep."

Adèle curled up in a ball – as if she could sleep out here in the forest! She closed her eyes, listening to the sounds around her. She prayed silently for Georges and his mother. She also prayed for her grandmother, her mother, and, most of all, for her twin. Where was Sophie – and was she safe?

TWENTY-TWO

To Adèle's great joy, 'Charlie' turned out to be Luc, come to take her to a camp where there were new recruits who needed training.

"It is nice to see you so healthy-looking, Elise – I mean Éléanor. Not many farmers look as attractive as you."

Adèle burst out laughing. He hadn't changed a bit – still as incorrigible as ever.

"How are you, Luc?"

"About the same, give or take a few of my nine lives, which may have disappeared. We are still starving; the men fish when they can and have collected dandelion leaves like the best farmers' wives, but we could all do with a good steak dinner. Not much chance of that. The Germans don't like us maquisards very much. No idea why."

Adèle smiled at the understatement. The enemy hated the maquis, or underground army, as they were also called. The Fritz found it difficult to fight an army of men and women who didn't wear uniforms, knew the local area, and could retreat into the shadows as and when required.

It was good to be around Luc, not only because she liked him as a person but also because he knew Georges.

"Luc, have you heard anything from Caesar?"

He shook his head, but he looked grim. Was he lying?

"I heard about Monique and her brother. I am sorry – you seemed to know them both well."

"Raphael was always weak; his parents spoiled him. Monique was a flirty little fool who cared nothing for anybody but herself."

Adèle winced. He could have been describing her back in Paris. That was the opinion Jean-Pierre had had of her.

"What is the situation? How many men do we have?" she asked as they reached the train station.

"Germans," Luc whispered.

Adèle stilled as Luc darted into the washroom. She waited outside and saw two German guards take position at the door to the station, while three others drew their Walther P38 9mm automatic pistols.

They arrested every man on the platform, herding them into trucks parked outside the station. Luc was nowhere to be seen, and Adèle couldn't think of a way out of this mess.

She had heard of this happening but had not seen it before now; it was what her fellow countrymen called a *rafle*. The Germans would bundle all the men off to the nearest police station, where they would be searched and their papers examined. Only those who had a genuine reason for not working in Germany – such as ill health or being a member of a vital occupation to the war effort, and in possession of papers certifying the same – would be released. Everyone else would be shipped off to Germany for the duration of the war. Families were left to guess what had happened if their loved ones failed to return home.

Adèle tried to keep calm as the minutes ticked by, seeing women torn from their men, crying and screaming, while the men – knowing they would be shot if they tried to resist – climbed into the trucks.

Where was Luc?

Finally, the Germans seemed satisfied with their haul and left. Adèle made her way to the platform, believing it was best to continue their journey. The train had pulled into the station before she felt Luc at her side. He pushed her aboard and came in after her.

"You smell disgusting." Her stomach churned.

"Better that than dead." He explained that a member of the train station staff had hidden him, but judging by the stench, Adèle was grateful to be spared the details.

They stopped at an abandoned garage used to store some of their weapons and explosives, picking up what they needed before heading to the forest to meet the new recruits.

* * *

Luc hadn't been joking. There were more men than she could have imagined waiting for her when they finally arrived at the new camp. They were a rowdy group who argued about everything, from the progress of the Russians and the Allies, to who their allies actually were. Some of the men were fanatical communists, while others were fighting to get back to their families and didn't much care who ran France after the war.

She glanced at Luc, and he gave her a thumbs up as a sign of encouragement. She clapped her hands for quiet and, when that failed, put her fingers into her mouth and whistled.

Silence fell as they stared.

She began to speak. "You must forget I'm a woman. I've been fully trained and am here to train you in sabotage and other areas so that when the Allies land, we are ready to help in the fight for France."

A man jumped up from the ground, his beret falling off in

the process. "What are we waiting for? They've been promising to come back for years."

Adèle ignored the comments coming from the field; she didn't blame them for their frustration, but nor could she do anything to change the situation.

"I know some of you have been involved in destroying transformers, but, as you have seen, it's not effective. The Germans have them back up and running in no time. What we need to do is blow holes in the transformers and then set fire to the oil inside. That should shut off the electricity to the factories for several weeks."

"And how do you suggest we do that? We just walk in and ask permission?" The young man who spoke out laughed, looking around at his comrades, encouraging them to laugh too.

Adèle took a second before she put the explosive she was holding gently onto the ground. Then she marched over to the man, pulled him to his feet and had him lying back on the floor in seconds. The same men who had laughed with him now jeered.

"You need to shut up and listen. I won't repeat myself. These are real explosives, and if you want to kill yourself planting them, who am I to argue with Darwin's law?"

"Huh?" The man's confusion was painfully obvious to all.

"She means the survival of the fittest. She's calling you stupid."

Adèle turned a furious look on the speaker, who wisely apologised. She walked back to where she had left the explosive, picking it up and starting over. "This is the box into which you put the explosive. As you can see, it is fitted with magnets. These will allow you to fix the bomb to the most sensitive part of whatever you wish to destroy." She held up the box to show the crowd of men. "You will set the bomb off using a time pencil, which will allow you to distance yourself from the explosion. The pencil, this short metal rod, is pushed into the box like so. Inside the rod, there is a mix of acid, which, when pushed – for obvious reasons, I won't demonstrate that part..." She waited for the laughter to die down. "When pushed, it will wear away the wire, causing the spring to release the detonator and then, boom."

A young man of about nineteen asked, "What about the people working in the factories, the innocent Frenchmen?"

"We will break in at night to plant the devices. Any night-watchmen will be taken away and tied up to show the Germans they couldn't stop us. Of course, if those nightwatchmen willingly work with the Germans, I won't risk the lives of my men to save theirs. They can go to their maker and make peace with him."

The men cheered.

"But before we let you loose with live devices, you all need to train together. We need small teams of four or five men, who will act as one. Pick those you would trust with your life."

The men broke off into groups as Luc came closer.

"You're good. You had me believing that bit about the traitors."

"Good, because I meant it. This is war, and we don't take prisoners." Adèle handed him one of the Bakelite boxes. "Every team should know how to set these up."

"Yes, sir." Luc saluted, but his grin showed her he was teasing. Then his grin faded. "You scare me. Your thirst for revenge is..."

"I learned my lesson from the Gulliver incident." She broke out in a cold sweat just mentioning the name of the agent Luc had told her to terminate. She'd hesitated, not wanting to kill one of her own countrymen. Gulliver had, by his bragging and total lack of security, brought the Gestapo to his resistance circuit, leading to the torture and deaths of several resistants. She held herself partially responsible and vowed never to make that mistake again. "They won't get a hint of sympathy from me." She spoke coldly so he'd get the message.

After a few hours, most of the men had gained the skills necessary to take down a target. Now it was a question of identifying some targets. Luc would accompany her on the tour of the area to find them, his local knowledge being superior to hers.

"Luc, you will come with me while Romain stays here." She turned to the young man, who seemed to stand taller, enjoying the extra responsibility. "You take over the training. I want these men grouped into companies of ten. Each should be responsible for a task such as digging latrines, gathering food, cooking and so on."

"Cooking? That's women's work."

Adèle raised an eyebrow. "I only see one woman here. Believe me, you'd rather starve than have me cook for you. If you were in the army, you'd have rations. Out here, we must fend for ourselves."

"The men can go home to eat." Romain looked at Luc for backup.

"Send them home, let them get arrested. If they are lucky, they will be shipped off to Germany as workers. More likely, they will be passed over to the SS for questioning, and then some will sing like canaries, and you can expect your whole new army to be caged like mice."

Romain flushed, but it was the warning in Luc's eyes that caught her attention. She wasn't going to win any friends with sarcasm.

"Sorry, Romain, I've been out of action too long, being stuck on a farm." She fell back on her usual method of dealing with men. "I know you have the skills needed to lead these men. I trained you well." She joked to ease the tension. "The men look up to you. Use what you learned and teach them." Romain stood to attention as he listened. "Their lives, and yours, may depend on it."

"I can do it." His tone was much more civil than before. "When will you be back?"

"A few days at the most. Tell the men who do go home to be careful. The Germans want nothing better than to smash us further into the ground."

TWENTY-THREE

SEPTEMBER 1943

Sophie checked the bandage on the little girl's leg, relieved to see the cut wasn't as red as it had been but looked like it was healing. "Well done, Aimée, you were so brave. It will heal nicely now." She wanted to reassure the little girl, who'd fallen onto a barbed wire fence at her father's farm. The poor man had carried his daughter to the convent himself. His horse had been taken by the Germans, and the walk took several hours, allowing infection to set in. Sophie had had to wash out the cut with iodine and apply numerous poultices, which the child endured bravely.

"Your daughter won't lose her leg, Monsieur Chastain."

"Thank you, Sister. We are so grateful for your help. I left some eggs and some vegetables for the kitchen. It is only a small gesture for what you did."

"The sisters and I are grateful. It is difficult to feed so many nuns." Especially when those nuns were sheltering several children and families in the dungeons below the convent. Not that she could tell anyone that. Those people relied on their discretion for their lives.

Loud music caused her to look out the window. The sight

before her made her shudder as wave after wave of soldiers marched through the streets of Nice. The announcement on 8 September of the Italians signing an armistice with the Allies had resulted in scenes of jubilation, especially in the Italian section of Nice. The men had come through the war unscathed, and they could go home to their families in Italy. The parties went into the small hours of the night, but the celebratory mood didn't last long. Stories reached Nice of the Germans capturing entire battalions of Italian soldiers and marching them away as prisoners of war. Now the martial music and sounds of the goose-stepping SS troops took her thoughts back to Paris. She couldn't believe they were here in Nice.

Aimée's father came to look over her shoulder. "Who is this man?"

"Hauptsturmführer Brunner, former commander of the camp at Drancy. His arrival here can only mean bad news for our friends." Sophie fingered the crucifix at her neck. She'd found she was able to play her part of a Catholic nun convincingly, given her Catholic upbringing. In fact, she wasn't sure anyone in the convent knew her real identity.

The nun next to her prayed. "May God have mercy on his soul."

"It's the souls of his victims I'm worried about." She might not want to kill a Nazi, but she wasn't about to pray for one either. She hurried back to checking on the sick children. Here in the convent, she didn't have to hide her experience as a doctor. People just assumed that, as a nun, she had spent many hours nursing the sick. Things had been difficult in Cannes, but it was worse here in Nice.

"Can Aimée come back to the farm now?"

"She should stay here for a few days to make sure the wound heals properly." Sophie smiled at him, she could see he was torn between staying in town near his daughter and checking on his farm. "Go back to your farm and come back in three days. She should be ready to go home then. She'll be well looked after."

"Thank you. I'll just go say goodbye to her."

Bea, one of the helpers, distracted her. "Sister Agnès, Claudette left you a note. She said she was taking some packages to her husband."

Sophie took the note, not reprimanding Bea for reading it as she didn't understand the code. Claudette had left Nice and taken some of the more Jewish-looking children to her husband at the orphanage in Izieu. Given its relatively remote location, they should be safe there.

The Germans weren't their only concern. The mortality rate had shot up over the last six months, the brutal winter and the starvation diet taking their toll. The Italians, while more pleasant to deal with, had been dreadful administrators. Rumours flowed of parcels of aid sent from Northern France being opened and distributed amongst the Italian soldiers rather than the intended recipients in Nice and other areas on the Riviera. Children were dying of malnutrition as well as falling prey to scarlet fever, mumps, and other illnesses.

* * *

Later, Mother Superior entered the ward and greeted a few of the children before making her way to Sophie's side.

"Sister Agnès, it is time to go to the market. I thought you might like some fresh air."

Sophie nodded as she finished up with a sick child.

"Sleep well, Patrick. Tomorrow you will feel like playing football again."

"You promise?"

"Yes, I do." She pushed his hair gently out of his eyes. Such a sweet little boy – Patrick never complained, though his whole family was missing. His parents had given him into the care of the nuns at the start of the war. He couldn't remember his last name.

She hurried after the Mother Superior.

"I thought you might need to seek out your friends." The Mother Superior whispered, handing Sophie a shopping basket. She never spoke loudly.

"Thank you." Sophie wanted to see for herself what was happening on the streets of Nice. She didn't enjoy listening to rumours, but the stories about what the Germans and the French Milice were doing were horrific. If only half of them were true, the Jews – and any resistance members living in Nice – were in real danger.

Mother Superior didn't like chit-chat and preferred to walk in silence. Sophie adopted the older woman's manner and pace; to the outside world, they looked like two nuns going on a short walk to the market. They walked in silence past the Baroque-style Chapelle de la Miséricorde.

Sophie couldn't help but think the Chapel of Mercy should be filled to the eaves with people praying for the souls of those around them.

As they walked on through the streets surrounded by the yellow and orange buildings, Sophie wished they were visiting at a time of peace. Nice had such a blend of cultures and history to explore. She'd heard the tzar of Russia had set up a flower market in St Petersburg after being inspired by the beauty of the flower markets at Cours Saleya. If he was alive, the tzar and anyone else who'd heard his stories would be disappointed if he had to visit now. There was no sign of the famous flowers but rather stall after stall of provisions, many of which were half empty. She lifted the basket she was carrying higher on her arm, hoping that the stallholders had kept aside some of the produce as promised. In her head, she could picture the array of strawberries, fresh juicy melons, bitter lemons and her favourite, plates of chickpea pancakes called *socca* that had been part of her childhood holidays to this region.

With no papers or ration cards, the people they were sheltering depended on what extra the nuns could source, either from donations or by visiting the markets and buying up old vegetables at a cheap price. Some of the market traders gave willingly, perhaps thinking they were securing a place in heaven. Sophie shook her head to rid her mind of the cynical thoughts. Most French people were doing their best to stay out of trouble and survive. They didn't inform on their neighbours, but neither did they go out of their way to help.

Suddenly, with a bunch of whistles and gunshots, they were surrounded by German troops. A roundup, or *rafle*, as the locals called it – and they were caught in the middle of it. Mother Superior grabbed onto Sophie's arm as they were jostled by the crowd. People began running in a desperate attempt to escape.

Sophie whispered, "Stand still; they might not question us." They stood watching as the soldiers and Milice, dressed in their blue trousers and jackets, brown shirts, and trademark blue berets, stopped and questioned members of the public. The members of the Milice were more dangerous. They understood the local accent and knew the people. Did they have to be so eager to help the Boches?

Sophie watched, horrified, as the soldiers instructed men to stop and drop their trousers in the middle of the street.

The Reverend Mother covered her face, "What are they doing?"

"Checking to see if they are circumcised." Sophie quickly explained to the old nun, who hadn't seen so much as a boy's legs since she had joined the convent fifty-odd years prior. Sophie's heart went out in sympathy to the Mother Superior, as well as the men now being thrown into the backs of vans. She moved quickly when a German soldier pointed a gun at a young child whose father was frantically trying to keep his family from being arrested.

"Stop it! Can't you see the man is a Muslim?" Sophie's tone suggested the soldier was stupid.

The soldier stopped in surprise, clearly shocked that a nun was approaching him.

"It isn't only the Jews who are circumcised, you know. Didn't you learn anything at school?"

"No, Sister. I mean, yes, Sister." The soldier tried again to speak in French, but his limited vocabulary didn't work for him.

"Let him and his family go. God is watching you." Spying the crucifix around the young soldier's neck, she appealed to his beliefs.

The soldier looked from her to the man and his family, and back again. He reluctantly stepped back, but before Sophie could shepherd the family to safety, a Milice officer barked out, "What is going on here?"

Sophie listened as the soldier explained in German what she had said about the family being Muslim. The officer's response to the soldier made Sophie blush, and she had to keep her face straight so the officer would not know she had understood their exchange in German. She decided to ignore them, and once more took hold of the smallest child's hand and went to lead them away.

"You stop." Sophie turned at the sound of the man's voice. She stared at him in silence. His jaw clenched, the knuckles whitening on the baton he carried. "I don't care if you're a nun; you don't interfere in German business."

"You are wrong. You cannot arrest this man and his family – they are Muslim, not Jewish." Sophie's voice was firm, although her legs were shaking under her robe.

"We will decide who we arrest. We might just arrest you." The malice in his eyes astounded her. Even now, this far into the war, she was surprised at the level of hatred people could hold against their fellow man.

Sophie returned his glare, not about to be intimidated by this jumped-up piece of garbage.

"You can do whatever you wish, but you are not taking this family into custody. I will go and see your German superior myself."

"That can be arranged, Sister." He spat the word out as if it offended him.

"What is the meaning of this? How dare you speak to one of my nuns like this! Show respect."

Sophie couldn't believe it. The Mother Superior wasn't whispering but speaking in a firm tone that commanded deference. The crowd that had gathered inched forward, their mood turning against the soldiers. They might not protect 'the Jewish foreigners', as they saw them, but nobody would treat their beloved Reverend Mother with anything other than the utmost reverence.

"I apologise, Reverend Mother, but keep your young nuns on a tighter leash. She has no business getting involved with our arrests." The Milice officer didn't take his eyes off Sophie.

"Sister Agnès has a generous soul and can't help but wonder at what you are doing. Jesus wouldn't stand by and let an innocent man and his young family be terrorised. Why should Sister Agnès?"

"Since when does your God like Muslims?"

"Their faith is of no concern. They are human beings, just like you – although your behaviour reminds me of an animal's. Now, good day." Mother Superior turned to Sophie. "Come now, Sister Agnès, let us escort this poor family to the convent. We may not have food suitable for their religious beliefs, but we can provide a nice cool glass of water."

The Reverend Mother took the father's hand and led him away, the small crowd parting to allow her through. Sophie grabbed the other child's hand, and they followed, with their mother bringing up the rear. Sophie glanced behind her; the crowd had closed the gap behind them, making it difficult for the Milice to follow them. Without saying a word, the community had sent a message to the Germans and the Milice to leave their nuns alone.

Only once they were out of the street did the Mother Superior stop. She was gasping for breath. Sophie went to her in concern; the woman was much too old for such stress. "You must rest, Reverend Mother."

"I will sit here for a while. Take the family and go. Don't return. Go to Father Tobias, in Saint-Just. He will find you a new place to stay. You have made an enemy of that man. But God will favour you for your bravery. I am in awe of you, my child."

Sophie kissed the Mother Superior's hand. A woman behind her said, "Go, Sister. That officer, Oscar Dubois, would sell his own mother to his Nazi friends. I will look after the Reverend Mother. May God go with you."

With one last look, Sophie left the nun with the other woman. She took the children's hands once more and led them away.

"You know I am not Muslim, Sister?" the father said in a low voice as they moved further away from the scene.

"Just as I am not a nun."

The man's mouth dropped open, but thankfully he didn't make a sound.

She whispered, "For now, you must pretend. All our lives depend on it."

"Thank you. Whoever you are."

* * *

Sophie escorted the young family to a safe house, only once she had made sure they weren't being followed.

"Are you sure they won't report us?" The father held his youngest child asleep in his arms.

"No, she won't. Just do as she says, and you will all be safe. She's not Jewish, so her food and home won't be kosher."

The man nodded as a tear fell from his eye. "We are grateful. God will understand. Thank you, Sister ... I mean, whoever you are."

Sophie knocked on the door, looking around as they waited to enter.

A woman opened the door, saying, "Sister Agnès, come in, please. Your friends too. Oh my, what beautiful young children. My name is Rose, and my home is yours." The middle-aged woman ushered them all inside and, with a last look around, closed the door to the street.

Sophie spoke quickly. "There's been a *rafle* down near the markets. This man and his family were caught up in it. We need to get them new papers and a way out. Can you keep them here until then?"

"Yes, of course. I've made a large pot of soup; we can water it down, and it will last a couple of days." Rose turned to the man's wife. "I apologise – it will not be what you are used to."

The Jewish woman burst into tears and stepped forward to embrace Rose. "Please and thank you. My French is not good, but you are wonderful to my family. I am so happy to be here; we all are. Merci."

Seeing Rose was speechless, Sophie spoke quickly in German, reassuring the young wife and mother her message had been understood. Then she switched to French. "Rose, please spread the word among the Jewish community that the men should not appear in public. If they must go out, tell them to leave their families at home. A man on his own has a chance to escape."

The woman of the house promised she would pass on the message. She would also try to find out if anything happened to the convent.

"I must go now. I have other people to look after. Be safe. Rose, look after yourself too. We need you and others like you more than ever."

Rose gave Sophie a kiss on her cheek. "Pray for me, Sister Agnès. They took my boys away. Every person I help, I do so in the hope someone will help my boys." Her gaze went to the fire-place, above which were two photographs, one of a young family taken shortly after the last war, the second of two boys in French Army uniform. They hadn't returned after the armistice. Rose had no idea where they were.

Sophie wished the family and Rose the best of luck before taking the back door, walking out through the small garden into the next street.

She kept her head down until she'd walked through several backstreets to the church where Father Tobias officiated. She'd only met him once in passing.

Now he stood in front of her, looking as if he wanted to throttle her. His bright red cheeks and clenched teeth warned her to expect a lecture, which was delivered as soon as he escorted her to the empty sacristy. She kept her eyes on the crucifix on the wall behind him as he gave her a verbal dressing-down.

"I can't believe you took the man on in public. You not only blew your own cover, but put the convent at serious risk."

Sophie winced but let him speak. She knew his anger wasn't all directed at her. She kept her eyes on the wall as he paced up and down the small space, muttering all sorts of things. Only when he fell silent did she speak.

"I know, Father, and believe me, if I could go back, I would hope I would act differently. But I couldn't watch them take the children." She lifted her eyes to meet his. "They were so small and scared."

The priest looked at her, his eyes full of sadness. She said nothing. She was sorry for involving the nuns, but she wasn't about to apologise for trying to help children.

"I know that, and in truth, I would probably have reacted in the same way," he said quietly. "I will plan for our friends to be moved, but you must lie low. We cannot risk you bumping into that man again. He is a bad enemy – worse than any German."

Sophie nodded, not about to disagree. She had seen the hatred in the man's eyes. She knew he would do his best to track down Sister Agnès.

"We shall have to think of a new identity for you. But for now, I will take you to an enclosed order where the Nazis are not likely to visit. Those nuns have taken a vow of silence and do not engage with the outer world. I know you will find it difficult, but you must blend in. We can't help anyone, not even the children, if your actions expose all our hiding places."

Sophie nodded.

"The sisters may have withdrawn from society, but the convent is home to many of our young friends. You will teach them how to be Christians, Catholics. They will have to learn our prayers, make the sign of the cross and all the other things the Nazis could test them on. For the older children, a certificate of baptism is no longer enough protection. We must make it seem real."

Was this what the parents she'd met back in the camps dreaded? The Christianisation of their children. Sophie pushed aside her doubts. Parents who loved their children enough to give them to strangers would agree to anything that would save them.

TWENTY-FOUR

Luc and a new man, Tomas, escorted Adèle to a new maquis camp. They left the bikes behind and walked through the forest in the pouring rain. The wind rustled through the trees as they ploughed their way around the large, thickset trees.

She jumped at the screech of an animal, causing Luc to flash her an amused grin. Some special agent she was, getting spooked walking in daylight in the woods. But the farther they walked, the denser the trees became and the more difficult it was to walk over the uneven ground pitted with rocks and tree roots. Her clothes caught on the thick brambles.

After about five miles of trekking through the forest, her nose picked up the scent of smoke before she spotted the small encampment. About twenty men, most of them between eighteen and twenty-five, milled around the clearing. She saw a few tents but more makeshift shelters formed with tree branches. Tomas raised a hand in greeting as they were spotted by a lookout holding what Adèle recognised as a rifle from the last war. While the men greeted each other, she appraised the area, noting a couple of defensive trenches but little else by way of security. The men looked like a group of circus performers or schoolchildren dressed up in their fathers' old uniforms. Most didn't have guns or any weapons that she could see. Was this the French army the leaders of SOE had told her to expect?

Luc put a hand on her arm as more of the men came forward, their eyes lit up with curiosity. "Claire, these are the men we spoke about last night. Their leader, Moise, is coming now." Luc whispered, "Treat him with respect."

Moise was older than she expected, a vivid scar where his left eye should have been.

"This is what London sends? A girl young enough to be my daughter." Moise spat some tobacco on the ground beside him.

The men around him muttered in response to their leader's displeasure.

Ignoring his rudeness, Adèle stepped forward and held her hand out. "Yes, I'm here to help. London is committed to providing you with everything you need. All you have to do is provide me with a list." She let her words sink in for a second. "On the condition you agree to follow orders."

His eyebrows rose at her response. He clearly hadn't expected her to speak, never mind challenge him.

She held his gaze, determined not to be the first to look away. He laughed. "What are you going to do? What do you think I need? A new dress?"

His men laughed, but Adèle didn't flinch. Instead, she let her gaze move from one face to another before returning to his and responding, "Dresses can be arranged. I'd suggest guns, ammunition, explosives, blankets, food, cigarettes, and money. But you are in charge." The men laughed but quickly muffled their reaction when Moise ground out his cigarette in the dirt.

"You mock me?"

"It's not my intention to upset you or remove your authority, but I will do both if I have to. I'm telling you I'm your connection to supplies. Respect is a two-way street."

Heart hammering, she spotted Luc's disapproving look from

the corner of her eye, but her main focus was on the giant of a man in front of her. He stared at her before he burst out laughing. "It seems like London sent me a spitfire. Come, have a drink – or don't young ladies like you drink?"

"I can drink anything you give me."

"This way." The crowd of men parted like the Red Sea as Moise led the way to a small wooden cabin. Entering it, Adèle forced herself to breathe through her mouth as the smell assaulted her nostrils, threatening to make her breakfast reappear. The bed in the corner moved with a life of its own. A dirty glass sat on top of a dirtier plate on the floor. On the other side of the room, a table with some rough-hewn stools were the only other furniture.

Moise kicked out at a dog as big as a wolf. "Get out, you stinky rat."

The dog barely glanced at his master as he left the room. Adèle kept her hand on the revolver in her pocket, not trusting a man that could mistreat an animal. Tomas and Luc, sporting similar looks of disapproval, took their seats, leaving Adèle sitting opposite Moise. The bearded man uncorked a bottle with his teeth before pouring it into four dirty tumblers. Forcing herself, Adèle picked it up and knocked back the contents before slamming the glass back on the wooden table.

"These are my terms. You need to reorganise your camp. The location is good, well-concealed from nosy intruders, but you couldn't defend it against an attack." Moise growled, but she ignored him. "You need to set lookouts around the perimeter of your camp. These sentries should do a four-hour tour of duty, day and night."

Moise poked Luc with his elbow. "I like your woman."

Again, Adèle ignored him. "We were in your camp before anyone spotted us. Your men need to be properly armed. They don't look or act like a disciplined army."

"Claire." Luc's disapproval warned her she may have gone

too far. She changed tactic, adopting the old Adèle charm. Smiling at the giant, she stared into his eye. "I know you've done the best with what you have, and I'm here to help. You pick the phrase, and I will get it to London to arrange a drop. You can then listen to the BBC; the night you hear the phrase you picked, the supplies will drop. On top of getting you weapons, I will also get explosives and help train your men."

"You?"

"Yes, me."

"What does a little girl like you know about weapons?"

Before he could finish his sentence, Adèle pulled her pistol, and shot and shattered the glass on the ground by his bed. He leaped to his feet, cursing loudly.

"Your men should have searched me before they let me near you. Another breach of security I will fix." Adèle stood up and marched outside. Furious at her loss of control, she berated herself. A few of the men whistled, some made a couple of disparaging remarks, but she pretended not to hear.

"Come back here, woman."

The command made her turn around, not because she wanted to but because she had to give Moise back some dignity. She needed him on their side.

"I agree to your terms."

Suspicious at his rapid change of mind, she waited in silence.

"I have a condition."

Here it was. Again, staying silent, she held his gaze.

"You move in here. Live among us. Share my ... hut."

The men cheered amid ribald comments. Adèle pretended to consider the offer as she tried to stop her body shaking with revulsion. "Alas, that won't be possible. If I stay here, I won't get the supplies I promised."

The men groaned, but she added, "I will be back. To bring your weapons and show you how to blow a bridge to smithereens with a charge of plastique." The men cheered, and even Moise cracked a smile. She walked up to him and, holding her hand out, said, "I assume we have a deal."

He eyed her for a moment before giving her his hand.

"If France had men with the same will as you, the Germans would be where they belong. Back in Germany."

"On that, we can agree. Now, please excuse us. Luc and I have another job to do. Tomas will work out the details of the drop."

With that, Adèle turned on her heel, and as she walked, she reached down to pat the dog, whispering in his ear, "Bite him hard the next time he mistreats you."

* * *

Adèle didn't say a word as she and Luc made their way back to the cottage. She strode through the forest wishing for a hot bath. She felt contaminated having spent time with that man.

Luc broke the silence. "He's a hero. They don't all come looking like film stars."

"He's an animal. No – worse than one."

"His manners leave a lot to be desired, but his bravery can't be questioned. He lost his eye in 1940 in a shoot-out with Gestapo agents who shot his wife and son. The child was three years old."

Adèle hesitated for a second before she strode on. "He needed to know he shouldn't underestimate me."

TWENTY-FIVE
OCTOBER 1943, NICE

Sophie lay low for weeks, using her time to help train the Jewish children to become 'Christians'. They had to learn how to act like Catholic or Protestant children, so they could be hidden in plain sight.

The older children knew the risks and were generally good students, but Sophie's heart went out to the younger children, those who cried for their parents. They couldn't understand why they were no longer called Yael or Yacob and instead had Christian names. Over and over, Sophie and other volunteers drilled them so that if they were questioned, they would not betray both themselves and the people protecting them.

Jacqueline Ardent and her sister Giselle were two of the children living at the convent where Sophie was hiding. Their story was becoming all too familiar. Their mother had been caught in a *rafle* when she went shopping; she had left the girls at home for their own safety. They didn't know where their father was. He had disappeared the year before, believing his presence would only bring danger to his family.

Jacqueline stared at the painting, asking softly, "Why do they hate us so much?"

"The Nazis hate everyone, but for some reason, they hold the Jews responsible for everything wrong in the world. It is not fair, and someday they will see they are wrong."

The girl looked unconvinced. Sophie put her arm around her shoulders. "What is wrong? Don't you like it here?"

Sophie knew it wasn't ideal to have children living in a convent, but these weren't ordinary times. The sisters were taking great risks sheltering these youngsters, risking death or deportation not only for themselves but for all the members of the order. But children wouldn't understand the danger, and probably thought the nuns were callous, not letting whole families shelter inside the walls of the convent.

"Most of the nuns are kind, but some of the children have been mean to Giselle. They say she looks like a Jew, so she must be pretending to be Catholic."

Horrified, Sophie tried to hide her fear from Jacqueline. "What were they saying?"

"They called her some horrible names. They measured the size of her nose and told her the Germans would come. It was Bella and her friends."

Sophie hugged Jacqueline as the girl gave way to tears. The whole idea of being able to tell a person's race from the size of their head or their facial features was just part of the Nazi nonsense.

She would have to do something about Bella; the young girl was a Nazi in the making. She was often behind the cruellest taunts, but Mother Superior deemed it too dangerous to remove her from the convent. Bella's only surviving relative, an uncle she never saw, was an important man in the local town. He could cause trouble if he wanted.

"I will see what I can do, but for now, just keep looking out for your sister. Don't let the hatred of others change your heart, Jacqueline. You have a kind soul. That is worth more than anything."

The girl looked unconvinced. Sophie gave her one last hug before she went looking for Father Tobias. He was holding confessions for the nuns.

She entered the confessional box but, instead of confessing her sins, told him she needed his help.

"Kneel outside – the nuns will think you are doing penance. I will speak to you after I've finished."

Sophie nodded and, leaving the box, walked into a pew and took to her knees. Blessing herself, she looked the picture of a well-behaved nun. As she kneeled, her thoughts flew around. Where was Adèle? What would she make of her twin dressed in a nun's habit, kneeling in a church? What would papa say if he saw her now? And Jean-Pierre. Her throat caught, thinking of her brother. Was he somewhere looking down on her? And then her thoughts went to Jules. She could barely bring his face to mind now – it seemed like decades since they had been lovers. She missed him, and the chance to be a wife and mother. Being around children made her realise how much she wanted to have a child of her own one day – but only when it was safe.

A cough alerted her to the fact that confession was over. She waited for the small chapel to empty before following the priest into his sacristy to the left of the altar.

"Father Tobias, we have a problem, one that may lead to the discovery of all the children hidden here."

The priest frowned when he heard the story. "It is true, Giselle is more Jewish-looking than most of the children staying here. Maybe she should be moved?"

"But where to?"

"Father Jacques has offered to take more children. His town is high enough up in the mountains to provide a haven for the girls. We need to get them there. Giselle is bound to attract attention. Would Jacqueline stay here? It would be safer, as she is less Jewish-looking."

Horrified that the priest was even contemplating splitting

up the girls, Sophie shook her head. "Jacqueline will never leave her sister. The last thing her mother said to her was to mind Giselle. She has taken that to heart. I will take them to Father Jacques if you tell me where to go."

"Are you sure? You risk torture and death if you are caught with them."

"I cannot send someone else in my place. I will take them. Plus, I have an ulterior motive. I wanted to help get children to safety, but I'm not able to do enough here. I am tired of looking at the walls of the convent rather than using the skills God gave me. I'm a good doctor, and with due respect, it's a better use of my time than the continuous prayers."

He burst out laughing. "You are a breath of fresh air, my dear." Then his expression turned serious again. "Don't take any risks."

"I won't. Are you sure this Father Jacques is the best person to look after the girls? I know we shouldn't favour any of the children, but the Ardent girls have become special."

"I'm certain. With Bella making life difficult for Giselle, the best thing we can do for the poor child is to let her live happily somewhere else."

Sophie went to find Jacqueline to tell her the news. The young girl was lying on her bed in the room she shared with several others, staring at a drawing she'd made.

Sophie sat on the bed next to the child. "Your mother?"

Jacqueline nodded, wiping a hand across her eyes to clear the tears. "It's not very good, but they took our photographs away. I keep thinking I will forget her. And papa."

"Come here." Sophie wrapped her arms around the girl and let her cry. Only once she stopped sobbing did Sophie explain why she was there.

"But how will we travel? Anyone looking at us will know we are Jewish."

Sophie ran her hand up and down the girl's arm. "No, they

won't. Most people are too worried about themselves to think of anyone else. I will be with you. You will be safe." Sophie hoped that was true. She crossed her fingers.

"I'm scared, but it will be worth it to get away from Bella. I hate her. I know I mustn't, but some days I want to wipe that smirk off her face."

Sophie knew she shouldn't encourage the child, but she was human. "I know that feeling, Jacqueline. I think even Sister Beatrice has felt the same."

The comment lightened Jacqueline's mood: Sister Beatrice was the kindest, softest soul in the convent. As they were chatting, Giselle ran in but came to a stop seeing Sophie sitting on the bed with Jacqueline.

"You've been crying. What did you say to my sister to make her cry?" Giselle turned an angry gaze on Sophie.

"Don't be rude, Giselle." Jacqueline admonished her sibling, but as she did so, she moved away from Sophie to draw her sister closer.

"We are leaving the convent and Nice."

Giselle pulled away, crossing her arms across her chest. "I'm not leaving here. Papa knows to collect us here."

"Papa will find us, Giselle. We must go to this new place. It will be safer, not just for us, but for the nuns and the other children. We don't want to be the reason the Germans raid this place and capture everyone, do we?"

The eight-year-old shook her head. Sophie had to look away to hide her tear-filled eyes. What sort of world was it where a child had to make a choice based on the safety of other children?

Sophie helped dress the children in good but worn clothes so they resembled every other child in France. She found them wooden clogs. It was almost impossible to find leather shoes now, so wearing them could cause suspicion.

The girls were tearful as they hugged some of the nuns

goodbye. Sister Beatrice gave Jacqueline an embroidered hanky and Giselle a new rag doll.

"Go with God, children." The nun didn't hide the tears running down her face.

Sophie escorted the girls from the convent to the nearest tram stop. The Nice authorities had reopened two lines after the buses got requisitioned, but it wasn't enough to provide for the demand, so the tram was crowded. A kind man stood and let Sophie sit down with Giselle on her lap, Jacqueline standing to the side.

* * *

Their journey passed without incident, apart from Giselle generating a couple of curious looks. Sophie was sure some people suspected the child was Jewish, but nobody said anything.

She left the children in a pretty little town, with the beaming, elderly priest waving goodbye to her.

Her faith in mankind was rekindled. She returned to the convent, convinced that the power of good would overcome the evil of the Nazis and their accomplices.

TWENTY-SIX

While Sophie loved helping the children, what she had said to Father Tobias was true: she was getting bored and restless. It wasn't just the endless queueing, which had become a national pastime. Everyone spent hours every day queueing for something, be it food, travel permits, or for the monthly coupons. You had to either keep an eye on the newspapers to see what coupons you were entitled to and for what, or else you consulted the posted announcements at the town hall.

Women vented their frustration in the queues. "What's the point in having ration coupons when the shelves are empty? Says here I can have a litre of wine every ten days; at this rate, it might as well be every ten years."

"I need more food; I've got a hard labourer."

The others in the queue smiled. That coupon was given to male workers and pregnant women but, in reality, what wasn't hard labour when you had to survive on less than 1,200 calories a day? And that was on the days you could find food.

And then there were the checkpoints, which seemed to be increasing in number.

Sophie missed working with patients and thought often of

her time at the hospital with Dr Murphy. She couldn't help feeling she could do more – but every time she suggested going back into the field, her request was turned down.

She tried to keep busy until, finally she got permission to collect some children from a safe house and move them to another one.

When the transfer was completed, she took the bus back to the convent.

Sophie looked around her as she took her seat and couldn't believe her eyes. The sisters she had left with Father Jacques, Jacqueline and Giselle, were sitting on the bus. What on earth did they think they were doing? They could be picked up at any time.

She was about to stand up when Jacqueline stared right at her and blinked rapidly. Without moving her face, the girl looked to her left. Only then did Sophie spot it: the girls weren't alone. They were surrounded by Gestapo agents. She had almost walked right into a trap.

She wanted to rush towards the girls and rescue them, but she knew that would be fatal – not just for her, but for the girls and for the rest of their group if the Gestapo made her talk. She forced herself to get off the bus at the next stop.

Please, God, look after those girls. Please, she prayed silently. Jacqueline was only thirteen, but she was very protective of her younger sister. She wouldn't leave Giselle's side. But now Sophie had to warn the group. The children didn't know many details, but if they were questioned, they could compromise some members – not least Father Jacques.

She sent word, via one of the children who took messages between the convent and the church, that she needed to see the priest urgently. Changing out of her habit and into her own dress, she took a side exit out of the convent. Rather than meet at a church, she had told Father Tobias to go to a small café on the seafront. It would be quiet now; she missed the noise and smell coming from the fishing boats as they brought in their fresh catch. Her mouth watered at the thought of her mother's speciality: bass with garlic and lemon butter. How long had it been since her family had sat down to a meal together? Three years? It felt more like twenty.

She walked there, making sure she wasn't followed by taking a circuitous route. As she approached, she spotted him sitting alone at a table outside. He saw her coming and stood up.

"There you are – I was worried." Father Tobias held out a chair for her.

She took a seat to his left, her eyes not leaving the street. The café owner arrived with two ersatz coffees before leaving them to talk.

"You were right to be. I just saw the Ardent girls on the bus. They were surrounded by agents. What on earth happened? They were supposed to be safe in Father Jacques's village."

Father Tobias wouldn't look her in the eyes.

"You knew?"

He nodded. "I was going to tell you today. Father Jacques couldn't keep his mouth shut. He was heard boasting about saving young Jewish children. He was lucky he wasn't arrested."

"Why did they not take him?" Sophie asked, hating herself for putting her suspicions into words. "He wouldn't be the first priest to take the side of the Nazis."

"No, he wouldn't – but in this case, I don't believe he meant any harm. He just couldn't keep his mouth shut." Father Tobias paused for breath. "You can't know how bad I feel. I was the one who suggested you take the girls to him. I trusted him."

"You are not to blame; he is. What happens to him? He is a liability." Sophie tried to choose her words with care. What she wanted to do was scream from the rooftops how wrong it was, a priest letting children fall into the hands of the Gestapo. "Why wasn't he arrested too?"

"The bishop has contacts. He agreed to send Father Jacques

to Rome on some sort of visit to the Papal office. It's legitimate enough to please the Germans and gets rid of the priest. Hopefully, he won't return."

Sophie wasn't happy. The bishop's solution wasn't enough; he had protected one of his own while innocent children had been sacrificed.

"Hopefully, no one else will trust him either."

"I don't think they will, Sophie. Information like that passes quickly."

"Can we rescue the girls?"

"We can try, but it will be risky. They are well known around here. It might be more prudent to wait until they reach Drancy. Our people up there may be able to help them."

Sophie couldn't stand the thought of the girls being sent east but knew she couldn't risk more lives trying to rescue them, either. There were too many other children who needed their help.

"I have had enough of hiding, Father. It's time I went back to work properly. I can do more than just move the odd child from one house to the other."

"What of the risk?"

"I don't care about the risk. I can't stay safe while children like Jacqueline and Giselle are in danger."

Father Tobias took some time to acknowledge her response. He stayed silent for so long that she was worried he was trying to think of a way to talk her out of her decision. She was about to argue all her reasons for wanting to be more involved when he turned back to face her, an agonised expression on his face.

"I hate sending young people into danger, but you are right – the need is great. I will shortly be transferred to Lyon. You will come with me. But for now, return to the convent. I will be in touch very soon."

TWENTY-SEVEN

True to his word, a week after their conversation, Father Tobias summoned her to a meeting at his home next to his church. When she arrived, another man with dark curly brown hair and brown, almost black eyes, sat on the couch in the living room. He stood when she entered holding out his hand as the priest introduced them.

"Sophie, this is Joël, a friend with another resistance circuit. He helps me with the children.

Sophie noted the man's firm handshake and tried to smile in greeting but she was too anxious to find out what he knew about Jacqueline and Giselle.

"Have you news of the girls?"

Father Tobias shook his head. "I'm sorry, but the girls were sent directly to Poland. They didn't get off the train in Drancy. There was nothing that could be done."

Anger threatened to overwhelm her but it wasn't this kind man's fault. He couldn't have known what the other priest would do. She gritted her teeth in a bid to keep a lid on her temper. She counted to five before speaking.

"I hope you have asked me here to tell me I can work again."

He shook his head. "It is too dangerous. The Germans have offered a bribe to anyone willing to denounce Jewish children."

"But nobody would take a bribe like that."

"Thankfully, most of our compatriots are as horrified as you are, but there are those who would sell anything to make a profit. The resistance has just removed a concierge who boasted of selling out three young children for five francs a head."

Sophie's voice trembled, "What has become of the world – innocent children sold to be murdered?"

The priest clearly couldn't answer her question; he had probably asked himself the same thing if his expression was anything to go by. He stayed silent with his eyes closed for a couple of seconds, and she assumed he was praying.

When he opened them once more, he took a loud, deep breath before saying, "The good news is that, by doing such horrendous things, the Germans have played into our hands."

"I don't understand."

"Many, perhaps the majority, of French people would have stood by while the Germans arrested the adults, particularly the foreign Jews. But few can stand by and watch them take away young children. Nobody knows where they send these young-sters, but no one believes it is anywhere pleasant. By insisting on targeting the youngest and most vulnerable children, the Germans have succeeded in uniting the French people to our cause."

Sophie didn't know if the priest was right. The whole conversation, and the theory behind it, was too horrific.

All she knew was that she wanted to return to active work – even if she couldn't use her medical skills, she needed to be useful – so she pleaded her case once more. "I am fed up with sitting around here doing nothing. I must be of some use."

Joël surveyed her silently for a few moments before asking, "How would you feel about a trip to Switzerland?"

"I want to help, and you are sending me out of the country?" Sophie didn't modulate her tone, her scarlet face high-lighted her frustration.

"Yes, but with the intention of having you come back and maybe doing the trip again and again. The Swiss have agreed to take some children." Father Tobias glanced at his companion. "Joël has some valuable contacts."

"But I thought they were sending refugees back to the Germans."

"They are, but mainly adults. The boss thinks it is worth the risk. Especially for the younger and more Jewish-looking young-sters. They are harder to hide, but their appearance also means it is risky to move them out of France. They could be picked up immediately." Joël looked directly at Sophie, but it was Father Tobias who spoke.

"It will be very dangerous, for you to be seen with these children. You will be risking arrest and deportation. You may even be tortured."

Sophie didn't have to think about it. "I know the risks, but I want to help. I will do it. I have a certain advantage. I speak fluent German." She glanced at Joël and added, "Thanks to a German grandmother." Sophie turned her attention to the priest, who looked unconvinced. "You know I can do it. These children need to get out. It makes sense. I look German and can easily pass for a Swiss person. If you get me the right papers."

Joël grinned at her. "I happen to know just the right forger."

* * *

Sophie found herself escorting her first group of children to Switzerland. Father Tobias brought them to her along with two older boys and made the introductions.

"Robert and Daniel were both members of the Boy Scouts. They are excellent skiers, and they both know the area so well, they don't need maps. They will go with you." Father Tobias gave the boys a look of approval before turning his attention back to Sophie. "Unfortunately, they cannot come back. You will be on your own when you return."

"Thank you for your help, boys."

The teenagers nodded but didn't smile. The shadows in their eyes hinted at the troubles they had already lived through.

"Right, children. Are we ready?" she asked.

"Yes, Nicole."

It took her a few seconds to remember that was her new name, and Sophie grinned. Changing identities was exhausting, but at least Nicole Samson was closer to her real identity than Sister Agnès had been. She didn't have to fast or say prayers for hours on end, as she had done at the convent.

"One last thing – Mother Superior said to tell Sister Agnès she was praying for her." Father Tobias said, "Robert brought us the message."

At once, Sophie felt the weight of guilt leave her shoulders. The convent that had sheltered her was fine. She smiled at Robert. He obviously had no idea who Sister Agnès was.

* * *

At first, the children treated their expedition like an adventure, but as the terrain became more difficult and the weather colder, their high spirits wore off. Sophie, Robert, and Daniel carried the younger children to help make their journey a little easier. Sophie had to keep the whole group moving, as any delay could spell disaster. Robert and Daniel were lifesavers. The boys took turns scouting ahead, and more than once, they had to change their route to avoid a patrol.

Soon they had arrived at the crossing – but there was no sign of their guide. They waited for a day and a night, but still, no one came. Robert inched closer, aware this voice could carry on the wind.

"I don't like this. He should have been here by now. I will go and check."

"No, you can't. It might be a trap." Sophie wasn't sure what to do. The children were exhausted, having climbed all this way. They could turn back, but it was almost certain they would be caught and deported. At least they had a chance if they went ahead.

Robert stood firm. "If it is, then it is best I walk into it alone."

Sophie considered the young man's words. He was only sixteen, and the thought of sending him to his death didn't sit well with her. On the other hand, she had ten children, all under the age of eight, who would perish if it was a trap.

"Let Robert go. If he doesn't come back, I can try to find another route," Daniel said. "You know it's the only way."

Sophie agreed reluctantly. What other choice did she have? She hugged Robert and told him to take care and come back alive.

Then she waited. The children all stayed more silent than usual, not fully understanding what was happening but aware that it wasn't good.

* * *

Time passed slowly. Night came, and the snow fell again. Sophie sheltered the children as best she could, using tree branches to build a sort of canopy under one of the taller trees. It kept the worst of the snow out but did nothing about the cold. She couldn't risk lighting a fire. The hours passed slowly, and she was tempted to go and find Robert herself.

Sophie checked again prompting Daniel to whisper, "Give him time. We didn't hear any shots. That's a good thing."

Sophie was about to respond when she saw someone

coming towards them. Thankfully her state of alarm lasted only
a few seconds before she recognised Robert.

"The guide is dead. I found his body some way to the north.
I scouted around to see if I could find anyone else, but the snow
covered all the tracks."

Sophie was thrilled that Robert had returned safely but
disheartened at the news of the death of their contact.

"We have no choice. We will have to go back."

Robert shook his head. "We can't get this far and return.
That would be more dangerous. We must keep moving forward.
Daniel and I know a place we can cross. It isn't ideal, but it is
better than waiting here to be discovered."

Sophie realised he was speaking sense. She woke the
sleeping children, and together they made their way forward.
The snow was a blessing; it helped to shelter them from sight as
well as covering their tracks. Hopefully, it would also keep the
Germans away from the mountainside.

They came to a river, and Robert took charge. "The crossing
is just up ahead. We will help the little ones."

Sophie eyed the river dubiously. "It looks so deep."

"It is. But it can be done. We don't have a choice."

Sophie glanced at the river, wondering if she could even
cross it, let alone the younger children.

"We have no choice." Daniel echoed Robert's words.

Together they moved forward. The boys took turns taking
the younger children across. Then it was Sophie's turn.

"You should leave now, Nicole. We will take the children
the rest of the way," Robert said. Daniel nodded his agreement.

"No, I must come with you."

"You can't. There is nobody to help you get back across the
river, and you are needed here. We will be fine. The border is
just up ahead. Go. Please."

Sophie hesitated torn between proceeding with them or
going back to help the others.

"You might find my brother – he is six. He needs your help, as do other children. Leave us." Daniel hugged her before turning away. Then he crossed, leaving Sophie alone with Robert.

"Be safe, Nicole, and thank you. We will see you soon."

"Thank you. I couldn't have helped these children without you and Daniel."

Robert didn't reply. She saw his eyes glisten with tears. He shook her hand and left without another word. Sophie watched until the little group had disappeared. Then she turned and walked back down the mountain. The boys were right. There were more children to help. Too many more.

TWENTY-EIGHT

Sophie reached Annemasse station without incident and waited for the train to Lyon. She noticed no one paid her any attention, although there seemed to be more of a police presence than there had been the day they'd arrived. She bought a newspaper and settled into her seat to read it. But the train didn't leave. That was unusual.

She kept turning the pages of the paper, but if anyone had asked her what she was reading, she wouldn't have been able to answer. Her hands were clammy, her heartbeat racing. When the men in raincoats finally boarded the train, it was almost a relief.

They demanded papers. She took hers out in readiness and handed them over with a smile. She made the mistake of looking up into the coldest blue eyes she had ever seen. They widened with recognition. She clasped her clammy hands together, pushing her feet into the floor to stop them shaking.

"Have we met before, Mademoiselle Samson?"

"No, I don't believe so."

"I could have sworn you came to my Paris office to speak to

me about a young man arrested for terrorism back in November 1940."

Sophie nearly swallowed her tongue. This must be the man Adèle had seen about Léo. What bad luck. She had to keep her head clear.

"Me, ask an officer to help a Frenchman? No, I don't spend time with young men – other than the ones in German uniforms. The Frenchmen, they are all in Germany, aren't they?"

She forced a smile to her face, ignoring the gasps of outrage from her fellow passengers.

"We didn't meet in Paris?"

Sophie made herself look at him, her gaze not flinching once. He looked so confused she nearly felt sorry for him.

"I have never been that far north. My parents, God rest them, were very protective and didn't like me leaving our town. Then the war came, and travel is so difficult now..." She shrugged.

The man finally gave up and walked away. It was terrifying the man had such a good memory; it had been almost three years since Adèle had gone to see him after Léo was arrested. Adèle was difficult to forget, but still.

The old woman sitting beside her leaned in and whispered, "You are a disgrace, flirting with those animals. I'm glad your mother is dead. She must be turning in her grave to see the way you behave."

Sophie ignored the woman. It was safer for the other passengers to believe the story she had given the Gestapo.

TWENTY-NINE

When she arrived back in Lyon, she didn't go to the arranged safe house. For a second, she was tempted to go to her grandmother's home but dismissed the thought as soon as it entered her head. Much as she missed her family, she couldn't risk it.

Instead, she took the precaution of booking two nights in a hotel. She told the concierge she was expecting her German boyfriend to meet her. He didn't seem too concerned, but then hotel staff were often the best actors. Hopefully, he would pass the information around the staff. If the Gestapo had followed her and asked questions, her cover story would hold tight.

Up in her room, she lay down, glad to be in a real bed, but her mind wouldn't stop turning.

Had she handled the situation properly? Would that man remember anything more about their meeting? Did he know Adèle had a twin sister? The questions went round and round.

She got up and pulled her coat over her nightgown. She ran to the bathroom down the hall to check if it were empty and the water hot. She was in luck. Feeling rather more alive after her wash, she headed back to her room. But upon entering, she discovered she was not alone.

A menacing air radiated from the young man sitting on her bed. His eyes smouldered with hate, his lean face making his features more prominent. Although she guessed he was as young as Jean-Pierre would've been now, his hair was prematurely grey in contrast to the dark stubble on his chin.

"About time you showed up. I was tempted to come and join you."

The lascivious gaze accompanying his sardonic tone turned her stomach. He wasn't a soldier; his hair was too long. His shabby clothes suggested resistance, but he could be undercover. Milice or SS? Either way, she was in trouble. She opted for the haughty defence.

"Who are you? What are you doing in my room?"

"I ask the questions! It's not often people like you are so blasé about their German boyfriends. What's it like, sleeping with the enemy? Does he buy you nice clothes and pretty trinkets?"

Sophie held her arms against her chest, feeling naked despite her coat covering her nightdress. The man's gaze raked her from head to foot. She couldn't move – the pistol in his hand saw to that.

"You are mistaken." She glanced at the string tying his stained trousers. He'd lost a lot of weight. His appearance suggested he was a maquisard.

"Really? I don't believe so. Half the staff heard you tell the concierge. Perhaps you didn't know, but we don't like traitors in Lyon. They have a nasty habit of dying."

Sophie had to think quickly. This could be part of a Gestapo trap, or she might be at the mercy of a resistance cell. Either way, she was in deep trouble.

"What are you going to do with me?"

"I am tempted to have a taste of what you so freely give to the Germans, but it will have to wait. You're coming with me.

Don't think you can scream for help – this will be pointed at your stomach the whole time. A single shot is all it takes."

"I won't do anything, but I assume I can dress first?"

"Be my guest."

The man stared at her, as if expecting her to dress in front of him.

"The least you can do is turn your back."

"And risk a knife between my shoulders? No can do. You are some actress, Nicole Samson. One might almost believe those blushes are real."

Sophie hadn't undressed in front of a man since Jules. She tried her best to get dressed without giving the man anything to look at.

"Put a smile on your face. You can pretend I am your boyfriend."

She glared at him. "Over my dead body."

"That can be arranged, my dear."

Sophie walked from the room with her head held high, the man's pistol pressed close to her side.

They walked through the hotel, some of the staff giving her distasteful looks. The rumours about her had spread. Nobody tried to stop them from leaving.

"Where are we going?"

"For a short drive. The truck will be here in a minute. I shall blindfold you; don't try anything."

"I won't." Sophie was tempted to explain who she was. She was almost certain he was resistance, but still, it wouldn't be good to be careless. Besides, she sensed the man wouldn't believe her anyway. When the truck arrived, he pushed her into it and quickly blindfolded her. Then another man – a farmer, judging by the stink accompanying him – got in beside her. He tied her hands together in front.

They didn't drive for long, the bumps in the road telling her they had left the town behind, though Sophie had no idea what direction they were travelling in.

The truck stopped and she was pulled roughly from the back, her captor taking advantage of her bonds to feel her body. She kicked out at him, making him laugh.

"We go the rest of the way on foot."

The road was rough, barely more than a trail. Exposed tree roots threatened to trip her up, and the branches of nearby trees tore at her clothes; she held up her hands, trying to protect her face.

Sophie moved as quickly as she could but judging by how often the man behind her hit her, she wasn't walking fast enough. She was almost at a run when they came to an abrupt standstill. She could hear men talking, and smell smoke from their cigarettes. She listened carefully but recognised none of the voices.

"Take it off, Denis; she won't be going anywhere."

"I told her we'd kill her, Maurice."

He wasn't much of an agent, given he had revealed his boss's name. But she kept quiet as Denis pulled the blindfold roughly from her face. She winced and held up her bound hands as a light was shone directly into her face.

"Claire? What on earth are you doing here?"

THIRTY

Claire? Who's Claire? Could it be Adèle?

"My name is Nicole Samson. I do not understand why I am here. Your friend suggested I would be raped and killed as punishment for consorting with the enemy. An accusation I find offensive."

The man Denis had called Maurice stepped closer to her, taking her chin in his hand and forcing her to look him in the face. His dark brown eyes were full of suspicion, yet she didn't flinch. She didn't have the same fear of him as she felt for the man who had kidnapped her.

"Cut it out, Claire. I would recognise you anywhere. Is Nicole a new code name? You worked with Georges."

Sophie stared at the man. Adèle was in England – at least, that was the last she had heard. She couldn't compromise her sister as she knew nothing. But her desperation for news of her family won out.

"You saw a woman who looked like me?"

He looked confused and a little annoyed. "Yes ... do you have a twin? Georges knew her brother. He was shot in early '42, his name was—"

"Jean-Pierre. Our brother's name was Jean-Pierre." She threw caution to the wind. "Is my sister here?" She looked around at the camp, almost expecting Adèle to jump out.

"How can the sister of two resistance fighters be in bed with the Germans?" Denis asked. His leader just stared at Sophie.

At his question, one of the other men spat in her direction, but thankfully his aim was off.

"I am not in bed with the Germans."

"You were heard speaking to the Gestapo on the train, and then you booked into the hotel and told the concierge your boyfriend was joining you. He will get a real surprise when he finds a girl with a loaded gun in his bed instead." Denis smirked, but the expression in his eyes made Sophie take a step away from him. He looked demented. She focused on Maurice since he appeared to give the orders.

"I told the concierge that to cover my behind in case the Gestapo had followed me. The German officer on the train questioned me because – like you – he recognised me but thought I was my sister, the woman you know as Claire." His eyes widened; he was listening. She kept talking, "When Léo Favreau, my sister's beau and friend of Jean-Pierre's, was taken prisoner, she thought she might be able to rescue him. She went to Gestapo headquarters on avenue Foch and met this man. He didn't help her, but she obviously made an impression on him."

Maurice's eyes narrowed. "You expect me to believe this? Why did Claire never mention a twin? Particularly one working in the same region of France. You're not with the resistance; you don't have a gun. So why are you travelling under false papers?"

"Why does anyone have false papers? Although thanks to your boneheaded operator, my cover is now completely blown." Sophie glared at Denis, but he simply bowed back as if laughing at her.

"You're with us?" someone asked.

"Not with your group, thankfully – but yes, I am in the resistance too."

"Who can vouch for you?" Denis's tone suggested nobody would.

"You expect me to give you the names of my people? I don't think so."

Maurice smiled. "Aside from the obvious physical resemblance, you are clearly related to Claire. She is a spitfire too."

"Do you know where she is? Is she safe? What about my parents?"

Denis's gloating tone filled the forest. "Your father is at the bottom of the Seine."

Sophie gasped, bringing the sneer back to Denis's face.

"He was a traitor." Maurice glared at Denis before turning his attention back to Sophie.

"Yes, he was – but he was still my father." Sophie said a quick prayer for his soul. Whatever he'd done, he was still her blood. She forced herself to ask, "What about my mother?"

"We don't know about her. Your sister said she was safe but gave no more details."

Sophie felt faint with relief. "And Claire?"

"She is due here in a couple of days." Denis gave her a look filled with loathing. "She'd better vouch for you, or you can join your father in the afterlife."

Sophie ignored him. She couldn't believe it – she would see Adèle shortly.

Maurice turned to address Denis. "Take her away. Lock her in, but see she is treated respectfully. I mean it, you knucklehead. If her story is true and she was dodging the Gestapo, we owe her a sizeable apology."

Her kidnapper shrugged; he obviously thought her guilty.

"Can you send a message on the BBC?" She ignored the others, speaking again to Maurice.

"Sure we can." Denis took a step nearer. "How about we

ask your friends in the Gestapo to come and visit us too? Maybe they would bring some real coffee." Once again, she ignored him appealing instead to Maurice, the man who seemed to be their leader.

"Please. It is imperative I get a message to my group. All your man must do is get it to London; they will be able to pass it on."

"What is it about?"

Sophie held his gaze, willing him to believe her. "I can't tell you."

Maurice ordered the rest of his men to leave them alone, waiting until they had moved some distance away before he spoke.

"Tell me. I can't risk you transmitting something unless I know what it's about." He cut her bindings.

The blood returning to her hands was painful, but she refused to let him see. She breathed through it before saying, "I know nothing about you. How can I trust you?"

"You know I worked with your sister. I've been honest about your father. Perhaps this will convince you?" He pulled open his shirt to display some nasty-looking scars. "I got those courtesy of a spell in a camp here in France. I escaped from a cattle train."

"You are Jewish?"

"Yes, and I can prove that too if you deem it necessary."

Sophie looked away as her cheeks flushed – not at what he had said but at the obvious invitation in his eyes. "That won't be necessary. For the last year, I have been working to hide Jewish children."

Maurice's eyes widened, but he didn't speak.

"I was returning from a trip escorting children over the border to Switzerland when I met our Gestapo friend. I couldn't risk going to our safe house in Lyon, as I thought he might follow me – hence the hotel. But I must let our people know that the children went ahead."

"You let them go alone?"

She bristled at his tone. "I couldn't stop them. There were two older boys with them, both accomplished skiers and Boy Scouts. The guide who was supposed to help had been murdered. When we came to the best place to cross the border, it involved crossing a deep river. I wouldn't have been able to get back across alone, and my group needs me here."

He stared at her in silence. She wasn't sure if he believed her or not.

"What makes you so precious?"

The combination of exhaustion after her trip and the stress of almost being arrested took its toll. Stung, Sophie felt the tears in her eyes but blinked them away. She refused to let the man see she was hurt. "I am a doctor – well, almost. I worked in a Paris hospital and would have qualified if it weren't for this blasted war. As you know, there is a shortage of doctors in the resistance."

"Which hospital and who did you work with there?" He seemed interested, but she wasn't about to give out information about her previous colleagues. She didn't know him.

"Lots of people."

"You worked with Dr Murphy, didn't you?"

Shocked, she tried her best to hide her reaction. What had she said to give herself away? Her conversation with Monsieur Brenner, the first member of the resistance she'd met after fleeing Paris and heading south, came back with a vengeance. He'd tricked her by mentioning Dr Murphy.

"Don't look so shocked. You are a woman studying to be a doctor." He leaned in, his breath warm on her skin. "In this country, that alone suggests you worked at a foreign hospital. I know Dr Murphy's views on women."

Sophie didn't move a muscle. She waited for him to continue, to explain how he knew her old friend so well.

"I used to study at that hospital. Michael is an amazing doctor. I qualified five years before the war started and went to work in a small hospital near here." Suddenly, as if he realised he had said too much, he stopped talking.

"You're a doctor too? Then you believe me?"

"Yes, Nicole. But we will still need your sister to convince the others. Denis – the man who brought you here – he lost his two brothers to the Gestapo just recently. They were betrayed and burned alive at the farmhouse they were sheltering in."

Sophie shuddered at the barbarity. Losing your brother was bad enough, but to die like that... "No wonder he is out for blood."

"He doesn't always think before he acts. At the rate he is going, his mother will bury another son." He paused, then said, "I knew some of the men who died with your brother, although I never met Jean-Pierre."

Curious, she asked, "How did you end up here?"

He looked at her sadly. "I was sent south to set up this network around the time they set up the one at the museum. I was lucky – well, at least until the Germans caught me the first time." He crossed his arms, his voice tightening. "I was arrested for being Jewish, not for being with the resistance. Thankfully they didn't guess the real reason I was here. I was sent to Drancy and was on my way east. When I escaped, I came back."

"You are the boss?"

"Yes, and if you are working with who I think you are working with, you have been in my group for a long time."

"Will you send my message?"

He nodded, so she quickly gave him the coded message.

"You can share my room until your sister shows up. You will be safer there."

"I can look after myself." For some reason, she did not want him to see her as someone weak or in need of protection.

"I have no doubt, but some of my men haven't seen a woman for a while. I would prefer to keep an eye on you."

Given the look in his eye and the electricity between them, Sophie didn't want to ask who would protect her from him.

THIRTY-ONE

While they were waiting on Adèle, Sophie used the time to treat a few of the injured members of this cell. Maurice was too busy to carry on anything but the most urgent doctoring, and though they had access to a local doctor, his visits had been limited recently by the heavy German presence in the neighbouring towns.

"Why are the Germans building up such a presence?" Sophie asked as they ate one evening, having heard some of the men commenting on it.

"They are planning something, but as yet, we don't know what it is."

She knew he wouldn't tell her anything else. She'd seen the way he interacted with his men; he was careful and security-conscious. He obviously knew more than he gave away. He was protective towards her, as if they were sharing more than a room. She noticed little gestures, like sourcing hot water for her to wash in the morning. He had someone find an extra set of clothes for her. They didn't fit too well, but it was the thought that counted, and it gave her the chance to wash her own clothes.

He gave the impression to his men that she was his: little touches on the arm, a brief kiss on the lips when they were around, although he never treated her like a harlot.

At first, she went along with it; she'd taken the warning about how long the men had been without a woman to heart. But she found herself yearning for his touch, and he seemed to feel the same. The little touches became more commonplace and lasted slightly longer.

They shared his shed; he gave her as much privacy as he could despite the small space, sleeping on the floor a little distance away, while she slept on the straw bed. They talked about this and that at first, but over the few days, their conversation became more intimate. He told her a little of his life before the war, and she made him laugh with stories of her siblings and growing up in Paris. His presence gave her comfort, and she admitted to herself she liked him being close to her. He was the first man she'd been interested in since losing Jules.

* * *

A few days later, the door to Maurice's hut burst open and there, standing on the doorstep, was Adèle.

"I can't believe it! You look awful. You are so thin." She rushed to Sophie pulling her to her feet.

"Thanks. I could say the same about you."

The sisters held each other, crying with happiness. "I can't believe you are in the resistance. Mémé told me you were heading to London, but I assumed you would have changed your mind and be somewhere with your feet up, having everyone else running around." Sophie teased as she hugged her sister close.

"I do that with the boys. Some of them are quite good at cooking dinner or making coffee."

"How is maman? And mémé?"

Adèle's face fell. "I don't know. I haven't been able to contact them. They're not in Lyon any more. I've been told they left before the Germans came, but I don't know where they went."

Sophie covered her face with her hands. She couldn't bear to think about anything bad happening to her mother and grandmother.

"Don't fret. They must be hiding somewhere." Adèle's tone hardened, "You heard what happened to papa?"

Sophie sat down on the bed, and Adèle sat beside her. "Maurice said he was at the bottom of the Seine, but he didn't explain why."

"The SS rounded up a bunch of Jewish men and boys, and took them to Mont-Valérien, and shot them – in retaliation, they said, for two German soldiers being shot dead. Our side knocked out a few of their known informants, darling papa being one of them."

Shocked at Adèle's callousness, Sophie chided her sister. "Don't talk about him like that. He was our father."

"He was a traitor." Adèle didn't meet Sophie's gaze, but looked out the window.

"Yes, he was – but before the war came, he idolised us. Especially you. You know that. Think of how many times he protected us from maman's wrath."

Adèle shrugged, and Sophie let the subject drop. She didn't want them to fall out. She changed the topic.

"What of Zeldah? Is she safe? Did she get to America? Did she have a boy or a girl?"

Adèle's face brightened. "Yes, didn't maman tell you? A boy. Both are in America now."

"No, maman was too upset to speak to me when I went to see her after Jean-Pierre's death. Mémé was better, but she didn't mention the baby. Maybe she thought it would upset me. But how did you get her to America? I wanted her to go, but I wasn't sure it could be arranged. There was a lot of talk about visas being denied."

"The Quakers helped us. Zeldah got papers to say she was a nurse and disguised her pregnancy. She may have given birth as soon as she landed on American soil."

"I hope both of them are well." Sophie couldn't help but think of her brother. If it hadn't been for the war, he would be a father now. And she would get to see her nephew.

Sophie's tears were mirrored in her sister's eyes. Adèle found her voice.

"I miss him, more than I can possibly say. I know he thought I was stupid and selfish, and he was right. But I wish he could see that I have changed."

As her sister's voice cracked, Sophie hugged her.

"He can. He knows. He loved you despite everything. He loved both of us."

They talked of old times, catching up on each other's news.

"You can trust Maurice with your life, but I wouldn't give Denis the time of day." Adèle took Sophie's hand. "I know Maurice trusts him, but I think he's unstable. The loss of his brothers was horrific, and it's understandable he wants revenge. But he takes pleasure in killing people. He had been reprimanded a couple of times for making people suffer more than required."

"I don't like him. The way he looks at me makes me want to take a bath. A hot deep soak."

Adèle grinned. "It's been so long – and to think you were working near me the whole time!"

"You must be careful." Sophie told her twin about her encounter with the Gestapo agent. "He remembers you."

"Jean-Pierre tried to stop me from going, do you remember? I wouldn't listen to him. I probably got Léo killed."

"No, you didn't. They were going to shoot him all along as

an example. The only people responsible for his death are the Germans."

Adèle sighed. Sophie wasn't sure her twin believed what she had said, but it was pointless to blame herself. War meant people died – the good and the bad. Unfortunately, it appeared more of the good were dying in this one.

"Maurice told me you are involved with the Jewish children." Adèle stood up and walked to the door of the small shed. She was claustrophobic. "Come outside and walk with me. I need fresh air. I have spent the last few weeks in hiding."

Sophie followed her twin out of the building, chatting as she went. "Yes, I escorted some to Switzerland, and have been helping to hide others. It is so horrible, taking the children from their parents. The adults know they are giving their little ones a chance to live, but the children, they don't understand that. If I had a franc for every child who asked me what they had done to make their parents hate them so much they gave them away..."

Sophie glanced at the weapon her sister carried. She wondered if Adèle had killed anyone, but something stopped her from asking. She didn't want to know the answer. "Do you think they would let us work together?" Even as she asked, she knew the answer. Twins would be too conspicuous and attract too much attention.

"I am leaving the area," Adèle whispered, even though the men around them were engaged in other tasks. "I have to go back to Paris for a while."

Sophie stopped walking and grabbed Adèle's arm. She pulled her around to face her. "You can't. People know you."

"They know Adèle, the spoiled brat daughter of the traitor. They don't know me. I will be fine. Where are you going next?"

Sophie knew it was pointless trying to talk Adèle out of anything. If she was intent on going to Paris, she would go, whether Sophie argued against it or not. She didn't want to spend their precious time together fighting.

"I am not sure. There were volunteers working in the camp at Rivesaltes before it closed. I have some contacts working with the Jewish orphanages, trying to keep the children safe. I enjoyed my time with Mary Elmes, and I'd like to spend more time working with that network. But this sounds selfish – I am thinking of myself – the skills I learn working with children will help me when I qualify."

"Sophie, there isn't a selfish bone in your body. You were always the saintly twin, remember!"

"And you are living up to your reputation as the daredevil. I used to wish I was more like you."

THIRTY-TWO

Adèle couldn't believe her ears. "Really?"

"Yes. Why is that so hard for you to understand? I know papa and maman found it difficult, but I always loved how brave you were. You let no one tell you what to do. Jean-Pierre and I admired you for that."

"Jean-Pierre admired me?" She couldn't believe that. She knew Jean-Pierre had been annoyed and upset with her. He had blamed her for Léo's death – or at least that was what she believed. Could Sophie be telling the truth?

"Yes, he did. He thought you were very brave."

Adèle blinked away tears. "I thought he saw me as a selfish, self-centred brat."

"Well, he may have thought that on occasion." Sophie poked Adèle in the arm. "He was very proud of his sister. He said you would surprise us all!"

"You are the one who became a doctor."

"Well, not yet I haven't. I never got to qualify."

"Still, I didn't have any career. I was happy to play around waiting to meet the next man who could keep me in the style to which I was accustomed."

Sophie stared around the forest at their current living arrangements. "Wouldn't be hard to do that now, would it?" She giggled.

Adèle laughed too, then asked her sister gently if she was still in touch with Yvette, Jules's sister.

"She's dead." Sophie crossed herself. "The Gestapo took her. I was almost caught too, but a farmer was watching the road. That's part of the reason I ended up down here."

"Poor Yvette. I know we didn't like each other, but I wouldn't wish the Gestapo on my worst enemy." Adèle hugged her sister. "I am sorry about Jules too; I liked him."

Sophie gave a wry smile. "No, you didn't."

"Well, I tried to."

"What about you? Anyone special?"

Adèle breathed slowly, trying to stop her heart from racing. She didn't want Sophie to guess her feelings. She hadn't told anyone about Georges. "In my line of work, not likely."

But Sophie wasn't fooled. She hugged Adèle and jumped up and down. "There is someone! You've fallen in love. Who is he?"

"Nobody you know."

"I do know him, don't I? That's why you won't look at me. Who?"

Adèle didn't answer. Sophie nudged her and said, "Go on, tell me. Give me some good news."

"Do you remember Georges Monier?"

"Georges – he was a communist, wasn't he? He and his mother lived near mémé for a while until they moved to a farm or something. No! You can't have fallen in love with him, have you? He hated us. Both of us."

"He never hated you, just our money and our father. He hated me for what I was. He was right."

"Now you have met again, and he knows the real you. Is he in love with you too?"

"I don't know. I didn't have time to ask him. The cell was blown, and he insisted I leave. He went back for his mother. She was a sweet lady."

Sophie's face said everything. "Georges's mother was a battle-axe. Sweet? You have changed."

"She looked after me, and she is so brave. She is as much a part of all this as we are." Adèle couldn't stop her voice from shaking. "I don't know if she is still alive, or him. I can't go back, and I can't ask."

Sophie hugged her. "I wish this war was over. I can't stand it – losing everyone we care about. Why won't the Germans just give up?"

"Maybe one of these days. I guess we have to do our best to help them on their way."

They walked in silence before Sophie voiced one of Adèle's worst fears.

"Do you ever wonder about what would happen if you got caught? I mean, as a resistant? The rumours of what goes on in the prisons are horrible. Maurice showed me his scars."

"Can't think about things like that. Anyway, if they get me, I won't let them take me alive." She hoped her words sounded more confident than she felt. She'd seen too many agents rounded up and heard the stories of the torture they endured.

Sophie's face turned ashen, her eyes filling with tears. "Don't say that. I can't bear to lose you too."

Adèle swallowed hard to regain composure, she couldn't start crying. Not here, not now. "Do you have one of these?"

Sophie stepped back as she recognised the pill. "No, and neither should you. Only God has the power to decide when you die."

Adèle fingered the capsule. "I believed that too when I was first given it. But it's not for my sake. I don't want the Gestapo to take me alive. I'm afraid I would betray people under torture. You know how squeamish I am."

She couldn't bear to look at Sophie as she admitted her weakness. The men thought she was so brave, but in truth, she was terrified of what would happen if she were captured.

"Nobody can withstand torture – we all know that. Just make up a story to give them. Use people who are already dead or those who are safe back in Britain. That will delay them long enough for your people to get away. You're braver than you think." Sophie's tone was reassuring, but Adèle wasn't convinced she could hold out for any length of time. She would never have admitted that to anyone else, but this was Sophie.

"I don't know if I could make them believe me. It would be easier this way."

Sophie gave her a stern look. "Promise me you will never take it – at least not unless you are certain all is lost. Where there is life, there is hope. I want us both to go to America to see our nephew. When the war is over."

Adèle nodded. She would like that too, but somehow she couldn't imagine a world after the war. It was time to change the subject.

"Do you have a gun? Want to go do some target practice? We are safe enough out here, although we don't have much ammunition to waste."

"I don't have one. I refuse to carry one."

Adèle's stomach churned. How could her twin still be so naïve? "That's stupid. What if you get caught? If you had one, Denis might not have taken you."

"If I had one, I would be dead. If he hadn't killed me, the Germans would have. And I am glad he took me – it means I got to see you. I love you. Much more than you will ever know."

Choked up, Adèle pulled her twin to her and held her close. "I love you too. I wish I could stay with you, but I have to go now."

"Already? But I thought you were staying for a while. A minute ago, you were offering to take me shooting."

"That was before my contact showed up. He has just got here."

Sophie looked towards the new arrival at the entrance to the camp. He was only a boy of about thirteen, his light pasty skin suggesting he was used to living in a city rather than in the outdoors. His blue eyes and mass of curly hair could make him look younger than he was, but she doubted he was an adult.

"That boy? He's your contact? He looks barely thirteen."

"Yes, they get younger by the day. Laurence is fifteen. It's safer as the older lads get picked up by the Germans and sent to Germany for labour or used as hostages. They tend to leave the children alone – at least for the moment. I must go – him being here spells trouble. You take care. I love you."

Adèle walked away without looking back. She couldn't let her sister know how worried she was. Laurence knew never to come to this place unless it was a real emergency.

Heading towards Laurence, she passed Denis on her way out of camp. He was sitting outside one of the tents, cleaning his weapon. "You touch a hair on my sister's head again, and pieces of your anatomy will decorate my ears."

His sudden pallor meant her threat, combined with her reputation, had hit home. He had heard of the White Witch, even if Sophie hadn't seemed to have heard her sister's nickname or her track record. Thankfully her twin appeared to have no idea of just how far Adèle had gone to the other side.

THIRTY-THREE

Laurence never smiled; he was far too serious for his age, but he wasn't easily spooked. So his pale complexion combined with his clenched teeth suggested the news was bad. They walked away from the camp to a sheltered area under some trees. She sat and indicated he take a seat beside her. They looked out on the valley below; it all looked so peaceful. So deceiving. "Tell me."

"The new agents, the ones London dropped two days ago..."

"Yes?" She wanted to shake the news out of him, he was speaking so slowly.

"The Germans have them."

"What? How? When?"

"Luc isn't sure. The landing seemed to go well; the Germans didn't turn up until the agents were in the safe house."

The hairs rose on the back of her neck. That was worse than she'd thought. If they'd been at the landing zone, they could have reasoned it was the sound of the planes that alerted them, but to wait until the next day to pick up new agents at the safe house suggested a traitor in the group with intimate knowledge of their procedures.

Laurence watched her face closely, and when she didn't speak, he prompted, "There must be a traitor in London. It's happened too many times to be the Germans getting lucky." The boy must have heard the men discussing what had gone wrong; he wouldn't have jumped to that conclusion alone. For one thing, he didn't know about the other times – unless security had really broken down.

Adèle agreed, but now wasn't the time to worry about that. They had to secure the remaining cells.

"Laurence, you get to the boys and tell them what's happened. They must disperse. Head for Spain. You should go with them."

"I am not running away."

"I need you alive. You are no help dead." Adèle's desire to keep him alive caused her to snap.

"What are you going to do?"

"I have to go back to Lyon."

His eyes widened as he brushed his hand over them. "That's suicide, Claire."

"I'll be careful. Just do as I ask. Go."

* * *

Taking her time to process the information, Adèle walked slowly back to the camp, searching for Maurice. She quickly explained what had happened. He would have to take his own precautions.

"Get my sister to safety. Sophie is too innocent to be caught up in this mess."

"She has her own agenda. She is not that different from you – she won't be told anything either."

Adèle grinned. Sophie shared her stubborn streak.

"Fair point. Can you make up something about her being

needed in Perpignan? She lived there before and will be less conspicuous down there."

Maurice nodded before hugging Adèle. "Take care."

"I will. You too. And look after my sister."

She left and didn't look back.

THIRTY-FOUR

Thankful she had been able to see Adèle but wishing she could have stayed, Sophie helped to prepare some food. The men had caught some rabbits and a few squirrels. All had been cleaned and were currently roasting over small fires. Sophie placed potatoes in the embers of the fire. Baked potatoes kept for a few days. She mixed up a batch of green leaves, not looking too closely at what they would be eating. Nobody could afford to be fussy.

Maurice called to her, asking her to come for a walk. The men whistled as Sophie blushed. They walked in silence for a bit until he said, "You need to rest up tonight. Tomorrow we are heading out."

"Where?"

"I am sending you to Perpignan. They need your help there."

"You mean my sister told you to send me somewhere safe."

Maurice coloured. "I pity your father. His life with the two of you must have been a nightmare. You are both so stubborn."

"We are not children. I have a job to do, and I intend to do it."

He turned to her, his eyes flashing. "You don't have a gun. What will you do if you walk into a trap? Barbie has people everywhere."

Sophie shuddered at the mention of Klaus Barbie, already nicknamed the Butcher of Lyon. He took cruelty to a whole new level. He especially hated the Jews, even the children.

"I will talk my way out, if possible. What about your group? Are you safe, considering the news?" Her heart beat faster as she took a step closer to him.

He pushed her hair back from her face, his eyes fixed on hers. "For now. As safe as we can be."

Still looking at her, he lowered his lips to hers. She reached up to put her arms around his neck, pulling him to her. The passion exploded between them; it was like nothing she'd ever experienced.

He was the first to pull back. "I don't want to stop, but..." He shrugged, looking around him. She wanted him just as much, but he was right. Now was not the time.

"Be careful. I couldn't bear it if anything happened to you."

"Please go to Perpignan."

She ran her fingers over his lips. "Don't ask me to do that. We both have a war to fight."

He pulled her close, resting his head on hers. She didn't know how long they stood like that, both staring into the distance, not wanting this moment to end.

THIRTY-FIVE

Sophie met with Father Tobias as soon as she got back to Lyon. The priest was delighted to see her, although he worried when she told him about her experiences with the Gestapo and her spell with the maquis. She was careful not to reveal names, and she didn't mention having seen Adèle.

He suggested she stay hidden for a while, but Sophie could see that he needed her help. The sheer number of people coming to see him requesting assistance made her nervous. What if an undercover agent were to unmask the kindly priest? She suggested numerous times he take more care, but he kept telling her God would look after him.

"I can't turn my back on anyone looking for help. It is not my nature." The priest reprimanded her one day when she brought up security once more.

She was saved from arguing when the priest's housekeeper told him someone wanted him in the confessional. Sophie waited for Father Tobias to finish.

He returned fairly quickly, his face as pale as his collar. An elderly man dressed in black accompanied him.

Afraid the priest would faint, she took his arm and led him

to a chair. "What's wrong?"

"Thank God you didn't leave." Father Tobias coughed to clear his throat, his eyes filling up with tears as fast as they rolled down his cheeks. "It's the worst news. Robert and Daniel have been captured; they returned from Switzerland to try to help other children. Now they are in the hands of the SS."

Sophie's throat thickened with emotion, but she had to stay strong. "How did the SS catch them?"

"The Germans set up a trap in Nice. They put one of their own French-speaking staff on the phones at the OSE office. If someone telephoned, they said they couldn't speak on the phone but to come in person. Daniel and Robert went to the office to find names of children who needed rescuing. They were arrested along with thirteen other boys."

Sophie paced, trying to clear her head. She didn't want to think about the boys in the hands of those sadists. "We have to rescue them, but how?"

The elderly man nodded as he addressed his comments to Father Tobias. "We should be able to rescue the French ones. The Germans have said they aren't going to transport French citizens."

Sophie bit her tongue; how often had that promise turned out to be a lie?

"One of our pastors has requested an appointment with Hauptsturmführer Brunner; he's the man in charge in Nice."

Sophie paced. "We wait?"

"No, we pray." Father Tobias knelt and started to pray. Sophie and the other man exchanged a glance before joining the priest.

* * *

A week later, Arthur, a young Scout leader about the same age as Daniel but without his natural charm, arrived at Sophie's safe house to tell her Father Tobias wanted to see her.

"Did they get the boys out?" Sophie couldn't help the excitement building in her chest.

Arthur shrugged. "I'm just the runner."

Sophie ignored his surly expression. She locked the door behind her and together they walked past the Parc des Hauteurs, heading for the old tram station. From there they would meet Father Tobias for a walk through the Loyasse Cemetery. Meeting so often in his church was causing unnecessary talk.

Father Tobias looked greyer than usual. Sophie didn't need him to tell her it was bad news; she read that in the new lines on his face, the desperation in his eyes.

"We had no luck with Brunner. He gave up all pretence that the Germans were only interested in foreign Jews. Nobody is safe. The boys are going to be shipped to Drancy for onward transport."

Arthur scuffed his boot against an old stone. "We tried to tell you that, but you wouldn't listen."

Sophie turned on the adolescent. "Mind your manners."

The boy scowled but didn't respond. Father Tobias walked on, his black cassock trailing on the dusty ground, his hands clasped behind his back as he walked.

Sophie couldn't let Robert and Daniel die without trying to help them. Sophie decided to use the papers for Nicole Samson once more. She figured the chances of meeting the Gestapo agent again were minute, and the papers were good forgeries.

"I am going to Marseille; that's where the train from Nice will stop before it goes on to Paris. If I have to go to Drancy itself, I'm going. There must be something I can do."

"But what?" Arthur asked. Despite his tone, his eyes had widened with hope. Had she misread his surliness for despair?

"I don't know, but I sure as heck am going to try. I owe those boys my life."

* * *

The train trip – although lengthy due to several stops – passed without incident until she got to Marseille. She left the train but, after an hour spent in a nearby café, returned to buy another ticket, this time to Paris.

She made her way over to a friendly-looking guard on the station platform. She turned on what she called the Adèle charm, making the man feel like he was Gilbert Gil, the actor.

"The train is delayed due to troop movements, you understand?" The man winked at her but whether it was his idea of flirting or a reference to members of the resistance blowing up the tracks, she didn't know. She pretended it was the former, laying her hand on his arm as if deeply attracted to him.

"Do you think it will take long? I really need to get to Paris. To see my sister."

He took her hand and kissed it. "I will go and check for you."

After some time waiting on the platform, she was called to the stationmaster's office. "Telegram for Nicole Samson."

Sophie took the piece of paper and walked back outside, but the friendly guard moved to her side, reading the telegram over her shoulder. *'The babies are on your train.'*

What did it mean? She stood staring at the piece of paper and then looked at the train. Then she spotted the prison car attached to the end of the train. The man was waiting – for an explanation or an invitation, she wasn't sure.

"My sister, in Paris, she is having her baby; she isn't due for another two weeks."

The man glanced at the telegram.

"Maman always makes mistakes on telegrams. She suffers from hysteria." Sophie illustrated her point by twirling her finger at her temple.

The man smiled. "Aren't all mothers like that? Good luck

with the baby. I hope it is a boy. For France. You'd best get on the train; your sister will need you."

Sophie smiled and pocketed the telegram, thanking him for his help before walking away and boarding the train.

There were more passengers in the carriages this time, which made Sophie feel less conspicuous. If only she had a way to tell the boys that she was on the train too. She took a walk through the carriages towards the back. The prison car was a carriage just like the others but with grilles on the windows and locks on the door.

There were armed guards who appeared whenever the train stopped at a station, but otherwise, the prisoners seemed to be allowed relative freedom to move from the prison car to the bathrooms shared with the other train travellers. Sophie put her bag down and sat on top of it, positioning herself close to the window as if she needed air. Given the crowding on the train, she didn't feel too conspicuous.

Her patience paid off as she spotted Robert going to the bathroom. He glanced around himself, his eyes widening as he recognised her, but he looked away so as not to bring the guards' attention to her.

She rushed to pass him, sliding him a nail file from her bag as she did so. Then she walked back the way she had come, asking another passenger if they knew where the other toilets were located as the ones at this end of the train were disgusting.

She made her way through the carriages and smiled as a man stood up to offer her his seat. Would Robert be able to get off? Could she cause a diversion, or would that be too obvious? As she pondered the problem, the train slowed down. She waited, her mouth dry, for the sound of shots, but it seemed to be some issue with the line rather than a prisoner escape.

As the train moved farther north, she regretfully realised that she couldn't afford to be seen in Paris – Adèle had said she was heading there. The last thing she wanted was to compromise her sister's safety. Given their respective backgrounds, there was too much risk she would bump into someone she knew. She would have to get off at the next stop.

As she went to leave the train, the chatty guard stopped her. "Mademoiselle Samson, this ticket is for Paris." His previous friendly chatter was replaced by a suspicious tone.

"Yes, I know, but I have become quite ill on the train. I can't continue with those public bathrooms. I need a real bed and a bucket." Sophie turned away from him, holding her hand over her mouth. She quickly put her finger down her throat and, gagging, turned back in time to vomit all over his shoes as he jumped backwards. Satisfied at the disgusted expression on his face, she opened the door and stepped off the train.

Thankfully there was only a bored soldier on duty at the exit; when he questioned her about her ticket, she gave him the same excuse as she had the train guard. She didn't have to pretend to be ill – she could smell the vomit from her clothes. The soldier nearly pushed her through the barrier in his haste to put distance between them.

She had enough money to secure one night in a hotel, but first, she had to find out where she was, as she didn't recognise the area from the name of the station. She stood at the gate, holding her stomach, but in reality, she was watching the train leave – with the prison car still attached. She couldn't stop a tear from rolling down her face, and she prayed Daniel, Robert, and the other boys would escape.

* * *

She decided not to find a hotel and took a train back to Lyon after a couple of hours. She made her way back to a safe house, feeling lucky. The previous occupants had taken care to change the bed and leave some basic provisions in the kitchen. Taking a quick cold bath – she didn't know how to heat the water – she crawled between the clean sheets and slept for two days straight.

It took a week before she felt it was worth the risk of travelling to Saint-Just to see Father Tobias. He was delighted to see her.

"You did it!"

"What?"

"Robert and Daniel escaped. They jumped off just before Arles, where they made their way to a safe house. They are now in hiding – thanks to you. Robert told me all about it."

Sophie listened as the priest explained how the boys had used her nail file to pry loose the window of the bathroom. They had tried to persuade the other boys to escape with them, but they'd refused, telling Robert and Daniel they were bound to be shot while escaping – that it was all a mistake and they would be released once the authorities knew they were French.

"Thank God our boys knew to try to escape. How brave they are!"

"They were lucky." Father Tobias fingered the crucifix he wore around his neck.

"What of the others?"

Father Tobias's delighted expression fell. "They were placed on the first transport out of Drancy. Destination Poland."

Sophie put her hand on the priest's arm. "Don't lose hope. They are young and strong. They may come back at the end of the war." If this blasted war ever ended.

"Where you off to next? Are you going back to the forest to the maquisards? I wish we could do more for our brave men; they are all so thin and look like they need a good rest. I feel rather helpless." The priest crossed himself.

"You are doing the best you can; we all are. We will rest when we can."

Or when we are dead.

THIRTY-SIX

All pretence that the Germans were only interested in foreign Jews had gone. The Nazis were clearly working from the census lists drawn up in the early years of the war. More people were caught in the occupiers' sweeps. Sophie couldn't help but think of Monsieur Litwak from her old apartment. How many more Jews would be deported because they had obeyed the laws and registered?

The demands on Father Tobias and the rest of their group increased, leading Sophie to become even more concerned about the security of their network. She went to see the priest, intent on telling him he had to take a step back. He was old, in need of rest, and putting everyone at risk, not just himself.

* * *

As she suspected, the priest refused to scale back his activities, but assured her he was being more careful. He asked Sophie to sit and have a coffee with him. To her surprise, he had real coffee and not boiled chicory. The scent was heavenly.

The priest poured the coffee. "A gift from a friend. He is an administrator in the current regime and very devout."

"I find that hard to believe." Sophie blew the steam off her drink to cool it down quickly. Her taste buds were impatient to enjoy the delicacy.

"Nicole, we all know there are good and bad on both sides of this war. Some of the Germans I have been dealing with are no fans of Herr Hitler. But they have families back home in Germany and are worried about them. They must obey orders."

"Not all the orders, surely?"

"Well, I guess they try to avoid the worst of them. But we cannot sit in judgement. Not until we have worn their shoes. But you didn't come here to discuss the morals of the occupying forces. I have been trying to be more careful, especially after the last few days."

Sophie sat straighter. "What happened?"

"I was warned already about the phone being tapped. But it was a visit the other night that put me on high alert."

"Who came to see you?"

"They call her Alice la Blonde."

Sophie gulped her coffee, burning her throat before whispering, "The Gestapo agent?"

"Yes. She had two Jewish-looking children with her. She called at night, telling me she had heard I was sheltering Jews. I could hardly bear to say no, not to those poor little mites, but I knew I had to." The priest stirred his coffee, a look of profound sadness on his face. "I can still see the fear in their eyes."

Sophie's mind returned to the children at the Rivesaltes camp. She could just imagine what the poor priest felt. She pushed down her own feelings and tried to reassure him. "You couldn't have taken them."

He continued as if he hadn't heard her. "I wanted to send her packing with a flea in her ear. Instead, I stayed the picture of calm. I told her she was misinformed. I said that, while I would love to help, I could not in all conscience disobey the law."

"Did she believe you?"

"Who knows? I wasn't destined to be an actor. I am but a simple priest."

Sophie thought he might have underestimated his abilities. The fact he was still here in his office said a lot.

"You must continue to act on your instinct. It might not do any harm if you talk as if you support the regime, at least a little. In mass and at other times. That way, suspicion may fall elsewhere." Sophie waited for her words to register before she added, "You cannot come to the camps any more to say mass. You could be followed."

"I think you are right." He looked so devastated. She wanted to give him a hug. Instead, she sat in silence.

"I have already made a start." He gestured to the signed photograph of Pétain on his desk.

"I know it is difficult, but what else can we do? We cannot give up on the children."

"I know, my dear Nicole. I wonder where it will all end."

She didn't answer that; she could only hope it would be soon and all those she loved would survive. Father Tobias, Adèle, and now Maurice. Her cheeks flamed as she thought of him. She turned her attention back to the priest.

They discussed some other issues, and the priest gave Sophie a sizeable amount of money. "It is probably a sin to buy things on the black market, but I think God will forgive us. Mother Superior and Father Baptiste are finding it a strain to feed their visitors. Perhaps your contacts could help them?"

"They can; thank you."

Sophie walked away from his residence with her head bent low. She loved the priest – most everyone who met him held him in high regard. But there were so many others in his position, and higher, who were alarmingly silent on the Nazis and their mistreatment of the Jews. She couldn't help wondering where God was in all of this. The Pope and the rest of the Catholic Church didn't seem to want to get involved with saving the children. How many Germans were Catholic? Would they listen if the Pope called on them to rise against Hitler? Not that he would do that. One priest had tried to explain to Sophie that the Pope was helping in secret, but in public, he had a duty to protect his people. Sophie wasn't convinced. One had a duty to protect every human being, not just those who followed a particular faith.

THIRTY-SEVEN

Adèle shivered, her sweat clinging to her skin, despite the light shower of rain falling on them as they waited in the forest. Her heart raced as she slipped on the moss-covered old stones, wondering for a split second what the ancient ruins they were hiding among had once looked like in all their splendour. She concentrated on the sounds coming from the road below. There were lorries, petrol ones, which meant the enemy.

She bit her lip as she waited with her men to see if the unit of soldiers would drive on past. Were they lost, or had someone betrayed her men? She glanced up, catching Tomas's pale face. He whispered to the man beside him, who nodded before taking off at a faster pace than she'd seen on their training courses.

Tomas crouched down and made his way to her side, tripping in some animal scat, judging by the smell of him. "He's our fastest; I sent him for help. Moise will come if he can."

"He's too far away. Luc and Romain are nearer, but even they aren't going to be able to help us."

Tomas didn't argue but instead asked, "Permission to go ahead? I want to see what we're up against."

"That's suicide."

"So is staying here." Still, he didn't disobey her. He picked up his rifle and fell back in with the others. The lorries stopped, and all her men seemed to hold their collective breath. The guttural sounds of German intermixed with French accents floated up through the trees. Her group were surrounded by a combination of Milice and Germans. Adèle couldn't believe their bad luck. They had obviously been betrayed, but by whom?

She stared at the boys she had by her side, all brave and desperate to avenge France, but sadly lacking experience. Should she surrender? Would they spare her men?

"We cannot sit here and roll over for them." Paul, a new addition to her group, glared at her. The youth had led his own smaller maquis group and had issues taking orders, especially from her. "We must attack."

"You wait for my order."

"You're a typical woman – all talk," Paul said. "Now is our chance. I want to avenge my brother, his wife, and their children. I say we go now."

"Shut up." Adèle checked her tone. "I understand the need for revenge, but how will I look your mother in the eye if she loses you as well? Patience is a strength."

"Surrender isn't an option. They will slaughter us all." He spat at the ground.

He was right. The Milice would take pleasure in killing their French brothers if they surrendered. If it had only been Germans, they might have had a chance.

Adèle split the group into three. She would command the first, Tomas the second and Paul the rear. By splitting up her men, she hoped to convince the enemy they were a larger force. Then maybe they would back down and retreat, allowing her men to escape.

Paul countermanded her order. "We must stick together."

"You have my orders. It's our only chance of getting men away. We've walked into a trap." Even as she said the words, she saw he wasn't paying attention. She snapped her fingers in his face.

"Paul, do as I say."

Gesturing to her men to follow her, she climbed up the slight hill. At least they would have the advantage of height.

She hadn't banked on the sight that greeted her. The enemy were fighting dirty. They had gathered a group of women and children, probably from one of the local villages, and were forcing them to march up the hill. With the hostages protecting them, they were gaining ground. Adèle and her men couldn't fire for fear of hitting the innocent people. She let loose a stream of unladylike language as she sent Laurence back to the second and third groups with orders to abort their mission.

But it was too late. Instead of waiting, Paul had his group come into battle right behind her, cutting off their avenue of escape. Tomas, no doubt seeing what had happened, tried to engage the enemy on his side, perhaps hoping a show of force would make the enemy retreat. They were overwhelmed, but worse, her men had no avenue of escape. Adèle couldn't tell them to stand down. Her men fought valiantly, doing their best to avoid the civilians, but the enemy didn't care who they shot. It was soon clear the maquis were losing, but nobody surrendered. They fought on. It was every man for himself as they engaged the enemy one-on-one.

A bullet entered her shoulder, and she collapsed at a soldier's feet, praying he would think her dead. He didn't give her a second look. In the ensuing chaos, ignoring the pain and loss of blood, she wriggled and crawled her way a couple of inches nearer to a pile of bodies of the hostages, hoping the enemy wouldn't check to see if everyone was dead.

Her men fought hard, but they were outnumbered. She saw

their young faces hit the dirt, each one adding to her pain. Had it been worth it?

* * *

Adèle woke some time later, lying on the ground, her thirst raging. The battle was over. She heard someone ask in German if the hostages were all dead. A man came forward and bayoneted a couple of the bodies, then said, "They are now." Through half closed eyes, she saw him smirk.

Adèle didn't even breathe. Night came, and the Germans withdrew. Adèle didn't dare move. She had to be sure they were gone. She drifted in and out of consciousness. She could hear Jean-Pierre talking in her head. '*Adèle, wake up. It's not your time. You still have so much to do. Sophie needs you.*' But it couldn't be her brother; he was dead. It just sounded like him. She leaned back, letting the blackness take over, but again she could hear his voice. '*Fight. Don't give up. Not now.*'

She tried to move, but her body wouldn't listen. "I can't. Too tired. Everyone's dead. I..."

A hand passed over her mouth. She tried to move her face; she couldn't breathe. "She's breathing. She's alive. Quick."

That was Luc's voice. What was he doing here? She tried to open her eyes, but it felt like her eyelids were stuck together. He needed to run. The Germans ... they could come back. She kicked out.

"Claire, lie still. You've lost a lot of blood. We are taking you to the hospital."

Adèle knew that wasn't a good idea. She might say anything under the influence of drugs. She didn't want to bring any more death or destruction to innocent people. Any doctor or nurse who helped her could, if discovered, face execution. She tried to protest, but she was too tired. Her brain wouldn't obey basic commands.

"Relax. I have you." Luc's voice penetrated her brain. She knew he wouldn't put others at risk. She closed her eyes, glad to be able to finally sleep.

* * *

She squinted at the brightness, the light overhead hurting her eyes. She was lying on clean, starched sheets, a feather-filled pillow under her head. Where was she? She tried to speak. Her scratchy throat, furry tongue and the horrible taste in her mouth made her want to retch. She opened her mouth to lick her chapped lips. *So thirsty. Water.* She moved and bit down on her lip in agony. She wanted to swear at the pain in her chest.

A cold hand touched her forehead as a woman spoke soothingly to her, telling her to lie still. She opened her eyes again, this time looking at a white-coated doctor.

"Welcome back to earth." He smiled. "It will hurt for a while, but you are lucky. The pleurisy is gone. You won't be fighting for a while, though, or climbing any mountains."

"Where am I?" Her voice sounded croaky.

"In England."

Adèle stared at the man, wondering if it was a trick despite his public schoolboy English accent. But she'd have known if she'd been flown out of France. He picked up two newspapers and held them out to her so she could see the dates and titles. *The Times* and the *Daily Standard*.

She stayed silent, twisting her head to look around the room. There were no other beds; was it a private ward? King George VI looked down at her. No pictures of Pétain or, worse, Hitler. Pain thundering through her head made her thinking foggy.

"I'm Dr Warwicker, and you're a patient of Guy's Hospital London, although we've relocated to Kent for the duration."

She closed her eyes. She was too tired to argue with him.

"Don't go to sleep just yet. There's a woman here to see you. She's been rather impatient to speak to you."

The door closed behind him. Adèle fingered the newspapers. Was it a ruse?

The door opened again to admit Miss Atkins, her usual stern countenance sporting a concerned look. Adèle burst into tears of relief, her arm shaking as she reached out to touch her guest, who clasped her hand before pulling up a chair closer to the bed.

"At last! You had us all worried. For a time, we thought you weren't going to pull through."

"I am in England?" But where else would Miss Atkins be?

"Yes. Don't you remember getting here?" Miss Atkins didn't mask the concern in her eyes. "We had a devil of a job bringing you out. The Germans really want to speak to you."

Adèle shrugged, having forgotten for a moment about her shoulder and chest. As she closed her eyes at the pain, her memories overpowered her. The massacre. She couldn't look at her friend, not wanting to see condemnation in her eyes.

"The women, children – they died because of us."

"Stop that. You did nothing wrong."

"They used them as human shields. I should have surrendered; maybe that would have saved them?" Adèle plucked at the bedsheets with her fingers, seeing the bodies of the innocents scattered over the forest floor.

Miss Atkins took her hand to stop her moving. "If you had surrendered, you and your men would have been tortured, and goodness knows how many brave people would have landed in enemy hands." Miss Atkins used her other hand to push the hair from Adèle's face. "Look at me," she commanded. Adèle opened her eyes and held Miss Atkins's gaze.

"They died because of the Germans and those traitors in the Milice. You have been cleared of all responsibility. You were in an impossible situation, and did the only thing you could do. It was a victory – a costly one, but a victory all the same."

"We won?"

"Not that battle, but the men you helped train went after those murderers. I don't think any Milice member lived to tell their families of their work for the Boches. Your bravery, leading from the front, doing your best to protect your men ... it sent a message, too. The resistance groups in that area have joined forces, forgotten about their petty squabbles between communists and non, and are armed and ready to fight as a group. That is down to you. Buckmaster is thrilled."

Given his reputation, Adèle didn't think the head of Special Operations Executive, known as SOE, would ever be happy, but she wasn't about to say so.

A tear escaped and rolled down her cheek. Miss Atkins wiped it away with a hanky.

"Look at me, crying like a baby."

"Like a human being. Stop trying to be brave and concentrate on getting better. That's an order."

Adèle tried to smile but failed. "It was horrible. There were wounded people around me and the Milice, they just came over and bayoneted them. I only survived because Jean-Pierre saved me."

"Jean-Pierre?"

"My brother. I know it sounds stupid, but I talked to him. He said it wasn't my time to die."

Miss Atkins patted her hand as the doctor returned. Adèle's eyes closed as she surrendered to the weakness taking over her body. The last thing she heard were Miss Atkins's words to Dr Warwicker.

"I think you'd better give her something. She's talking but not making sense."

THIRTY-EIGHT

Adèle recovered slowly. Miss Atkins came to visit often, bringing small treats and whatever information she was allowed to pass on.

"We got a message from Luc. He said Laurence is fine, Romain is fighting hard, and Caesar has a sore head."

Adèle giggled at the message as Miss Atkins waited for her to explain.

"Luc is the man who met me after my first jump. Laurence is a child – no, actually, he isn't. Not any more. He's a young man of fifteen. Romain is one of the men who fought by my side."

"And Caesar?"

Adèle hoped her cheeks didn't look as flushed as they felt. "He's the area leader. Bit of an old grump."

"Hmmm." Miss Atkins raised an eyebrow.

Adèle ignored Miss Atkins's response. She didn't want to talk about Georges and how much she missed him. He was still alive. Was he missing her? She needed to get back.

"I'm glad your friends are still alive and fighting hard. Now do what you're told, and I will be back in a month."

Adèle said goodbye, not promising anything.

Dr Warwicker insisted on bed rest. She pretended to agree but every time she was alone, she got up and walked. At first, she could barely put her weight on her feet before falling back on the bed. But over the next few days, she pushed herself. She'd been in peak physical condition prior to being injured; all that cycling had paid off.

She paced the room to build up her walking speed, and used the wall to practise the get-fit exercises they'd completed in training, sit-ups being impossible with her shoulder bandaged up. She ignored the pain; it was a small price to pay for getting home.

* * *

One day, the door opened as she was practising, having first removed her bandages, to admit Dr Warwicker and the matron, who now looked like she'd taken a bite of a lemon.

"I knew it. You couldn't stay in bed, could you?"

Adèle sat back up on the bed and tried to look contrite. "You've no idea how boring it is. I'm not used to sitting around all day doing nothing." That hadn't been her life for a long time. Not since everything changed after Jean-Pierre... She pushed that thought from her mind and focused on the doctor. "I'm recovering, aren't I?"

He examined her, first listening to her lungs while instructing her to take deep breathes. Then he took his time inspecting the shoulder wound. She clenched her teeth rather than scream at the pain his probing caused. Eventually, he seemed satisfied. "Yes, remarkably, actually."

Adèle's smile of triumph didn't do anything for the matron's demeanour.

* * *

Miss Atkins's face was a picture when Adèle insisted on walking her friend out of the hospital and into the grounds outside. She took a moment to appreciate the beauty of her surroundings, the rolling green fields, the rain clouds dominating the sky. The air smelled of trees and flowers rather than bleach. She led Miss Atkins to a small bench.

"It's time. I want to go home."

"Buckmaster and I were just discussing that. A friend has a nice house near the sea in Scotland. It will be the perfect place for you to recover."

She would have laughed, but she thought it might hurt Miss Atkins. Sitting by the sea when her country was under the boot of the enemy? Not a chance. Wait a minute, didn't they send agents who didn't pass the training courses to Scotland. She wasn't going to the 'cooler'.

"I'm not going to the 'cooler', I'm getting back in the fight in France. I can't stay here for the rest of the war."

"Impossible. You are not sufficiently recovered. It would be suicide to send you back."

"Dear Miss Atkins, our chances in the field are grim anyway. Didn't you once tell me the lifespan of a pianist, sorry wireless operator, was about six weeks? And that of a courier or other operative not much longer?"

"I never said that about wireless operators." Despite her protest, they both knew it was the truth. Most agents were lucky to survive for longer than six months, but those who acted as wireless operators faced higher risks, especially with the new technology the Germans had developed for tracing the radio transmissions.

"You need agents. You know you do. I am perfectly fine."

"Adèle, you've worked hard. I should have known you'd disobey the doctors but ... walking out of the ward is..." Adèle glared at her, making Miss Atkins falter. "In time, when you have regained your strength—"

"By then, the war will be over. The invasion could happen any minute. I will not miss that fight. I am going home – with or without your approval."

Miss Atkins's lips pursed, her eyes narrowing. "I could have you locked up."

"You could, but you won't. Now please work your magic on the boss and get me back out there. I hate English food, and the weather is just too grim altogether." Adèle's impression of a bored housewife made them both smile.

Miss Atkins stood. "Are you sure?"

Adèle gave her a look.

Miss Atkins threw her hands up in defeat. "They don't pay me enough to argue with you. I will tell Buckmaster."

"Thank you, Miss Atkins. Now, how about you break me out of here and let me come back to London with you?"

"No can do. Get the doctor to release you, Adèle. Not even Buckmaster can overrule him."

Adèle knew Buckmaster could find a way if he wanted to, but it was best she make his life as easy as possible. She could charm the doctor – he was a man, wasn't he?

* * *

The next morning, she brushed her teeth before pinching her cheeks to make them flush. Thanking Miss Atkins for having given her the basics, she added a little powder and a touch of lipstick before picking up a book and settling in the chair near the window. She flicked through the pages, not reading anything but thinking of her men. Soon she'd be back with them.

The door opened, admitting a doctor who was eighty years old if he was a day. What was he doing here?

She stood up, putting the book on the windowsill. "Where's Dr Warwicker?"

The man frowned at her tone, saying brusquely, "His wife went into labour. Darned inconvenient if you ask me – doesn't she know there is a war on? Please lie on the bed."

Adèle stayed silent as she got onto the bed and lay down. How was she going to convince this crotchety old bear to let her out? She waited as he conducted his examination before sitting up.

"Will I live?"

Her joke earned her a look of scorn. She tried to smile and use her looks, as her mother had once taught her, but perhaps his eyesight was waning.

She wasn't about to fail. Some agent she was if she couldn't break herself out of an English hospital.

"Doctor, I know how busy the hospital is. You have a shortage of beds. I can be looked after at home by some very capable friends. Can I please leave?"

She held her breath as he glanced through her notes before nodding. "Absolutely. You need to rest, but there's no point in a pretty little thing like you taking up a bed when one of our lads needs it. Would today be too early?"

Adèle had to resist the urge to hug him.

* * *

When Miss Atkins turned up, Adèle was waiting with her bag packed. She wasn't about to tell her friend that dressing had taken every ounce of energy she possessed, it having been the first time she'd got dressed properly without the shoulder strap. She would get stronger. She had to.

Miss Atkins's driver drove them up to London. He waited while Miss Atkins escorted Adèle into a small hotel where she'd secured her a room with a bathroom next door.

"I'll send the car for you tomorrow at ten. Get some rest, or you will need more than make-up to convince Buckmaster tomorrow." Miss Atkins kissed her cheek.

As soon as she left, Adèle fell into the bed fully dressed.

* * *

The next day, Adèle sat at the round table in the main London office while her bosses in SOE discussed their plans for her. Nobody seemed interested in what she thought. She tried to keep still, her hands folded in her lap so she didn't tap the table.

"We will send her to Paris." Buckmaster glanced in her direction before turning to a uniformed man whom Adèle didn't know. His grey skin suggested he spent all his time indoors, perhaps in this office. He wasn't a field operative. She didn't look at Miss Atkins but kept her eyes on a spot just above her head. Until the unknown man protested.

"You can't do that. She is known to the Gestapo."

Buckmaster dismissed the protests with a wave of his hand. "Adèle Bélanger was known to the Gestapo. We will give her a new identity. Anyway, the Germans swap their people around. It is highly unlikely she will meet the same people she met back in '41."

Adèle coughed, causing the men to glance at her. "I am still here, you know. I want to go back. I know Paris well. I can do good things there – I know I can." She'd prefer to go back to her old network, but Paris was better than London.

Buckmaster nodded. "We need you to re-establish the network. It's risky, as we don't know who has been blown. We don't even know the real traitor."

She nodded, but it seemed it wasn't her choice. The officer shook his head, pushing his chair back and getting up to head over to the map of France hanging on the wall.

"Paris is not ideal; someone who has experience with building networks in a city would be better. We need people with battle experience like Adèle in Corrèze and the surrounding area. The local leaders say they have men, but they're untrained and lacking leadership."

Adèle looked up at the compliment offered by the stranger, but neither man was paying attention to her as they argued the merits of where she should go. She glanced across at Miss Atkins, who shook her head in warning. Adèle picked up on the non-verbal message. *Stay silent. Let them sort it out.*

Foot tapping, she placed her palms face down on the table, adopting a picture of deference to their senior position. She listened as they argued. Finally a decision was made. She was going back after a spell in training school. Buckmaster stared at her for several uncomfortable seconds.

"You should see the latest gadgets the boffins have come up with. Leo Marks wants a word with you too. With the invasion imminent things are going to get hotter over there. Are you sure you're ready?"

"Yes, sir." She crossed her fingers at the lie. She wanted to go home but first she needed to sharpen her skills and stamina.

THIRTY-NINE

APRIL 1944

Ever since Adèle had left, Sophie had worked closely with Maurice's group. She brought them food when she could, and medical supplies, and tended to their wounded. Father Tobias didn't come anymore but sent a priest he trusted, every fourth Sunday, to say mass and hear confession.

One sunny morning, she and Maurice were enjoying some precious time alone by the river running adjacent to the campsite. It was difficult to do anything but talk given the sheer number of men now in the camp, but they stole a few kisses. The alarm – a shrill whistle – broke the mood.

Maurice jumped to his feet. "Someone's arrived. Don't look so worried; they aren't a stranger." He held out his hand to help her to her feet.

Despite his comforting words, she sensed the tension radiating from his shoulders. She stayed quiet, following him back to the large table the men had carved from some tree trunks.

The man panted, trying to catch his breath. "Please send someone to check it out. They need to get those children out of there. All of them together in Izieu is just asking for trouble."

Maurice stepped over to the barrel and, taking the dipper, fetched the man a cup of water.

"Calm down, Antoine, and speak slowly from the beginning."

"I met a friend earlier." The man flushed a little but continued. "She entertains some Germans, but she's on our side. She said they were planning to go to Izieu. They said they were going to burn it down."

Sophie thought her heart had stopped; she put her hand on her chest. *Izieu.*

"I am telling you—" Antoine stopped talking as Sophie approached. She didn't recognise him and his eyes showed no sign of recognition either.

"What is wrong? I heard you mention Izieu." She turned to Maurice. "I worked with Claudette, helping to evacuate children. She left Nice to go to the orphanage in Izieu to join her husband."

Antoine glanced at Maurice, who nodded his head. "She is with us. You can speak."

"My contact, she said the Germans have been boasting that the best way to eradicate the Jews is to kill our women and children. That way, there will be no tomorrow."

The bile burned in the back of her throat. "That's horrific. But they can't mean to go to Izieu. It's miles away, and the orphanage is hidden."

"I still think we should send someone to warn them." Antoine rubbed his hands together, clearly agitated. "I would go, but they'd miss me from the garage."

Maurice's face flushed. "Everyone is needed here. We have orders from London."

"I can go," Sophie said. "I will need new papers and a bicycle. I have been there a few times before. Even if Barbie isn't set on targeting the children now, we know he will. I think we should move them – and assuming it's a false alarm, I can discuss moving the children with Claudette. The more people who know about the orphanage, the more dangerous it is."

Maurice patted Antoine on the shoulder. "Get back to the garage. Thank you for coming." Then he pulled Sophie to one side. "Are you sure? It could be a trap."

"What better excuse do I have? If you get me papers as a nurse, it would be my job to check on children." Sophie knew Maurice was trying to protect her, but she would not turn her back on children in danger. She would not pick up a gun, either. This was her way of helping.

"Let me go, please. I have my war to fight too."

He nodded, but she could see he wasn't pleased.

* * *

It took Maurice two days to provide her with new papers and a decent bike. When she was packed and ready to leave, he blind-folded her at her insistence and took her to the edge of the forest. Removing the blindfold, he kept his hands on her shoulders.

"I must leave you here. It would compromise your safety if you were seen with me."

She nodded, not trusting herself to speak. He pushed a strand of her hair behind her ear. She wanted to grab his hand and insist he came with her. She didn't want to lose him too. She'd bared her soul to him after learning he knew Adèle's identity.

"Sophie, take care of yourself."

"I will."

"You'd better, or Adèle will rip my heart out. With her teeth." His mouth was smiling, but his eyes were full of something else. Concern, and maybe...

No. It wasn't the right time for love. They'd agreed on nothing serious until the war was over.

"You be careful, too. Don't get too friendly with the wrong end of any guns." She tried to joke to dispel her fears for him. "I heard you are losing your doctor."

He uttered an oath, and the next thing she knew, she was crushed against his chest, his mouth on hers in a demanding kiss. And then he was gone.

FORTY

8 APRIL 1944

Sophie cycled her way through the peaceful countryside. It was hard to imagine there was a war on; everything looked so quiet. In the distance she saw some small farms, but she didn't see any people. She didn't see any soldiers.

Her new papers were in the name of Sylvie Henriot – someone's idea of a joke, given Henriot's reputation as a Jew-hater. Her cover was that of a nurse who was taking time off to recuperate. She would stay with an old friend of Maurice's. The elderly lady wouldn't ask too many questions.

Sophie couldn't stop thinking of Maurice. He was an enigma – one minute ordering a raid or the execution of known informants, the next planning the rescue of children.

As she cycled along the road, she couldn't help wondering what it would be like to climb to the top of the mountains and hide for the rest of the war. She could take all the children with her and hide in the forests up there. Maybe the Germans wouldn't bother coming after them.

It took three hours' hard cycling before she spotted the small town. She stopped to eat before making her way to the orphanage, knowing that otherwise Claudette would insist she have lunch there. Everyone was short of food, and she didn't want to increase their burden.

Sophie dismounted and walked her way into the town, pushing her bicycle by her side. There weren't many people on the streets, and those present stared at her. She kept moving, conscious that everyone seemed to be looking in her direction.

Stopping outside a café, she leaned her bike against a table and sat down.

The owner was beside her almost before her behind hit the seat. "What do you want?"

Taken aback by his unfriendliness, Sophie asked for some soup and bread.

"We have none. You should leave."

"I am on my way to visit someone. Can I please have water? Maybe a coffee?"

"Why are you here? What's your name?"

"Sylvie Henriot. I am a nurse."

"Show me your papers."

He had no authority to check her papers; he wasn't a gendarme. He wasn't Milice either unless he was out of uniform. But she did what he asked.

Showing him her papers, she asked, "What is wrong? Why is everyone so unfriendly?"

He ignored her questions. "Who sent you?"

A chill that had nothing to do with the slight breeze blowing down from the mountain went through her. Something was very wrong.

"Nobody. I am just coming through on my way to see a friend. I shall leave." She stood up to go.

"Sit down. Who did you come to see? Nobody just lands in our small town."

Sophie looked around her. There had been no one around when she first cycled in, but now a small crowd was gathering.

They didn't look friendly, either. She didn't want to blow her cover, but she needed them to see she wasn't a threat.

"I wanted to check on my old friend Claudette. We knew each other growing up, and I remembered she had moved here." She really hoped Claudette wouldn't call her Sister Agnès. Surely she would realise the fact that Sophie was no longer in a nun's habit meant she'd had to switch identities?

But the look on the man's face sent chills through her. Had something happened to Claudette?

"You are scaring me now, monsieur. Please, is she here? Find her, and she will explain."

The man said something to his wife so rapidly that Sophie didn't catch every word. It sounded like he had told someone to come quickly.

Claudette came running, but she didn't look pleased to see Sophie either. Sophie stood and took a step back, seeing the furious expression on Claudette's face.

"You're too late. The children – they are gone."

Gone? No, they couldn't be. That had been a rumour, surely?

"What? Who took them and where?" Sophie asked.

"Barbie sent his goons to the orphanage two days ago. They took forty-four children and seven adults, including my husband. We heard they were put on a train to Drancy."

Sophie sat back down on the chair. She was too late; why had she waited for new papers? But even if she had left immediately, she wouldn't have arrived in time; it seemed Antoine had been too late warning Maurice.

She whispered, "All the children are gone?"

"Everyone but Leon, a medical student. He managed to escape. His parents and nephew were taken, as well as his sister, who worked as the orphanage's doctor. Leon told us what happened. I wasn't there. I had gone to another town to check on some children. Why didn't you come last week?"

Claudette's anger was replaced by tears. Sophie stood up and caught the woman in her arms. She pulled her close and whispered, "The name on my papers is Sylvie Henriot. I will explain when we are alone." She kept her arm around Claudette's shoulders. Turning to the café owner, she said, "I got caught up in something else."

"Like what?" The man, clearly suspicious, wasn't prepared to let the matter rest. "The children were denounced. Some traitor gave Barbie the information he needed."

"It wasn't me. I had my own issues with the Gestapo, who intercepted another trip involving children. I then fell foul of the maquis, who also seemed to believe I was on the German side. Frankly, I'm getting sick of being taken for a Nazi-lover." She saw the shocked look on the café owner's face.

There were way too many people around now, all staring at her. She wanted to leave, but she wasn't going anywhere without Claudette. Whoever had betrayed the orphans knew this village well. She would bet her life on it.

Sophie turned to Claudette. "You and Leon will have to come with me. Who knows if they will come back and try to track you down?"

Claudette frowned, her hands moving up and down the sides of her dress. "Where will we go?"

"I have a friend who will get you papers. We can try to get you to Switzerland."

Claudette shook her head. "I should go to Drancy. I can't just walk away from those children."

Sophie sensed someone watching them too closely but from a distance. Was it the traitor? Because it had to be someone known to this village. She had to get away and take Claudette with her. It wasn't safe. "Claudette, you can't do anything for them now. We have some friends who may be able to help the children. Come now. There is no time to delay. I must get back to warn the other orphanages. It seems nowhere is safe now – not with Klaus Barbie in charge."

"He will pay for this." The café owner spat on the ground before moving away.

Claudette whispered to Sophie, "You must forgive Claude. His close friend worked in the orphanage with us. He is grieving for her. We are all in shock."

"I understand, but we must leave." Adrenaline surged through Sophie, her gut tightening. The longer they delayed, the greater the risk the Germans would return.

Claude came back with a small bag of food, and handed it to Sophie. That action alone told her he knew her to be in the resistance. "My apologies, mademoiselle Henriot, but one cannot be too careful."

"I know – but I believe you will find your informant closer to home. A stranger wouldn't have been able to give such information to the SS." She spoke softly so the rest of the villagers wouldn't hear her. She saw by the look in his eyes he shared her suspicions.

Sophie picked up her bicycle, only then realising how much her hands were shaking. Claudette followed on foot, saying goodbye to a few friends as they left. They would pick Leon up from his current hiding place on their way.

Claudette hesitated, staring at the ground. "Perhaps he would be safer here?"

"The traitor is someone who knows you all. Of that, I am sure." Sophie was positive someone in the village had alerted the Boches, maybe in return for extra food or to save their own child from the dreaded STO. Or maybe just because they hated the Jews – but she still found it hard to believe anyone would knowingly send a child away to what was, at best, a horrible camp.

* * *

Sophie took Claudette and Leon to the meeting point at the edge of the forest. She couldn't risk bringing them to Lyon; if the Germans knew they had left witnesses behind, they would hunt them down. She made sure the lookouts saw their approach, then waited for someone to come to them.

"They will blindfold us, but that is only for their protection. That way, we can't give them away if we're caught."

Claudette didn't say a word; she hadn't spoken since they'd left the village. The boy nodded, his eyes wide. Two men came forward, their hands releasing their guns as they recognised her. They put on the blindfolds and escorted them into the camp.

"Sophie." Maurice's whisper broke her resolve. The tears fell as he removed the blindfold. "What happened?"

She moved closer to him.

"I was too late. They are all that is left. The Germans took everyone else."

He wrapped his arms around her and held her as she sobbed, only now giving in to her grief for the little ones.

Maurice spoke over her head, "You are safe here. Go with my men; they will find you food and water."

Maurice's men took Claudette and Leon away.

Sophie couldn't stop crying on his shoulder. She had told no one, but as Sister Agnès, she had placed four children in that orphanage, two sisters and a brother and sister. Their parents had entrusted their precious children to her care, and she had let them down.

"This isn't your fault, Sophie."

"Why didn't I take them to Switzerland? I should have insisted they leave. But they were so young – the oldest was six, Maurice. Six years old and a target for an animal like Barbie."

Maurice picked her up and carried her to his shed, then lay on the straw mattress with her, holding her in his arms. "You did the best you could. Nobody could have done more. Now you need to rest."

He held her tight, and she closed her eyes, not expecting to sleep, but relief came. She woke a few times, her sleep tormented by the cries of the children she had taken to the orphanage. He held her tighter as she sobbed until, too exhausted to think, she fell into a dreamless sleep.

The next morning there was no sign of Claudette or Leon. They had already been moved, on their way to another network in a different region. Sophie was determined that no other orphanage would fall into the same trap. She had to get back to her contacts and spread the word about Izieu. They had all believed it was far enough away from anywhere to be safe. But nothing was safe any more.

FORTY-ONE

Adèle got off the train to find a car waiting to drive her to the stately home. It was odd to be back at the training centre not least as the new recruits knew she had been in the field. They pestered her with questions. She answered those concerned with tactics, the enemy and their perceived weaknesses but refused to discuss her actions or her last mission. Major Hunter barely raised a hand in greeting at his first talk to the recruits. But later, she was summoned to his office where he poured them both a stiff drink.

"Well done, Adèle. The reports from the field were truly impressive not that I doubted you."

She smiled at that. She was glad she'd proved him wrong.

"Thank you, sir."

"Baker Street tell me you are heading back to the same area. That's suicidal. Have you met with the head doctor?"

"Yes, sir. My men will keep me safe. I've built up a regular army over there and we'll need them when the invasion comes."

He leaned back in his chair, his eyes contemplating the whiskey in his glass. "And there is the old Adèle. Still believe you are better than anyone."

She rushed to correct him. "No, sir, that's not what I ... oh you're teasing me."

He drained his drink before pouring another. She declined when he offered a refill, she needed to keep her wits about her.

"Yes, I am. It is suicidal but given the whole of France is about to blow up anytime, I guess no more than sending any other agent over there. We're desperate. Have you heard the news about Salesman?"

She knew the circuit by reputation. They had blown up trains, destroyed substations and factories and scuttled a German minesweeper used as a submarine tender to deliver food and water to U-boats, right under the nose of the offices of the Kriegsmarine. Their exploits were legendary.

"I've heard of their expertise in the field."

"They've been blown. The lead agents were injured and, in their absence, something went wrong. An informant perhaps or they just ran out of time. We lost a lot of agents in the Gestapo roundups including Newman. I believe you met him."

She shivered remembering the wireless operator, hoping he had died rather than being subjected to torture at the hands of the Gestapo. Major Hunter lit up a cigarette, changing the subject. "You've been given your orders?"

"Yes, sir. The gloves are off. We're to raise havoc and cause as much disruption as possible. The boss wants the Germans to be kept busy and away from all the ports." She locked eyes with him. "Do you know the location of the invasion?"

"No and even if I did, I wouldn't tell you. You will be dropping back in with another agent who has also returned from the field. First, Buckmaster has asked me to make sure you are ready to go back. Not just physically but emotionally. They nearly killed you last time."

* * *

She didn't get to see the Major again, she was summoned to RAF Tempsford to fly back to France. They had to take advantage of the full moon. The light rain dribbled down the back of her flying suit. She found Miss Atkins pacing back and forth, lighting one cigarette from the other. The news must be bad. Before Adèle could speak, Miss Atkins kissed her on the cheek in greeting, enveloping Adèle in a cloud of cigarette smoke.

"The Nazis have been busy, they've broken a few more circuits. We're dropping you in blind, no reception committee. We need eyes on the ground. Steer clear of your former contacts until you know they haven't been compromised. Understood?"

"Yes." She didn't mention she was the one with the field experience like the old Adèle would have done.

Miss Atkins looked tired, no worn out was a better description. The circles under her eyes were darker, her expression more haunted. Adèle couldn't believe she had once thought this woman to be cold. Not only did she care about every agent but she took every disappearance, death or injury to heart as if she was personally responsible.

"Take this with you." Miss Atkins held out the L pill. Adèle's thoughts flew to her conversation with Sophie who disagreed with suicide. She hesitated for a brief second before accepting the tablet.

Miss Atkins grasped her hands. "Take care, mon amie. Next time bring me back some fresh eggs."

Adèle laughed. Powdered eggs, the only sort available in London, were an acquired taste. She kissed Miss Atkins on both cheeks and with a whispered "Merde alors" ran, bent low and with as much grace as she could given her parachute gear, to catch up with the other two agents climbing into the Liberator B-24. This giant could fly further and faster and more importantly was not vulnerable to flak damage from the ack ack guns. Soon she was sitting on the cold floor of the aircraft, shivering, desperately trying to keep all thoughts of what lay ahead out of her mind. She knew circuits had been blown. Was Caesar dead? Or captured? Luc, Romain, young Laurence. So many of their faces flashed through her head.

FORTY-TWO

The plane hadn't alerted the Germans and the drop went well. After disposing of her parachute and flying suit, she picked up the satchel, checked the money was still in the pouch around her waist and made her way toward the nearest village. There were supposed to be several thousand members of the maquis in the area. She hoped she'd stumble over one of them rather than a German checkpoint. Despite having the names of a few safe houses from London, she'd decided to find her own. She didn't trust anyone but the men and women she knew personally.

Rain clouds covered the moon, both a blessing and a curse. She strode along, watching the path in front of her so she didn't stumble over anything. Every so often an owl screeched and she heard rustling in the overgrowth but no engines. It looked like her arrival had passed unnoticed.

Arriving at a small farmhouse she had used previously, on the outskirts of a village, she knocked tentatively on the door. It took a while for the occupants to answer, long enough for her to wonder if they had been picked up in a raid. She heard the scrape of the lock and a curly grey-haired man peered out. His eyes widened in recognition.

"Claire, you're back. You're alive." Jean-Claude poked his head out the door checking behind her. "You're alone."

She smiled as despite the rush of words, he left her standing on the step. "Oui. Can I come in."

"Of course, come." He pulled the door open and enveloped her in a bear hug. The smell reminded her of the local lack of soap and toothpaste.

She waited while he pushed the warped door closed behind her, the sliver of moonlight just bright enough to highlight the mess on the table. Where was Maxine? The couple weren't rich but she was house proud. Her heart beat faster.

"Jean-Claude, I heard..."

"Of the raids. I'm surprised you came. They could come back." He sank into a chair gesturing she sit in the other. The fireplace was bare, she shivered despite herself. As her eyes grew accustomed to the dark, she saw the room had been ransacked.

"Maxine?"

"Gone. Neighbours complained to the Germans in the garrison in the next town that the maquis were thieving. Maxine was furious, those lads are starving out there. She and some of the women from the town took some food up to the camp. They must have been followed or else the Boche got tipped off. They surrounded the whole lot of them." He shuddered. Adèle held her breath, waiting for him to recover his composure. His eyes glistened as he looked up. "They put the women in prison, someone said they're being sent to somewhere called Ravensbrück. The boys... they slaughtered them, Claire. They weren't content with just killing them." He put his head in his hands, mumbling, "I couldn't do anything. I couldn't protect my family."

She moved to comfort him. "Jean-Claude, there was nothing you could do. Maxine is a formidable woman. She made her own decisions. Andre too."

"I couldn't find him. I searched but nothing. When I was gone, they came here. Took everything that wasn't nailed down."

She glanced over at the table. "Do you want a drink?"

He nodded. She stood up and walking over to the table, poured some red wine into a mug. Handing it to him, she asked, "Do you know who escaped? Where they are now?"

"I can guess but I'm not sure. There were agents among those captured. They've been sent to Paris already. The local gestapo obviously thought they were important."

Adèle's stomach churned. "Did you hear about Caesar?"

"Who?"

"Doesn't matter. Are we safe here tonight?"

"I waited for them to come back. I was ready for them." He indicated his rifle lying on the table. "I hid it when the Boches first arrived. It's been days and no sign of them. I thought Andre might..." His voice trailed off.

"First thing tomorrow, we are going to find the maquis. Both of us. I'm not leaving you here."

He didn't answer just stared into his drink.

* * *

At daybreak, they left through the back door, Jean-Claude carrying his rifle. Neither had anything to eat, not even water. The Boches had thrown something down the well. She didn't want to think too much about that. They moved in silence through the countryside, Jean-Claude sticking to the lesser worn paths. The animals they passed couldn't betray them. As they walked, he told her of the increased presence of Germans. "It's like they are expecting something to happen."

She'd spotted a stream up ahead and gestured for him to follow her. "The invasion."

"Le jour de la libération!"

She hated the bitterness in his tone. He'd been such a bright cheerful bear of a man. She patted his arm. "It's coming. We just need to hang on a little longer."

* * *

The sentries spotted them first. They asked for the code word but she didn't know it. Then a voice piped up. "Claire, you came back." Laurence ran down the embankment and almost knocked her off her feet.

"What are you doing here? Is Luc or Romain with you?"

The boy shook his head. He looked at the sentry. "She's the one they call the White Witch."

The sentry rolled his eyes but at least he let them pass.

Laurence chatted non-stop as he led them into the camp. She tried to listen, but her eyes were taking in the men surrounding them. They were too lean, dressed in rags with a hunted look about them. Their weapons consisted of some rifles left over from the Great war, knives at their waists and a couple of wire garottes. How could they be expected to fight against the German machine guns. Her heart ached for them. They'd given up everything, taken to the woods to fight for their country.

Laurence stopped talking. "That's the boss. Bastien doesn't like women."

Adèle felt the leader's eyes on her. She waited for him to finish his assessment and speak first. Bastien stayed silent, leaving it to her to make the first move.

"I'm Claire. I think you're the man I was looking for. London said you had a huge army behind you."

He waved his hand around. "It was bigger but you missed the fireworks. Lawrence knows you?"

"We've fought a few times together. I worked with another circuit but was injured. I'm fully recovered and was due to meet with someone, but the circuit was blown. Do you have a radio operator?"

"Yes."

"Good. London wants to send you as many guns, grenades, and explosives. As much as you can handle."

His eyes widened as he clasped his hands to his chest, before resting them on the rifle strung across his chest. "When? My men are itching for revenge."

"As soon as you agree to two things. I train your men and you wait for revenge until the Allies have landed."

He snorted. "Which century is that likely to happen? If I had a sous for every time I heard of this promised invasion. *Frenchmen* will free France, Mademoiselle Claire."

"They will but only with help from Frenchwomen and the rest of their allies. Now do you want the weapons or do I find another group?"

He muttered something she pretended not to hear.

"You are the white witch?" White Witch.

Not a muscle moved in her face. She hated her reputation - it had grown legs over the last year. According to Lawrence, she was credited with killing over a thousand Germans, but if it changed his mind so be it.

He clapped her on the back. It took everything she had to stay standing. "Welcome to our family."

* * *

Over the next days, Adèle worked with the men insisting they trained like soldiers so they could act as a cohesive force. She arranged drop zones picking out suitable spots and sending the co-ordinates via the radio operator. Her credibility grew as London delivered the promised Bren guns, rifles, grenades, some clothing and cash.

"Bastien, take this and pay the local people for the food you take. Your men can steal whatever they want from Fritz but we pay the French. We need their hearts on our side over the next months. Pay above the going rate and..." the man gleefully counted the francs, "bring me back a receipt."

* * *

Lawrence followed her around. "Why do you keep hitting the sides of your hands against the table like that?"

Adèle looked up from the table she was working at. One of the men, a former carpenter, had hewn one out of a tree and she hadn't been aware of what she was doing.

"That's to make sure if the need arises, I can kill someone."

"Teach me."

"You know enough already." She sent him off on some errand.

"You treat him like a child." Bastien continued cleaning his Bren gun.

"I treat him as a young lad who deserves to grow up. He's our future."

Bastien's eyes held hers. "You truly believe the invasion is coming?"

"Yes." Though when she didn't know.

"The men are growing restless."

She knew that for herself. Petty squabbles broke out almost every day. The men were sick of waiting.

She stood picking up her Bren gun. "They aren't the only ones. Let's go make life difficult for the occupiers. London said to keep them nervous."

His face broke into a grin as he lifted her off her feet and swung her around. "Now you talk my language."

* * *

They waited, watching as a convoy passed. Bastien went to stand but she put a hand on his shoulder. "Wait, let most of them through. We attack the last two only, with everything we have."

She watched and then she gave the order to attack. The men lobbed grenades at the two trucks before opening fire. Everything exploded at once, the screams of the German soldiers drowned out by the warrior cries from the maquis. By the time the Germans realized and turned their front trucks, the maquis had fallen back and dispersed.

"We didn't lose one man." Bastien clapped her on the back. She listened to his recounting of the attack but didn't join in the glee. Young men had died, they may have been the enemy but she hadn't expected them to look so young.

FORTY-THREE

Sophie was due to meet Arthur, the Scout leader, in the market square that morning, but that wasn't the reason she was awake so early. It was only a ten-minute walk away. She couldn't sleep. The last few days she'd had a bad feeling, and she couldn't shake it. It wasn't being back in Lyon, although it was clear the locals were nervous. There was something in the air as the constant gossip about Allied landings flew around. Some people complained the Allies had forgotten all about them, while others swore they would land any day.

She wondered if something awful had happened to Adèle. There were those who believed you could tell if your twin was in danger or pain.

Then she heard the boots. Jumping out of bed, she ran to the window. Her apartment building seemed to be surrounded. She grabbed the papers in the names of Sister Agnès and Sophie Bélanger and quickly burned them in the tiny fireplace. She'd been using them to collect rations in different areas to aid Maurice and his men. She had nothing else incriminating, did she? Before she had time to check, the loud knock on her door nearly splintered the wood.

"Open up."

She opened the door, hiding behind it as she wasn't dressed.

"Papers."

Her heart hammered – she recognised his voice even before looking into his eyes. Oscar Dubois, the Milice officer from the market.

Sophie held out her papers, her hands steady despite her heart beating so fast. Had her veil and wimple been enough of a disguise? Her hopes were crushed when he spoke.

"We meet again, Sister Agnès – or is it Nicole Samson?"

"I have no idea who you are. My name is Nicole Samson."

"I think you recognise me. I remember you from that day in the market when you saved that *Muslim*."

His stale breath made her stomach roil, but she didn't move an inch. She knew that fear would excite him further. When he put his hands on her arms, she kicked out.

"Get off me, you brute." Her protests only encouraged him.

"Fight me!"

His hands patted her body down, taking pleasure in the intimate search.

She restrained herself with difficulty. If she continued the pretence of being Nicole, she had some chance of escaping.

"Take her away. The Gestapo wants to speak to her – about her love for the dirty Jewish pigs." He addressed the young man standing in the doorway.

The youngster's eyes bulged. "Aren't you going to let her get dressed?"

Sophie couldn't believe the guard cared, but his question worked. Oscar handed her a coat, his sneer telling her what he thought of her.

Sophie couldn't stop herself. She spat at him.

He rubbed her spittle off his face. Coming closer, he put his finger under her chin and roughly forced her head up to meet his gaze.

"You will regret that, mademoiselle." He then backhanded her so forcefully that she fell over. His men picked her up and manhandled her down the stairs, leaving the others behind to search her room. She raced through her thoughts, trying to reassure herself that there was no written evidence waiting to incriminate her.

As they made their way inside a local hotel commandeered by the Milice, she protested her innocence, but the men didn't take any notice. They pushed her into a room stripped of its furniture. She saw the marks on the walls against which a bed had once been placed, perhaps a mirror and some paintings. But now it was empty but for the presence of another prisoner, a trim but not skinny woman in her mid-thirties wearing a filthy cotton dress with bare feet. Was she a German plant? She certainly wasn't starving like most French citizens.

"What you in for?"

"I don't know. They keep saying I am some nun. Do I look like a holy sister to you?" Sophie kept up the conversation while trying to work through her story for the interrogation coming. The Gestapo would be thorough. She had to be prepared. She couldn't afford to trust this woman, who might be working for the Germans.

The woman shrugged her shoulders. "They caught me with extra food. I know you shouldn't use the black market, but I have children to feed. They are going to be so scared." The woman started crying, immediately making Sophie feel sorry for her. At least she didn't have children relying on her – not children of her own, anyway.

The Milice returned with news that they didn't intend to interview Sophie, but hand her and her cellmate, whose name was Michelle, over to the Germans.

"You'll wish you spoke to us." They laughed as they pushed the women through the door of their hotel room, down the stairs and out to a waiting truck.

Sophie was surprised to find another prisoner already sitting in the truck, slumped against the side. She recognised Denis, despite his face and every inch of exposed skin being covered in welts and bruises. Some of them were still bleeding.

"Can I help him? I am a nurse."

She inched her way towards the injured man.

"No talking."

The soldier hit her with the butt of his rifle. Denis didn't acknowledge her presence.

The sun shone in a bright blue sky as they drove across Lyon, but she didn't feel any warmth. Her heart was as cold as ice hearing the men say they were to be taken to the Hôtel Terminus, the beautiful castle-like building on cours de Verdun. Sophie tried to breathe slowly to stop her heart from racing. This once beautiful hotel was now the home to Klaus Barbie, the hunter of those in the resistance. He was responsible for the raid on Izieu.

It was said, despite the soundproofing incorporated into the walls of the hotel, that the screams from torture victims could be heard streets away. What would they do to her? Would she be able to keep quiet? She closed her eyes, seeing Maurice and Adèle. She couldn't betray them. She wouldn't.

* * *

They entered by the front, but instead of heading to the reception area, they were taken down a backstairs to the basement. They made slow progress, given their shackles, but the guards refused to release them. Denis was led off for interrogation, Sophie and Michelle were dumped in an old hotel room.

"Don't get too comfortable, we will be back for you shortly." The guard leered at them before he shut the door.

Michelle bowed her head, her lips moving. Sophie took advantage of the brief respite to go over her story.

* * *

The guard came back, pulled Sophie to her feet telling her she was going to be the first to be questioned. Michelle shuddered not able to hide her relief before sending Sophie a guilty look.

He prodded her in the back as she walked along a corridor, deliberately shuffling her steps to delay the inevitable. Over and over, she silently hoped for the courage to withstand whatever was waiting for her in the room at the end of the corridor.

On entering, she stilled as she recognised the tall man with the coldest blue eyes she'd ever seen, standing against the desk. "Good afternoon." He spoke excellent French with only a trace of an accent. "Do you prefer to be called Nicole or Sister Agnès – or perhaps Adèle Bélanger? My men call you the White Witch." Sophie had heard of the White Witch, the woman rumoured to have killed hundreds of Germans single-handedly, but she'd always believed her to be a myth. He couldn't mean Adèle, could he?

He came closer to her, lifting a strand of her hair. "They say you are Jewish. You look nothing like a rat."

Sophie tensed, trying to subdue her impulse to pull away from him. Her stomach hardened with fear as her chest pains grew worse due to her racing heart. She couldn't believe her bad luck. She recognised him; he was the same Gestapo agent she had spoken to on the train.

"I see you recognise me. Oberführer Max Mueller, in case you have forgotten. Back when I met you and your beau, Favreau, I was with the Wehrmacht. As you can see, I've been promoted. Quite a runaround you gave us, Adèle."

Sophie didn't react. The SS man patted her down as he spoke. His hands were far more thorough than those of the Milice, and even more intimate.

"I could never have forgotten such a pretty face. Pity, it is

Jewish and therefore verboten. I would have enjoyed making you squirm beneath me."

Despite the weakness in her legs, Sophie stared back at him, not sure who she was trying to convince of her indifference – him or herself. How did he know Adèle was Jewish?

"You have been a real thorn in our side, Mademoiselle Bélanger. I believe you are responsible for the deaths of over a hundred of our loyal German soldiers."

"I have never killed anyone."

She made the mistake of glancing around the room, flinching when she saw the bath filled with water in the corner. She'd heard of what they did to prisoners to make them talk: half-drowning a person before reviving them and asking them more questions. She bit back on the scream wanting to escape from her throat.

"You would say that, but my sources tell me otherwise. Your skills with your rifle are legendary."

Bemused, Sophie listened as he listed out her crimes. Had Adèle really done all those things? She couldn't see her sister as a cold-blooded killer, yet this man wasn't lying. He clearly believed every word he told her.

"Do you still plead innocence?"

"I have never killed anyone." Sophie held his gaze. It was a better view than the torture implements lying casually around the room.

"You know, you are quite believable. What an actress – not even a glimmer of sweat or the blink of an eye to show you are lying. Yet we both know you are."

Sophie didn't argue. He wouldn't believe her anyway.

"You will give me the names of your contacts. You can do this the easy way or the hard way; it is up to you."

"I have nothing to tell you."

He put his hands on her shoulders and pushed her onto a

chair. Her tailbone ached in protest, but she remained silent. For that, she got a slap across the face.

"That is not helpful. I intend to get the information I need – and, believe me, nobody fails to spill their secrets."

Sophie believed him, but she remained silent.

"You have clearly forgotten how Favreau looked when you last saw him. Perhaps you should see another example of my work – it may make you talk. Bring in the prisoner."

Sophie stifled a cry when they dragged Denis in. He looked ten times worse than he had in the lorry. He couldn't stand; they had to prop him up as they taunted him.

"This is the famous Adèle you wouldn't tell me about."

Denis smirked – or at least he tried to. The lack of teeth ruined the effect somewhat.

Sophie begged him silently to stay quiet, but Denis couldn't resist.

"Hah! Fooled you again. That's not the White Witch but her twin sister, a doctor. See, you Germans are the fools."

His remark earned him a punch in the stomach. And another one. Sophie closed her eyes as they beat him to a pulp in front of her. She prayed he would black out soon.

"Take him away."

They dragged him out of the room, leaving just Sophie and Mueller.

"A sister?" The man stepped forward and pulled Sophie back up to a standing position by the hair so she was up close and personal to him. "Is this another ploy, Adèle?"

She didn't answer.

"You've seen how enthusiastic my men are about their job. If that imbecile speaks the truth and you are her sister, as a doctor, you know the human body can only take so much pain. Spare yourself. Tell me what I want to know."

But Sophie stayed silent.

He forced her back into a seated position, but this time her front was facing the back of the chair. A knife swished through the air, slicing the blouse and undergarments from her back, leaving her naked. She shivered as the cold air hit her skin, but the sensation was nothing compared to the pain when he first whipped her. Again and again, the whip splayed across her fragile skin. She bit her lip until it bled in a bid not to cry out. Squeezing her eyes shut, she pictured the people she loved, Maurice and Adèle, together and separate. She could cope with anything to keep them safe. Blackness finally descended, releasing her from the pain.

FORTY-FOUR

A blast of freezing water revived her as she sputtered her way back to consciousness. The stinging from her back drew tears. She flinched at the sound of his voice.

"I can stop. You can have treatment for your back, but only once you tell me what I want to know."

"I don't know what you are talking about." Every word took all her energy, but it was pointless; he didn't believe her.

"My arm's too sore to continue."

She breathed a sigh of relief, but it was temporary as the next belt of the whip hit her.

"I can rest, but Theo here, he loves what he does. Takes great pleasure out of the pain he inflicts. He can go on for hours. Can't you, Theo?"

Sophie screamed as the whip hit her back again and again. She maintained her innocence, denying all knowledge for the next few hours. Her lack of co-operation drove Theo to hit her harder. Over and over again, the whip flew through the air. She shrieked in pain but her agony seemed to encourage him.

She fainted but each time they revived her. The pain never ended, her shredded skin raw. Her grip on reality started to slip as her body bled. Just as she was about to give in, they stopped. A guard dragged her along the stone floor back to her cell. Michelle was still there, she didn't look any different. She gasped in horror, rushing to help Sophie as soon as the door was closed.

"What have those animals done to you? Here, lean on me. Let's get you to the bed."

Trying to control her shaking limbs, Sophie took the woman's arm and hobbled to the bed. She lay on her stomach, her back a bloody mess. The woman did not try to clean her wounds; she couldn't. They had no water or cloths. Instead, she stroked her hair.

"What could you have done to deserve this? Can't you tell them what they want to know? Or make something up? Anything to stop them from doing this again. You need a doctor."

Sophie wanted to scream that she was a doctor, but despite the woman's kindness, she knew she couldn't be too careful. She pretended to lose consciousness. The pain was agonising; not a single part of her body seemed to be free. How much more of this could she endure? Tomorrow would be worse – the man who called himself Mueller had promised her that.

"They shot someone earlier. Just like that, in full view of all the windows. Didn't even bother to hide it. Poor man had to be carried to the execution point."

Was it Denis? She hoped so, for his sake. If she was in pain, he must have been in agony. Then she gave herself up to the darkness.

* * *

They came for her early the next morning, rousing her with a bucket of ice-cold water. They didn't like the fact that she walked so slowly, so they carried her down to where Mueller and the grinning Theo were waiting. The smell of real coffee did little to mask the smell of blood and other bodily fluids in the torture chamber.

Mueller set his cup of coffee on the table. "Good morning. Have you had a change of heart?"

Could it hurt Adèle if she told him her real name? No, she didn't think so. She had no idea where her sister was, so she couldn't betray her. She didn't know her code names either. Sophie said a silent prayer that she was doing the right thing.

* * *

Taking a shaky breath, she started to talk. "My name is Sophie Bélanger, and I am a doctor. Or at least I would be if the war hadn't started."

He smiled as she spoke, probably thinking he would get all the information he wanted.

"Where is your sister?"

"I have no idea."

"I don't believe you."

"I don't care. It's the truth. I haven't seen my sister since you took my brother in 1941."

Sophie outlined how she had left Paris to look for her friend, and Adèle had gone by the time she returned. It was close to the truth. But he didn't believe her, and gave her a sound slap for lying to him. She repeated what she had said, again and again.

"You are lying, Mademoiselle Bélanger. Last night I did investigations of my own. You and Adèle were seen together in 1943 – two years after you claim to have last seen your sister."

Sophie didn't flinch. He couldn't be that sure of his information, as his eyes kept flicking. They would have remained steady had he been speaking the truth.

"Your information is wrong. I haven't seen Adèle. Until you mentioned her, I assumed she was dead. Everyone else is."

He didn't hit her, so she could only hope he believed her. But he had another card to play.

"Not everyone. Your mother, for instance."

Sophie crumpled inside. He couldn't have found maman.

"Perhaps if we bring her in here, you will tell us what we want to know."

"I told you, I know nothing." She forced her voice to stay steady. She couldn't betray her mother.

"Or were you a daddy's girl? Maybe we should bring him in and give him some of our special treatment."

Sophie stopped herself from reacting, although she wanted to laugh in his face. Maybe he didn't know her father was dead, or maybe he was just lying. But did that mean he was also lying about her mother? Either way, she wasn't falling for his tricks.

"I don't know anything. You could bring anyone in here, but I can't tell you what I don't know."

Her insolence earned her another beating, but she refused to speak again. This time, as his gaze raked her from head to foot, he finally seemed to accept she couldn't tell him anything.

"I tend to believe you. Pity – if you don't have any more information for me, now that you have told me what you know, you're worthless. Take her away."

Sophie couldn't believe her ears. He wasn't going to hurt her any more. She didn't even try to resist as the soldiers grabbed her and bundled her back to her room.

Her cellmate, Michelle, was surprised to find her back so quickly. "You told them what they wanted, I guess."

"I told them the truth. I know nothing." Sophie turned her head towards the wall and let the tears come. She didn't know what the next step was; she was just relieved that she didn't have to face any more questioning. She shut her eyes and thought of Maurice. How they could have been happy, living together, working as doctors, raising a family together. Then she thought of her grandmother and mother. Were they still alive?

And then there was Adèle. Always her twin. Had she kept her safe? She couldn't face any more torture, so she hoped they would shoot her. And soon. Before she broke and destroyed those she loved.

FORTY-FIVE

The days passed, and nobody came for her. Michelle asked for water and clean cloths, and surprisingly the Germans provided them. With Michelle's help, Sophie was able to dress her wounds. Her cuts and bruises slowly began to heal.

Then it was Michelle's turn. Her cellmate went and never came back. Sophie hoped it meant she had been set free and returned to her children. Although she still hadn't trusted Michelle with any information, she wasn't convinced any more that the woman had been a plant.

Weeks passed – at least Sophie thought it was weeks, as she lost track of time. Her wounds caked over. Every day she forced herself to pace the cell, back and forth, to build up her strength. To keep her mind from breaking, she recalled precious memories from her childhood. Times with those she loved, back before the war when their family was happy. She pictured papa taking them for a walk along the Seine to get ice cream. Everyone was laughing and talking, papa holding Jean-Pierre in his arms when his little legs got too tired. Other days, when it was too painful to remember her family, she thought about the hospital. How were Dr Murphy and Elizabeth faring in occupied Paris? She hoped they were safe. Her mind flitted over memories of Jules and how innocent their love for each other had been. They'd believed their love could change the world. She cried, remembering his loss and that of his sister. Then her thoughts turned to Maurice. He reminded her of Jules, but in other ways, he was so different. Jules would never have taken up arms. Her first love had been a dreamer, not a fighter. Maurice, although a doctor too, wanted revenge and freedom. Would he get it? Was he thinking of her, and what their life together could have been?

And every day, she thought of her twin. In her worst moments, in the early hours of the mornings, she imagined Adèle was dead. Was that why she couldn't feel anything when she thought of her? In the past, she'd got hints when Adèle was in pain, happy or sad, but now she'd lost that connection. Did that mean...?

"Out. Schnell. *Schnell.*"

Sophie staggered out of the cell, her legs still too weak to walk properly. She followed the guard to the back of the building. Expecting to be taken out and shot, she prayed for forgiveness for her sins.

Instead, she was pushed into a truck full of other women and girls. One of them gave her a seat.

"You look rough," a familiar-looking woman said.

Sophie stared. "Esmée? Is it really you?"

Tears fell as she recognised the woman who'd been working with her at the camps. She'd left to help move the Jewish children to safe houses. They hugged, Sophie trying her best not to flinch, her back was still tender in places. Esmée stepped back to look at her.

"My goodness I didn't recognise you. What did those animals do to you?"

"I am fine. Call me Nicole, for that's what they are using," Sophie whispered. "What are you doing here?"

Esmée shrugged. "Who knows? My time was up. They caught me with a bundle of clothes and food, and I couldn't explain it. I was lucky. Nobody tortured me. They figured to send me to Drancy instead."

"Is that where we are going?"

"I think so. That's what the guards said."

Sophie's heart plummeted. She'd heard from various escapees that the conditions in Drancy were appalling, worse than those at Rivesaltes, and she imagined they hadn't improved any in recent months.

* * *

It took days for the train to arrive at Drancy, having been delayed by blown-up rails and stops to allow for more important trains to pass by. It was so hard to breathe in the cars designed for horses, not people. Not only were there too many people but with the lack of toilet facilities, the not-very-clean straw floor was soon destroyed. Sophie did her best to look after the children in the train car. She and Esmée took turns holding them up to the wire-covered windows so that they could get a little air.

Once they arrived, the women were ordered down from the train. When they didn't move fast enough, a soldier fired above their heads, causing panic. In the chaos, Sophie missed her footing and fell heavily on her left arm. The pain made her eyes water, but she didn't scream, not even when a guard pushed her roughly into line.

"Lean on me." Esmée offered her arm as they were marched into the camp. "It's broken, isn't it?"

Sophie couldn't respond. It took every ounce of energy to keep walking and not faint. She knew she could be shot if she didn't keep up with the other prisoners.

* * *

Drancy was everything she had imagined and worse; there were prisoners from all areas across Europe with only one thing in common, their being Jewish. It was a pit compared to Rivesaltes – and that had been bad enough. But word spread about her broken arm, and it turned out there were many doctors among the prisoners, one of whom offered to examine it.

"You're lucky. It's a clean break, and you haven't punctured the skin."

"Thank you." She wondered how long the older man had been in Drancy.

"You won't thank me when I pull it into place. Here, bite on this – we have nothing for the pain."

Sophie bit down on the cloth offered by his female assistant. The pain took her right back to the torture chamber. She broke out in a cold sweat. Then it was more bearable, but she still couldn't speak.

The doctor patted her good arm. "That should heal now – though who knows if it will have time."

"What does that mean?" She breathed heavily in a bid to overcome the nausea caused by the pain.

"Haven't you heard the rumours? We are to be gassed on arrival in Poland." The doctor didn't lower his voice.

"Don't be ridiculous." His female assistant corrected him. "Nobody kills thousands of innocent people. They want us to work for them."

Sophie looked into the doctor's eyes and saw the truth. The woman walked away, leaving Sophie alone with the doctor.

"How do you know?" she asked.

"We heard the reports on the BBC."

"You listen to the radio here?"

"No, before I got caught. Some people escaped from a death camp in Poland and got word back to London."

Sophie couldn't believe her ears. She knew being deported wasn't pleasant – but murder?

"Everyone who is sent east is murdered?"

"I don't think everyone, but you can see it makes sense. Who needs old people or pregnant women and children as essential workers?" Despite the question, he didn't expect her to answer as he continued talking. "Try not to get on a transport until that arm is healed. Only those who can work will have a chance."

She nodded in response to his warning, but she knew once her name was on the list, she would have to go – and that would be that.

FORTY-SIX

"This is better than the old days, no?" Bastien looked up from the package at his feet. The field around them was covered in similar packages, everything they had asked for and more. In addition to the arms and ammunition there were also uniforms. Her maquis could exchange their ragged clothes for basic khaki uniforms with black boots. Now they looked like the army they were. Her heart swelled with pride. They were winning the hearts of the locals as well not just by distributing the cash coming from London and paying for the items they needed. By turning up in public wearing uniforms they lifted public morale. Adèle knew the invasion was coming but each hour the anticipation grew so did the nervousness of the Germans. It was difficult keeping the men in hand, they wanted to fight now.

On June 5th, their group gathered in a safe house where they sat around the T.S.F listening to the BBC French broadcast.

"The crocodile is thirsty."

One of the men scratched his head. "What is he talking about?"

"Shush." The group leaned in as the announcer paused. Cigarette ends glowed as the tension rose. "I hope to see you again, darling, twice at the Pont d'Avignon... You may now shake the..."

Adèle jumped up. "That's it. The invasion is on. Grab your things, we have targets to hit."

The men stopped to raise a glass in a toast then drifted off to where their men were waiting. Bastien put a hand on Adèle's shoulder.

"Thank you." He kissed her on both cheeks with one more for luck. "To victory."

The sky lit up with explosions as power cables, rail junctions key to the effective movement of German troops and factories at Clermont and Montluçon blew up. Adèle spent day and night setting explosives blowing bridges and railway lines, laying booby traps on the roads. Men who excelled as sharpshooters took position as snipers on either side of the main routes harrying any Germans who dared to travel.

They made life difficult for the enemy but their main focus was to slow down the panzers on route to Normandy.

The Germans responded aggressively, turning on any French local found in the vicinity of any sabotage attempts. They burned down homes, rounding up hostages who were shot or hanged. Adèle tried not to think about these innocents. Rather than stop the maquis, the actions of the Germans fuelled the uprising with the local resistance papers telling the people that they would take 'two German eyes for every one French.'

But despite the brave actions of her men, it didn't take the occupiers long to rally. They had more sophisticated weapons and behaved like cornered rats. Within days of the Normandy landings, they turned their artillery, armoured cars and tanks on the maquis and everything else in their path.

Adèle knew it was time to contact Luc. She sent him a message '*send chickens to Gatère.*'

Luc would know it wasn't a person, but it meant she was aiming for an abandoned farmhouse not far from Figeac, owned by one of his father's friends. The previous owners had emigrated to America at the first opportunity.

She wanted Luc to check out the rumours about a local factory that was working for the Germans. She'd also teach him how to use the new explosives she'd brought from London.

Romain arrived with him; they were like the terrible twins that pair. They put their bicycles down, and both lifted Adèle off her feet and swung her around, celebrating like it was Christmas. She assessed the impact of the last week on them both, taking in the shadows on their face highlighting their lack of sleep. Knowing her men, they'd been working flat out since London had increased the drops in preparation for the invasion. They had to rest, if only for a few hours.

"Can you make some lunch?"

In response, Romain took some pâté, apples, figs, and a few olives from a bag before handing her a small parcel. "Madame Abreo said you'd appreciate it. She wouldn't let me open it."

Adèle hugged the parcel close, wishing she could hug Josette Abreo in person. She hadn't seen them since the German spy incident. That night seemed like a lifetime ago.

"Let's sit and enjoy our meal. Then, Luc, you can cycle to the town to check out a factory, and you, Romain, will stay with me. I'll teach you how to use the explosives, and you can train the men back in your camp. I'll be down in a minute. Help yourself to that bag. There's cigarettes, chocolate and a few other things in there."

Romain beamed at the mention of chocolate; rationing was difficult for everyone but especially for those with a sweet tooth.

She climbed the stairs carefully, the creaking floorboards protesting under her weight. Reaching the room she'd chosen, she pushed the warped door as closed as it would go before she opened the package. Inside was a beautiful, embroidered nightdress more suitable for a honeymoon than nights on the run. She held it close, her tears threatening to run over at the kindness of the gesture. A note fell out.

Tu as un coeur de lion.

It wasn't signed, but Adèle could see her friend writing it. She kissed the note, wishing for the day when this was all over and she could see Madame Abreo again. To visit her now would place her in danger.

* * *

The squeaky hinge of the stove reminded her of her visitors. Soon some men from the next town would visit too. She hid her present deep in her bag and, drying her eyes, came back downstairs to see Luc carrying in a load of firewood while Romain kicked the stove. "It won't light."

"You need to treat it kindly." She sent him a teasing look as she took over. They caught up on each other's news.

"What about Caesar? Have you seen him?"

Romain and Luc exchanged a glance at her question, their eyes bright with curiosity. She ignored them and waited.

"Last we knew, he was visiting Clermont-Ferrand, recruiting more men. Does he know you are back?"

"No, Luc, and it's best it stays that way. I don't think he'd approve."

* * *

Adèle looked up from the kitchen table where she'd laid out their supplies. "Are you ready?"

Romain nodded, his lips twitching nervously.

"You won't blow us up, don't worry." Despite her confident words, she said a quick prayer. Explosives were volatile by their very nature, and it had been a while since her training.

Romain followed her instructions, and soon they had seven sixteen-pound plastic charges ready. "I wanted to be an engineer, you know, before the war." Romain picked up one of the charges. "I thought I would be designing things not blowing them up."

"Don't feel sorry for the factory. They make propellers for Heinkels and Focke-Wulf aircraft. They should have been careful about putting money above French lives."

She felt Romain glancing at her from under his eyelashes. "What?"

"You've changed so much since that first day I met you."

She brushed her hair back, a good reminder they needed to wash their hands carefully. "In a good way?"

He shrugged.

"Romain?"

"Maybe. You're tougher now. You don't seem to think about the Frenchmen who could die either in the factory or in the reprisals after."

She brushed aside the crushing impact of his comment, was that what he thought of her? "They don't call me the White Witch for nothing, do they?" She forced herself to turn it into a joke. The thought of any more innocents dying because of her actions churned her stomach. But what could she do? They had to win the war. "Luc is over at the factory using his considerable charm. The only men who will die tonight will be the Germans and anyone who decides to stick to their side." She turned back to focus on the job. "You'd better take a bath and try to get rid of the smell before you head back to your camp."

"I wish you would let me stay with you. Go on the mission."

Luc hadn't returned, but she'd ordered Romain to go back to his old camp to protect his cover. The network couldn't afford to lose both.

"Thank you for your loyalty, but Luc needs you now. You can teach him how to use the explosives London sends. The circuit in the next village is sending four of their most trusted men; that's all we need for this job." She watched from the door of the farmhouse as he cycled off. This was a dangerous mission, and she couldn't bear to put either of them at risk.

FORTY-SEVEN

The four men sent by the other group were all eager and ready to play their part. One of them had copied the foreman's keys and knew the factory inside and out.

She showed them how to blacken their faces before she handed out the explosives. "We need to be in and out as fast as possible. I don't want to have to go back in for any of you."

The men nodded, holding the explosives rather gingerly. She pushed down her reservations and headed out. A local garage owner had lent them a Citroën, just like the Gestapo liked to drive. The irony!

They parked close to the factory and walked the rest of the way, not wanting to alert anyone to their presence. The streets were deserted. Adèle waited, Sten gun at the ready, while one of her men opened the factory door with the foreman's keys. There appeared to be no security.

She pointed out the two machines and two furnaces they needed to destroy. They placed the explosives and ran, tossing the last one just behind the door they'd used. The man had the presence of mind to lock it before they left.

"That was a good idea. Hopefully, the Germans will think

something went wrong inside rather than blame the locals for sabotage."

He nodded as they got into the car and drove back to an abandoned farmhouse. From there, one man would drive the car back to the garage. The other three would disappear into the surrounding countryside.

They heard the boom in the distance just as the black car drove away. She shook the other men's hands before they melted into the darkness of the countryside. She'd sleep at the farmhouse before moving on to meet up with Luc.

* * *

The next morning, Adèle walked outside into the garden and stilled. There was something wrong. It was too quiet. Why weren't the birds singing? Or animals rustling in the undergrowth. Did they sense something. Her hand cradling her Sten, crouching low, Adèle studied the view as she moved to the shelter of the largest tree in the garden. She'd learned to listen to her gut, and it was screaming. There was something wrong, but she couldn't put her finger on it. Was it too quiet?

She spotted someone crawling on his belly towards the farm. Laurence!

"What are you doing here?" It didn't make sense; the boy should be with Luc's group near Tulle.

"We've got trouble." He pulled at her arm and pointed in the direction he had come. She stared into the trees, trying to see what he had seen. He pulled her down closer to the ground, almost rolling on top of her.

He whispered into her ear. "Milice."

She burrowed further down, her eyes straining now she knew what to look for, her hand on her Sten. The Germans were one thing, but the Milice were something different. They were locals and would know the area better than she did. How many were there? Had they arrested the men from last night?

"Laurence, get out and warn the others."

"No. Luc told me to stay in the nearest town to keep an eye on things. He had a bad feeling. He said I was to stay nearby."

"I'm in charge, not Luc. Leave now. That's an order."

Laurence stared at her with a mutinous expression on his face.

She kicked at his leg. "Go. I can handle it. I'll cover you."

He gave her one last look before racing away, running low through the long grass and trees to the west of the house, ducking down as he ran to avoid detection. A few shots rang out from the trees, but she fired back to give him cover.

She held still, watching the trees, waiting for someone to show himself.

She tried to remember what she had studied of the local territory. The woods became denser farther to the west. Should she head that way or go east? The eastern route offered less shelter, but she had more contacts there. As she wavered, a shot pinged off a branch just above her hairline.

"You are surrounded! Come out with your hands up."

She responded to the order by firing off a shot in the direction of the voice. They already knew where she was, so she wasn't giving away her position. She smiled as a grunt told her the shot had found its target.

Another shot went wide, hissing as it sailed past her ear, but the next one hit her. Thankfully, it was her left arm, so she could still shoot. She grimaced but didn't make a sound. She fired again rapidly, in the direction where the shots had come from. But more shots came from her north, south and east. She was surrounded on three sides. The only way out was through the same field Laurence had used, and that would be suicide.

"Give yourself up. We will not kill you," the French voice said. "We admire your bravery."

Adèle's thoughts flickered to the pill she carried.

No, she wouldn't take that way out. They could shoot her, but she would try to escape. She stood up, raining fire on them as she ran. Her actions seemed to take them by surprise.

"Shoot to injure. I want her alive!" The orders came through loud and clear. Adèle didn't stop to wonder why; she concentrated all her efforts on getting away.

Running out of breath, her lungs screamed, but she kept going although at a slower pace. They were gaining ground; she turned to fire, but her gun clicked. Out of ammunition. She had to outrun them, but how?

"Down, Claire!" a voice she recognised screamed. She hit the ground fast, just in time to avoid a hail of bullets. The groans and shouts behind her told her that her pursuers had been hit. She stayed flat on her face until the firing eased off a little.

"Laurence, what on earth—"

"Come on. You don't have time to lecture."

The boy half-dragged, half-carried Adèle to a waiting car and bundled her into it. The car took off, hitting every bump on the road as her arm screamed in pain. Behind her, the battle in the forest continued. She looked around for Laurence, but he was nowhere to be seen.

She hoped the boy would make it. That was her last conscious thought.

The pain in her arm woke her. She looked around and found she was lying on a makeshift bed in the middle of a camp, surrounded by the trees of a forest.

"At last, Sleeping Beauty is awake."

"Luc? What are you doing here?" Adèle looked at her second-in-command. "I thought you went back to Lyon."

"Charming. Doesn't sound like you missed me," he teased before turning serious. "I should have known not to trust you with men you didn't know."

"It couldn't be one of them; they were with me in the factory."

"Someone talked."

"It might have been a coincidence."

"It wasn't. Laurence heard them talking about you. At least he thought it was you."

"Where is he?" Adèle tried to still her racing heart. She didn't want to be told the boy was dead.

"He's like a cat – nine lives and more. He brought the men to where the English dumped the arms, and he's back in the village. He's safe."

"He is until I catch up with him. He disobeyed a direct order."

"Be thankful he did. The house, the arms would have fallen into the hands of the Milice, and you wouldn't be here. We drove you back to Maurice's group. He's patched you up best he can."

Hope sprang into her chest.

"Maurice. Is my sister with him?" Adèle sat up straighter, ignoring the pain in her arm.

Luc wouldn't meet her eyes. Her stomach roiled.

"Tell me, Luc."

"She's not here."

"Where is she, then?" Adèle looked from Luc to Maurice, who was walking over to join them. She noted that he wouldn't meet her gaze either. "Tell me."

"She was arrested some time back," Maurice answered.

Adèle's stomach sank. "Arrested? When? What are you keeping from me?"

"Claire, calm down. I only recently learned of her arrest."

Adèle stood up, tossing the blanket aside. "I swear, if you don't tell me, I will shoot you."

Maurice didn't look up from the ground. "They thought she was you. She was seen being shoved into a van; Denis was there too. His body was dumped outside Gestapo headquarters a few days later. He'd been shot."

"And..." Adèle couldn't continue.

"She was kept for a while. The Gestapo..."

Adèle had to turn quickly to empty the contents of her stomach. Her darling sister had been in the hands of those monsters! And it was all her fault. They had mistaken Sophie for her.

She had to know. "Is she dead?"

"We don't know. She was put on the trains."

Adèle's head came up hard. "Trains?"

"We think she convinced the Gestapo they had the wrong woman. A lady who shared her cell spoke of her terrible injuries, but said they left her alone after that. She says she helped nurse her back to health."

Adèle moved to gather her things, her first instinct to get to Sophie.

"Drancy? Was she sent there?"

"Nobody knows – or if they do, they aren't telling." Maurice looked away, but not before she saw the expression in his eyes. He loved Sophie.

Adèle couldn't believe he wasn't pursuing the lead. "This woman who helped her – can I speak to her?"

"There is no point. She was released over a month ago." Luc put his hand on her arm and turned her to face him. "She can't tell you anything."

She hated seeing the pity in his eyes. She didn't want to acknowledge what he wasn't saying: Sophie was probably dead.

"She can tell me who betrayed my sister." Adèle gripped the knife by her waist. "They will pay."

"We don't have time for that now." Luc held her stare, his brown eyes boring into hers, begging her to listen to him. "The invasion is on. Our people need us. Personal vendettas will have to wait."

"Easy for you to say – this is not your sister." As soon as she said the words, she wished she could swallow them. Luc's family had been sent to Drancy, for onward deportation, early in the war.

His hands grabbed his own hair. "Listen to yourself. You think you are the only one whose family has fallen victim to the Gestapo? Look around you. Tell me who hasn't!"

Shame engulfed her. What Luc said was true. Each member of their troop had their own horror story to share, yet they were all focused on the job in hand. Unlike her.

She filed away the news about Sophie to deal with when the time was right. But whoever had betrayed her sibling would pay. That much she promised.

"What now?" she asked before she saw the men exchanging glances. "What? You are keeping something else from me. Tell me."

Luc shrugged his shoulders. "I am as much in the dark as you are. Maurice, tell us?"

Both looked to Maurice. Adèle couldn't read the expression in his eyes – was it loathing, disbelief, shock? She leaned away from him, not wanting to know what he had to say.

"We can't. We have to show you."

Foreboding swallowed her. Gritting her teeth, she let Luc tie her wounded arm in a sling; then, picking up her Sten with her good hand, she followed her men.

They were too silent. What on earth had happened now?

FORTY-EIGHT

10 JUNE 1944

The men's silence was disconcerting, but soon Adèle realised there were no other sounds either.

"It's Saturday, market day. Where is everyone?" Luc's question went unanswered.

The local people should be heading towards Tulle to buy whatever provisions they could find. Even in these times, people liked to sit at the cafés, drinking a tisane of peppermint or lemon balm while they caught up on each other's news.

Sweat trickled down her back, her stomach caught up in knots. Determined to fight the fear of what might lie ahead, she walked faster.

Luc caught her arm. "Let me go ahead."

Even in the middle of war, he was still behaving like the gentleman he had been raised to be. She knew he was trying to protect her, but these were her men. Some came from this town and the surrounding area.

"I must take responsib—"

But her words failed as they reached the main street. Although she could see clearly, she refused to believe what her eyes were telling her.

"Mon Dieu."

Luc's whispered prayer confirmed that the horrific scene was real. A body hung from every lamppost, and from some of the balconies. Every man – some only boys – had his hands tied behind his back. Their bodies swayed in the gentle breeze.

Adèle noticed a curtain twitching here and there, but the townspeople remained behind their shuttered doors. No one ventured out to greet them – too broken by the events of the previous few days.

She stopped walking. The men who had been following her caught up, their silence saying everything she couldn't put into words. Bile rose in her throat, and her stomach roiled, but she swallowed hard. She would not disrespect these victims further. Now was not a time for weakness.

A door banged somewhere behind her, and it was as if the people of Tulle took it as a signal to pour out onto the street. Grief-stricken women keened at the bases of the lampposts, their white faces traumatised. The silence of the town was broken by animal-like sounds of pain. The tears running down Adèle's face were mirrored by those of her men.

Adèle stared at the women. There were some elderly men shuffling around and some young children, but there were no able-bodied men left in Tulle.

She spotted ladders lying on the ground near the corpses – probably the same ones used by the Germans to commit these murders.

"Luc, get everyone into teams. We need to cut these bodies down and see to it they each have a Christian burial. Maurice, can you send someone for a priest? Maybe the next town?"

Maurice nodded grimly before turning to carry out her request. He didn't remind her he was in charge, not her.

Gently and with great respect, the men and boys of Tulle were released and laid to rest on the ground in front of the *mairie*. Adèle's maquisards stood waiting to carry the heavy bodies as the ropes were cut. The women brought sheets and blankets and gently wrapped their husbands, sons, and brothers, readying them for their final journey.

About two hours later, Maurice's group returned with the priest, and together they buried the victims. Adèle counted ninety-nine graves.

"There would have been more, but they ran out of lamp-posts." An old woman told her. "They took the rest away. A hundred and forty-eight men, all deported."

"You did this. You and your FFI." Another woman came at Adèle, hitting her across the face. "Where were you when they took my Noël and Constant? He was only sixteen last week! Yet they killed him, my poor boy..." The woman collapsed against Adèle, who held her tightly, and their tears mingled until an older woman came forward to lead the grief-stricken mother away.

As she stared at the graves, an old man shuffled nearer, dragging one leg behind him. Had his old injury saved him?

"It is time for you to leave."

"I am so sorry..."

He held up a hand to stop her apology. "The Boches did this. No one else. Finish this war. Make sure it is the end this time. They told us in '18 that it would never happen again. It is your job to keep that promise."

Adèle nodded, not knowing what to say. She gestured to the others, and together they walked out of the small town without a backwards glance.

* * *

"What now?" Romain lit up a cigarette but ground it out almost immediately, putting a hand to his mouth.

"We regroup and get the swine who did this." Adèle forced

the tears back as they sat around the campfire. No one had any appetite.

"But—"

A runner came in, distracting them. Romain and Adèle watched as the men crowded around the new arrival. They saw Luc howl with grief – raw pain unbearable to witness – and some of the other men began to break down too.

Adèle rushed forward but soon wished she hadn't. The runner told them the 2nd SS Panzer Division Das Reich, not happy with the cruelties inflicted on Tulle, had attacked Oradour-sur-Glane. In that town, they'd tried to make sure they had left no witnesses by killing everyone – men, women, and children. Adèle ran to the closest bush and emptied the contents of her stomach, not bothering to hide her tears. Luc's fiancée lived there.

She wiped her mouth before she walked over to him. "Go, take some men with you. She may have got away."

"But ... after what I said about your sister." Despite his words, his eyes strained on the distance.

"Go, Luc. Take Romain with you. Come back when you can. Be careful." She kissed his cheek, his tears mixing with hers.

FORTY-NINE

The group split up, some heading to Oradour, others heading to their own villages. They'd evacuate those they could, sending them into the hills or forests until the threat had passed. Adèle, Laurence, and the rest of her team made their way north.

They broke the march near to the Trochet family farm, to have a rest and eat something. Laurence and Adèle stood together apart from the rest of the group. Feeling dizzy and warm, Adèle stripped off her jacket, only to put it on again a few minutes later as she was shivering.

"Do you think what we do is worth it?" Laurence murmured.

"You mean with the reprisals?"

"Yes. I heard the men talking about Tulle."

Adèle threw the rest of her bread to the watching birds. She hated wasting food, but her stomach churned.

"What happened there was murder. Not war. The people who did it will be punished. It is not our fault."

"But if the resistance hadn't killed forty Germans, those men would still be alive." Laurence took a deep breath. "My uncle and his sons lived in Tulle."

Adèle noted his use of the past tense. She knew she had to be careful.

"What happened was an atrocity. Many will blame the resistance for bringing the Germans to Tulle. But the Nazis have murdered hundreds of thousands of people. They must be stopped. This is the only way."

"But what of the children in Oradour-sur-Glane? They will never get to grow up, have families, live in freedom."

"No, they won't. It was the same group of men who committed that atrocity too. The massacres at Tulle, Oradour-sur-Glane, and elsewhere will be avenged, and those men prosecuted if the war ends before they die in battle. Now, let's get moving. We have a job to do. The sooner we do it, the sooner this war ends."

"Claire?"

"Yes?"

"Thank you for not treating me like a child."

"You are a man, Laurence. Age is only a number."

Adèle wanted the war to be over now. But she kept that opinion to herself. She cycled back alone, sending Laurence on with a message to yet another group. Her eyes glazed over a few times as she wobbled precariously on the bike. She couldn't wait to get to bed.

* * *

The Trochets greeted her return like the prodigal son, all smiles. But the smiles dropped when Madame Trochet saw that she was injured. She fussed around Adèle, telling her of the home remedies she would use to heal her arm.

Adèle asked the couple to sit down, then told them the news of Tulle and Oradour-sur-Glane. Madame Trochet cried, and even crusty old monsieur's voice had a gruffer edge than usual.

"You will make them pay. You and the rest of our people. They will not be forgotten."

Adèle nodded as she made the promise. She wasn't feeling very well; the wound in her arm was aching, the skin all inflamed.

"I think I should go to bed. I feel rather tired." She stood up and promptly lost consciousness.

* * *

"She's coming around. Get the doctor." The smell of garlic and onions made her nauseous. When she opened her eyes, she couldn't believe who was in front of her. His hair was greying at the edges, a little too long on the sides, and the lines around his eyes were etched into place. He'd lost too much weight, it didn't suit him, but his eyes were still the same.

"Georges! Am I dead? How did you get here?"

"That's charming. I save your life, and you wish me dead?" He chuckled as he pulled her closer. Although he stank, she snuggled into him, relieved to know he was alive.

"Shush now. Rest. The doctor will be back in a few minutes. You have an infection. The doctor tried to cut out a bullet, and you have lost a lot of blood, chérie."

He had called her '*chérie*'. It made her ridiculously happy.

Closing her eyes, she let herself fall back into the deep blackness.

* * *

She came in and out of consciousness over the next few days, her thirst raging as she was unable to keep anything down. She had been moved from the Trochets' farm to protect them. It wasn't safe for the doctor to come and visit her at the farm; too many people knew the Trochets and would call at the farm to check on them.

Georges dealt with all her intimate needs – something that would have been too embarrassing for her to bear, but now she didn't care.

She was aware of being moved again and knew that they were travelling; the cart swung back and forth like the ship that had once carried her across the English Channel. She heard the men discussing her, but she couldn't focus on what they were saying. All she wanted to do was sleep.

When she next woke, they had arrived somewhere, and she was in Georges's arms.

"Georges, where are we?"

"Shush. We are at the nuns' hospital." Then he turned to the doctor. "Dr René, our capitaine, needs your help."

"Get her onto the bed."

"See to the others first, Doc; I am fine. It is a graze."

"I will be the judge of that. You might be the boss out there, but this is my kingdom, my rules."

Adèle attempted a half-salute, but it hurt too much. She lay back and let him assess her.

Madame's herbal remedy had helped remove the poison from the wound, but he told her he thought there might be fragments of the bullet left in her arm. He would have to operate.

"Georges, don't leave me." She begged, not caring how fragile she sounded. She didn't want to lose him.

"I won't."

FIFTY

She shifted in the bed and opened her eyes. Georges was asleep in the chair by her bedside, his head on the bed by her hand. He seemed to have aged twenty years in the eight months since she had seen him. She reached out and traced the wrinkles on his face, her fingers working gently over a new scar just under his eye.

"You're awake," he said, smiling as he opened his eyes.

"Where are we?" She tried to sit up, but the world spun violently, so she soon gave up on that idea.

"Near Meymac. How are you feeling?" Tenderly touching his hand to her forehead, he leaned in closer. "Your fever has broken. About time. You gave me a fright."

"I did?" She raised an eyebrow as she looked at him.

He gave her a stern look. "Adèle, now is not the time for flirting. I'm serious. Doc had a hell of a time getting that bullet out. I don't know how many times we thought you were gone."

"Only the good die young, Georges."

That wasn't true, everyone died in war.

He didn't respond, just kept staring at her. Uncomfortable with what she thought she might see, she asked, "Georges, your mother? Is she..." She stopped as the pain filled his eyes. "I'm so sorry."

"She didn't suffer; for that, at least, I am glad. She shot two before they got her."

"She had a gun?" Adèle couldn't hide her surprise. The Germans had insisted all weapons be confiscated, but she knew people had buried theirs. Obviously, Georges's mother had been prepared.

"It was my father's. Left over from the war. I didn't even know she knew how to shoot."

She held out her hand to him in response to his pain-filled voice. He glanced at her, his eyes wet but no tears on his cheeks. Despite the pain it cost her, she reached up to kiss his cheek.

"I am sorry. She was so good to me."

"She liked you. Said you grew on her."

Despite her wound and her sadness at the news, Adèle gave him a self-depreciating smile. "Like mould."

They lapsed into silence for a few moments, just staring at each other.

"How have you been? Before you got shot, I mean."

"Fine." What else could she say? He didn't really want to know the answer. How would he react if he learned she was responsible for the deaths of hundreds of men? They were Germans, of course, but they were still human beings. At least for the most part.

* * *

Several days passed by before the doctor allowed her to get up and move around. She was transferred out of the private room into the maternity ward, the doctor deciding that would be safer for everyone.

She pushed the bed covers aside. "I need to get back to my men."

"You need to rest. The—" The rest of the doctor's sentence was cut off by the sound of explosions. Almost simultaneously, they heard hammering on the outer doors.

Adèle slid her weapon from under the pillow, thankful she had kept it concealed in her clothes and refused to part with it. She wasn't going to be taken alive.

A young nun came rushing onto the ward. "Dr René, gather all the men here. The Waffen SS are in the town. They are looking for maquisards." The nun's words spilled out but she remained calm.

"There is no way to get the injured out. Evacuate as many as you can." Adèle added, "I will stay."

"It is not possible to evacuate anyone, mademoiselle." The nun crossed herself. "The town has been surrounded." The nun turned to leave.

They were caught like mice in a trap. Was this the way her war would end? She looked at the patients in the beds around her, women who had recently had their babies. Would the Nazis kill them where they lay?

"Wait."

The nun turned at her command.

"The boys who alerted you, can you send them to me, please?"

The nun stared at her for a second, possibly considering the consequences of her Mother Superior finding men in a female ward. But then she nodded.

The boy was younger than Adèle had expected.

"There's about three hundred, armed to the teeth. They jumped out of the trucks, shouting 'Où sont les maquisards? Où sont les terroristes?'" The boy's eyes gleamed with excitement.

"Where are the maquisards?"

"In the forests. I will join them."

Adèle stared at the boy. Was he walking into danger or away from it? She couldn't tell, not from her hospital bed. "Tell them to stay in the forest and wait for reinforcements."

"They will not take orders from a woman!"

The boy sneered, earning him a clip around the ear from Dr René, who had just come back into the room.

"Tell them I told them to wait. And watch your tone when talking to a lady."

The boy gave him a dirty, resentful look before rushing out of the ward. Adèle hoped he would get away. For all his chauvinistic tendencies, he had spirit.

"Mon Dieu."

The doctor prayed as he glanced out the window. Adèle's eyes filled as she stared out of it too. She'd blame it on the smoke filling the air. How many innocents would die at the hands of the SS tonight or in the flames? The SS had set the town alight; the convent beside them hadn't been spared either.

Her chances of evading the SS were minimal, but she couldn't stay here. "They may be looking for me. I should leave."

"Get back into bed, Claire, quickly. Hold still." Grabbing a roll of bandages, Dr René wrapped it around her face, loosely enough she could breathe but tight enough to fool a casual observer. "You hit your head falling out of a barn. You lost your baby, and you haven't regained consciousness." He left little gaps at her eyes, so she could still see.

She lay back, despite every instinct telling her to fight. She heard the marching boots on the cobblestones as they made their way into the hospital. She prayed over and over that the nuns and other patients would not pay a high price.

"Where are the terrorists? We know you are sheltering them." The German officer had a good command of French, his accent better than most.

She heard the Mother Superior speak softly, denying that

the hospital was used for any purpose other than to nurse sick people.

The door to their ward opened, and Sister Marguerite grabbed a newborn baby. Adèle peered through the gap in the bandage, ready to react if she needed to. She would surrender rather than let these brave people die. She saw the nurse pinch the baby's little leg, and the child wailed on cue. The German officer took a step back.

"Maternity? My apologies. Please excuse me."

Adèle couldn't believe it. The monsters who had killed women and children respected the fact it was a maternity unit. She lay there, trying not to breathe, as they left the hospital miraculously intact.

"Claire, you can open your eyes now. They've gone." Dr René removed the unnecessary bandages.

She helped him as best she could. "We'd better get out of here. They may come back."

Dr René didn't answer but continued working.

"I wonder why they didn't burn the hospital? They burned the convent," she said, wondering if she would ever understand the mindset of the SS forces.

"Considering what I have seen men do to other men, I have given up wondering. Just be grateful."

Adèle couldn't be anything else.

* * *

Dr René arranged a car and driver to collect her. He refused to leave the hospital. She kissed him goodbye. "Thank you for saving my life."

He waved, and they were off. She must have fallen asleep as, two hours later, she woke due to the bumpy trip over old tracks. She saw the men with rifles standing guard as the car came to a standstill. The driver got out and held the door open for her. The lookouts whistled, and two men came running.

"About time you showed up. Were you having too much fun?" Luc teased, hugging her. He released her with an apology as she flinched.

Romain held out his hand to shake hers. "We were sure you were done for when we heard they had entered the hospital."

She blew the hair from her eyes. "It was a little close even by our standards. The nuns saved our lives – the nuns and a little boy who is only a day old. The youngest hero of the resistance."

Luc smiled. "Speaking of young heroes, we have a boy here who seems to think women should be at home minding the children. We thought you might like to speak to him."

Adèle knew he was teasing her, but she didn't want to talk to the boy. He already had an idealised view of what the maquisards did. The last thing she wanted was another child caught up in their war against the Germans.

She walked with them towards the camp, the thirty-odd men cheering her with their hands in the air but not using their voices. She waved back in acknowledgement, tears of pride stinging her eyes. They were so much more security-conscious now. Firing rifles and loud cheers would have alerted everyone to their position. They also didn't have any supplies to waste.

She sat with the men for a meagre meal of rice mixed with some sort of meat. She didn't want to identify what it was. To a man, they welcomed her back.

She pleaded tiredness and headed for the tent they had given to her. She wished Georges was here, but he had gone to lead another attack. Her dressings remained intact, but she missed the hospital bed as she curled up on the straw mattress and tried to sleep.

FIFTY-ONE

DRANCY

As fate would have it, the doctor was sent on the transport before Sophie was, so she took over many of his duties. There was little she could do for the inmates, given the lack of medical supplies. All they had was whatever people had carried with them into the camp and were prepared to give to those in need. Some aspirin, a couple of bottles of iodine and the odd crutch or two, the latter being left behind when their owners were transported east.

"How did they manage when there were over seven thousand people living here? It's overcrowded already, and there are only about two thousand prisoners left now."

Esmée looked up from the pile of rags she was sorting, trying to find some clean enough to use as slings for broken arms or shoulders. "Someone said they used to send people into Paris to live in smaller camps. They weren't like this; they were like warehouses where they had to sort out Jewish clothes, furniture, bed linen, or anything that could be sent to Germany. They worked them in twenty-four-hour shifts, and those who couldn't keep up got transported. But then I guess they ran out of stolen stuff as they sent them back here. Or maybe it was the bombings."

Esmée helped her with the tasks that required two hands, such as bandaging a wound. The guards seemed to be as frustrated at being locked up as the inmates and regularly took their anger out on the prisoners, using their rifle butts or whips.

The younger woman began to speculate about their chances of avoiding the transport altogether. "They say the Allies will be here any day, Nicole. They have landed in France. They will free us all."

Sophie didn't respond.

Everyone at the camp called her by her false name. For whatever reason, the Germans hadn't registered her as Sophie Bélanger but as Nicole Samson. Sophie wondered again about her sister's reputation. Perhaps the Gestapo agent hadn't wanted to admit to his superiors that he'd held the sister of the White Witch in custody but still couldn't trap the Witch. Whatever the reason, she thought it was best not to argue the point.

Esmée insisted, "It's true. The Allies landed at the beginning of June. Pierre heard from a contact on the outside. We will be free."

Sophie couldn't get excited like Esmée. Her hopes had been dashed too many times before. The arrival of the Allied forces didn't seem to bother the Germans. They were still shipping people East.

The sound of buses arriving at the camp broke the monotony. Sophie wanted to scream as she watched the over two hundred children disembarking from the buses. She rushed forward to help.

Whispering, she asked one of the adults alighting from the bus, "Where have you come from?"

"The SS emptied the Jewish orphanages in Paris. We thought the children were safe; the Allies are almost at Paris.

But these monsters arrived, and now..." The woman looked around. "Why are we here?"

The answer came all too soon. The camp was being emptied; all the children and the thirty adults who'd arrived with them were set for deportation. Along with over eight hundred remaining prisoners at Drancy, Sophie and Esmée among them.

Esmée was distraught and became suicidal, begging Sophie for help.

"I can't do that; don't ask me. There's still hope. Someone must live to tell the next generation our story. You have a duty to do that, Esmée. You will do an excellent job, too, just like you did helping all those children."

"How did you become so brave, Nicole?"

"Brave? I am not brave; I am terrified. But I refuse to let them see. Then they will have won."

* * *

Sophie repeated her own words over and over for the duration of the transport. Esmée had been pushed into another car. In the darkness, she could only see others by the whites of their eyes. The stench from the one overflowing pot that served as a latrine was making many people vomit.

These people weren't from prisons; they had come to Drancy via other camps. Some were immune to the feelings of their fellow sufferers, but most still looked out for one another, attempting to give whatever relief they could. Fathers and husbands encircled their families with emaciated arms to protect them. Some children appeared to be travelling alone – Thomas, a small child of about four with chocolate-brown eyes, struck at her heart. He reminded her of Maurice. Would their child, if they were lucky enough to have one, look like this boy? The thought made her long to survive, long for the future. She held Thomas as he cried, the tears streaking a white path down his grubby face. He'd been separated from his family; his mother and siblings were on the train but not in this car. She held his hand, promising him she would stay with him. The continuous stopping and starting of the train, the heat, the despair, and the blackness – it all threatened to overpower her, never mind a small child.

Finally, the train screeched to a stop. And then the nightmare truly began.

The noise was deafening as the doors slid open. The light hurt her eyes, but she saw barking dogs straining on their leashes, teeth bared to show bright pink gums.

SS men with whips ordered the prisoners out of the cars. They stumbled, some falling to the ground. She gripped Thomas's hand tightly as they climbed out into the dirt.

What was this place? At first, she thought it was snowing, but it was ash that fell, covering their clothes. In the background, she spotted enormous plumes of black smoke coming from chimneys. Was it a factory? Were they to work for the German war effort?

Sophie gazed at the pile of suitcases being sorted by gaunt prisoners dressed in striped suits, small caps covering their shaved heads.

"Let the child go; save yourself." One scarecrow mumbled as he passed to move a case. She didn't believe she'd heard him correctly. Her mind must be playing tricks on her.

Thomas pulled her hand as they moved to join the queue. The selection split families, with aged parents – or were they grandparents? – being sent to the right, along with children and pregnant mothers. Sophie held Thomas's hand tightly, asking him if he could see his mother. He shook his hand, his eyes wide as he took in his surroundings.

Someone stumbled, knocking into Sophie. She fell forward, losing her grip on Thomas. The crowd carried her along, trying to escape the blows of whips as the SS tried to get the group back into formation. Frantically she tried to turn and find Thomas, but it was no use. He was gone.

They were forced into lines. Sophie could see a man in a white coat up ahead, telling people to go left or right.

"Make yourself look less attractive, or you will be sent to the brothel," a male worker in a bedraggled, striped uniform murmured as he helped people into the lines.

"Go to the left." His eyes shifted from left to right before he whispered. "Stay away from the hospital unless you want to end up in cahoots with the devil himself." He stood back before screaming at her loudly to move along.

She spotted Esmée up ahead in the queue; with a determined effort, she reached her friend. They held each other tightly as they were sent to the left.

FIFTY-TWO

Her group was herded into a column and marched away. She looked around for Thomas, but there were no children with them. Maybe he would find his mother – in the meantime, someone was bound to look after him. Who could resist those chocolate-brown eyes?

Glaring white lights lit up the barbed wire surrounding the camp; the wire seemed to be draped in places with pieces of fabric. Sophie glanced over once, but squeezed her eyes shut as she realised she was looking at hapless victims who had made an attempt at escape.

The constant yelling, and the chaos of the new arrivals being beaten by sticks by other prisoners, created panic and confusion. What manner of place was this?

She glanced up to read the sign above her head. *Arbeit Macht Frei*: Work will make you free. What kind of work would she be assigned to do?

She didn't have time to consider that. The column moved forward into a wooden building.

"Undress, undress, *schnell*, *schnell*."

"This is it. The showers." Esmée's eyes filled with terror.

"But they may have water."

"And I might be a princess. You heard the stories. If you believe in God, you had best get praying now."

Sophie didn't want to believe what she was hearing. She concentrated on taking off her clothes as quickly as possible. Finally, she stood naked in front of a desk. The inmate sitting behind it didn't look up.

"Name? Where are you from? Sign here."

Shaking, she scrawled her name; then it was on to the next queue. They were to be shaved. Three men, one for each underarm and the other...

Sophie closed her eyes. It was pointless to protest. She forced herself to remember better days back in the Paris apartment with her siblings.

Her long hair was the last to go. She stared at the white-blonde threads on the floor, feeling lucky that at least the man shaving her seemed to be gentle, if the number of nicks on the other women's heads were anything to go by.

Then they were ready for the showers. She held Esmée's hand as they walked in.

"Did you see Maria from the camp?" Esmée asked. "She was with the children."

"Yes, brave girl. They told her to leave the children, but she wouldn't. She insisted on going with them. Said she was all they had."

Sophie wanted to believe the children had been taken somewhere safe, somewhere all the older women, mothers and babies had been routed to. She closed her eyes, praying silently as they waited. Gradually, the muted whispers stopped as everyone stared at the shower heads. Then it started. Freezing cold water dripped down on them.

It wasn't gas. They were saved.

They exited the room, dripping wet. The SS were still present, but this time they were women, dressed in riding boots and carrying whips. Sophie shuddered as the whip came down across Esmée's bare back. She grabbed her friend's arm to keep her from sliding to the floor.

The SS barked orders to get dressed. Sophie rubbed her skin, trying to get the circulation going again. They were each given a shapeless brown dress to wear.

"Not quite the latest fashion." Sophie joked trying desperately to be cheerful.

An SS officer screamed, "Silence."

The women stood huddled in silence as the last of the prisoners dressed hurriedly.

Once again, they formed a queue, and were moved to another wooden building. Here they had numbers tattooed into the outer side of their left forearm. Sophie shuddered and not just at the pain. Cattle were branded to show ownership.

They were given consecutive numbers, Sophie's one number higher than Esmée's. As she stared at the blue number, she couldn't help but wonder why the Nazis felt the need to mark them like this. It seemed like a lot of time and effort to process people in such a way.

"It's a good sign, yes?" Esmée said as Sophie continued to stare at her arm. "They cannot mean to kill us after going to all this trouble."

Sophie hoped her friend was right.

FIFTY-THREE

Their joy was short-lived as they were escorted into their new homes. Their group was to be held in quarantine – not a safety measure for the camp occupants, but a means of rooting out those who would be selected for gassing.

The guards screamed and abused them as they were put to work breaking stones or hauling the pails full of rocks to make cement for new barracks. The work was backbreaking, and when combined with a diet of thin soup and mouldy bread, the death rate soared during the first ten days they were there. Sophie watched helplessly as, one by one, the women she knew on the train fell victim to the Nazis until, of their original group, there were only four left, including Esmée.

Two weeks after they had arrived, a screaming female guard was beating a prisoner, who slid to protect herself from the onslaught. Sophie watched in horror, unable to move as events unfolded; Esmée didn't see the stricken prisoner until it was too late, and in a last-ditch effort not to hit the woman with her pail full of stones, she pivoted – right into the path of another worker's pickaxe. Esmée's scream as the axe hit her arm was enough to stop the guard in her tracks.

Sophie dropped what she was doing and raced towards her friend. "I am a doctor; let me through." She shoved past the other prisoners, falling to her knees beside her pale-faced friend.

She pushed Esmée's threadbare uniform aside to gauge the injury, but Esmée was too dirty. The mud mixed with the blood. Sophie's own hands would only contaminate it further.

"Get water. I have to clean it to see how bad it is."

"Get up now. Move away. There is nothing to be done," the guard yelled in her face.

"I am a doctor. I can help her. Please," Sophie begged in German. She stared at him and, taking a risk he may be a Christian, said, "I beg you in the name of our Lord, please let me help her. She is like my sister."

But the guard didn't have time to reply. There was a loud bang, and silence descended.

Shocked, Sophie looked down at her friend, now prostrate and bleeding into the ground. The red tinge at her head contrasted with the ash-covered earth.

"Get back to work, all of you – except you. Take her away."

Sophie stared at the female guard shouting at her. The woman had murdered Esmée, just like that. She couldn't move.

"I said move."

"Schnell, this way." The male guard had recovered and was pushing her roughly with his rifle. Sophie didn't know where she was going. She didn't care. Esmée was dead. Everyone else was gone.

FIFTY-FOUR

"You shouldn't have done that.' The soldier pushed her down the path, using his rifle to prod her in the back. "Now I have to shoot you too."

So shoot me. Why make me walk any farther?

She wanted to be with Esmée and the others. She didn't want to be alive when they were all dead. Briefly, she closed her eyes, her twin's face swimming in front of them, mingling with Maurice's. They were probably both dead, too.

"You are French. How did you learn to speak German so well? How do you know our prayers?" The guard's questions surprised her.

"My grandmother was German. She married my French grandfather. We were brought up Catholic."

His eyes widened, and he looked more troubled than before. "You are one of us – yet you are here? Wearing that?"

Sophie looked down at the yellow marking on her chest.

"Even Germans get things wrong sometimes." She wasn't sure where the words came from.

He looked around furtively, then prodded her in another direction. She didn't ask why. She didn't care any more.

He took her to Barrack 19, a small blockhouse near the camp hospital. "Do not question what I say and tell no one what happened."

He was helping her. But why?

"What's your name?"

He glared at her for a second before muttering, "Karl." Then he prodded her forward.

"Walloschek, French doctor for you." Karl pushed her inside.

"I didn't call for a doctor." The man in charge looked at Sophie, scrutinising her from head to foot.

"I don't question my orders." Karl's voice sounded gruff, different to how he'd spoken to her. He didn't like this man even if they wore the same uniform. "She's your problem now. Speaks German and says she's Catholic."

And then Karl was gone, leaving Sophie with the Walloschek.

"A German-speaking French Catholic in a Jewish uniform in Auschwitz? Wonders will never cease."

Sophie didn't respond. She didn't like the look in the other man's eyes. Perhaps it would have been kinder for the soldier to have shot her.

"You'd best get cleaned up. You can't go anywhere looking like that. Get food, too. You're too skinny. Won't last long."

And then Walloschek left, leaving Sophie standing there wondering what had just happened. She sat on the floor, not wanting to risk sitting on someone's bed.

Shaking, she put her head in her hands and wept. What type of world was this where someone as lovely as Esmée could be murdered just like that? Where children disappeared? The tears came, and she let them, no longer trying to be brave. She was terrified.

The time passed incredibly slowly. Nobody came looking

for her. She wasn't sure where she was supposed to be, so she assumed it would be safer to just wait.

* * *

She must have fallen asleep; the sound of low voices woke her.

"Look what the cat has dragged in. What are you doing here? You'll get us all into trouble." The inmate pushed at her with her foot.

"Leave her be."

Sophie looked up at the woman, who had spoken with a voice full of authority.

"Someone's looking after you. Come this way. Name's Gena."

"Nicole."

Gena took her to have a shower and get a fresh uniform – which, although not new, was in much better condition than the previous one. Then she gave her food, including, to Sophie's surprise, some cheese and a small, bruised apple. Gena spoke the whole time Sophie ate, explaining the rules and who to watch out for.

"Trust no one. Even the inmates. Some in here would sell you down the river for some apple peel."

"What of the guards? One brought me here; his name was Karl."

"Karl doesn't belong here. He is no more SS material than I am. His father is someone high up in Berlin – sent his son here to keep him safe, is my guess. Watch out for Otto Walloschek. He has a scar above his right eye. He's meaner than he looks. He works closely with Mengele."

Walloschek, the man she had encountered when the Catholic soldier had dropped her off. Shivering with revulsion, she asked Gena, "Why are you telling me all this?"

"I was a friend of Esmée's too. I heard what you did."

"Already? That was fast. How did you know Esmée?"

"It pays to keep your ear to the ground. Esmée and I were at school together, same class, in fact. Anyway, you've got a friend in me, Nicole. You've got to keep out of the way of the guard who killed Esmée. She's been in trouble before with her superiors for shooting workers."

Sophie couldn't follow what Gena was saying.

"I know it seems odd when they don't mind gassing us, but the commandant gets upset if his guards take matters into their own hands. Who pretends to understand how their minds work? Maybe he is worried we will revolt." Gena shrugged her shoulders.

Sophie couldn't believe her ears. A man in charge of murdering millions cared if one of his guards shot a prisoner. Weren't they trying to kill everyone anyway? Why did it matter how the prisoners died?

"The female guard doesn't like leaving witnesses to her loss of temper. The women you were working with were all sent to the gas this afternoon."

"All of them?"

"Yes." Gena was looking at her grimly. Sophie reached up to touch her cheek self-consciously. She couldn't believe the women she had arrived with were all dead. If given a chance to live, wouldn't they have fought for it? She was letting them down by giving up.

"You clean up too well, Nicole. You won't be left alone for five minutes if the guards spot you. Rub some dirt into your face. It would be better if you could get a couple of sores as well. Anything to make you look less attractive."

"What work will I be doing?" Sophie asked.

"You're a doctor, right?"

"Almost," Sophie explained.

"Tell no one that. Just nod. Believe me, you have more experience than most. Not that you'll need it – precious little can be done for our sick. The Nazis have two alternatives: get the workers back to work or ship them to the gas."

Horrified at Gena's emotionless tone, Sophie asked, "How long have you been here?"

"Since '42. I've been lucky. But nobody's luck lasts. Right, let's get back. The Blockführer will not wait around to count us."

"Thank you, Gena."

Gena didn't smile or acknowledge the thanks. Was that how she had lived so long, Sophie wondered, by closing down her emotions? She wished she knew how to do the same. Every thought was related to her family, her twin or Maurice unless she got distracted by those suffering in the camps.

FIFTY-FIVE

The next few weeks of the war were the worst to date. The Waffen SS clashed violently with every town they had the misfortune to enter. Luc told Adèle of how they had come to his chateau, determined to raze it to the ground with him inside, but on arrival had found it empty, Luc and his men having got wind of their intentions and escaped just in time.

Luc bragged, "I didn't leave a rat behind for those devils to torture."

She didn't challenge him, having seen the hurt in his eyes at the loss of his home.

The Germans had adopted a scorched-earth approach, leaving a trail of destruction in their wake. They were defeated, violent, rash, well-armed, and dangerous.

Adèle was desperate for supplies from London, but none were forthcoming. They were holed up in a makeshift camp in one of the many abandoned châteaux dotting the Corrèze region. There was little furniture, but the men appreciated being able to sleep on the floor of an old bedroom rather than in a tent or under the open skies.

She rubbed the back of her neck, trying to ease the kinks of frustration. "How do they expect us to fight them?"

The man she addressed didn't answer her but stared over her shoulder. She turned to look and couldn't believe what she saw: a man dressed in a British uniform, walking towards her as if walking down Oxford Street. Two of her men walked behind him, their guns trained on his back. Another small group hung back behind them.

She leaped to her feet.

"What on earth?"

"Jedburgh team, mademoiselle." His French was excellent, with only the slightest hint of an accent. "Pleased to make your acquaintance. I am looking for Alex."

Adèle stared from him to Luc and back again. "What?"

"London has sent me to take over this sector. I was due to meet with maquis Saint-Flour but they were decimated in a battle. We were lucky, a farmer saw us and hid us from the Germans. He sent us to you."

She walked slowly towards him, trying to calm her racing blood pressure, already high due to too many demands and not enough supplies. He towered above her, but she held his gaze. "Take over? Are you serious? An Englishman wearing a uniform, and you expect to walk in and take over my men after all this time? Who do you think you are?"

His eyes flickered around the group before coming back to her. "Your men?"

"Yes, my men. This is my group. Why don't you sod off and find your own? The Germans are that way." Adèle pointed in the general direction of the Boches before storming off.

"My apologies, mademoiselle, I seem to have got off to a bad start. I—"

One of the new arrivals stepped forward into the light. She recognised him as he mock saluted her in greeting before moving to kiss her on both cheeks. He whispered so only she heard, "So relieved to see you're still alive. My code name is Florent."

Only then did he address the Captain, "With all due respect, sir, you shouldn't mess with this lady. We trained together and I'm not ashamed to say she kicked my butt on several occasions." Florent held out his hand to Claire. "Come sit and tell me what I've missed. I've heard the Germans call you the White Witch. How many kills has it been?"

Despite her hatred of the enemy, the number of men she'd killed didn't sit well on her conscience. She wasn't one to boast about it.

"Never mind that. How are you, Florent? And Madame Robert?"

He reached into a pocket causing one of her men to point his pistol right at Florent's heart. Claire rushed to avert disaster. "I know him, from years ago. He's a true Frenchman."

Her protector blushed, muttered something and walked away. Florent retrieved a photograph of a beautiful young woman carrying a baby. "She's in Wales. They thought it would be best. My baby, she'll never recognize me."

"Of course, she will. She has your eyes." Adèle handed the photo back to him conscious of the Englishman's eyes on her. She didn't want him to think she was a sentimental woman.

She sat cross-legged on a wooden chair at the table, thankful that her scruffy trousers allowed her to take up such an unlady-like pose. She wasn't going to show any deference towards their guest. Luc held out the other chair for the new arrival.

"My name is Thomas Reynolds. You know Florent and that's our radio operator, Borkowski. He's Polish but speaks fluent French." The Pole nodded but remained silent. "We were sent here to ... provide whatever assistance you may need."

"We need weapons, ammunition, plastique, medications – take your pick."

"I meant military expertise, but I shall certainly mention your request to my staff."

Florent coughed. "Sir, I think we can skip the military expertise and just move straight to supplying Claire and her men with everything they need. This maquis is in good hands."

The captain shifted position. "My orders are to stop General Elster from reaching the Alps. He is in full retreat."

Romain spoke up before she could. "We know that. Why do you think we need the ammunition? I hate to tell you this, but we have been fighting this war out here for the last four years." He was clearly riled by the man's attitude.

Adèle couldn't blame him; he'd more or less taken the words out of her mouth.

"Our teams have been here in France for some time but undercover until the invasion."

Adèle looked at Reynolds with fresh eyes. She could see the strain on his face. He'd seen or done things he wouldn't brag about too.

"I assure you we are on the same side. I didn't mean to imply otherwise." The Englishman apologised. "Blame lack of sleep for my bad manners."

"Not to mention generations of the British imperial mentality." Romain, voiced more than one man's thoughts. Florent laughed, quickly turning it into a cough at a glare from his captain.

"Romain, enough. This man is our guest." Adèle turned away from Romain, her attention resting on the officer once more.

"Where are you staying?" she asked.

"I had rather hoped you would put us up. I feel somewhat conspicuous."

Everyone laughed, including Adèle. She gestured towards the tents. "It's not luxurious, but I am sure the boys will share. Now tell me what your orders are."

She listened as he explained what he knew of the current situation. She was gratified to hear that London was happy with their work to date.

"We could do more with proper supplies." That was the understatement of the century. In the week prior to D-Day, London had kept them well supplied but these days, they were running short. If he wanted their help, Reynolds would have to provide help in return.

"I have a contact for that. Leave it with me." Reynolds then quizzed her on how many men she had at her disposal, their training, and other related questions.

* * *

Later that evening, when Adèle joined her team at the fire where they were brewing something resembling coffee, she spotted the Englishman. He now looked like a regular Frenchman, wearing a short jacket, white shirt and dark trousers, clean-shaven apart from a small moustache and a beret, of all things, on his head.

"It suits you."

He grinned, looking down at his clothes for a second before looking her in the eyes. "Forgive me for my first impression. My mother was a suffragette; she would kill me for assuming the person in charge was a man."

"You wouldn't be the first nor the last."

* * *

The next day, Adèle proved herself worthy as his equal. The group hid in the trees, watching as the trucks came, one after the other. She hoped her team would hold their nerve; it was tempting to press the detonator, but they had to time it properly. They had hidden the plastic explosives by placing them in small holes and covering them with horse dung. Simple but effective.

Boom.

The third truck blew off the road, the men inside disappearing in the flames. Chaos ensued among the surviving Germans. Adèle gave the signal to attack. Only when there were no survivors in the German unit did they retreat. They couldn't afford to leave witnesses.

Reynolds cast her a glance of approval. "That was nice work."

"I don't enjoy killing wounded men, but we can't afford to take prisoners."

"I wouldn't lose any sleep. At least you are humane – you don't torture them first."

Adèle had seen evidence of the treatment these soldiers had dished out to injured maquisards. Still, deep down, she felt her actions were more suited to a Nazi than a Frenchwoman.

FIFTY-SIX

The maquisards attacked continuously, wave after wave, but still, the Germans came. Reynolds called in RAF bombers, which helped. But by the end of August, despite their best efforts, the enemy hadn't surrendered. The resistants were low on food, ammunition, guns, clothes, and sleep – but the need for revenge spurred them on.

Reynolds reappeared in the camp and headed to her side. "Heard the news?"

Bone-weary, Adèle could barely talk to him. "What now?"

"Elster refuses to surrender to the FFI." To be fair, his eyes didn't move from her face. Others might have looked away when delivering such news, but he treated her like he would a man.

"He can't choose who he surrenders to. We are the only outfit here." Exasperation was making her short.

"They want safe passage to the Americans."

Adèle swore under her breath. Safe passage – after what they had done? These men had murdered innocent men, women, and children, and now they expected her men to stand by and let them walk to the Americans? That would never happen.

"After Tulle, Oradour, and every other atrocity their compatriots committed..."

"I know."

"I don't think you do. I am not even sure any of my men would obey my command not to touch these Germans." Did she want them to? If she was honest, she wanted to track and kill every single man responsible for the horror imposed on the civilians.

Reynolds moved closer, lowering his voice. "We have orders. Keep our eye on the main prize."

"Even if that means complete betrayal of my people?" She couldn't believe he expected her to agree to this plan. He'd seen what those animals had done to the men under his command.

"What do they say? It's for the greater good." He ignored her muttered response. "You want Fritz out of France. This is not ideal, but ... Well, it may be all we get."

Adèle thought for a few minutes in silence, then whistled. Luc and Romain both arrived in seconds.

"Effective. Crude but effective," Reynolds observed.

"The Englishman has something to tell you." She felt guilty at the look he gave her, but she wasn't about to break this latest news to her men. Thinking about what she had seen in Oradour-sur-Glane and Tulle, she wasn't sure she could resist killing a member of the SS squad if she had the chance, never mind waving at them as they marched right past her.

She listened as he explained it. Her right-hand men reacted just as she predicted. Romain nearly had apoplexy, his face turning various shades of red. Luc was more reserved but still furious. In fact, she was more worried about his reaction, if she were honest.

"You will not agree with this?" Romain asked.

She looked at him.

"Claire" His composure faltered.

"I don't like it. I don't – but the Englishman has a point." She paused, trying to find the right words to explain why she was asking her men to leave even one occupying soldier alive never mind watch them walk out to surrender to the Americans, a foreign power. "We want our freedom. We want the war to be over. For our families to come back."

"You want that. This is because of your sister, isn't it? You will sell the rest of us out on some vain hope she will return from the camps."

"No, Romain, it's not that. I am tired of the fighting. We all are."

"My cousins were hanged at Tulle. My sister-in-law and her baby were in the church at Oradour-sur-Glane. I cannot let those brutes just leave. I won't."

"You can, and you will." Adèle stood up and faced Romain. "You are a soldier. You will obey orders. These are the orders." She walked away.

"Where are you going?" Reynolds asked.

"To tell my men."

"Want backup?" Although he offered without hesitation, it was clear Reynolds was reluctant to face the others.

"This is something I have to do alone. But thank you."

She strolled towards the centre of the clearing. With a few sharp whistles, she soon had people's attention. Romain followed her; she could feel his glare burning into her back. His body language caused ripples of consternation to move through the crowd. Luc came to stand beside her. She glanced at his expression, but he was stony-faced and impossible to read.

"I have our new orders. You will not like them."

A man shouted out. "Tell us."

"Elster has agreed to surrender."

Cheers broke out, and a few of the men began to dance, but

they soon realised that Luc and Romain weren't joining in, and
Adèle hadn't moved.

"What's the catch?"

The same man called, looking from her to Romain and
back.

"They have sold us out. That's the catch."

"Stand down, Romain. Now," Adèle ordered. She fixed her
attention on the crowd, several muttering, their frustration
evident. She shared their feelings but now was not the time for
emotions.

"I have been ordered to ensure safe passage for Elster and
his men. They refuse to surrender to the FFI; they wish instead
to meet the Americans."

"But they are in Loire. We are here." The same man spoke
again, but this time his tone was confused.

"Why should they get a choice?" another man asked
belligerently.

"We can take them now. Kill the lot. What's better than a
dead Fritz?"

The last remark whipped her men into a frenzy. They
wanted blood, and she couldn't blame them. Gritting her teeth,
she had to find the right words to convince them. How, when
she wasn't convinced herself? Would letting the German
soldiers walk freely through this countryside help the war end
faster?

The comments flew thick and fast. Adèle whistled again. "It
is a measure of how much the Fritz fear you that they refuse to
surrender into your hands. You have made me proud to be part
of your team, and to be French. I dislike this deal, but I don't
have any choice. I want the war to be over. We all do."

"But these men—"

"Yes, these are the men who killed our friends, families,
innocent women and children. Come the end of the war, they
will be held responsible for their crimes."

"You don't know that."

"I hope they will be held responsible. I have only ever been honest with you. Now I need you to stand by me and let the Germans pass unmolested to the Americans."

"That's sixty miles away."

"Yes, it is. I will leave you to make your decision." Adèle waited to see if anyone would argue with her directly, but the men were too angry. They spoke to one another, some of them becoming very heated.

"Hey, Luc! What say you to all this? Are you going to stand by and let her get away with this betrayal?"

Adèle watched her second-in-command. The others would follow him without question. But what would he decide?

Luc stepped forward without glancing at Adèle.

"My family was killed early in the war. Like many of you, I expect no one I know to return from prison. I had extended family in Oradour-sur-Glane, including the woman I hoped to marry. I want to avenge her death. I want to kill the man who killed her with my bare hands."

The crowd cheered and surged forward. But Luc wasn't finished.

"But I swore an oath to follow our leader to the death. Otherwise known as Elise, Éléanor or Claire, Adèle Bélanger has given everything to our cause – she has stuck by us no matter what. She returned to the field despite being so badly injured that she doesn't remember being put on the flight to England. Many of you here were with me when we carried this woman to that plane. Many others have seen how she cares for everyone. She is the reason we have been so successful. There-fore, where she goes, I follow. I stand with Adèle."

With tears in her eyes at his words and the use of her real name, which said more than anything that their war was almost over, Adèle watched as he moved to stand by her. Romain came forward as well; he didn't say a word, nor did he look at her, but he stood at Luc's side.

One by one, the men fell in behind them. She was too choked up to speak. By the end, only a few held back, their desire for revenge stronger than their loyalty.

Adèle decided they were best ignored. They might change their mind, or they would vanish overnight to join another group. Either way, she had to take back control.

"Thank you, Luc, Romain – and you all. Believe me, this order leaves a bitter taste in my mouth. But someone – maybe someone more knowledgeable than I – believes it to be the best for France. Vive la France!"

The cheers resounded throughout the forest.

Luc walked away, and she went after him. "Luc?"

"Not now, Adèle, please."

She let him go.

* * *

On 17th September, she watched with pride as her men lined the route the Germans marched down. Despite the swagger of the Wehrmacht, she had seen them glance nervously at the sheer number of uniformed maquisards, all watching them with steely expressions.

Romain growled, "They don't look like they are surrendering, do they?"

Adèle understood his frustration; her own finger wasn't too far from the trigger. She almost wanted them to give her an excuse to shoot.

"They might strut and sing their marching songs, but they know it's over. For them, anyway. We have won. And they have to live with that knowledge forever."

She spoke confidently, but Adèle wondered if these soldiers thought they had lost. They were good actors if they did. She was proud of her band of maquisards and rather amazed that they didn't rise to the bait. She turned away from the spectacle in disgust.

She later heard the Germans had been met by the Red Cross in Loire and given cigarettes, chocolate, and oranges. She couldn't remember the last time she had seen an orange, never mind real chocolate. Presents for murderers while her fighters, heroes every one, starved. Why was the world so messed up?

FIFTY-SEVEN

AUSCHWITZ

The days passed, and with them came one horror after another. Just when Sophie thought she couldn't bear anything more, another atrocity reached her ears.

She made the mistake of walking into a barracks full of twins one day. It was like going from a street café into the Ritz. None of the inhabitants were wearing a uniform; they remained in ordinary clothes. Their heads weren't shaved, and they were eating normal food in quantities Sophie hadn't seen since before the war. She couldn't help but think of her own twin. If Adèle was here, would they have ended up in this barracks?

She spoke to the women. They didn't know why they had been singled out and treated so well. Everyone had a story to tell her, and she listened to each one as she examined them. They were healthy, in the main, and while not happy, they were relieved not to have to be out working in all weather.

Yvonne, a young girl, asked, "Why do we deserve special treatment?" She spoke fluent French with only a slight accent.

"Why not? They can see we are of a different quality to the people who came before us," another answered, in a voice Sophie recognised as the type Adèle had used back before the war started. She couldn't judge the woman, though. God only knew what torment she had been through; if she wanted to believe she was special, who was Sophie to say otherwise?

"Regina, I am serious. Why us? Why here? They took my parents and siblings away. They sent my brothers to the quarry. But we end up in here. Treated like this. Why? I demand to know." The woman caught at Sophie's sleeve.

"I do not know. I cannot tell you, as nobody has told me. But keep calm, or your blood pressure will rise. It is already above healthy levels." Sophie tried her best to calm her patient, but she wasn't listening. And who could blame her? Despite the pleasant surroundings, Sophie couldn't wait to leave that barracks. Something was wrong.

* * *

A week later, she returned to find the twins gone. Nothing remained but Regina's scarf. Sophie didn't ask what had happened to the occupants. She didn't want to know.

Gena proved to be a godsend, although she wouldn't have liked being described that way. Virtually every evening, she would appear with a gift for Sophie. Often it was something Sophie desperately needed for a patient, such as aspirin or heart medications, or cigarettes, which could be used for bribing guards for extra food for the patients.

Trying to fight malnutrition and the spread of diseases such as typhus with a few blankets, soup, and mouldy bread didn't work. These extra gifts gave some a lifeline.

Some of the doctors and nurses had medical training, like Sophie, and others pretended to have medical qualifications. The Germans didn't ask for certificates.

Regardless of whether they held qualifications or not, the care they provided depended on the individual. Some did their best to help the patients, while others viewed being a medic as a way to save themselves. They rarely touched a patient if they could avoid it.

"What do you think you are doing?" Sophie asked one of these so-called nurses one day.

The woman didn't even try to look guilty as she continued to rifle through a patient's bed, finding two half-smoked cigarettes.

"She doesn't need them, does she? She's on the list for today."

"Let me see that." Sophie swiped the list from the bed. The woman quickly pocketed the two cigarettes and continued rummaging through the patient's meagre belongings.

The patient, a young woman, looked at Sophie, her glassy eyes a testament to the fever devouring her body. Her chances of survival in a proper hospital would have been slim; here, they were zero. Still, Sophie couldn't just toss her on the scrap heap.

She brought a bowl of water and sponged the woman down. The patient mumbled, trying to say something, but Sophie couldn't understand her. She kept bathing her, soothing her as if she were a child.

Eventually, the woman spoke. "Save yourself. Don't worry about me. I want to die. My children, my husband – they are waiting."

Sophie couldn't stop the tears as the woman murmured quiet syllables over and over – the names of her family, Sophie assumed. A cold rage consumed her, and she stared at the nurse who had stolen from the dying patient. "I will tell the guards."

"Tell them what?" the woman retorted, although her fear was evident.

"You are not a qualified nurse. I am guessing you may have done a few months working as a nursing assistant, or perhaps you are married to a doctor. But you, madame, have no medical training."

"You're wrong. I am just as good a nurse as anyone else.

You're the one who needs to be careful. We all know Gena's looking after you. Her little pet. What do you think they would do if they knew you two were lovers?"

Sophie leaped at the woman, clawing at her face. "You are a disgusting piece of garbage. How dare you say something like that about Gena? That woman is the reason we are still alive, all of us – but you are too blind, selfish, and stupid to see that. Aren't you?"

Then, as quickly as she had grabbed her, she let the woman go. Horrified, Sophie watched her sink to the floor. Then she dropped to her knees beside her victim.

"I'm so sorry. I can't believe I did that." Over and over, Sophie apologised, but the woman wouldn't look at her.

Sophie was sure she would scream for the guard. Instead, she hissed, "You are right in everything you said. But I am not as brave as you. Or Gena. I want to survive. I want to go home to find my little boy – if he still lives. How will I find him? He must think I abandoned him. He has no papers; I have no proof he is mine."

The woman rocked back and forth on the floor. Sophie put her arms around her, and together the two of them shared their tears.

FIFTY-EIGHT

Gena woke Sophie up, rubbing her shoulder. "Nicole, be careful. Something is happening."

Bleary-eyed, Sophie stared at Gena. What now? "Another selection?" she asked.

"No, not this time. The kitchens are preparing macaroni and milk."

Sophie couldn't believe her ears. Macaroni and milk? She sat up straighter, trying to ignore the pain in her chest. "Gena, you know that what means? The Allies must be here – the Russians, maybe. They will liberate us."

Gena shrugged, but her expression said everything.

Sophie wanted to cling onto the slight hope of rescue. "You don't believe it."

"I won't know what to believe until the Russkies march through those gates. But I don't trust the Boche."

The shrill whistle interrupted them.

"Come on, lovebirds – up you get."

They ignored the slur commonly aimed at anyone who became close friends. The block leaders preferred to rule by a policy of divide and conquer and did their best to disrupt real friendships.

They walked out to line up. Sophie looked around carefully, avoiding eye contact with the guards. They did seem different, but was she reading too much into things? When she had been captured, the war hadn't been going well on the eastern front. Had the Russians broken through? Were they coming?

The day progressed as usual, apart from at mealtime. The prisoners looked on in awe as they were served bowls of macaroni and milk. Sophie did her best to tell people to eat slowly; their stomachs wouldn't be able to cope with the rich food after starvation rations for so long. But most paid no attention. They couldn't believe their luck. The women smiled, their hopes soaring. Things were changing. They would be rescued. People who had never spoken about their past lives shared their stories. They spoke about their hopes for the future, yet the day before, many wouldn't have thought beyond the next hour. It took too much energy to stay alive; there was none left for dreams.

One inmate poked Sophie's arm. "What's wrong with you? Your face is a picture."

"Nothing. Just eat slowly, please. Otherwise, you will be sick." Sophie repeated the warning over and over.

"Stop telling us what to do. If you're not eating yours, I'll take it." A prisoner grabbed Sophie's bowl.

Sophie didn't stop the woman. She couldn't force down another mouthful. Her stomach revolted, but thankfully she didn't vomit – she would have been punished if she had.

She looked up to meet Gena's glance of understanding and pity. The other woman wasn't eating too much either.

They didn't have time to speak before the guards sent them off to work.

* * *

Later, when they were lying on their allotted bunk bed, Gena whispered, "The Red Cross was here today. That's what the macaroni was all about."

"But why? What good would it do?"

"Nicole, for someone who has been here so long, you are still so naïve. The Nazis are trying to convince the outside world this is something other than a death camp. By feeding us decent rations, they hope to fool the Red Cross into believing it."

"It can't work. Surely someone told the officials?" Even as she spoke, Sophie knew no one would be brave enough to do that. Maybe when they had first arrived, but months in the camp took away everything but the will to survive. She had learned to spot the ones who were going to die next; they smiled. It was as if they were happy to escape.

"The truth? Who would do that? Not only would that sign their own death warrant but likely everyone who shared their barracks."

The Blockführer barked an order. "Silence."

Sophie curled up in a ball, trying to squeeze the tears back. Even though she had told herself over and over, it was a ruse, a tiny part of her heart had hoped. Now that was gone too.

FIFTY-NINE

OCTOBER 1944, AUSCHWITZ

A nurse shouted at her, "Nicole, quick! Mengele is coming."

She looked out the window to catch a glimpse of the most feared man in Auschwitz – all five foot ten inches. She watched as he came nearer, her eyes drawn to his brown hair and eyes. Wasn't he walking proof that all Nazis weren't blue-eyed, blonde master-race types? Her blood chilled as she caught herself staring at him, a man so evil he conducted the vilest of experiments on living subjects.

She glanced at the list in her hand. She'd been instructed to mark off those patients who weren't expected to survive the next two weeks. She had marked no one in her care, not even those with typhus. She refused to be responsible for anyone's death.

She moved quickly around the beds, trying to offer comfort where possible. The women knew what the arrival of the camp doctor meant. She almost passed Claudette, not recognising the other woman, who didn't look a bit like she had that day in Izieu.

"Sophie, it's you, isn't it?" Claudette whispered.

Sophie rushed to her side, hoping nobody had heard the girl call her Sophie. "I thought you got away. Leon?"

"He went to Switzerland. I don't know if he got there or not. I can't believe you are here."

They didn't have time to chat. Mengele would arrive at any moment. Sophie pulled Claudette from the bed.

"Stand by yourself." Sophie forced the harsh tone, her friend would die if she didn't obey.

"I can't. Leave me here." Claudette sagged back against the mattress.

"You can and you will. Someone has to give evidence at Barbie's trial. Think about Izieu. The children. They need you to get them justice."

Claudette stared at her, a sole tear running down her face.

Another patient distracted Sophie. "Help me, pinch my cheek. Yes, that will put colour in it."

"I look better today, Doctor, don't I? You will tell him I will be well enough to work tomorrow, won't you?"

All around her, the patients clamoured for her help. She couldn't get back to Claudette, but a glance told her that her old friend had listened. She was pinching her cheeks and brushing her hair with her fingers. She moved to tend to Freda, a thirty-one-year-old woman who'd gone deaf due to mumps. Freda had helped her fellow patients as much as possible until she had become too sick to continue; she was now bedridden.

Sophie believed Freda's tireless efforts had exposed her to greater infection. She had held the patients' hands, hugged them and wiped their brows when they were raging with fever, stripped their dirty beds without complaint. Kindness had once radiated from her deep brown eyes – those same eyes that were now growing large with horror. Sophie could see something was wrong. The fear of Mengele penetrated through her silence. She grabbed Sophie's arm and pushed something into her hand.

A shred of paper, two names and two dates of birth. An adult and a child.

"Your husband?" Sophie spoke slowly, emphasising the word in an effort to help Freda understand. She nodded, then mimed holding a baby.

"Your family?" Sophie said. "You want me to take it?"

"Tell them ... I love them." Freda pulled Sophie closer, her efforts to squeeze out the words sapping all her remaining strength. "Thank you." Freda kissed Sophie's cheek.

Sophie clasped her hand, about to tell her not to worry, but the look in Freda's eyes stopped her. The woman knew she couldn't stand without assistance, and that was enough to put her in the wrong group. Sophie hugged her.

"I promise to try to find them. I will tell everyone about you. I won't forget." Sophie repeated the words slowly, hoping Freda understood her. Then the door swung open.

A female guard shouted, "Achtung." The nurses and doctors stood to attention, and into their midst walked the devil himself.

Sophie knew she was not supposed to look at his face, but she couldn't help herself. How could such a decent, normal-looking man be so evil? She quickly lowered her gaze to his shiny black boots. Despite the mud and disgusting conditions of the camp, those boots remained clean.

Sophie stood as her patients' numbers were called. Each patient had to strip naked for a cursory examination by Mengele or his team before getting redressed and back into bed. With each examination, Mengele made a mark in his notebook. No one else knew what decision had been made.

Claudette faltered as she tried to undress. Instinctively, Sophie stepped forward to help her, but a guard shoved her roughly back.

Mengele reprimanded the guard. "Let the doctor do her job. She is responsible for this woman's well-being."

Sophie glanced up and locked eyes with Mengele, swallowing at the look in his eyes. Then she moved to help.

Mengele made his notation in his book, and then moved on to the next patient. Had she done the right thing? Had her actions condemned Claudette or saved her?

The examinations continued until the guard shouted, "Achtung!" again signalling the inspection was over. Sophie leaned against a door, watching as the Nazis walked away, laughing and chatting as if they had just been to a garden party. Behind her, the patients tried to reassure themselves.

"He saw I was looking so well. He will know I can work."

"He smiled when he looked at me. I will be fine."

The women who had not been able to stand knew that they were doomed. But the others? No one knew who would be saved or not.

Sophie spoke a little with Claudette, catching up on her news and sharing what little she knew with the other woman. Seeing how weak Claudette was, she told her to sleep and they would speak more tomorrow.

If they had a tomorrow.

* * *

Sophie waited all day for something to happen, but there was nothing. The soup and bread arrived that evening as usual. The next day also passed as if nothing had happened.

Just as everyone had decided they were safe, the nightmare resumed.

SIXTY

Sophie sat near the single light, working on her notes in the almost silent ward. Claudette and some other patients were snoring, others lying halfway between sleep and wakefulness, when the door burst open, and the guards piled in. "Achtung, change barracks!"

The women screamed, as did the guards. One woman was struck in the face with a rifle butt before Sophie could calm things down.

"All those on the list will move to Barrack 25." Mengele's assistant held out the page as he called out the women's names one by one. Those who could stand lined up. Those who couldn't walk would be carried to the new barracks. Some tried to run and hide, but there was no escape. Those who had been spared pulled their covers further up their chests as if the blanket would stop the guards changing their minds.

Sophie held her breath, ignoring the palpitations of her protesting heart. She stared at the floor rather than her old friend for fear of motivating the guards to take Claudette. She willed strength to her friend. *Keep quiet and keep standing. You will be fine.* She repeated the mantra over and over until the selection was finished. Only then did she look at her friend and see the tears of relief on her face.

Sophie exchanged a look with Claudette before stepping towards the door. She wasn't going to let her patients leave without giving them her support. Every woman deserved to live.

A guard stepped in front of her, barking, "Stay with your patients."

Sophie stared into his face, seeing the surprised look he gave her as she did so. Inmates did not look guards in the eye. She gestured towards the people being removed. "These are my patients too. Can I not check on them?"

The man recovered, smirking. "You are keen to die."

"I am a doctor, and these are my patients."

He shrugged and let her follow. She helped a couple of the women by linking her arm through theirs, supporting them on the short walk to the new barracks. Once everyone was inside, the guards left.

The condemned women sat in their new barracks, some weeping and wailing, others were silent in shock. Sophie moved to each one, in turn, trying to give comfort where she could.

"It's a mistake. Why would they kill us? We are still useful. We can work..." One woman muttered over and over, some of the other women nodding in agreement. Sophie stayed silent; she couldn't make empty promises.

One woman, who looked to be in her sixties but Sophie knew was only thirty-five, pressed a note into Sophie's hands. "Can you please take this? If you can get it to my husband and son, they are in the men's section..." The woman rocked back and forth as she sat on the floor. "If you can't find them, tell the world about me when this is all over. Don't let me be forgotten."

She checked on Freda, but she appeared to be sleeping. Her eyes were shut tight.

Sophie wished over and over she had something to give all

these women. A single dose of morphine would be enough to give a peaceful death – but that was murder, and she had sworn not to take another's life. Had she really been so naïve as to believe she would never break that oath? She closed her eyes, picturing Mengele. She believed she could kill him with her bare hands without hesitation.

"You should go. Otherwise, they may take you with us."

She looked at the woman addressing her, a timid lady whom she had never heard speak before.

"How can you tell me to save myself?" Sophie asked. "I should go with you. I took an oath to save lives, not stand by while people died."

"You must live." The woman gritted her teeth, shuffling closer to Sophie, her injured leg dragging behind her. "To tell the world what you have seen, what happened to us. So it can never happen again."

Sophie shook her head.

The woman gripped Sophie's arm. "You must survive. Live to tell our story. Go now. Before it is too late."

"I wish ... Oh, why can't I help you?" Sophie's chest hurt, and her throat was dry. She ground her teeth, trying to release the rage she felt at this senseless slaughter.

"Nobody can help us now. God has a plan, and we must follow it." The woman squeezed her arm, but this time in a gesture of support.

"You are so brave."

The woman looked up, her eyes shining with tears as she shook her head. "Brave? No, I don't think so. I am terrified – but tonight I will be with my husband and my parents. I have missed them. Go now. Live your life for me. For all of us." The group fell silent as they heard the truck engine stall outside their barracks. The woman shoved Sophie. "Go," she shouted as the sounds of the guards and barking dogs grew closer.

Sophie ran. She didn't look back.

SIXTY-ONE

The next day, Sophie returned to Barrack 25 with the group of cleaning women selected by the guards. The whole ward had to be disinfected. It was deserted, but the presence of the women could still be felt. She glanced around at the precious mementos they had left behind: a ragged hair ribbon, a metal pin, a clasp – and the bread. Bread. In their last moments on earth, these women had surrendered their most precious possessions, lumps of mouldy bread.

Sophie didn't know how she got through the days afterward. Even Gena couldn't pull her out of the slump. Claudette had been moved, but Gena convinced her she was alive and would be fine. Sophie didn't believe her, but she didn't have the energy to argue.

Gena forced her to eat and wash herself, but Sophie had given up. She didn't want to live any more. She didn't feel worthy.

* * *

Mengele left the camp a week later with some of the other doctors. Sophie didn't know where he was going, and she didn't care.

As the days passed, Gena took to force-feeding her. Sophie just wanted to be left alone. She didn't believe in anything or anyone any more. Every time she closed her eyes, she saw Mengele making his selection that horrible day.

* * *

Then one morning, everything changed. "Nicole ... wake up. Do you hear that? The battle is much closer. The Russians are coming; they will be here in days."

Sophie shook off Gena's hand. In the distance, they could hear heavy guns. It was true the battlefront was moving closer, but it was too late.

Gena pulled at her. "The camp is being evacuated. Get on the trains, Nicole."

Sophie closed her eyes, trying to go back to sleep. That's all she wanted to do now. Sleep and never wake up.

"Wake up."

"I am not going back on a cattle train. Leave me be." Sophie turned her head away.

Sophie had told Gena everything. If her friend survived, she would find Adèle and tell her what had happened.

"Nicole Samson, or Sophie Bélanger, whatever your name is, stop being a selfish witch. You can't give up – I won't let you. You have a job to do. You can help save lives. Now quit feeling sorry for yourself." Gena gave two hard slaps to Sophie's face.

Sophie flinched but didn't defend herself, shocked at Gena's shouting. Gena took advantage of her shock to pull her to her feet and push her towards the door of their almost empty barracks. The other inmates had already left.

"They need doctors. You are a doctor. Now go."

Sophie moved towards the door – and only then did she realise that Gena wasn't following her. She stopped and turned back.

Something was wrong, but her fuddled brain couldn't work out what it would be. Why was Gena forcing her onto a train yet not leaving? "What about you?"

"I will be on the next one," Gena said and turned away.

Sophie walked towards her quickly. "What are you doing?"

"I am not a doctor; I haven't been selected. Go, Nicole."

Sophie stood her ground. "We go together or not at all. I am not leaving you here. I refuse to do that."

"You don't have a choice. Your name is on the list; mine isn't. Now go."

The list. All of Auschwitz seemed to survive on lists.

Not this time.

Sophie went, but instead of heading to the train, she ran in the direction of the camp hospital, racing into one of the barracks to rummage through a shelf.

"What are you looking for?" a soldier asked. "You are supposed to be on the train. You must hurry. It will leave soon."

Sophie pulled herself up, quick recognising him. It was Karl, the soldier who had helped her before.

"I need something to get my friend on the train. Help me, please."

"The names are on the list. Unless her name is there, there is nothing you can do." He stared at a point above her face.

"Can't you add her? Please, she has helped so many people," Sophie begged. He didn't respond. "Karl, help me." She touched his arm.

He looked at her hand and then at her face. "Who is it?"

"Gena."

A closed expression came over his face as he took a step back and stood straighter. "No. She stays."

"But why? What difference does it make who stays and who goes?"

He refused to meet her gaze, but his neck turned red. She watched as it took over his whole face.

"She is not my concern," he muttered, a stubborn expression on his face. "You are on the list. I was the one who got your name on it. Cost me ten cigarettes. Go now. Save yourself."

Ten cigarettes – was that all her life was worth? What was Gena's worth? She had nothing of value left. "I won't leave without her. Why can't you put her name down? Help her instead of me?"

"She is ... special." He wouldn't look at her.

The way he said that word made her skin crawl. She eyed him.

"Not to me. No, I am not like that. To Walloschek, Otto Walloschek."

The guard with the cruel eyes and scarred face. As understanding dawned, Sophie's stomach twisted. "Never. Gena wouldn't have anything to do with that evil piece of garbage."

Karl eyed her sadly. "You are still so innocent. So naïve, even in the midst of this hell. How do you think your friend has survived for so long? Did you never question her freedom to come and go from the sorting sheds, the area you women call Canada? Her ability to smuggle in medicines and other gifts? Prisoners have been shot for eating bread found in the clothes from the transports, yet she was never caught with valuable property. You think we are blind?"

SIXTY-TWO

Sophie staggered back until she came to rest against the wall. Gena had prostituted herself to save Sophie and the others. Tears came to her eyes, and she balled her fists so hard the nails dug into her flesh.

"We have to save her. He will kill her."

"He will kill me if I put her on that train."

Sophie stared at Karl. He could be right. She wouldn't put anything past Walloschek. She waited, watching as Karl's emotions played across his face. She didn't move when he came closer to her, nor when he put his hand out to touch her face. He caressed her skin, his touch as gentle as a butterfly's wings. "In another time, you and I might have been friends. I admire you. Not only are you a doctor, but you care deeply for your fellow man."

Sophie saw her chance. Despite her stomach turning as her body flinched at his touch, she forced herself to suppress her feelings. She'd do anything to save Gena. She owed her friend.

"So do you," she said. "You have proved that again and again by not killing us when others wearing your uniform did. Help me now, please. I can't – I won't live without her."

Sophie watched the battle in his eyes. She stepped closer to him. "Please, help her. If she stays, I will die."

"You could die anyway. We are all going to die."

"Yes, but we have a chance. And when you die, you can face Saint Peter at the gates and look him straight in the eye. You can save her life. Only you, Karl."

Sophie forced herself to kiss him gently on the lips. She let herself go limp as he pulled her to him, deepening the kiss, demanding her surrender. Just as quickly, he let her go. He touched his lips briefly before he stood straighter. "I apologise. I shouldn't have done that. Go now."

"And Gena?"

"Get her on the train without Walloschek seeing her, and you have a chance. I will do my best to distract him."

"Thank you. You have done the right thing today."

Sophie didn't look back. She ran to where she had left Gena, hoping and praying her friend hadn't moved. But she was gone. She ran back out of the barracks, stopping some women who knew her friend.

"Where's Gena? Have you seen her?"

The women took a step back from her, fear in their faces. One of them snapped, "Quit pushing. We must get to the train. Didn't you hear? We are being evacuated."

"Yes, but I have to find Gena. Think – where did she go? She was here fifteen minutes ago."

Sophie ran from person to person, but nobody seemed to have seen Gena. She had vanished. The whistles grew louder, and the guards' shouting escalated. She rushed back to their barracks, even looking under the beds, but she wasn't there. She was running out of time. Where was she? Where would Gena have gone?

She headed out of the barracks towards the old hospital barracks. It backed onto a small space that was never used and rarely patrolled. Gena had shown it to Sophie a while back as a place to go to get away from the incessant over-crowding.

Sometimes Gena sneaked out at night; Sophie had believed she just needed some space. Now that she knew about Walloschek, she understood what her friend had been doing. But she had a suspicion Gena would have gone to what she called her special space.

As she rounded the corner, she nearly fell over her friend in her haste.

"Sophie! For goodness' sake, I thought you were on the train. What are you doing here?"

"Looking for you. Come on."

Gena didn't move. "Where are we going?"

"On that train."

"I can't. I am not on the list." But she stood up.

"You are."

Hope flared in her face for a second before it became an expressionless mask once more. "Sophie, you don't understand. I can't leave. I will be shot as soon as he sees me."

"Then we can't let him see you. Trust me, Gena, just as I have always trusted you. I am not leaving this camp without you. Are you going to argue with me, or are we getting that train?"

Gena stared at her, understanding dawning. "You know. How?"

"It doesn't matter. We don't have time for this; come on."

Sophie grabbed Gena's arm and, half-pulling her, ran back the way she had come. She prayed Karl had managed to distract Walloschek. She didn't want to think of the punishment he would impose on them if they were caught.

But their luck held. They were pushed into a smelly, filthy cattle truck, but neither cared. Nobody was checking the list any more as the distant battle sounds got louder. Hundreds of prisoners were pushed in on top of them, but they didn't complain – the extra bodies hid them well.

Then a shot rang out, followed by two more.

The people in the truck froze. Had someone tried to get off the train? Those nearest the doors tried to look out, but the guards closed them quickly – so quickly that one woman got her hand caught. Sophie pushed through the crowd to help her as Gena pushed some other women aside to peer through a hole in the door.

"Oh my. It's a guard, not prisoners."

Sophie was busy wrapping a makeshift bandage around the injured woman's hand to pay too much attention. The train jerked, then moved slowly out of the camp. Sophie finished what she was doing, and then shuffled back to stand beside Gena. To her amazement, her friend was crying.

Sophie pulled Gena into a hug, "What's wrong? We are safe now. Well, relatively speaking." She tried to sound light-hearted as she glanced at their surroundings.

"It was Walloschek. On the ground. Karl too. Karl must have shot him first and then himself."

Gena was racked by sobs, shaking violently. Sophie wrapped her arms around her friend, protecting her as much as possible as the train jerked along the tracks.

Karl had done as he'd promised. He had saved them giving up his life in the process. She said a quick prayer for him. Yes, he had been part of the nightmare of Auschwitz, but he had retained a glimmer of humanity. If not for him, where might she and Gena be now?

* * *

Their journey lasted three days. Gena and Sophie did what they could, but they couldn't keep people from dying from lack of water. At first, the bodies remained where they fell due to the overcrowding. Sophie persuaded her fellow travellers it would be best to move the dead to the corner of the train car if they could. Working together, the women moved their fallen friends to one side. The bodies were laid on top of each other. The mound of the dead grew bigger daily.

Although they had been deemed the healthiest of the Auschwitz camp, they were, in reality, half-starved and full of disease. Rumours were rife about their destination, but one thing was certain: they were headed into Germany. Sophie was getting nearer to home.

For the first time in months, she allowed herself to think of seeing France again. Just one more time.

* * *

Bergen-Belsen was different to Auschwitz, yet somehow still the same. There was no gas chamber; to Sophie's disbelief, the camp shipped prisoners back east to gas them.

The prisoners were called by their names, not their numbers – something that got Sophie into trouble on the first day. So used to being called by her number, she missed her name and was given a beating by the guards. But even the beatings were less severe than at Auschwitz.

In other ways, though, the camp was much worse. Sophie was again put to work in the hospital, but there was no running water, and they regularly lost electricity. Diseases, including typhus, spread rapidly among the prisoners, and this time there was no means of getting extra medicine. Gena worked at the hospital with Sophie, neither of them believing they could survive without the other. The weather grew slightly warmer, but Sophie almost preferred the freezing temperatures. At least when it was frozen, they were not covered in mud.

Soon after she arrived in the camp, she was overjoyed to find some Frenchwomen among the inmates able to give her some news of home. They knew no one in common, but still, these women were a link to the life she had left behind.

SIXTY-THREE

APRIL 1945

After helping to clear the last of the Nazi strongholds in the French countryside, Adèle and her two self-styled bodyguards accompanied her back to Paris. Neither Romain nor Luc believed they had any surviving family. Luc had seen Caesar shot and fall in a battle. It hadn't been possible to search for his body, but there had been no word from him since. Nobody had seen him.

All three wanted to go to Germany to search the camps for Sophie and any of the men who'd been captured over the years, but they knew it was futile.

"The best we can do is move to Paris. That's where those returning from the camps will be processed." Adèle looked up from the newspaper she'd been reading. "At least that's what London suggests."

"Has London released you from your duties yet? I thought you had to stick with them until it was all over."

Luc had put her worst fears into words, but thankfully, as a woman, she wasn't expected to continue fighting. She was tired, heartsick, and exhausted. They'd trekked miles scouring the countryside not just for Germans but for bands of the hated Milice. She wanted life to return to normal.

Romain got them tickets on a train from Lyon, and together they headed to Paris. As they left Lyon station behind, Adèle couldn't stop a tear running down her cheek.

"He'll turn up. Caesar is too clever to get himself killed." Romain's belief in Georges was annoying. Luc had seen him shot, and if he was alive, he'd have found her.

Everyone was dead or missing. Georges was the only person who knew where her mother and grandmother had moved to. She'd visited mémé's old home, and spoken to Dr de Guelis, but all he could tell her was that both women had disappeared in late 1942, and he hadn't seen or heard from them since. She promised to write to him with her address in Paris, and he agreed to pass it on if they turned up.

The train was packed; they had to squeeze on with Adèle sitting on their bags. Romain and Luc flanked her on either side. As the train meandered through the countryside, the numerous stops reminded them of the damage done by the maquis, the Germans, and the Allied bombings. It took three days to reach Paris and another week before Adèle could reclaim her old home.

As they entered the old apartment, Romain said, "Good job you kept that letter from London proving what you did in the war. They could have arrested you for collaborating."

"Romain, that's not funny," Luc said. "Adèle, are you sure you want to stay here?"

Adèle looked around the ransacked rooms, the antique fireplace ruined by deep gashes, disgusting graffiti on the silk wallpaper, and empty spaces where the paintings and Sèvres vases used to stand. None of that mattered; it was the missing people that hurt the most. She closed her eyes, seeing her family sitting down for lunch, Jean-Pierre and her father arguing by the fire,

Zeldah and Sophie laughing in the kitchen, maman ... She wiped the tears from her eyes with the sleeve of her coat.

"Hey, look at this. What a monstrosity." At Luc's shout from the bedroom, Adèle and Romain rushed in.

Adèle burst out laughing. "That used to be my favourite piece of furniture. Mémé brought the dressing table with her from Germany and gave it to me when she left Paris. I wanted to ask my father to take it when we left during the *exode*." She ran her hand over the now defaced black wood, fingering the body of the angel, all that was left of the china pair that once decorated the now-shattered mirror.

"Looks like someone destroyed a Dresden china dressing table. They obviously didn't realise how much it was worth. Didn't the Germans love that sort of thing?" Luc said. Romain went out to the hallway.

Adèle wasn't listening; she was too busy reliving memories. Where was Sophie? Was she ever going to come home?

"Adèle, a woman here wants to talk to you," Romain called from the hall. "Says she knows you."

Adèle ran out but stopped when she saw it was Madame Garnier in the doorway. She froze. "What are you doing here?"

"Please, Adèle. I was good friends with your family. I need..."

Adèle turned on her heel. "Romain, take her to the local police station. She's a collaborator just like my father."

"No ... I tried to help. I didn't tell on those Jews, the Litwaks, or your sister for what she did. You were worse than I ever was. You went dancing with them, took their food, their flowers..." Her words filtered up the stairs as Romain escorted her out of the building.

Luc whistled. "She wasn't expecting that. Not from an old friend."

"We were never friends, but she did know the old me. And I

guess in her eyes and those of many others, I was a collaborator, at least before they murdered Léo and then Jean-Pierre."

"Léo?"

Adèle could see Léo's face, his gentle smile. "He was an engineer, caught in the wrong place at the wrong time." She raised her eyes to meet Luc's. "He was a lovely, honourable man."

Luc turned away. He hated talking about those who had died. "So, are you going to move in here?"

"Are there any alternatives? You saw how hard it is to find accommodation. You and Romain are welcome to move in too. It not like there isn't plenty of space."

Space was about all they had. The apartment had been stripped bare except for a couple of tables that appeared to have been used for firewood. Adèle didn't care. None of it mattered. She had to find her sister.

SIXTY-FOUR

There were several centres set up in Paris for those who were returning from the camps. Every day, Adèle trawled through the lists of survivors, looking for news of her sister, but as yet, no one had any firm leads.

Luc came back to the apartment one day, sporting two shopping bags. He held them up in triumph. "I met Félix Abreo; his parents send you their regards. He gave me these and said he would call around to meet you in person soon." Luc grinned. "I think his mother may want him to marry you, but he's heard rumours about the White Witch and isn't too keen."

Food was scarcer now than it had ever been. Acres of farming land had been destroyed by the bombings, leaving a shortage of wheat, fruit, and vegetables. There was little meat too, so people starved unless they could afford the black market.

Romain grabbed a bag, exclaiming as he emptied it, "Pâté and some stale bread. Well, guess it's better than nothing."

Luc pretended to give him a clip around the ear.

"Adèle, Félix suggested you try the Hôtel Lutetia on boulevard Raspail. He said that's where they are taking survivors from the camps."

Adèle knew of the Left Bank hotel. It had been requisitioned by the Germans, and so had survived almost intact.

"Thank you." She tried to subdue the urge to race to the hotel and find Sophie immediately.

"Adèle, be ready. The stories – of the gas chambers and everything else – it is all true."

Luc wouldn't meet her gaze, and she guessed he was struggling with his fears for his own family. They had been among the first to be deported from Drancy following the Vél d'Hiv *rafle* in July 1942.

Adèle couldn't believe her ears. They had all heard the rumours, but nobody wanted to believe them. But if the people returning from the camps were telling the same horrific stories, they couldn't be lying, could they?

"How would Sophie know to go to the hotel?"

"They have volunteers meeting the trains at Gare de l'Est. Everyone – resistants, political prisoners, and Jews – are being guided to the hotel. Well, all those who don't have families or homes in Paris, at least. They are in such a sorry state – too weak to lift their feet to walk. They seem to move by sliding in a mass of prisoner uniforms." Romain's description painted a graphic picture.

Adèle had heard enough. Picking up her bag, she hailed a cab to take her to the hotel. All the way, she prayed as hard as she could that she would find Sophie.

* * *

She had believed that she had seen every atrocity known to man and was prepared for what she would encounter at the hotel, but she was sadly mistaken. The sheer numbers of people were frightening to behold. She pushed her way inside to the lobby, where reception tables had been arranged to process the returning prisoners and determine their needs.

Glancing at the queues, Adèle decided that was too slow a process for her.

Then she spotted someone she knew in the crowds and made her way over to her. Adèle tried to hide her shock at the woman's emaciated appearance, her shaved head, and her dress several sizes too big. She was a shadow of the young, laughing nurse Adèle remembered. "Noémie, it is you, isn't it?"

The woman only stared at her.

Adèle persisted. "You were a nurse; you worked with my sister." Was she brain-damaged or in shock? Adèle tried to temper her impatience; she spoke slowly in a calm voice. "It's me, Adèle, Sophie's sister. Have you seen her? Please help me."

"I know who you are." She turned away.

Adèle swallowed her hurt. Noémie must believe she had spent the war as a socialite. "Please help me."

The woman shook her head sadly. "Everyone is looking for someone. Those with the resistance look for one or maybe two adults. But Adèle, the Jews! We are looking for entire families. Look at this list. Twenty members of the same family, three generations – all gone." Noémie buried her head in her hands.

Adèle couldn't deal with other people's pain. She had to find Sophie. She mumbled something and moved on.

Romain and Luc also asked questions. Luc's family had been taken at the start of the war. Romain's had been shot, but he was looking for the men and women who'd worked with the resistance but had been captured. There were crowds of people.

"How does anyone find someone here?" Romain's frustration bubbled over as Luc turned to speak to more survivors.

Adèle sympathised. She couldn't find anyone who'd seen Sophie. Not in Drancy or in Auschwitz. It was as if she'd never existed.

A man answered Romain. "They have a system. Everyone is registered. After registration, the survivors are provided with proper identification papers and ration books. They are also given a sum of money and some vouchers for Le Bon Marché, the department store around the corner."

As Adèle listened, she spotted a gendarme treating the survivors roughly. She looked at him closer. It was the man she'd met with Luc the day she had first met Jozef. Nobody knew where Jozef was now; he had disappeared like so many others. Luc had warned her this man was closely associated with the Germans. She broke away from Romain and walked closer to him.

The gendarme's scathing tone and attitude withered at the look on her face. Before he could react, she challenged him. "Cheval! What are you doing here?"

"Same as you. Trying to help." His confident tone didn't match the way his eyes glanced from side to side as if seeking an escape.

She couldn't believe the man had the audacity to be alive and pretending he was helping people.

"Help? You were responsible for putting these people on the trains in the first place – you and the rest of your force. You should be ashamed of yourselves!"

The man grabbed her arm. "Don't make me arrest you, mademoiselle. I won't have you cause a scene. I had orders. I had no choice."

"Get your hands off me. Is that what you tell yourself? I saw what you did. You bribed those poor unfortunates, promised them they would be safe, and once they paid, you handed them over to the Germans."

He flushed. "We all did what we had to do to survive. From what I've heard, you enjoyed more than a cuddle at the hands of our occupiers."

Adèle snapped. The man was on the floor with her knife at his throat before he knew what had happened.

"You swine! I was not a collaborator. I fought with the resistance, got shot twice and lost many of my friends due to

your despicable actions. You will answer for what you did,
Cheval."

Two gendarmes came forward to disarm Adèle, but after
hearing what she'd said, they stood waiting. Then she sensed
someone move closer to her.

"She speaks the truth. He took pleasure in working for the
Boches. Get that piece of filth out of here and put him where he
belongs." The man put his hand gently on Adèle's arm. She
knew his voice, but through her fury she couldn't place it or
bring herself to look at him. "Let the knife go, Adèle. He will be
tried properly. You are not a murderer."

Adèle couldn't speak, the red mist in front of her eyes
seeming to take forever to disperse. The gentle pressure on her
arm increased. "Do as I say."

Gradually, Adèle came to her senses – and then, at last, she
recognised the voice.

"Georges? Georges!" She let him pull her away from the
collaborator, thus allowing the French police to do their job. She
saw them deliver a couple of well-aimed kicks to the prone
figure before he was pulled to his feet, handcuffed and escorted
out of the building.

"Thank God. I thought you were dead." He folded her into
his arms and held her before releasing her and standing back a
little as if wondering if this was real.

He looked much older and had grown so much thinner
since she had seen him last. The scar running from his ear down
his neck was new. She leaned in and traced it with her finger.
"You got shot?" A shiver ran through her; the bullet must have
come close to killing him.

"It was nothing; you should see the other guy."

His attempt at humour fell flat as the look in his eyes gave
away the real horrors. Lines etched around his eyes and
mouth stood out against his tan. He'd shaved off his full
beard, leaving a shadow. It suited him, as did his now fully

grey hair. She drew her eyes away from his toned, muscular arms.

"What are you doing here?"

"Looking for you. And others." Georges stared at her as if waiting for her to do something. She wanted to pull him close and kiss him, but now that he was standing in front of her, she felt shy.

"I'm looking for Sophie. She was taken by the Gestapo – they thought she was me."

"I'm sorry. But why here? If the Gestapo thought she was you – I mean, your reputation..." Georges fell silent, as if realising he wasn't helping.

"Somehow, she convinced them she wasn't me. They sent her to the camps. That much we know. But how she fared is another question."

"We will find her. I will help you." Georges took her hand, but his formal tone kept a distance between them. Was he feeling awkward too? As if it was too much to seize their chance of happiness with misfortune and loss all around them. "It is so good to see you. I didn't think we would both live to see this day."

She hadn't thought so either, but she felt guilty for feeling joy. She had to find Sophie – she would deal with Georges and her feelings afterward. They were interrupted by Luc's cheers as he came over and greeted Georges. "I thought you were dead, my friend. Romain, look what the cat dragged in."

The three men hugged, ignoring the gentle smiles of those around them. In this place, it was rare to get good news.

"Was that Cheval being elbowed out the door?" Luc asked.

"Yes, Adèle floored him. I had to stop her from cutting his throat."

"You should have let her. That man is..." Luc choked up, his eyes filling with tears. Romain lit a cigarette and handed it to him.

Adèle changed the subject. "Sophie is a doctor; maybe she is helping with patients. Do they have a hospital set up in here?" she asked Georges.

"Of sorts. They provide beds for those who are too weak, either physically or mentally, to be alone. The nurses have insisted on a special diet, too. Most of these people have been surviving on bread and water, so rich food would kill them."

"Can you show me where they would be?"

Georges nodded and took her hand. His touch made her yearn for him to take her in his arms. But for now, just having him by her side was enough to make Adèle feel stronger. "Luc and I will catch up with you at home. Georges, we're living at Adèle's old apartment." Romain escorted his friend out of the hotel.

Adèle and Georges moved through the crowds, hearing snippets of heartbreaking conversations along the way.

"Yes, I knew your brother. He survived Auschwitz – we were on the same march. But I am sorry, he was shot by the SS. I told him he was too slow, but he would not listen. He was stubborn, you know?"

The people spoke in monotone voices, making the horrors they described even more harrowing. Adèle wanted to cover her ears and run from the building, but she couldn't.

The hotel rooms were stifling with their radiators turned up to full blast. The returning prisoners were skin and bone; the heat kept them alive. Again and again, she asked for news of Sophie, but nobody knew her.

"Come on, Adèle, let's get you out of here. We will come back tomorrow."

"I can't. I have to find her."

"Yes, you do – but not at the cost of your own health. You don't look well."

She gave him a look. "Compared to these people, I am in the prime of health." She knew he didn't believe her, she saw his eyes narrow as she failed to swallow a yawn. Her severe exhaustion crippling her.

He leaned in, pushing a strand of her hair behind her ear. "For once in your life, will you do as you are told?"

Adèle was about to argue but gave up. She didn't have the will to fight any more. She let him escort her out of the hotel.

"Wait! Please wait."

A shaven-haired woman wearing the striped concentration camp uniform threw herself at Adèle, saying, "Sophie, you survived! How well you look. I can't believe it."

Adèle stared at the woman in front of her, trying not to shudder at the sight of the shaved head, sunken eyes and rotting teeth. The woman looked like a walking skeleton. She took a step back.

The woman's joyful expression faltered. "You don't recognise me? It's Claudette."

"I am not Sophie. I am her twin sister, Adèle."

The woman looked confused.

"Claudette, did you hear me? I've been looking for Sophie – do you know where she is?"

"You aren't Sophie? But you look like her."

"We are twins. Did she not tell you she had a twin?" Adèle realised how stupid she sounded – obviously Sophie had been protecting her.

Georges put his arm around Adèle. "Claudette, where did you last see Sophie? It's very important." Georges used a very gentle tone. "Sophie and Adèle are twin sisters, friends of mine from long back. We are not trying to confuse you, I promise."

"She was in Auschwitz. Working in the hospital. She saved my life." The woman would have collapsed but for Georges moving quickly to grab her. He carried her into the hotel, past the reception and straight to the hospital area, Adèle following close behind him.

"Has she registered?" the nurse asked.

"I don't know. She fainted, so I thought I should bring her straight here. She was in Auschwitz, and her name is Claudette. That is all we know." Georges laid the woman gently on the bed for the nurse to assess her.

"She is a friend of my sister's. Please look after her." Adèle took Claudette's hand in hers. "I will come back to see you tomorrow, I promise." She didn't know if the woman had heard her or not. She let Georges lead her back out of the hotel, her vision swimming with tears.

"Sophie in Auschwitz. Oh, Georges, what have I done?"

"You are not responsible for this. Sophie was helping Jews. She could have been arrested for that reason. Adèle, you know that during the war, you could be arrested for looking at a German the wrong way. There is nothing to be gained by you taking responsibility for any of this. Come, I am taking you to a doctor. I don't like your colour."

Adèle gasped as he gathered her up in his arms. It was nice to be cuddled and treated like something fragile, despite having spent the last three years fighting and behaving like a man.

That was her last thought before the blackness descended.

SIXTY-FIVE

When she came round, she was back in the apartment. Maurice, his face a picture of concern, stared at her. Romain and Luc hovered it the background like fathers at the birth of a baby. Georges sat beside her, holding her hand.

"Maurice? You're here. How? Why?"

"I came back to Paris to work at the hospital. Dr Murphy and so many of the other staff have disappeared. I thought I might find news of Sophie and the others while helping where I could. So many of our men just vanished. There's no records."

Adèle turned her head away. She couldn't bear to think about the men she'd fought with and lost.

Maurice continued his physical examination.

"You need to stay in bed, or you'll suffer a relapse, maybe get pleurisy again. Luc told me you haven't stopped searching. Let us do that for you, and you rest."

She refused to listen.

How could she think about herself when Sophie might be out there somewhere? What horrors had her twin endured?

Maurice put away his stethoscope. "Adèle, you must eat. Build up your strength. The fight is not over."

"The war is won; my fight is done."

He turned her head, forcing her to look at him. "Are you going to let the people who destroyed our families get away? I am not talking about the Nazis, but the French who collaborated, who sent our people to their deaths or to the camps."

He was not above using guilt. She would have done the same if the roles were reversed.

"I don't have time for revenge. All I care about is finding Sophie. I must look maman and my grandmother in the eye and tell them I found her."

At her words, his gaze flickered to Georges standing to the side before Maurice moved back. "I'll let you tell her."

"Tell me what? Georges?"

"Nothing. I am just disappointed. I thought you would listen to Maurice—"

"Stop it. You know something." She dropped his hand. "My mother. Grandmother. You do, don't deny it. I can see it in your face. Where are they?"

Maurice coughed. "Tell her, Georges. I'm due back at the hospital." He looked at her sadly before picking up his doctor's bag and leaving. Her eyes returned to Georges.

"Darling, you must be brave." She let him take her hand. "The house they were living in was hit by a bomb. They didn't suffer; they would have died instantly."

She stared at him in disbelief. "A bomb? But the Germans..."

"It was an Allied plane. Apparently, it got hit, and the pilot had to let the bombs go to land. He picked what he must have thought was an isolated spot, but one hit the farmhouse. I am so sorry."

Her mother and grandmother had been killed by their own side after escaping from the Nazis. How could that happen?

"Adèle, let the tears come. You can't be brave all the time. Let the feelings out, or they will poison you."

She knew he was talking, but she didn't care what he said. She couldn't feel anything for anyone any more. The last bit of hope had just died inside of her. She turned on her side and stared at the wall. Her whole family was gone. There was nothing left to live for. She closed her eyes, willing him to leave. She wanted to be alone.

Georges refused to leave her side for long. When he did have to go out, he made sure Luc or Romain was there. At first, she didn't care. But after a couple of days, it became irritating, she wasn't a child. But despite her protests and the men insisting it was just the way things worked out, she was never alone.

People arrived at the apartment at all hours. Members of the maquis visiting Paris or those returning from the camps. Despite several requests from Luc and the others, Adèle barely left her bedroom.

"How long are you going to sit in misery? You could help us. We have so much to do."

"Like what?" Adèle didn't even bother to look up from her book although she wasn't reading.

Georges walked across the bedroom and took the book from her hands. "Enough. I know you're hurting but you're not alone. Our men, those who died, left families behind. They need help. The survivors from the camps, men and women who supported us, they need us."

"What about what I need? I did my bit," Adèle screamed. "I've lost my entire family, my friends. Almost everyone I loved."

"You still have me. I love you. Together we can forge a new France."

"I've no interest in politics. All that sitting around talking and making plans ... I'd be bored in an hour."

"I don't see you do anything useful now. You stay in bed all day."

She jumped up, getting tangled in the sheet in her haste and fell straight into his arms. "You ...You..." Her words stopped as she registered the look in his eyes. His gaze shifted down to her mouth and lower before raising to meet her gaze. He took things slowly, giving her the opportunity to stop him if she wanted. He pushed her hair behind her ear, his touch making her shiver. His breath grazed her cheek, his expression full of tenderness and longing.

"I love you. I can't bear to live without you." His fingers traced her jawline, before his lips followed. Butterflies exploded in her stomach, her limbs trembling in anticipation. She was a widow, not a naïve maid but the intensity of the feelings he created was like nothing she'd experienced. She wanted his kiss but he took his time, brushing his lips against the hollow of her temple, pushing her hair out of the way as he kissed her ear. Desire flooded through her as losing patience, she twisted her hands in his shirt dragging him closer, standing on her toes to reach his mouth. He shuddered, emitting a low groan as he folded her into his arms. Her grin of satisfaction was fleeting as his mouth descended onto hers removing all ability to think of anything but him. Georges. She ran her hands up and down his muscular arms, before using her lips to trace the scar under his eyes. His body trembled as she traced his face with her lips, kissing his closed eyes and all the way to his mouth.

He broke their kiss. "Marry me." He kissed her again, this time his lips barely brushing hers as he repeated, "Please be my wife. I want you. I need you."

She ran her hands down his shirt, her fingers opening the top buttons, wanting access to his bare skin.

"You can have me, we don't have to get married. Not after everything we've been through."

His hands stopped hers. "I want you as my wife. Nothing less than that." He put his finger under her chin and looked straight into her eyes. Then he bent down on one knee and took her hand. "Je t'aime. Veux-tu devenir ma femme?"

"Oui, oui." Tears ran down her cheeks as he jumped to his feet, his mouth crushing hers in a kiss. "Today? I find it hard to resist you."

She laughed, drunk on the power she had over him, more exhilarating as she loved him just as much.

"As soon as we can."

* * *

Dressed in a short blue summer dress, Adèle walked up the church aisle on Luc's arm. The familiar smell of incense took her back to her first wedding. Not that this one compared to that huge society event with the church full of family, friends and associates. This time she was marrying for love, not a position in society.

She glanced at the almost empty pews on the bride's side. Some of the maquis had come to celebrate with them, many bringing their wives or girlfriends. She appreciated the gesture but would have given anything for her mother, mémé, Jean-Pierre, and of course Sophie to be there. She pushed the sadness aside, they were with her in spirit.

Her legs weakened when she caught sight of Georges standing in his best suit, clean shaven waiting for her. Maurice acted as his best man with Romain also standing by his side. Flowers adorned the altar including some blue Iris, the symbol of faith and love. She passed her small bouquet to Claudette, now sufficiently recovered to sit in the front pew of the church.

The priest smiled as he concluded the service. "It is an honour to join a couple in matrimony. Even more so when they are two heroes of France. May you live long and prosper and of course, I expect the children to be baptised here."

She blushed, not at his comment but at the look in Georges's eyes. He took her hand and together they walked down the aisle ready for whatever lay in front of them.

SIXTY-SIX

MAY 1945

A roar from the street outside alerted them to Charles de Gaulle's announcement, that and the church bells ringing out.

Luc carried over the tray of drinks. "See, I'm well trained after all." Although he joked, his smile didn't reach his eyes. Adèle knew he was struggling to get over his fiancée's death in Oradour.

Romain grabbed two glasses, passing one of them to Adèle before downing his drink in one go. "Anyone want another?"

Adèle and Luc shook their heads, watching Romain as he set off to find another bottle.

"Let him enjoy today. He's got his head fixed on right; he's going to be an engineer." Luc turned to Adèle. "All that training you gave him on explosives gave him ideas."

"Better that than a politician like Georges," Adèle tried to joke.

"He said he'd be home in time for the announcement." Luc wandered over to the window, looking down at the celebrations outside. "If only we'd had so many when we needed them. We could have won the war years earlier."

Adèle agreed with the jaded statement. It was amazing how

many so-called supporters of the resistance had come out in public now. Most were ordinary citizens who had been too scared to do anything, but some had been zealous collaborators. To protect themselves, these turncoats were often the most determined at dishing out punishments to those considered guilty of collaborating. Men were shot. Women who had slept with Germans – even those who had done it to feed their starving children or to save a loved one from being sent to Germany as labourers – had their heads shaved. These poor unfortunates were stripped, sometimes naked, beaten and marched through the streets. Retribution was swift, cruel, and often misplaced. Many used the chaos to settle old feuds.

"Adèle, where are you?" Georges shouted as he slammed the door to their apartment.

"Stop shouting. I am not in Spain. I'm in here with Luc. What is the matter with you?"

"Darling, sit down. I have news." He took a seat.

Doing as he asked, Adèle wished he wouldn't treat her like a china doll. She had recovered from her breakdown. The doctors had insisted it was a normal reaction after the stress of the war, but Georges continued to treat her as if she was fragile. She sat on the sofa beside him.

"Sophie is alive. She's been ill, but she is alive."

Adèle stared at him, wanting to believe him, but after all this time—! She had searched everywhere for her sister, but Sophie had just vanished.

"Alive?" Adèle whispered. "Where has she been?"

"Bergen-Belsen."

"The camp? But the newspapers said it was burned to the ground after it was liberated. How?"

"The prisoner camp was, but Sophie is in the displaced persons' camp. She's been there the whole time."

"She's alive and never tried to find me?" Adèle stared at him, horror dawning in her eyes. "She blames me for what happened to her, doesn't she? She hates me – that's why she didn't try to find me."

"Darling, stop it. Nobody hates you. Sophie tried to find you, but she was told you were dead. Everyone was dead. She stayed where she was. Now I have someone here who wants to meet you. Are you up to seeing her?"

"Who?"

"She was a friend of Sophie's in the camps."

Adèle jumped up. "Where is she? Why didn't you bring her inside?"

"She didn't want to upset you. She heard you had been ill and—"

Adèle ignored the rest of what he said, opening their apartment door and running down the stairs to the main door of their apartment building. She barely registered the new concierge, who walked out of her *loge*, saying, "What's the rush? Why are you making..."

Adèle ignored her as she pulled open the front door and ran outside. She saw the woman Georges had mentioned and stalled. This person was her link to Sophie. What would she tell her?

The pretty, albeit thin, woman sitting on the bench outside stood, then immediately sat down again as her face paled.

"Forgive me, but you look just like her." The woman's voice shook with emotion.

Adèle forced herself to go gently. She couldn't imagine the horrors this lady had shared with her sister. She waited, but when the silence lingered, she prompted, "You are Sophie's friend?"

The woman nodded. "I owe your sister my life. My name is Gena. We were in Auschwitz and Bergen-Belsen together. I was liberated, but Sophie was too ill to be released. She was kept in the hospital. She believes you to be dead."

Adèle's heart thumped, her breath coming almost too fast.

She took a seat beside Gena. Sophie was alive, or at least she had been when the camps were liberated. But that was months ago.

"I tried to find her and couldn't. There was no listing for her on any of the camp lists."

Gena struggled, speaking through her tears. "She didn't use her real name. She kept that quiet."

"To protect me?"

Gena didn't reply.

Adèle needed answers and, if she was honest, reassurance. Was she the reason Sophie hadn't come home? Did she hate her? Blame her for being caught and sent to the camps? "Why didn't she come back to Paris herself? The hospitals here are better. Her old friends—"

Gena interrupted. "It was too painful. Her friends are dead or missing. You were dead, or at least that is what she was told. She loved you so much, and I don't think she could return to Paris. Too many memories."

Adèle choked up. It took all her effort not to dissolve into a puddle of tears.

Gena's voice grew weaker, but she kept talking. "Once she got well enough, she helped in the displaced persons' camp. There is a huge need for doctors and nurses, and she knows better than most what the people have endured. She said she was going to move to Palestine after the trials. But first, she felt she had to find the children and their families."

Typical Sophie, looking after others before herself. Wait – what? "The trials? What children? Oh, I am not following."

"She is to be a witness for the prosecution in the Nuremberg trials. She will be called sometime next year. But first, she is trying to find the families of the children she cared for." Completely confused, Adèle could only stare at the woman. Families? Weren't all the children gassed at the camps? Overwhelmed, she could only stare at the woman. A shadow blocked the sunshine as Georges arrived.

"Gena, please excuse my wife for forgetting her manners. Won't you come inside? We can continue our conversation there."

He offered his arm to Gena, reminding Adèle of the woman's fragile state. Still, she couldn't just sit around. She needed Sophie.

"I don't want to talk. I want to go and find my sister."

Gena smiled at Adèle's reaction.

"You are alike. Sophie is impetuous and stubborn too. If she were not, we would both be dead."

"Adèle, go on up and put on some coffee for our guest." Georges pulled her to her feet and kissed her gently on the forehead before giving her a small push in the direction of their home. He turned to offer Gena his arm and assisted her climbing the stairs up to their apartment.

Adèle followed and then ducked into the kitchen area, not just to put on the coffee but also to take a moment to compose herself. What did Sophie look like if she had been too ill to leave? Gena was frailer than she'd first appeared.

Luc picked up his hat. "I'll find Romain, and we'll give you some privacy."

Adèle smiled through her tears at his kindness before she returned to the living room, carrying a tray with cups and some pastries Georges had purchased the previous day. Gena sat on the sofa, her head pressed back into the cushions, pale with exhaustion. Georges put a finger to his lips before he went into the kitchen and returned with the coffee. He poured while Adèle took a seat. Gena sniffed appreciatively. "Real coffee. I still can't get over the pleasure from smelling the beans."

Georges offered their guest a cup, which she cradled in her hands. "I find it difficult to talk about the camps."

To Adèle's annoyance, Georges interjected, "You don't have

to tell us anything. Relax and enjoy your coffee. There is plenty of time."

No, there wasn't. Sophie was out there somewhere, and this woman knew where. Adèle moved forward, but, at a look of censure from Georges, she forced herself to stay silent.

Gena smiled her thanks at his understanding before sipping her coffee. Then the words came stumbling out. "It's hard to describe what it was really like, back there. You know? The pictures you see in the papers and the cinema, they can only hint at how bad it was. Knowing that your life depended on a whim. You never knew which day was your last. Whether it was your turn, or that of the woman next to you or standing behind you. All you knew was that the killing machine never stopped. Those chimneys ... they never stopped smoking." Gena gulped, her hands shaking. The remains of her coffee spilled slightly. Distraught, she jumped up. "I'm so clumsy. I don't think it got on the sofa. I'll clean it..." Her eyes darted around the room, looking terrified.

Georges moved quicker than Adèle. He took the cup and put it down on the coffee table. "Please sit down. The sofa doesn't matter. You didn't burn yourself? No? Then no harm done."

Adèle moved onto the sofa beside Gena and took her hand in hers. "Please don't torture yourself."

Gena put her second hand on top of their clasped hands. "You need to know. By the time Sophie arrived in Auschwitz, I'd lost all sense of myself. I lost my soul. I didn't care what happened to those around me. I just wanted to live and was prepared to do whatever it took. I didn't have time, energy, or love to waste on anyone. The Nazis took everyone I loved to the Camps: my parents, my two brothers, and our older sister and her children. One was only a baby." Gena swallowed, closing her eyes for a second. "Then I heard about this new arrival. She'd taken on the worst female guard in history, all because of a girl I had once gone to school with. I couldn't believe someone would put themselves in danger like that. Sophie – or Nicole, as I first knew her – she was inspirational right from the start. She never stopped fighting for others, no matter the cost to herself. I lost count of how many times she gave blood to a patient to save them from one of the selections."

"Selection?" Georges asked.

"Yes, from the hospital. It wasn't anything like a real medical facility, just a hut with some beds. But Sophie gave the best care she could. She begged, bartered, and did whatever she could to save lives. Once, when a whole load of twins were condemned..."

Adèle cried out, "Twins?"

"Mengele liked to experiment on twins, and he kept an eye out for them when the trains arrived at the camp." Gena grasped Adèle's hand. "She was relieved you weren't with her. Not because it spared her the fate those twins were destined for but because she couldn't bear to have witnessed your suffering."

Adèle wiped a tear away. "She loved me so much and was always protecting me, even when I was too stupid to see it. If you knew how I behaved when the Germans first arrived in Paris..." Adèle exchanged a look with Georges, needing his gentle smile, the loving look in his eyes, to confirm she wasn't that person any more. "I danced with them, drank with them, ate with them, even shopped at the couture stores they patronised."

For the first time, Gena grinned. "Sophie told me."

"She did?"

"Yes. But she wasn't being nasty. She told me stories about your brother and you. How you argued and what different lives you lived. She was so proud of you; she'd heard you went to England to train to become a special agent, and when you returned to France, you fought back. You helped win the war."

Adèle cried and laughed as Gena told her story, and finally

hugged the woman. "Thank you for coming to find me. I can't believe Sophie is alive."

"She believed you dead. We lost count of the number of times we got false leads, and Sophie decided it was too painful to continue. People confirmed you had died, and she believed she had to let you rest in peace."

"But you didn't agree?" Georges asked.

Adèle was overcome with tears.

"I did at first; I wanted to spare Sophie more pain. She is rather fragile. The camp, it took a lot out of her. But then I heard a whisper that the White Witch was in Paris. I didn't tell Sophie as I wanted to check it out first myself. I didn't want to raise her hopes only to see her devastated again. I wish I had told her now."

"You did what you felt was right." Adèle tried to smile through her tears. "What of you, Gena? Did any of your family survive the camps?"

Gena shook her head sadly. "There is nobody left; Sophie is all I have. I think of her as a sister."

Adèle took a deep breath, wondering if Sophie had heard about their mother and grandmother. She would wait until she saw Sophie in person before discussing that.

"Where are you living?" she asked Gena.

"At a hotel. It isn't near here, but it is the best I could afford." Gena paused. "I am not planning on staying in Paris. My aim was to find you, or what had happened to you, then go back to Sophie with news."

"You must come and stay with us. We insist – don't we, Georges? Now, how can I get to Germany? If my sister can give evidence against the Nazis, so can I."

"But your doctor—"

"I don't care what Maurice says. He is an old woman."

"Maurice is treating my wife for injuries sustained during

the war. He has advised her to take things easy," Georges explained to Gena.

Gena's eyes widened in recognition. "Maurice? Is he the same Maurice as the man Sophie met?"

Adèle beamed, feeling so happy she could burst. "Yes, the same. I think he might take a trip to Germany too."

"Sophie isn't in Germany any more."

Adèle stared at Gena, horror making her feel ill. "You mean she has gone to Palestine already?"

"No, she is back in France. She's in Perpignan – at least she should be. That is where she was headed when she last wrote."

"Why didn't you say so before? Georges, how fast can we get to Perpignan?" Adèle jumped up. "Gena, come and help me pack. Then we will drive to your hotel and get your things. Georges will call Maurice."

Adèle hugged Gena as she lost her ability to speak. She let the tears flow – but this time, they were happy tears.

SIXTY-SEVEN

Sophie looked around the garden, trying to remember where she had buried the jars. She had to find the records; the children's real names and their last known addresses were on them.

"Sophie, you need to slow down. You will make yourself ill," Mary chided her softly. Since Sophie's return from the camp, Mary had insisted she live with her. She'd nursed and fussed over her every day, tempting her to eat and insisting she rest even when she wanted to do more. She treated Sophie as she did the children who'd gradually returned to the orphanages, coming out of hiding from the churches, convents, and families who'd protected them during the war. Now they were waiting for their own families to come back. For their fathers, mothers, aunts, uncles, cousins, siblings. Anyone at all who was related by blood.

Sophie glanced up. "I can't. The children are waiting. What if their parents believe them to be dead and move on with their lives? I have to find them."

"Sophie, you know the chances of most of the parents coming back are low. You were there..."

Sophie glanced at the ground. "I must do this. Otherwise it

was all in vain. Even if I can only reunite one family. I must try. You understand, don't you?"

"Yes, I do, but I wish you would slow down." Mary took a step towards her, hand outstretched as if to take the shovel away. "Just take things a little slower. Your body can't take much more."

"Listen to the woman, Sophie Bélanger."

Sophie gasped, the shovel falling to the ground as she and Mary turned to see who had spoken.

Sophie rubbed her eyes. "Adèle? You're here? But you're dead! I was told..."

Then the darkness swallowed her as she heard Adèle say her name.

* * *

Sophie recovered to find herself being carried from the garden into the house, heading for the living room in the arms of a man who seemed familiar. If this was a dream, she didn't want to wake up. She whispered, "Maurice? Is it really you?"

He kissed her forehead, gathering her closer in his arms. "Shh. You fainted. Let me take you out of the sun and get you a drink."

Sophie looked into his face – it was him. He looked just like he had in her dreams every night over the last eighteen months. She ran one hand along his chin ... he was real. She stared over his shoulder. She hadn't been dreaming. Adèle was here, absolutely glowing with full health. Her sister was alive, and Gena, dear Gena, was holding her hand. A man, vaguely familiar, but she couldn't place him in her memory, hung back as if not wanting to intrude, but not wanting to let the ladies out of his sight.

Her eyes returned to those of her twin. "Adèle, I thought..."

Adèle nodded. "I know. Gena told me. I looked everywhere

for you. It's all my fault. I'm so sorry. I can't imagine what you have been through."

Maurice gently placed Sophie on the couch, and sat on the corner, not leaving her side. Adèle moved to sit on the other side, taking Sophie's hands in hers. "I'm sorry."

Sophie brushed her thumb over Adèle's hands. "It's not your fault. None of it. I did what I had to do, what I wanted to do. It wasn't enough."

"That's nonsense." Georges coughed, his voice gruff with emotion. "If France had more citizens like the Bélanger sisters, maybe – just maybe – the war wouldn't have lasted five long years." Maurice and Gena nodded their heads in agreement.

Sophie stared at Georges, his voice sparking a memory. Him and Jean-Pierre, about ten years previously in mémé's garden in her Lyon estate ... Another lifetime.

"I know you." Then she looked at Adèle and caught the loving look she exchanged with Georges. "You and my twin?"

"Yes, I convinced her to become a communist and marry me."

Adèle laughed – a lovely sound – as she swatted her husband. "I married him all right, but me as a communist? I haven't changed that much."

Yet she had, and the changes were obvious, at least to Sophie's eyes. Despite the horrors she'd seen in her own war – and there had been many if the shadows under her twin's eyes were anything to go by – Adèle was softer, happier than before the war. She had a deep love for her husband, and judging by his infatuated expression, it was returned in spades. Sophie didn't have to worry about Adèle. Not any more.

Maurice moved so that his arm hung around her shoulders rather than on the back of the chair. She settled back, her head resting against it as if it was the most natural thing in the world. He leaned in and kissed the top of her head. Self-consciously, she put a hand to her scalp; the hair growing back was very patchy. "You're beautiful. I love you." His words were whispered in her ear just loud enough for her to hear them. She reached out for his other hand and clasped it, not able to speak.

Gena cleared her throat. "Sophie, I have a letter for you. It's from a Monsieur Litwak."

"The girls. Did they survive?"

Gena nodded, a big smile on her face. "The whole family survived. He and his wife hid in Paris; Arlette and Minette and young Samuel, the orphan you rescued, hid in the mountains, and they are now living in Palestine. The Litwaks adopted Samuel. They have asked you to come and stay with them. They wrote to you at your father's home, but their letter was returned. Monsieur Litwak heard of the project at Hôtel Lutetia in Paris. He visited the hotel before he left for Palestine."

"You saved so many lives." Adèle looked at her proudly.

Sophie gazed at her sister. "From what I heard about the White Witch, so did you!"

* * *

A month later, they gathered at the town hall. Maurice pulled at his collar with Georges grinning by his side. Adèle checked the doctor's tie. "You're more nervous now than you were leading a charge against the Germans."

"I didn't care what happened to them. What if I am rushing Sophie? You see how fragile she is, she should be resting not rushing here, there and everywhere."

Adèle tried to keep her voice steady. In truth, Sophie was frail and looked dreadful. She would take time to recover, like all those returning from the camps. "She's driven by what she saw. She wants to reunite the families and isn't ready to face that may not be possible." Adèle leaned in and kissed his cheek. "She will thrive with you at her side. As her husband, you will be by her side when she travels to Germany and takes part in trials. She is strong and she loves you. You've shown her she has her own reasons to focus on the future."

His eyes shone but she was the one who let a tear roll unchecked down her cheek.

Georges was the first to spot the bride's arrival. "Here she is."

Maurice inhaled sharply as Sophie stepped out of the car, Gena at her side. He stepped forward to take her hand.

"You look beautiful."

She ran her other hand over her hair. It was growing but slowly. Adèle gulped back the tears as her sister, blushing under Maurice's gaze asked, "Are you certain you don't want to wait and have a Rabbi marry us?"

Maurice shook his head, drawing her close to his side.

EPILOGUE

"How many people are coming to this reunion? Is the George V Hôtel big enough for everybody?" Georges asked again teasing, as Adèle fussed over her reflection. She felt queasy at the smell of food so had retreated to their bedroom. Should she tell him what she suspected or wait for a doctor to confirm her pregnancy?

She eyed him in the mirror as he paced back and forth.

"Georges, come here and sit down. I..."

"Adèle they're here. Come on." Gena's voice carried from the hall as she knocked on their door.

Georges offered her his arm. "Are you ready, Madame Monier?"

Her news could wait. She patted her lipstick, ran a brush through her hair and stood up. The ground tilted.

"Adèle, what's wrong?" He caught her in his arms.

"I got up too fast, that's all. I'm fine. Let's go meet our guests."

Georges muttered something but she pretended not to hear it. She took his arm as they walked along the hotel corridor and down the stairs.

"Isn't it wonderful how many families, Mary was able to reunite? Sophie was clever to hide the information she held on the families in the garden." Adèle spoke the whole time trying to distract him. Many parents didn't return from the trains, but some of Sophie's information helped to reunite siblings.

Sophie and Maurice were already standing at the door welcoming their guests. She kissed her sister's cheek. Sophie looked so much better, healthier than she had done at her wedding. This despite her instance on traveling to Germany for the Nuremberg trials.

"Gena worked so hard, gathering as many of the children as she could find – their parents, too, in some cases." Sophie's eyes filled with tears as she stared at the room full of people. "Is it wrong, I see ghosts? I'm grateful so many survived but it brings home those we lost."

Adèle understood exactly what she meant. She missed maman and mémé, Madame Monier and others all the time but gatherings like this drove home their loss.

"I know but we must celebrate those who lived. Those who died will never be forgotten." Adèle had barely uttered her words when a giant of a man stepped forward, his arms outstretched. Father Tobias introduced him. "Sophie this is Monsieur Ardent."

"Thank you for what you did for my girls. I will always remember you." Monsieur Ardent hugged Sophie.

"It was my fault, Jacqueline and Giselle died in Auschwitz. I wish we could have saved them." The man shook his head, interrupting Sophie.

"The Nazis killed my daughters, Mademoiselle Bélanger. You tried to save them. I will always be grateful." He brushed a hand over his eyes before Father Tobias led him off in the direction of the bar. Adèle watched how Sophie's eyes followed him.

"Georges, let's go find a drink." She pulled her husband away in a bid to allow Sophie time to compose herself.

* * *

Maurice fussed over her. "Are you sure you don't want to go upstairs and rest. Let the guests arrive and catch up with one another and you can come down later?"

"No, I don't want to miss a second. Could you fetch me a glass of water, please." She needed a couple of minutes alone. He hesitated before he agreed. She watched him walk away. She loved him deeply but sometimes the memories of what they had both been through were overpowering.

"I will be a pilot." A young boy came up to greet Sophie. "I promised you I would come back to see you."

"Szymon? Is it you? But you are so tall! And Hannah?" Sophie beamed at the eighteen-year-old. "Is it true you lived in hiding for the whole war?"

Hannah nodded. "We stayed on a farm with friends of Dr Murphy's."

At his name, Sophie couldn't hide her grief. Hannah hugged her, sharing her sadness.

"I am so sorry he didn't make it through the war."

"So am I, but at least his wife and son survived. For that, we must be thankful."

"Thank you for what you did for us." Hannah hugged her again. "Szymon is my little brother now. We are family."

Sophie smiled, deeply pleased.

Maurice came over, handed her a glass of water before he his arm around her shoulder. "Are you doing all right?"

"Yes, it is so good to see everyone looking so well. But ... I guess it makes it real that some of our loved ones will never come home."

Maurice held her close for a moment, but they were soon interrupted.

"Thank you for letting me help you free France." A young

man stood in front of her. She laughed and called Adèle over. "I think this young man is looking for you."

"Laurence, how tall you've grown!" Adèle greeted the young man, who flushed as he realised his mistake. "Luc is here and so is Romain. Both are married now." The boy grimaced as Adèle and Sophie exchanged glances and laughed.

Luc gave Adèle a big hug, as did his wife, Louise. They'd met on the streets of Paris during one of the celebrations of the end of the war. Louise held their newborn baby girl. "We called her Claire, but we hope she is slightly less stubborn than her namesake." Luc joked before he hugged Adèle again.

Adèle choked up on seeing Josette Abreo with her husband and Felix.

Georges shook Felix's hand as Madame Abreo gathered Adèle in her arms and hugged her tight. "I am so proud of you. Annoyed you married Georges and not my Felix, but proud all the same."

Everyone laughed including Felix and the young woman by his side. Luc whispered something to his wife before disappearing out the door.

"Madame Monier, please close your eyes." Adèle took a few seconds to realise Louise addressed her. She felt Georges's arm slide around her waist as she closed her eyes.

A very wet tongue licked her hands, barking in delight.

"Seb. You brought him. I missed you." Adèle bent down and cuddled the dog. "De Gaulle should have given you an award. You're my hero."

Seb barked in agreement.

* * *

The party was a great success, but Sophie still tired easily. She agreed readily when Maurice suggested they retire to their rooms. On their way out, they met Adèle and Georges, who had had the same idea.

"Next year, we sail to America to meet our nephew." Adèle's smile lit up her face. "Are you ready for it, Sophie?"

Sophie hugged her twin. "With you by my side, I think I can handle anything."

A LETTER FROM THE AUTHOR

Dear reader, thank you for reading my book. I hope you enjoyed Adèle's and Sophie's story as much as I liked writing it. If you'd like to be the first to find out about new releases, please sign to my newsletter!

www.stormpublishing.co/rachel-wesson

If you enjoyed this book and could spare a few moments to leave a review that would be hugely appreciated. Even a short review can make all the difference in encouraging a reader to discover my books for the first time. Thank you so much!

In school, I loved hearing about the female heroes of the Second World War but there weren't many books about them back then. This war was a defining moment in our history, and for far too long the heroic actions of the women – be they spies, resistance fighters, nurses, pilots, or women trying to care for their families – were overshadowed by their male counterparts. By using fictional characters like Adèle and Sophie, I hope to highlight the role played by women under exceptionally trying circumstances and to celebrate their courage, resilience, and sacrifice. Although Sophie is a figment of my imagination, what she endured in the concentration camps was the real-life experience of too many, most of their stories lost forever to the world.

By showcasing the immense courage and capabilities of women, I hope to inspire and empower future generations to break free from any glass ceilings and to pursue their dreams with confidence.

Thank you so much for reading my books and being part of this amazing journey with me and I hope you'll stay in touch – I have so many more stories and ideas to entertain you with!

Rachel x

www.rachelwesson.com

facebook.com/rachelwessonsreaders

twitter.com/wessonwrites

goodreads.com/15024927.Rachel_Wesson

HISTORICAL NOTE

Most of the people in my novel are products of my imagination, but some were real. I learned of their actions, described in this book, from reading other books.

As you already know from *Darkness Falls*, book one of this series, the character of Jean-Pierre is based on the youngest member of the Musée De L'Homme resistance circuit. In this book, I reference the ladies of the group being shot. In reality, five women were sentenced, three women were condemned to deportation. The three condemned to be deported were: Germaine Tillion, Agnès Humbert, Yvonne Oddon. All three survived the camp. Two others, Renée Levy was beheaded in August 1943, and Émilie Tillion, mother of Germaine Tillion, was gassed in Ravensbrück.

The story of the boys, Robert and Daniel, being arrested and escaping from the train actually happened and more or less how it is described in my book, including the telegram being sent. I've changed their names but they were real heroes having both helped other children to escape to Switzerland.

Dr Jackson, the heroic American doctor from the American Hospital whom Dr Murphy is modelled on, didn't survive the war but was murdered by the Nazis. His wife and his son Philip were also taken prisoner but survived.

Claudette is modelled on a woman called Sabine Zlatin, a Jewish nurse and OSE activist. She survived the Izieu *rafle* as she was away that day visiting Montpelier to find hiding places for the children. Her husband was deported and shot, along with two of the older boys. Forty-five younger children and five adults were gassed at Auschwitz. Sabine wasn't in Auschwitz; Claudette's journey in the camp and back at the hotel is entirely fictional.

For the residents of Tulle, France, June 9th marks a day of great sadness. Hardly a family in the town escaped the atrocity committed by the 2nd SS Panzer Division Das Reich. Between those who were hanged and those who were deported to concentration camps, never to return, the impact was devastating.

In my story, I show Adèle and her men taking down the bodies and burying each one in a proper grave, but in reality, the Germans stayed in Tulle for a number of days. The men were left where they had died, and the townspeople were forced to parade past them. After a day or so, the Germans cut down the bodies and threw them into a mass grave.

The tragedy of Oradour-sur-Glane, which took place on 10th June, is better known, having been covered in several films and books. A second unit of the Das Reich Waffen-SS Division were responsible for that atrocity.

The devastating events in Tulle and Oradour were made worse by the fact that no one was brought to justice for what happened. In the chaos after the war, the perpetrators – those still alive – escaped punishment. In fact, despite the large number of atrocities carried out in France, few of the men responsible were held accountable for their crimes.

The account of General Elster and his men being given a

safe passage to join the Americans is true, and the SS were indeed offered chocolate and oranges by the Red Cross.

The Nuremberg trials resulted in convictions mainly for prominent Nazi figures such as Göring, who died by suicide after being found guilty, and also those directly involved in the concentration camps, such as Rudolf Höss.

For some war criminals it took a long time for them to be brought to Justice. After the war, Klaus Barbie, the so-called Butcher of Lyon, was helped to flee to Bolivia. As the investigation of Klaus Barbie has shown, officers of the United States government were directly responsible for protecting a person wanted by the government of France on criminal charges and in arranging his escape from the law. As a direct result of that action, Klaus Barbie did not stand trial in France in 1950; he spent 33 years as a free man and a fugitive from justice. *https:// www.justice.gov/sites/default/files/criminal-hrsp/legacy/2011/ 02/04/08-02-83barbie-rpt.pdf*

France never gave up the fight to prosecute him and he was tried and sentenced to death in absentia. His victims and their families demanded justice. He was finally arrested and extradited to France in 1983 and tried from 1983 to 1987 when he was condemned to life imprisonment (death penalty had been abolished in France) and died in prison from cancer in 1991 at seventy-seven years of age.

In the years following the war, the world was consumed with fear of a third world war. The so-called Cold War began in earnest, and many former Nazis were recruited by the Americans, British and Russians.

Trials continued but with less publicity than the Nuremberg trials. Simon Wiesenthal and his team never gave up and brought many Nazis to justice.

Most people wanted to put the war behind them, that was true. Given what the people of France and other countries had been through, it is easy to understand why.

ACKNOWLEDGMENTS

To all my readers, especially those in my Facebook readers group. You don't know how much your lovely comments about my books inspire my writing. Thank you.

My editing team including my incredible editor, Vicky Blunden on the English side and Genevieve on the French side. Together they turn my scribblings into stories.

My father, who introduced me to books and the wonderful world they open.

To my husband for helping run our home and look after our children. I don't miss those school runs.

To my children for having patience while Mam works on her next book.

I am beyond grateful to be living the life of my dreams as an author and am truly humbled so many readers want to read my stories. Thank you.